THE BONE THIEF

V.M. WHITWORTH

EBURY
PRESS

1 3 5 7 9 10 8 6 4 2

Published in the UK in 2012 by Ebury Press, an imprint of Ebury Publishing
A Random House Group Company

\   er

T   )09

Addresses fo   n be found at:

A CIP cata   itish Library

The Ranc   tewardship
Council (FS   organisation.
Our books carry   paper. FSC is the
only forest certifi~   ~ntal organisations,
including Greenpeace. Our paper procurement policy can be found at:
www.randomhouse.co.uk/environment

Printed and bound in Great Britain by Clays Ltd, St Ives PLC

ISBN (Hardback) 9780091947217
ISBN (Trade paperback) 9780091948740

To buy books by your favourite authors and register for offers visit:
www.randomhouse.co.uk

ACKNOWLEDGEMENTS

No matter how many people I acknowledge, there are bound to be some meritorious names left off the list, if only because so many have contributed to the making of *The Bone Thief* in one way or another.

I was so lucky to have among my teachers in my last three years at school the inspiring writers George Szirtes, Peter Scupham, Neil Powell and Stephanie Norgate. From my Oxford days, I am endlessly grateful to Heather O'Donoghue and Ursula Dronke for my first lessons in Old English and Old Norse respectively, and to David Howlett for his valiant attempts to instil in me a proper understanding of Mediaeval Latin. At York, I had the great good fortune to be given a passion for archaeology by Martin Carver; a deeper understanding of Old English by Sid Bradley; and a sceptical approach to historical sources by Katy Cubitt and Edward James.

There are so many other friends in the academic world who have put up with me and my ramblings over the years: Helen Gittos; Sarah Semple; Sam Turner; Kate Giles; Farah Mendelsohn; David Petts; Jane Stockdale; Alice Jorgensen; Emilia Jamroziak;

Lesley Abrams; Hannah Collingridge; Heather Cushing; Simon Trafford; Katherine Lewis; Joanna Huntington; Claire Woozley; Anna Selvey; Felicity Clark; Noel James; Howard Williams; Sybille Zipperer; John Blair; Alex Sanmark; Dawn Hadley; Chris and Alison Daniell – it's been a great journey in your company and I hope you're not too disconcerted to find yourself cited in this context. (Anne Brundle, you are sorely missed.)

Harry Bingham and Sophia Bartleet of The Writers' Workshop were the source of tremendous encouragement in the early stages. I also have to thank the staff at Julia's Café in Stromness, Orkney, for letting me colonise a corner to write in even at their busiest times. Other friends without whom I would never have got this far are Lucy Blackburn, Susie Holden, Jessica Haydon, Janni Howker, and in particular Sophie Holroyd (thanks, Soph, for badgering me to write fiction).

I can't really credit my sisters or my cousins with support for this project as they had very little idea what I was up to until the last minute – but thank you anyway, Wendy Lord, Katie Thompson, Clive, Rebecca, and Alexandra Lacey, for so much, in so many ways, and over the last twelve years in particular. (And never, never forgetting Quentin.)

Laura Longrigg, my agent at MBA, has been amazing; and I am also blessed in my editor at Ebury, Gillian Green. My husband Ben has been the greatest help imaginable, particularly in keeping our daughter Stella off my keyboard. My debt to my late parents, Sheila and Miles Thompson, is beyond all calculation. But the deepest thanks must go to my aunt and my mother-in-law, who read early drafts with great patience and astute comments, and to them *The Bone Thief* is dedicated.

DEDICATION

Barbara Katherine Lacey. Angela Whitworth.
First readers. Toughest critics. Dearest friends

CAST OF CHARACTERS

NB These ethnic categories blur and overlap. Some people are identified according to where they are encountered geographically in the story, rather than by ethnicity. Historical characters are marked with an asterisk.

MERCIANS
Wulfgar of Meon, known to some as 'Litter-runt', a subdeacon trained originally at Winchester Cathedral, now secretary to the Lord and Lady of the Mercians. Son of a king's thane, a major land-owner with a wergild of 1200 shillings. His friends call him 'Wuffa' (Little Wolf/ Wolf-Cub)

*Athelfled, known to her family as Fleda, eldest child of Alfred the Great and a West Saxon princess, now Lady of the Mercians

*Athelred, the 'Old Boar' of Mercia, her Lord

Kenelm the Deacon, the Bishop of Worcester's nephew

*Werferth, the Bishop of Worcester. If he really had only one eye, no chronicler ever bothered to record it

*Ednoth of Sodbury, a young man from a gentry family, whose father has a wergild of 200 shillings

Heremod 'Straddler' of Wappenbury, a minor land-owner, whose mother is a singularly fearless and stroppy old lady

WEST SAXONS
*Athelwald Seiriol, Atheling of Wessex. His father was Alfred the Great's older brother and predecessor as King of Wessex. Anglo-Saxon laws of inheritance allow him to claim the throne. It is not clear who his mother was; I have invented a Welsh background for her, and a second, Welsh, name for him. He is known among the Danes as 'Athelwald the Hungry', also my invention

Garmund 'Polecat', son of Wulfgar's father and one of the field-slaves on their family estate at Meon in modern Hampshire

*Edward, King of Wessex, eldest son of Alfred the Great. Historians call him 'Edward the Elder' because there was another King Edward later in the tenth century, but obviously this did not apply in the first King Edward's lifetime

*Denewulf, Bishop of Winchester. Legend has it that he was the swineherd in whose hut Alfred burnt the cakes. But it's only a legend

LEICESTER

Gunnvor 'Cat's-Eyes' Bolladottir, whose father came from Norway as part of the Scandinavian Great Army. Only she knows where her father's loot is buried

Father Ronan, of St Margaret's Kirk, Leicester Cathedral, son of a canon of Leicester Cathedral and his house-keeper, an Irish slave-woman

Kevin, his altar-boy and son

Orm Ormsson, Norwegian chancer

Ketil 'Scar' Grimsson, Jarl of Leicester and younger brother of the late Hakon 'Toad' Grimsson. Hakon and his followers grabbed Leicester when Mercia imploded in the 870s

LINCOLN AND BARDNEY

Toli 'Silkbeard' (*Silkiskegg*) **Hrafnsson**, the young Jarl of Lincoln

Eirik 'the Spider', a slave-trader who moves between Lincoln, the Northern Isles, and Dublin

Thorvald the Reeve (Estate Manager) of Bardney, son of a Danish soldier and an Englishwoman, grandson of the last sacristan of Bardney when it was still a great church and site of pilgrimage

Leoba, Thorvald's English wife, and their two young children

The Spider's Wife, an Englishwoman of good family, originally from Northumbria, bought by Eirik when she was very young

CHAPTER ONE

Worcester, April, 900

Late again.

Wulfgar was still tugging at his choir robe as he hurried across the courtyard through the mild spring drizzle. He had pulled the robe straight on over his tunic, to save time, and now he was too hot and flustered, and there was an uncomfortable ruck of fabric somewhere round his lower back.

The bell summoning Worcester's clerics to Vespers tolled for the last time.

Despite his best efforts to scrub his hands clean with pumice, ink had now somehow transferred itself to the cuff of his white robe.

Why, he wondered, am I bothering? I could have just stayed at my desk in the muniments room. Heaven and the Saints all know I've got more than enough to do, with the shire-court commencing this evening. Now I'll be going in to Vespers late and all their horrible, smug faces will be staring at me. He found his feet were beginning to drag.

Come on, he encouraged himself, you've got this far! If you're ever going to be accepted by the Mercian minster-men you've got to show your face sometimes. He could hear their singing now, blessedly muffled by the cathedral's thick stone walls.

All the clerics might already be in the choir, but the courtyard outside the cathedral was bustling with activity, and he was nearly knocked over by a couple of harassed-looking palace servants staggering with trestles out of the Bishop's great hall. 'Look where you're going,' one of them shouted, just in time, and then laughed when Wulfgar had to jump out of the way.

He hurried through the gate, away from the thronged courtyard, his eyes on the cathedral's north door, the nearest one to his stall in the choir. He was so intent on it that he didn't notice the small boy running full pelt towards him. Likewise, the boy failed to notice Wulfgar because, as he ran, he was looking back over his shoulder.

Inevitably they collided. The little boy went flying across the slippery cobbles.

Wulfgar recovered his wits first.

'Are you all right?' he asked.

The child had gone crashing down with his arms extended, and he was now looking ruefully at two grazed and grubby palms. A pair of bigger boys had appeared out of nowhere and were gazing at them balefully from a short distance away. The expression on the little one's face told Wulfgar everything he needed to know, and he couldn't help but see his own past reflected in the young boy's terrified eyes. The difference is, he thought, that I'm no longer the runt of the litter.

He straightened up and started walking towards the older boys. Older, yes, but only by a year or two. All three of them were clearly cathedral oblates, though their tonsures, like his own, were grown out from the long Lenten weeks of neglect.

'You should know better,' he said, when he was close enough. 'Leave him alone.'

One of the boys looked as though he was backing down, but the other, a snub-nosed, freckled little monster, put on a pugnacious face.

'We don't have to do what you tell us. You're not the oblatemaster. You're just that West Saxon.'

'I'm the Lord and Lady's secretary,' he said sharply, 'and that's quite good enough.' Five months in the post, and it still gave him a thrill to be able to say it. 'And why aren't you in Vespers?'

'We're helping get the hall ready for the shire-court,' said the smaller, more conciliatory one.

'Then do what you're supposed to be doing,' he said curtly. 'Go on!'

The freckled one looked as though he were about to answer back again. Wulfgar wondered what he would do if the boys flatly refused to obey him. He rubbed his chin, trying to look stern and authoritative. Perhaps the six weeks' growth of beard would help. Maundy Thursday tomorrow – Shear Thursday, as some jokingly called it. Every cleric in Worcester would be shaven and tonsured again by the evening, and not before time, he thought.

The freckled lad was pulling a sulky face.

'Do what you're told,' Wulfgar said sharply, and at last the two older boys turned in the direction of the hall.

Hiding his relief, Wulfgar turned his attention back to the youngest one.

'Let's have a look at those hands. Why were they chasing you?'

The little boy was getting to his feet.

'They wanted this.' He dug down under the collar of his tunic and produced a leather thong with a small, trumpery, bronze cross on it. 'They said new boys aren't allowed to have anything of their own. But my mother gave it to me, before I left home, and I wasn't going to let them take it . . .' His chin wobbled, but he kept the tears at bay.

Wulfgar nodded. Mindful of the child's dignity, he only said, 'If they get at you again, you can always come to me.'

'Thank you, sir. But—'

'But what?'

He was shoving the cross back down the neck of his tunic and took a moment to answer. When he did, his mutter was inaudible, and he couldn't meet Wulfgar's eyes.

'What is it?'

'Well, sir, it's just – like they said – you're from Wessex. And they'll probably be worse to me now, because of what you said.'

Wulfgar nodded, suppressing a sigh. It was a familiar story. How many times had the palace steward, back home in Winchester, saved him from the clutches of Edward and his gang, only for them to redouble their efforts when they finally caught up with him? No, he couldn't fault the child's reasoning, but he did resent the way all Mercians, even the smallest, seemed to dislike West Saxons.

'If you went to Wessex,' he said gently, 'you'd find it swarming with Mercians, you know. Doing very well, some of them. Why shouldn't a few of us come here?'

'I don't know, sir,' the boy said miserably.

Wulfgar could have provided an answer, but it would have been a long and complex one, a tale of lost lands and faded glories, and a deep mistrust of Mercia's old enemy to the south. Another time, perhaps. He straightened up.

'Oh, run along,' he told the boy.

The other clerics were already midway through the first hymn as he slipped into his place in the high, narrow choir. He took a deep breath of the numinous air and felt his pounding heart slow, his ragged breathing grow regular enough for him to join in towards the end. *Unloose the bands of guilt within*, he sang, *Remove the burden of our sin*, trying his best to sound as though he had been there all along.

Why am I letting what those boys said get under my skin? he thought.

He bowed his head to pray, noticing as he did so that the ink stain on his robe had now been augmented by smears of mud. Sorry, he thought, glancing up to the image of the Mother of God in her blue, starry cloak, her Son nestled on her lap, which adorned the wall above the high altar. Most Blessed Lady, I shouldn't come before you like this, late and grubby and distracted. I'm such an ingrate. I should be counting my blessings, and being here in Worcester should be first on the list, he said to himself firmly, aware of her painted eyes on him. It was a beautiful cathedral, even if it was small. He looked at the glorious altar cross, with its gold, and rock crystal, and enamel. You can tell the Danes have never yet got this far, he observed. How many churches still have treasures like that? And look at you, Queen of Heaven, Star of the Sea. So beautiful . . . I do know when I'm well off, he told that friendly, painted face. Really, I do.

Queen of Heaven, help me get used to being here, he prayed. You don't have to remind me Winchester will never be my home again. That door's as closed as the gate of Paradise. He glanced up at the image on the south wall where Adam and Eve were turned away, weeping, by a stern-faced angel with a sword of fire.

But, he told himself, that doesn't matter. I'm at the heart of affairs in Mercia now. The Lady knows my worth, and I think the

Lord's learning to, as well. I'm doing what I've been trained for since I was younger than that child outside. I even have a desk of my own, at last.

So why am I restless? Why isn't this enough?

The choir began singing the Magnificat, reminding him to augment his list of blessings: he was involved in the solemnities and the splendour and the singing of one of the few great churches left to the English . . .

And my spirit hath rejoiced in God my Saviour, because he hath regarded the humility of his handmaiden . . .

Singing. Humility. Queen of Heaven, he thought, I really am striving to be humble. His bad temper was tightening his throat and hampering his breathing, marring his own true tenor voice. But it was as nothing compared to the grating notes coming from the fair-haired young deacon standing next to him. Kenelm, that was his name. I don't care if the Bishop *is* your uncle, Wulfgar thought impatiently, I was singing that phrase better when I was seven. He sneaked a glance at the precentor and the cantor and stifled a sigh. There was no chance those two would ever let him take charge of the choir, and doubtless they would live to be as old as Methuselah, just to spite him.

Oh, Winchester . . .

The old King's funeral – now, that had been proper singing. It had been the last gift they could give him, even though Wulfgar had hardly been able to see through his tears.

And that thought led to the equally bittersweet memory of the night before the funeral, at his dead Lord's wake, when the Lady of the Mercians, red-eyed and solemn-faced, had tugged at his sleeve and drawn him away from the mass of mourners drinking deep and singing raucous songs around her father's bier.

'I know it's customary,' Wulfgar remembered saying to the late King's daughter, 'but I wish they'd pray for him instead.' He had known she was one of the few souls present who would understand his squeamishness. He had looked back over his shoulder at the shrouded figure on the bier, surrounded by stands of guttering candles, the richly draped catafalque barely visible through the crowd. 'Not that he needs our prayers. If ever a soul went straight to God's embrace—'

'Come to Mercia,' she had interrupted, her grey eyes bright with tears.

He had just gaped at her.

'My Lord and I need a new secretary. We'd – I'd – like you.'

'Leave Wessex?' He had found an unstoppable tic tugging at his right eyelid. 'But my life is here.'

'Was,' she'd said.

'What?' And he'd remembered his manners. 'My Lady.' It was as though she had thrown open the door of a dark room and let the sunlight flood in. He had been dreading the changes the new dispensation would bring, with all the promises the old King had made him rendered null and void. Now, suddenly, the chance to redeem his future and his dignity was being put within his grasp.

She had offered him her hand, small and cool and hard. And he had taken it, his heart pounding. He had sworn his formal oath later, kneeling at her feet, her hands on his head, but the true vow had been made then, only yards from her father's corpse and rendered even holier by that proximity. He could still feel that calm, confident pressure on the skin of his palm. He treasured it yet.

'You know I'm right, Wulfgar,' he remembered her saying.

'There's nothing for you here in Winchester now Edward's taken the high seat of Wessex.'

He had tried not to flinch at the direct brutality of her words.

'Is that – are you sure it's inevitable? It has to be your brother?'

She'd nodded, her face sympathetic in the firelight.

'You must have seen it coming,' she had answered. He had heard her sigh. 'Not one of my cousins has so much questioned his claim.'

'Not even Seiriol—'

'*Ow!*'

Someone had *kicked* him. Hard. Right on the bone of the left ankle.

And the only possible culprit was his neighbour, Kenelm, the fair-haired deacon, who was now staring at the altar with studied innocence.

Wulfgar glared at him in speechless outrage, aware only of the shock and pain radiating from his ankle like cracks zigzagging through over-burdened ice. Belatedly, he realised every other man in the cathedral choir was falling to his knees.

Somehow, while he had been indulging himself in reminiscence, the door in the north porch, only feet away from him, had opened, with a cool, wet gust of wind. A pair of men-at-arms had come in from the twilit yard, and they were now standing either side of the door. Whom could they be heralding? Not the Bishop, not with armed men, not in his own cathedral.

It had to be the Lord of the Mercians. No one else would dare come bursting into the cathedral sanctuary.

Just in time, he cascaded into a graceless genuflection.

But it wasn't the Lord of the Mercians.

Queen of Heaven, it's my Lady. Interrupting Vespers? It's unheard of.

At first glance, she looked as serene as ever, her oval face smooth, head high, grey eyes calm, her veils neatly pinned back from her temples. But Wulfgar noticed how her top teeth were worrying at her lower lip, a mannerism he remembered from their childhood back in Winchester. As she stepped further into the candlelight, he thought, yes, something's terribly wrong. She'd been crying.

The precentor was leaving his stall, hurrying forward, hand on heart, head bowed.

'My Lady, to what do we owe the honour?'

She nodded to him, a hand returning to push at her gold-embroidered veils, but her eyes were elsewhere, peering into the incense-heavy air, scanning the ranks of clerics.

Wulfgar knew, somehow, that she was looking for him. He scrambled to his feet, hot and flustered, sensing twenty hostile pairs of eyes.

'Wulfgar,' she said. 'Oh, thank goodness.' She stopped, took a deep breath, lifted her chin. 'With your permission, precentor?'

'My Lady?'

She pointed an imperious finger at Wulfgar, who pulled himself up as tall as he could.

'My secretary. I need him.'

If the precentor was expecting an apology, or an explanation, he was disappointed.

'*Now*, my Lady?'

'At once.'

CHAPTER TWO

The first thing that struck him was a sharp metallic scent in the air – a scent he couldn't place, cutting through the heady fragrance of the apple-wood fire and the beeswax candles. The Lord's bower was dimly lit, and seemed crowded. Wulfgar's eyes went at once, apprehensively, to the great carved chair, but it sat empty.

The Lady had said nothing as she hurried him across the courtyard, the men-at-arms in close attendance, and he didn't dare ask what he might have done wrong. Nonetheless his over-active conscience foraged frantically through the work he had done for the Lord and Lady over the last few days. He must have made some appalling error, he thought, frowning, to make her come for me in person. His recent work had all been connected to the court cases to be heard after Easter. Endless quarrels about cattle, and grazing rights, and who had moved the head-stakes of whose ploughland . . . He shook his head. Dry, and routine, and fascinating in their minutiae, and absolutely nothing that might merit being hauled out of Vespers like this.

Kenelm and the others would be speculating wildly, he realised. Let them.

As they entered the bower, the Lady moved away from him abruptly, going straight over to the bed with its crimson canopy. Wulfgar hovered, unsure whether she would want him to follow.

That smell . . .

Then he knew it for what it was.

Blood.

Even as he recognised it, a waiting woman brushed by him with a bowl covered with a stained linen towel. He peered further into the gloom, and realised there was a figure in the bed. A fragile-looking, motionless figure, whose arm was being bandaged by a healer, to whom the Lady was speaking in low, urgent tones. Wulfgar saw the man gesture at the supine figure and shake his head, and the Lady sagged suddenly, shoulders dropping, neck bowed. Wulfgar, baffled, squinted harder into the gloom. The figure in the bed appeared to be an old man. Where had he come from? What was he doing, in the Lord's bed?

Understanding followed, a heartbeat later.

The Lady was at his side again.

'Wulfgar, what have you heard?'

He could hear the strain in her voice, like a over-tightened harp-string. He shook his head at her, distressed beyond words.

'There's been no gossip among the cathedral clerics?' she persisted.

He found his voice at last.

'None that I've heard, my Lady. Though they don't tell me everything.' They tell me nothing, that would be a better way of putting it. But he pushed the bitterness aside. Now was hardly the time. 'I've been at my work in the muniments room all day. I haven't seen many people.'

She was still wilting, her face tense and weary even in the kindly light of the candles.

'Wulfgar, he woke up like this.' She put her hand on the sleeve of his tunic. 'Come and see.'

The old man – and Wulfgar realised that, somehow, in the space of a few hours, the Lord of the Mercians had become a truly aged man – lay inert against the pillows, under the weight of lambswool blankets. His face was grey, his eyes filmy and elsewhere.

The Lady approached tentatively, as though he might launch himself at her, growling and biting.

'My Lord,' she asked, 'has the bleeding helped?'

She came up to the bedhead and bent over him. Even exhausted as she was, her smooth skin and bright eyes made a painful contrast with the haggard figure under the blankets.

'My Lord?'

The Lord of the Mercians opened his mouth to answer, and a stream of gibberish gushed forth. As he spoke, he became more and more agitated, struggling to sit up, waving an arm but so little in control that he threatened to hit both himself and his wife in the face.

The healer stepped forward and grasped the thick, bony wrists.

'Hush, my Lord. Drink this. It's only milk and honey,' he said in a softer aside to the Lady, 'but it may calm him.'

Wulfgar watched, open-mouthed, silent and appalled, as the Lord of the Mercians choked his way through the glass of sweet milk.

The Lady had her hand to her mouth. Wulfgar could see her

swallowing painfully, almost gagging, in sympathy with her husband. She turned away at last.

'Wulfgar, what should I do?'

'My Lady? I'm no leech!' He glanced at the healer.

'He's been like this all day. I've been waiting – hoping.' She, too, turned to the healer. 'He's not going to get better, is he?'

'Not yet, my Lady. Given time—'

'*Time!*'

The healer ducked, although the Lady hadn't raised a hand.

'We don't have time. He's hearing the first case in the court this evening. And how many – Wulfgar? Over the next week?'

'It must be at least thirty, my Lady.'

'Not to mention hosting the Easter feast on Sunday, with the Bishop.' She put her hands to her temples. 'Oh, my dear God, Wulfgar. The Bishop.'

He nodded, frowning, trying to understand, and wanting to help.

In a low, urgent voice, she said, 'He'll take over. He'll start by holding the court alone, against all precedent. Then he'll find his own candidate for the throne of Mercia. I can see it all.' She flexed her fingers in front of her like claws, as if she were trying to find something to which she could cling. 'I'll be all on my own. No one to watch my back.' She sounded ragged, on the verge of hysteria. 'Wulfgar, they hate us here, you know that.'

He didn't know what to do. He took a step closer to her. It still surprised him, to find that he was now more than a head the taller.

'My Lady, they don't hate you. You've been the Mercians' Lady since you were a girl.'

She had closed her eyes, and to his horror he saw her lips quiver.

'Girl? I was a *child*. Sixteen years I've been in Mercia,' she said, her voice a brittle whisper. 'And nothing to show for it. "Barren". It's almost as bad as "West Saxon", don't you think?'

His throat was tight with sorrow for her. The Vespers psalm she had just interrupted came forcefully to mind: *Behold the inheritance of the Lord are children: the reward, the fruit of the womb.* But if there were no children? What inheritance then? The significance of her words came seeping slowly through to him.

'My Lady,' he said, his shock audible, 'do you mean the Bishop doesn't know about this?'

She shook her head. 'I've been turning people away all day. They'll be talking, though. Only the healer and I have seen him, and my women – though they'll be blabbing it up and down the streets of Worcester as soon as I give them leave to go. I don't trust them. I don't trust anyone.' She looked up suddenly, and reached for his hand. 'Except you.'

'Me, my Lady?'

Her grip crushed his fingers. She looked up at him then, her sea-grey gaze suddenly steady and focused. Queen of Heaven, he thought, but you look like your father. So slight, and so beautiful, but you've inherited his unyielding gaze. He blinked, and tried to make sense of what she was saying.

'Wulfgar, I've known you since you were that funny little boy who used to sort my embroidery silks. You are oath-sworn to me, as you were to my father before me.' He nodded, trying to keep pace with her rapid words. 'You would never betray me.'

Was it a question?

He nodded again, swallowing.

'What do you hold most precious?' she asked, still clinging to his hand.

'My soul, my Lady. And – and you.' I'll swear on my soul and my hopes of Heaven, he thought, if you ask it of me. Let me help. Let me look after you. The words trembled unspoken on his lips.

She squeezed his hand again, and let go.

'I believe you. And I trust you.' She managed a faint smile. 'If only because you're a stranger here, as well.'

Did she have to add that *if only*? Wulfgar rubbed his hand, still feeling the pressure of her fingers.

'My Lady,' he said firmly, 'you are not alone. And you are loved. Very much loved.'

'And I'd forgotten that my cousin Seiriol is coming.' She closed her eyes briefly. '*Deo gratias*, I am not alone after all. He will protect me.'

She looked at him then, grey eyes calmer, her mouth pursed.

I've lost her, he thought. That moment of connection had vanished as though it had never been.

'The first case this evening. Bring us—' She stopped, and corrected herself. 'Bring *me* the documents.'

'For the shire-court, my Lady? Here, to the bower? Now?'

'Yes.' But she turned then, and looked at her husband, prostrate again in the great carved bed. 'No. To the great hall – to the little antechamber next to it, I mean.'

'What are you going to do, my Lady?'

Her eyes were still on her husband.

'*Do*? I'm going to pray, Wulfgar. You should, too. Mercia needs a miracle.'

CHAPTER THREE

'Wulfgar, my uncle wants you. Now.' Kenelm put out an arm to intercept him as he hurried by, but Wulfgar pulled away, his leather-soled indoor shoes threatening to skid on the rain-slick cobbles. It was already dusk, and the court would be in session soon.

'I have no time,' he said over his shoulder.

Kenelm refused to be so easily dissuaded from the task in hand, however. His long legs caught up with Wulfgar as the other hurried across the courtyard towards the muniments room, and he grabbed Wulfgar's arm again. 'I don't think you heard me, *subdeacon*. Your Bishop wants to see you.'

Wulfgar struggled, but Kenelm had him surprisingly tightly by the wrist, and he didn't want to make a scene. Enough curious eyes would be watching, as things were.

'Please, Kenelm, let me go. I'm on an errand for the Lady.' He made the mistake of adding, 'And my duty is to her, not the Bishop.'

Even in the half-light, Wulfgar could see Kenelm's pale blue eyes turn icy.

'You're a cleric in my uncle's diocese. Therefore, you answer to him, even if you do manage to wriggle out of most of your obligations.' Kenelm's lips tightened. 'You think you're so special, don't you?'

Wulfgar closed his eyes. His wrist was hurting in Kenelm's bony grip, and he could feel the soft April rain beginning to soak through to his scalp. He sighed with frustration. He had no idea what the Bishop might want, and he could only hope that it wouldn't take long. He knew exactly where to find the documents the Lady needed; he could see them in his mind's eye all neatly piled and docketed on his desk. 'Very well then.'

'I think I'd better escort you.'

'There's no need.'

'I think there is.'

Wulfgar had to suffer the indignity of being steered back the way he had just come, but towards the Bishop's private bower now rather than the royal apartments.

'Ah, Wulfgar. Good.' The Bishop looked up, and noticed Kenelm smirking at Wulfgar's side. 'You can go now, nephew.' He waved Kenelm away with an impatient hand. 'Wulfgar, come in. Don't hover in the doorway.'

Wulfgar, who had been hoping to leave as quickly as he had arrived, reluctantly stepped over the threshold and, at the Bishop's bidding, he swung the heavy door closed behind him.

'My Lord.'

'What's going on? Why was the healer summoned?'

Wulfgar could think of no reply that would not betray his Lady's confidence. He felt uncomfortable returning the Bishop's dour one-eyed stare, and concentrated instead on the ancient gold pectoral cross the old man wore round his neck.

'Pay attention, boy! Look me in the eye. Try and behave less like a cornered leveret, and give me an answer!' The Bishop knuckled his empty eye-socket with a ring-heavy hand. 'Is she ill?'

'Not the Lady,' Wulfgar said, prevaricating. 'Not ill, I mean.'

'Don't tell me she's with child at last?'

He shuffled his feet, embarrassed.

'Not – not as far as I know, my Lord.'

The Bishop squinted at him.

'Does that trouble you? She's a flesh and blood woman, like any other. Don't confuse her with a painted saint.' He sighed then. 'So, it must be my old friend who needs the leech. Is he dead?'

He shook his head.

'Oh, for God's sake! Say something, boy.'

'I think the Lord of the Mercians has been struck down,' Wulfgar said unwillingly. Speaking the words aloud seemed to give them some awful power. 'By sickness, I mean. Or something.' The Devil, he thought. That's what some would certainly say. And surely it would indeed require some malign power to turn the Boar of Mercia into that dribbling wreck. Wulfgar shivered. Demons. Elves. Or a human hand, as diabolical as any unseen power. Had the Lady thought of poison? Witchcraft? 'He can't speak, and he can't swallow, and he can't get out of bed,' Wulfgar admitted at last.

The Bishop sat very still for a long moment.

'Dear God,' he said at last. 'This is the end.'

'The end, my Lord?'

The Bishop sat with his head bowed over his folded hands.

Wulfgar wondered if he were praying. It seemed inappropriate to interrupt, but after a few moments, wondering whether he might be excused, he ventured, 'My Lord—'

Without looking up, the Bishop said, 'When I was a boy, Mercia was the undisputed overlord. We ruled from the Humber to the Thames. From the Wash to the Irish Sea and the Bristol Channel. Every king in the British Isles paid us tribute.'

'Yes, my Lord. I know, my Lord.' And he did know. He had spent the last five months immersing himself in Mercian history, Mercian charters, Mercian law . . .

The Bishop lifted his head.

'You smug little West Saxon brat. Crowing over the humiliation of Mercia, are you? You today, and King Edward tomorrow?'

And, quite suddenly, Wulfgar had had enough. I'm not a brat, he thought. I'm four and twenty, and I'm a subdeacon of the Church, and I'm sick and tired of this.

'My Lord, why does Mercia hate Wessex so much? Surely we're on the same side? The people you should really hate are the Danes. They're the ones who've stolen half your country. Not us.'

There, he thought, I've said it. I've been thinking it for ages, and now I've said it. What's the worst that can happen? He can't eat me, can he? But remembering some of the stories he had heard as a child, Wulfgar had to wonder.

The first time he had ever seen the Bishop of Worcester, he had been no more than nine years old. The Lady's wedding feast, he remembered with sudden clarity. The bigger boys – that unholy pair of Edward, heir to the West Saxon throne, and Garmund, Wulfgar's own slave-born half-brother – frightening him witless with ever more gruesome tales of how the Bishop had lost his left eye. Wulfgar had still never learned the truth of the story.

He shuddered at the memory, returning to the present moment

to find the Bishop staring at him, disconcertingly owl-like, with that one remaining eye blazing out from below its overhang of grey eyebrow. Then, to Wulfgar's astonishment, the old man laughed. There was no merriment in it, but at least it was a laugh.

'A good answer, boy. You've more spirit in you than I thought.' He gestured at a low stool.

Wulfgar drew it up reluctantly and sat at the Bishop's feet. It was cold in the little room, although the Bishop, swathed in his silk-trimmed lambswool, didn't seem to notice. His attention appeared to be entirely elsewhere. Wulfgar tried to see what it was on his desk that he was staring at. I need to get out of here, he thought. The Lady is waiting for me.

As though reading his mind, the Bishop said, 'Who's going to hold the court?'

Wulfgar stiffened. But he wasn't expected to reply.

'I'll have to do it by myself,' the Bishop said. 'Never mind the conflict of interest in the first case. We'll get over that somehow.' He drummed his fingers on his writing slope, then stood and took two or three paces across the room before turning and coming back. 'Wulfgar—' He stopped.

'My Lord?'

'You speak some Danish, don't you?'

His eyes widened. How did the Bishop know that?

'A little, my Lord. Why? Is there a Danish plaintiff—?'

The Bishop cut him off with an abrupt gesture.

'And have you ever been north or east of the line? Anywhere in the Dane-lands?'

'Never, my Lord. I've been to London, though.'

'London – hah!' The Bishop snorted. 'Can you ride?'

He blinked.

'I – a little, my Lord.' Greatly daring, he asked, 'Why?'

The Bishop's craggy face was closed and remote. Then he looked down at his hands, holding his gold cross. His lips moved. Wulfgar had the impression the old prelate was counting something. Was he trying to keep his temper?

Abruptly, the Bishop said, 'There's a task I need done. But I need someone – a churchman, for preference – who can ride, and knows some Danish, and who can leave Worcester for several days.'

Not me, then, Wulfgar thought with a wave of relief.

'Is that all, my Lord?' he asked. 'I'll let you know if I think of anybody. The Lady needs me now.'

He got to his feet, half-expecting a furious command to sit down again, but the Bishop's thoughts were elsewhere.

'I need a loyal Mercian. Not you, with your heart still south across the border.'

The Bishop turned away with a brusque, dismissive gesture, as if forestalling any further protest, and Wulfgar was able to retreat at last. At the threshold, however, he was called back.

'Wulfgar, the documents for the first case this evening. Fetch them here, to me.' He slapped his hand on his writing desk.

'But—'

'No buts.'

The Bishop's voice was flat and final.

CHAPTER FOUR

But I can't!

He hadn't said it, though. He had nodded, and bowed, and backed out of the bower. I simply can't, he thought again, really hurrying now through the damp dusk, praying for no more ambushes. The Lady had requested those documents first. And he didn't care what Kenelm had said; his allegiance was to the Lady, not the Bishop.

What did he mean, 'Can you ride?' Wulfgar thought, I can sit on a horse while it follows the horse in front. But I don't suppose that's what he had in mind.

Pushing the Bishop and his mysteries out of his mind, he lifted the latch on the door of the muniments room, going straight to the desk where he had stored the wills and charters and writs needed over the coming days. The opening of the court was tonight, and then half a dozen more cases were due to be heard tomorrow, and then there would be a three-day hiatus for the commemoration of Good Friday and the celebration of Easter.

22

The cathedral clergy would be busy tomorrow with the Maundy Thursday liturgy, but most of his own time had already been commandeered by the Lord of the Mercians, to attend him in the court . . .

Wulfgar paused in his rummaging, his eyes suddenly blinded with tears. It was only yesterday that the Lord had been in here with him, listening to Wulfgar explain the details of one tangled bequest after another. He had heard him out, that blunt, grizzled, warrior's face giving nothing away. And then, at the end, the approving slap on the shoulder, the gruff commendation that had had him blushing with pleasure. 'Good man. An eye for detail as well as a sense of the bigger picture. You'll do well here, Wulfgar.' A bluff, jovial man, the Lord of the Mercians. Not unlike Wulfgar's own father. But, he thought, my father – God rest him – never bothered to say anything like that to me.

The documents weren't where he'd left them. It's really only that will, he thought, and the rent returns – but the will's the important one; oh, this is exasperating – I *know* I left them here.

When he found them at last, they were right at the bottom of the iron-bound chest, folded inside a completely irrelevant sheaf of manumissions. He gritted his teeth against a curse. Kenelm, he thought, though it could equally have been any of the others. What made them so petty? Wulfgar was only just beginning to learn his way around the politics of Worcester's cathedral community, and he found the atmosphere devious at best, and all too often riddled with spite (although he admitted, if only to himself, that Winchester had sometimes been just as bad). Too many celibate, ambitious, well-born men who'd given up hopes of family and marriage and land. Men with their avid eyes fixed on the few wealthy abbacies and bishoprics left now after the English

Church had been shattered by the Danes. Every year in Winchester, he had witnessed one or two of the cathedral clergy falling by the wayside, exchanging their soaring visions for the life of a village priest or a canon at a small, poor, rural minster – an ordinary cleric who could marry and farm and raise his family away from the perilous world of bishops and kings.

Wulfgar's lips tightened. If only Kenelm would do as much.

Never mind. He had those documents now and he would take them to his beloved Lady, Kenelm and the Bishop be damned. He couldn't repress a small, triumphant smile. He pulled his cloak from its peg and, wrapping it over his choir robe, he went back into the dusk and the blowing rain.

At the door of the little antechamber to the great hall, though, his lingering smile vanished. At first glance the little room looked so enticing, with its woven hangings, its painted beams, the friendly glow of the charcoal in its braziers. But the air fizzed as though a lightning storm were brewing. He stopped at the threshold, clutching his sheets of vellum to his breast.

'Wulfgar. Good.' The Lady never took her eyes from the Bishop. 'A cup of wine for his lordship of Worcester.'

'This is my palace, Fleda. I give the orders.' The Bishop held out an imperious hand. 'Wulfgar, thank you.'

'But it's my kingdom,' she said.

'Your *kingdom*?' The Bishop creaked with mirthless laughter. 'Wessex has a King. Mercia doesn't, not any more. Don't try pulling rank on me, girl.' He looked at Wulfgar for the first time. 'I'm waiting.'

'My Lord,' he stuttered. 'My Lady—'

She closed her eyes, and, lifting her head under its weight of gold-worked veil, she breathed in.

'Leave us,' she said, eyes still closed.

Her two attendant women rustled to the door, where Wulfgar was also turning to obey.

'Not you, Wulfgar.'

Wulfgar still hesitated, clutching the will and the rent returns to his breast.

When she spoke again, there was a bitter edge to her voice.

'Oh, give those documents to his Lordship of Worcester, if his need of them is so great.'

Wulfgar bit his tongue, bowed, and did as he was told.

'The wine,' she said.

He slid past the Lady to the small table and picked up the heavy glass jug. His hands shook as he poured.

'Godfather.' Her voice was small but steady, her eyes still closed. 'Please. Don't be angry with me, not now.'

The Bishop was holding the documents close to his good eye.

'That land belongs to Worcester diocese. I have plans for it.' He stared over them at the Lady. 'Don't meddle with things you know nothing about.'

She stared back, her jaw set, and Wulfgar found himself fuming on her behalf, his fist clenching around the jug's handle. He forced himself to relax, hesitating for a long heartbeat before he dared to take the brimming cup of wine over to the Bishop, half-expecting the shell of fragile green glass to be dashed in his face. But he had under-estimated the old man. The Bishop sketched a cross over the cup, downed the wine in one swallow and handed it back.

'I have sent for my cousin Seiriol,' the Lady said. Her gaze was still fixed to the Bishop's face. 'He is with my Lord.'

'Your dying Lord.'

'He is *not* dying.'

A rap sounded on the outer door.

'Come in.' She looked up, her expression strained and eager.

Wulfgar's own heart also lifted as the door swung open to admit a familiar figure, a dark-haired, bright-eyed man in his thirties, with rain beading his hair and glinting on the silver of his sword and belt-knife. Athelwald Seiriol, the senior atheling of the West Saxon royal house, the Lady's cousin and oldest ally, and someone else, Wulfgar thought happily, who had no cause to love the new King of Wessex.

The Atheling spoke to the Lady first. 'My dearest cousin!' Taking both her hands in his, he kissed her warmly on the cheek. 'Your husband lives,' he assured her. 'No better, but at least no worse. The healer is with him.' Then, over his shoulder, 'Excitement expected in the court tonight, my Lord Bishop?' He turned, dropping the Lady's hands to give the Bishop his easy smile. 'Everyone out there –' he jerked his head towards the hall '– is wondering how you might keep the men of Sodbury loyal.' Then, 'Wulfgar!'

'My Lord?'

'Good to see you here! How are you settling in? I had a word with your uncle before I left Winchester. He wants you to know his lungs are bad again.'

Wulfgar, delighted and astonished to be noticed, bowed deeply.

'Thank you, my Lord.' He hesitated. 'My Lord Atheling.' Was Seiriol still allowed to claim that title, that status so close to the throne, now that his younger cousin Edward was King?

The Atheling, still smiling, acknowledged the title with a nod.

'And your brother Wystan's had a son,' the Atheling said, 'but that must have been before you left Winchester? All's well at Meon, they tell me.'

Wulfgar mumbled his gratitude again. He thought, oh, I've no worries on that account. Wystan will be all right under Edward's dispensation. Him, and his son and heir, his sheep, and his rolling acres of wheat, they won't care one way or the other that there's a new King in Winchester. But, he couldn't help wondering, what about my father's other son? What about Garmund, the Polecat? I don't need to ask, he thought bitterly. He'll be all right, too, damn it. More than all right. This will be his big opportunity.

The Bishop looked from face to face. 'Have you quite finished?' he said. 'This is no time for your petty Winchester gossip. We face disaster. This lethal blow, at the holiest time of the whole year. Why?'

'These things have no sense of season,' the Atheling said.

'You're wrong there,' the Bishop snapped. 'Our advocates in the court of Heaven have turned against us.'

'Save it for Sunday, Bishop. The Old Boar's not dead, not yet.'

The Bishop leaned back in the chair and squinted up at him.

'This isn't pulpit rhetoric, Seiriol. Mercia is being punished.'

The Lady, eyes closed, massaging her temples.

'Wulfgar, unpin my veils, will you?'

Me? But her women had been dismissed, and she could scarcely expect the Atheling or the Bishop to do it. His hands trembling a little at the intimacy of the task, he slid the gilt pins out of the fine gold-spangled linen and laid them on the table with the jug. She pushed at the veils and he lifted them away from her head, startled by their weight. Her corn-coloured hair was coiled in sleek plaits around the back of her head. 'That's better. That'll do. Thank you.' She looked up at him with a weary smile. 'Don't start counting the grey hairs.'

'It's as golden as it was on your wedding day, Fleda,' the Atheling said, smiling down at her.

'Flatterer. How would you remember? It's so long ago.'

'Forget the day you left Wessex? The day Edward was named as your father's heir?' He had stopped smiling.

'The Atheling is right, my lady,' Wulfgar heard himself say, filling the awkward silence. His face grew even warmer, remembering. Her wedding day had been the worst day of his young life, for so many reasons.

'You surely don't remember my wedding, do you, Wulfgar?'

Still blushing, he nodded.

'But you were only a little boy.'

Not so little, he thought. Nine years old, and I loved you already. He realised he hadn't once seen her bare-headed since her wedding, not until now. And there were indeed silver-grey hairs threading through the fair plaits. He felt disloyal even noticing them, to acknowledge even in his secret heart that she could be anything less than perfect. I was nine, he thought, and you were fifteen when the Boar of Mercia took you away.

You weren't the lofty Lady of the Mercians then. I just called you Fleda, like everyone else. From the day I arrived in Winchester to be fostered by my uncle, you took me under your wing, you and – he glanced at the Atheling – Seiriol. The two of you always seemed to be together in those days. For two winters, you protected me from Edward and Garmund and their little gang of bullies when the adults turned a blind eye. I loved you both then with an adoration verging on idolatry. And then you went away.

The old Bishop's gaze had been ranging around the room, as though looking for someone who wasn't there. Now he said, 'Listen to you gabble! West Saxons, every one of you. What do you care for Mercia, any of you? All my friends are dead.' He paused. 'Or dying.'

'He's *not* dying,' the Lady said passionately.

The Atheling shifted restlessly.

'Common enemies make unlikely bedfellows, Bishop, and have done these thirty years and more.'

The Lady turned to Wulfgar.

'Close the shutters, please. And feed the braziers.'

Glad to have something to do, he hurried to obey, pulling the shutters closed and drawing the curtains across with a rattle of rings, stoking the charcoal in the braziers and lighting more of the small oil lamps. The light glittered and danced across the Lady and the Bishop, but the Atheling was almost as dully dressed as Wulfgar, and the shadows drew him in.

Wulfgar busied himself with the lamps.

'Think of the great shrines of Mercia,' the Bishop suggested. 'Crowland, Ely, Bardney, Repton, Lichfield – what do they have in common?'

Lost, Wulfgar thought. Burned and ruined and looted and lost.

He must have spoken aloud, because the Bishop was nodding.

'All of them, *all of them*, destroyed by the Danes. Whom do we have left?' His hands were quiet now, but their knuckles were white, gripping his great cross and its tangle of gold chain. 'Petty saints unknown outside their impoverished minsters. The landlocked rump of our kingdom. And this new treaty with your brother shows you can't even be trusted with that.'

The Lady closed her eyes.

'Oxford and London are Mercian and always will be. Ceding them to Wessex is inconceivable,' the Bishop went on, remorseless.

The Lady lifted her chin.

'My husband knows what he's about. He knows my brother is our friend, just as my father was. Like it or not, Mercia needs the protection of Wessex.' Her voice was tight. 'And we need to keep the love of the Mercians who are still, somehow, loyal. Men like Ednoth of Sodbury.' She gestured at the discarded will on the matting.

The Atheling roamed around the little room, fingering a hanging, lifting and replacing a cup. He turned.

'If you have a point, Bishop, come to it. My cousin is tired.'

'The point, young man, is this: I can smell fidelity shifting direction out there.' He jerked his head at the white-plastered wall, the inner door and the hall beyond, through which the shuffle and rumble of the gathering court could be heard. 'Mercia could be lost without a battle, this time. Every hour your Lord lies ill, another dozen thanes will leave him to take their allegiance south to Wessex – or north, to the Danes. We need to remind them that they are Mercians, and Christians, and proud of it. We need a new leader.'

A sudden intake of breath.

A faint hiss and crackle from the braziers.

'What's your game, Bishop?' The lamp-flames glittered in the Atheling's eyes.

CHAPTER FIVE

'No game, Seiriol. I want to bring one of our lost saints home.'

There was a sudden, convulsive movement from the Atheling. He turned away, seemingly fascinated of a sudden by the elaborate coiled birds in a woven hanging.

Wulfgar could see his fingers clenching, his shoulders rising and falling with the long, slow breaths he was forcing himself to take.

'We have suffered enough,' the Bishop said. 'It's time to act. I want a new soul for Mercia. A new shrine. Pilgrims from all Christendom coming to Worcester.'

'Not Worcester,' the Lady said. 'Gloucester.'

'Worcester.'

'Gloucester. Not the old minster, either. Our new church.' There was a mulish look to her which Wulfgar remembered all too well.

So, it appeared, did the Atheling. Turning round, he shouted with harsh laughter. 'You'll not move her, Bishop.' He took the Lady's hand. 'Any particular saint in mind?' He echoed the question Wulfgar's own lips had been silently forming.

31

The Bishop closed his eyes and bowed his head over his hands, still clutching his gold cross. Wulfgar wondered if he was making them wait on purpose.

When he lifted his head again, the Bishop said, 'Oswald, King and Martyr.'

The Lady choked on her wine.

Wulfgar, even with no wine to choke on, found a lump in his throat. He stood very still, unwilling even to breathe in case he missed anything. The glory of the Bishop's ambition dazzled him.

The Lady wiped her mouth and regained her composure.

After a moment, she said flatly, 'You can't. Bardney was sacked thirty years ago. St Oswald is only a name.'

'Ah, but what greater name?' The Bishop paused for a moment, as though still unsure how far he could trust this rabble of West Saxons. He came to a decision. 'His bones still lie at Bardney. I had word in the winter.'

Wulfgar could feel his eyes widening almost to the point of pain. Was this what the Bishop had been hinting at earlier? Someone who can ride, he had said, and speak Danish . . .

'A raiding party, then?' The Atheling narrowed his eyes.

'Out of the question. A raid might lead to open war, and we can't risk that, not now. This must be secret. One man could do it, if he's the right man.'

And another man, Wulfgar thought, to organise the welcome of the saint to Gloucester. His heart galloped. Surely he himself was the obvious candidate? They would need the very finest silk vestments, bronze thuribles for incense, embroidered banners, processional crosses, all at very short notice. What did the Bishop have stowed away in the Worcester sacristy? Would he be able to track down some Greek incense?

'A trusted man,' the Lady said.

'A churchman,' added the Bishop.

The Atheling sounded thoughtful.

'Someone whom no one would suspect.'

Another prolonged silence.

Wulfgar's fingers were itching to get his ideas down in wax before he could forget them. *We could have singing boys outside the church, on a high scaffold. I wonder if I could borrow some proper choristers from Winchester . . .*

'Wulfgar?'

It was the Atheling's voice.

Wulfgar came to his senses, blinking. Someone had spoken to him, but he had missed the import of what had been said.

The Atheling smiled at him.

'I said, what about you?'

'Me, my Lord?' He smiled, buoyant with excitement. 'It would be an honour. St Oswald! But surely I'm not worthy—'

'Why not?' The Atheling interrupted, looking pleased with himself. He counted off on his fingers: 'Trusted, yes. A churchman, yes. And look at you. Who would suspect you of anything?'

They all looked.

Wulfgar squirmed under the onslaught of their eyes.

'But surely we need someone who can fight?' The Lady sounded doubtful.

The Bishop snorted.

'No, Fleda. We need someone who can tell the bones of a saint from those of a pig. But I'm not sure Wulfgar's our man.'

Despite the warmth of the little room, Wulfgar felt a wintry shiver of realisation ripple through him. *Fight?* They weren't talking about him arranging a magnificent *adventus* for the saint, were they?

'My Lady,' he said in sudden panic. 'I can't – I mean, I don't—'

The Atheling interrupted him.

'Wulfgar, a word outside?'

Wulfgar looked beseechingly at the Lady, hoping she would countermand this order masquerading as a request, but she only nodded, her face tense and wary.

Taking Wulfgar's arm, the Atheling slid open the bolt of the little door into the courtyard. They stepped out and he drew the door closed behind them. It was still raining, a light needle-prickle of water on the skin of face and neck and hands. There seemed to be no one else in the darkness but the guards around the glow of their brazier at the distant gate.

The Atheling stepped close to Wulfgar and murmured, warm into his ear, 'Believe me. I know. You are the man to do this '

He needed it spelled out.

'You mean I should go to Bardney, don't you, my Lord?'

The Atheling ignored his question.

'Who holds your loyalty?' He took hold of Wulfgar's upper arm again. 'Is it Edward, after all? You're still a West Saxon.'

Wulfgar, shoulders stiffening against the unwanted contact, shook his head in vehement protest.

'Mercia, then?'

He shook his head again.

'No, my Lord. At least—'

'Yes?'

'The Lady,' he admitted.

The Atheling lifted his chin and laughed softly.

'Ah, the Lady. Of course. Our lovely Fleda.'

Wulfgar caught a glint of teeth.

'God above, Wulfgar, does it make the Mercians happy, having us here?'

Wulfgar had to shake his head again.

'And do you want to go home to Winchester?' The Atheling didn't wait for an answer. 'No more than I do. I should be King in Wessex. And that little bastard Edward wouldn't even give me Kent.'

We shouldn't be having this conversation, Wulfgar thought nervously. Men have been exiled for less. But being invited into the Atheling's confidence was stirring deep, unfamiliar ripples of excitement in his soul.

'Would – would Kent have satisfied you, my Lord?'

He felt, rather than heard, the Atheling's soft laughter.

'Oh, no. But how I would have enjoyed throwing his offer in his face.' Now he gripped both Wulfgar's shoulders. 'Tell her you'll do it. Go to Bardney. Show her what you're made of. Make Mercia strong. Bring St Oswald home.' His voice was warming, softening. 'Show us you're more than that bookish little boy who used to believe there was a bear behind the need-house.'

Wulfgar found it hard to smile in return. That bear had been very real.

'Come back in, then? Tell her you'll go?' Wulfgar realised the Atheling was still laughing. 'What? Don't tell me you're afraid? Of the Danes?'

Wulfgar could feel his cheeks grow warm. He nodded, ashamed.

'Aren't you men of God supposed to go forth as lambs among wolves?'

Wulfgar bit his lip. It was no more than the truth. My Lord

Seiriol's right, he thought. Here I am, being offered the chance to do something of infinite value. I have to take it.

'Yes, my Lord.'

'That's the spirit!' The Atheling clapped Wulfgar on the shoulder. 'Good man. In we go, then.'

Wulfgar, hot and cold with excitement and terror, found himself dazzled, eyes watering in the sudden brightness of the candles.

'My Lady,' he said quickly, 'I'll go to Bardney, if it pleases you to send me,' half-hoping, half-fearing, that she was still opposed to the plan. 'If you can hold the court without me . . . ?'

But she nodded at him, her face sombre and composed, and yet looking so soft and young without the severe frame of her veils. 'You know I wouldn't ask you if there was anyone else,' she said gently.

He closed his eyes. What had he expected? *Well done, good and faithful servant?*

Behind him, he half-heard the Atheling saying, 'Wulfgar's loyal. He'll do as he's told.'

The Lady smiled right into his eyes.

'More wine? Wulfgar, pour a cup for yourself.'

Any other time the invitation to join them would have surprised and delighted him, but now it barely registered among the flurry of his thoughts. If he succeeded, it would show those smug place-men at the cathedral he deserved his standing in the Lady's favour. He would come home in triumph with the greatest king and saint the English had ever known, snug in his saddle bags. There would be new songs, stories, miracles. It would make his name for ever.

Miracles.

Mercia had never needed a miracle as badly as she did now.

The green glass cup turned round and round in his hands, the wine slopping close to the brim. He swallowed and felt the warmth of southern vineyards trickling through his veins.

'Then we'll have to find a Mercian to accompany him,' the Bishop said. 'I refuse to trust a West Saxon, not even this one. What if he finds St Oswald's bones and takes them to Winchester, to Edward?'

Wulfgar's mouth fell open in outrage.

The Lady looked up then. Her direct grey gaze met Wulfgar's full on. And her smile was like the sun coming out.

'He won't,' she said, with utter confidence. 'Wulfgar's loyalty is to me. We should go through to the hall,' she said, reaching for her veils. 'Wulfgar, pass me the pins.'

Wulfgar obeyed, his mind far elsewhere.

'How far is it to Bardney, my Lady?'

It was the Atheling who answered.

'Not much over a hundred miles north and east to Lincoln, and Bardney's hard by.' He sounded as though he rode it daily. 'Set off at dawn, hey, Wulfgar?' He smiled at the Lady. 'Give him a week. If he rides the fastest road.'

'A *week*?' The Lady put her hand to her mouth. 'What if my Lord doesn't survive a week?'

'The fastest road, my Lord?' Wulfgar asked, his cold fingers fumbling for a pin.

I don't know where I'm going, he thought, and I don't even know how to get there.

'Leicester,' the Atheling said. 'And on to Lincoln. Easy. There's only one road.'

'The Fosse Way,' Wulfgar said slowly.

The road into the dark.

CHAPTER SIX

The Bishop was concluding the prayers. Wulfgar, up on the dais, standing discreetly to one side, looked over the row of the Lord's armed hearth-retainers to the crowd. Two hundred men were packed in shoulder to shoulder like sheep in a penfold, cloaks giving off the stifling aroma of damp wool. The air was thick with the smoke from hearth and torches and clusters of candles on their iron stands. It was hard to breathe.

Enthroned, her little face framed in those thick-worked, shimmering veils, his Lady looked far more like an image of the Queen of Heaven than the flesh and blood woman the Bishop had called her. Her husband's massive seat with its lion-headed armrests had swallowed her up, the hems of her skirts barely brushing the floor. Wulfgar realised he should have brought her a footstool; there must be one somewhere in the Bishop's palace. He berated himself for his thoughtlessness. She cradled the will on her lap; he had picked it up for her after the Bishop had left the antechamber.

'Amen,' came booming from the floor, and Wulfgar realised the prayers were already over, and the Bishop was settling comfortably onto the purple-padded judgment-stool at the Lady's side. Her face was grim, her little hands gripping the arms of the chair. Wulfgar could hear the mutters coming up from the crowd, angry that the Bishop should apparently be judging a case in which he was also the plaintiff. The Bishop had to hear the grumbles too, but he ignored them. Now the young defendant came up to the dais to put his case. His voice was loud, his indignant words tumbling one over another.

'He told me I had to become a priest! We all thought he was making fun of us, at first. We'll pay you rent instead, we said, but word came back he –' a furious thumb was jerked at the Bishop '– wouldn't accept. And we've fed our sheep on those meadows for some hundred years. It's not *fair*!' The young man pushed a lock of chestnut-brown hair out of his eyes and took a deep, preparatory breath, but a look from the Lady silenced him. He still looked sulky though. A cocky brat.

He's doing himself no favours there, thought Wulfgar.

The Lady unfolded the old will now, the hall suddenly so quiet that the stiff vellum could be heard cracking. She kept them waiting, an unnecessary hand raised for silence, while her eyes flickered over the text. At long last she got down from the chair.

'Ednoth.' Her voice was so low that Wulfgar could hear the sparrows twittering sleepily on the roof beams ten feet above his head. He found it hard to breathe, overcome with a rush of anxious, possessive pride. She cleared her throat. 'Ednoth of Sodbury, I find evidence here in your ancestor's will that your kin did indeed undertake to provide Worcester with a priest in every generation, or the land at Sodbury would revert to the cathedral.

39

You and Bishop Werferth here agree that your family has failed to do this, and so he wants the land back. Is that right, my Lord Bishop?'

The Bishop nodded.

'But it's not about the land.' He swivelled back to Ednoth, stabbing at him with a bony finger. 'It's about souls. *Your* soul, boy. Your great-grandfather entered this pact in good faith, trusting you to pray for him. In refusing the priesthood, you betray your own blood and bone.'

Wulfgar could feel the hairs lift on the back of his neck. How could the boy resist?

'But surely, my Lord, you wouldn't want an unwilling priest?' The Lady was turning away from the Bishop without waiting for his reply. 'Wulfgar?'

Flustered, he stepped forward.

'Take this, please.' She held out the will. He could see her nervousness, the quick pink flicker of her tongue over her dry, pale lips. 'And make a note of my judgment.'

He scrabbled for the wax tablets at his waist as she turned back to the young man.

'Ednoth of Sodbury, this is the judgment of the court of Mercia. Your family has failed in its most sacred duty. The Bishop will tell you the cost of masses for your dead, and the penance for your sins. I see your father's wergild is two hundred shillings, and I would ask the Bishop to bear that in mind when assessing compensation.'

A satisfied growl from the Bishop.

But she hadn't finished.

'However, you keep the land.'

Ednoth whooped with delight.

What an arrogant young fool, Wulfgar thought. Didn't he care if he alienated the Bishop?

But the Lady smiled at the young man.

'We need loyal friends like your kin down on the Wessex border.'

A triumphant grin spread across Ednoth's face, reflected in the growing murmur of support from the floor.

'The bond in this will has outlived its purpose. Justice and common law dictate the terms be changed to an annual rent of fifteen shillings. Wulfgar, have you noted all that?'

He nodded.

'Enough. Let us adjourn for the feast, and the most solemn celebration of Easter. On Monday we reconvene, and, God willing, the Lord of the Mercians will be back in his chair.'

Ednoth raised a clenched fist in triumph, turning from side to side, playing to the crowd.

'I cannot allow this judgment!' The Bishop was on his feet now. 'Fleda, this is – Wulfgar, give me that will.'

Wulfgar clutched it to his breast, looking at the Lady. But she seemed to have forgotten about him. She swept around the screen, back to the antechamber, head held high, women flocking in attendance. Ednoth had already vaulted over the low rail that edged the dais, straight into a mob of whooping, back-slapping friends.

'Court dismissed,' the steward shouted.

Already the big doors at the far end were opening; the noisy factions of thanes and their kin, the gildsmen, the law-suitors, their witnesses and hangers-on, were collecting their weapons and heading out into the dark with their heavy burdens of gossip for the inns and hearths of Worcester.

She's done it, he thought. She's made them accept her in the judgment seat. Now we've a few days' grace to celebrate the Resurrection of our Lord – and perhaps that of the Lord of the Mercians as well. He looked up and blushed to encounter the Bishop's furious, one-eyed stare.

'That's it,' the Bishop said, 'I'm going to send him with you.'

Wulfgar blinked.

'Who, my Lord?'

'The Sodbury brat. His penance. Let him go hunting St Oswald, and much good may it do him.'

'I don't understand.'

'Don't you? Two birds, one stone. You need someone to watch your back. He may not be loyal to me, but he's loyal to Mercia. He'll do.'

CHAPTER SEVEN

Maundy Thursday

It was a cold, bright morning, the rising sun glancing off the weathercock on the cathedral's north-eastern tower, frost still lingering on the shadowed side of the roof. Jackdaws tumbled and soared around the cathedral towers, their shrill caws echoing off the white-plastered stonework.

The day of betrayal, Wulfgar thought. Judas slipping away from the feast to alert the soldiers. St Peter's heartfelt avowals of loyalty to his Lord, vows that were shattered before the cock had crowed three times. How could do they do it? I could never break my oath. Tears pricked his eyelids.

Wulfgar had sent a slave to collect his clean linen; he had his wax tablets and his belt-knife. He had asked the keeper of the cathedral's treasure-house to guard the box which held his little treasures: a little pile of books, his precious ivory styli, and the silver brooch the old King had given him on his ordination. No further prevarication was possible. He had to see the Bishop, and then he would need to set off on this frightening journey. There was no sign of young Ednoth, the boy from Sodbury, who had been so full of himself in the court, and whom the Bishop had chosen as his companion. Wulfgar wasn't sure if he was relieved or sorry. The young man hadn't seemed a likely ally.

'Hey, Wulfgar!' The voice came from one of a small mob of young clerics heading towards the cathedral. He half-turned towards them, despite not wanting to hear anything they might have to say.

'Did you ever hear the story about the West Saxon who went into an ale-house and asked for a yard of ale?'

'Aren't you coming to Matins?' another shouted.

He flinched, turning away again.

'I'm in a hurry. I've got an appointment with the Bishop.'

'With the Bishop,' another mimicked, sing-song and spiteful. 'You think you're so important, don't you?'

'No, I—'

'So the ale-wife says to the West Saxon—'

He walked away, stumbling slightly on the frosted cobbles in the cathedral's shadow, trying not to hurry, ignoring the burst of laughter. He was still rattled by the Bishop's anger last night over the Lady's judgment. He didn't want to provoke him further by being late now.

When the Bishop's door-ward announced him, he found the old man at his writing desk. The day's brilliance had penetrated even this dim room, the shutters standing ajar to admit long lances of light, falling across the notes and tablets on the Bishop's writing desk, including the sheet of parchment he was currently reading. The Bishop was alone.

'Look at this, Wulfgar,' the Bishop said, without looking up. He flipped the edge of the page with an irritated finger.

It wasn't the welcome he had expected. Where was, *Hail, my young hero! God speed you on your quest!*

'What is it, my Lord?'

'A report from the visitor I've sent round the uplandish minsters. He tells me – well, read for yourself.' The Bishop pushed the letter at him.

Wulfgar scanned the scrawl.

'Halfway down the page,' the Bishop said. 'About Diddlebury.'

'Ah, yes.' His lips shaped the words as he read. '"As I reached the minster of St Peter in Diddlebury, I found a baptism in progress. To my horror I heard the priest announce, *Ego te baptizo in nomine patriae, et filiae, et spiritus sancti.*"' What? The Fatherland and the Daughter, instead of the Father and the Son?' He frowned, interested now. 'But if it's just an honest mistake – a priest with inadequate Latin and no heresy intended – canon law states that the baptism should be valid, surely? Doesn't Pope Zachary write that—'

The Bishop grunted.

'Oh, the baptism is valid enough.' He rubbed a hand across his brows. 'But the Latin – *inadequate* is putting it mildly. It wouldn't be so bad if this were an isolated incident.'

Wulfgar nodded, agreeing but still puzzled.

'But, my Lord, why are you showing this to me, not one of your own staff?'

The Bishop growled, and then said, as though it were being dragged out of him, 'We've no one else in Mercia with your kind of scholarship. It seems we have need of you.' He brandished the letter.

Wulfgar tried to resist a smile. So, the Bishop did value him, despite all the evidence to the contrary. He wished Kenelm had heard his uncle's admission. Belatedly, he realised that the Bishop was still speaking.

'A task for when you return.'

'Return? Oh, Bardney.'

'Indeed,' the Bishop said. 'Bardney Abbey. What a tragedy.' He rubbed at his empty eye socket. 'I remember it well, in its glory days. On an island, surrounded by fen. Now the stronghold of a heathen called Eirik, known as the Spider—'

There was a thumping knock at the door.

Wulfgar jumped.

'Enter.'

Two armed men, framed by light, entered, thrusting a grubby and rumpled Ednoth of Sodbury between them. Wulfgar's nostrils twitched at the penetrating fumes of stale wine. A third man reached in to dump a bulky bag inside the door, its half-open flap revealing a glimpse of purple-stained leather straps, decorated with silver-gilt roundels. The boy's sword-belt, no doubt, and the rest of his gear.

'Good. Put him over there.'

The young Ednoth stood just inside the door, looking like thunder.

'Where was I?'

'Eirik the Spider, my Lord,' Wulfgar said, startled and distracted.

'Ah, yes. His reeve – a man named Thorvald – contacted me in February. He claimed that his mother's father had been the guardian of the shrine—'

'But Thorvald's a *Danish* name,' Wulfgar said, unable to stop himself, still rattled by Ednoth's sudden appearance.

'Oh, yes, his father was a Danish soldier. But his own loyalty is to his saint, he tells me. His grandfather entrusted him with the secret of where the relics lie. This Eirik has no idea – he is rarely there. His wife runs the estate. Thorvald's price is five pounds in silver. Under no circumstances will you let him know the true worth of the relics. We don't want him inviting other offers.'

Wulfgar blinked.

'Other *offers*, my Lord?'

The Bishop snorted.

'Name me a bishop in Wessex who wouldn't break half the commandments to have Oswald King and Martyr in his church. That jumped-up swineherd, Denewulf of Winchester, for one. But I've no cause to think he's on the scent.'

Wulfgar, bridling at the insult to his old superior, couldn't restrain himself any longer.

'But, my Lord, canon law forbids – *nemo martyrum mercetur*—' His bravado stuttered to a halt in the face of Bishop Werferth's unwavering glare.

'Don't tell me how to do my job, subdeacon.' The Bishop's mouth twitched.

Are you *laughing* at me? Wulfgar thought.

'Shall we say that Thorvald is giving us a present, and we're giving him one in return? No *marketing the martyr* there, eh? No *nefarious* haggling? So you can stop pulling that face.' He sighed. 'It's a dirty world out there, Wulfgar. Not everyone can afford the luxury of a conscience as freshly fulled and bleached as yours.'

Wulfgar nodded, shocked and unhappy. It wasn't a matter of conscience, but a matter of canon law, and the law could hardly be clearer. He could hear his uncle lecturing on the subject even now: '*Nefas est*, the clause says, *sacras reliquias vendere* – translate, Wulfgar?' And his own voice, piping: 'It is absolutely forbidden to sell sacred relics.'

He came back to the present moment with a frown. Absolutely

forbidden – and the Bishop knew it as well as Wulfgar did himself.
Wulfgar glanced at Ednoth, but the boy was still staring at the
floor, brows knitted and lower lip jutting. No help from that
quarter, but he hadn't really expected any.

The Bishop tugged the largest of his massive rings over a bony
knuckle. He held it out to Wulfgar.

'This will serve as your passport. Thorvald knows it. Take good
care of it. My steward will find you two horses and some supplies.'
He unlocked a small chest that stood by the side of the desk, and
removed one weighty and one smaller leather bag. 'Thorvald's five
pounds. Another pound for travel expenses. I'm being generous.
Don't let the Danes cheat you – but you speak Danish, you should
be all right.' He locked the chest again. 'When you have the relics,
bring them straight down to Gloucester, to the royal palace at
Kingsholm.'

So, the Lady had won that battle. Wulfgar felt a little smile
tugging the corners of his lips upward.

'Yes, my Lord. Gloucester, my Lord.'

'Don't smirk. It's revolting.' The Bishop reached out his claw-
like hand to grip Wulfgar's own with astonishing power. He
looked more like a fierce bird of prey than ever. 'Bring him back
to us. And hurry, boy. Your precious Lady can't hold Mercia on
her own. She's mad to think she can. But with St Oswald at her
side, she could bring the most rebellious thanes to heel.'

'Yes, my Lord.' He had clearly been dismissed. But he had to
ask. 'Does – does the Lord of the Mercians still live?'

The Bishop released his hold. He seemed to sag suddenly.

'If you call it living.' He turned then and looked at Ednoth.
'Young man, this pilgrimage is your penance. Your job is to guard
Wulfgar and support him in all he does. When you return with the

saint, then we will see about re-admitting you into the communion of Holy Church. Until then, be warned. Your soul is in mortal peril.' He snorted. 'And much you seem to care. Wulfgar, take that stinking boy outside, get on your horses, and *go*.'

Wulfgar bowed his head for the old man's rapidly sketched blessing.

As soon as they were outside, Ednoth burst out, 'How can you stand it?'

'What?'

He shivered violently, like a dog shaking dirty water from his fur.

'*Don't let him know the true worth of the relics*,' Ednoth mimicked savagely. 'My father warned me the Bishop was out to cheat us. I didn't realise he was out to cheat everybody.'

'Were the Bishop's men rough with you?' Wulfgar asked, concerned.

'I don't want to talk about it.'

'Did they hurt you?'

The boy shrugged, half-turning away.

'It was my idea to come.'

Wulfgar, feeling snubbed, kept his doubts to himself. He unclenched his fist and looked at the Bishop's ring in his palm. Greek work by the look of it, a heavy gold band, its chunky filigree setting holding a blood-coloured carnelian. Far too big for his finger, or even his thumb. He would have to find a spare thong and tie it around his neck.

'My uncle never gave you that?' It was Kenelm who had approached unseen, light-blue eyes avid with curiosity.

Wulfgar instinctively looked around for the rest of the Deacon's gild-brothers, but Kenelm seemed to be on his own.

'It's a loan, that's all,' he told Kenelm.

'It's a reliquary, you know.'

Wulfgar looked at it again, and shook it. A faint rattle answered him.

'Who's in there?' He felt very moved by the Bishop's trust. He lifted the ring to his lips, kissed it, and whispered, *I'll take good care of you.*

Kenelm shrugged, tight-lipped.

'Why should I tell you? Go back in and ask him yourself if you want to know.'

Wulfgar looked at the ring.

'I don't need to know.'

He wished Kenelm would go away. He didn't really want anyone to witness him trying to get onto a horse, let alone one of his fellow clerics who would be only too happy to tell the others what a spectacle he had made of himself.

The stable-lad led out two horses. Fallow and Starlight, he told them. Ednoth looked them up and down, and pulled a face.

'Do you want the gelding or that funny little mare?' he asked Wulfgar.

Which was which? Wulfgar wondered.

'I'll have the little one, the brown and white one,' he answered, after a pause. He tucked the ring away in his belt-purse and strapped the bags of silver behind his saddle before leading the mare over to the mounting-block and putting a tentative foot in her stirrup-loop.

Ednoth had already swung himself into the saddle, ignoring the block.

'Which way?'

'Where are you going?' Kenelm asked, his eyes narrowing.

But before Wulfgar could respond to either question, there was a flurry of movement at the gateway.

'Wulfgar!'

It was the Atheling, riding in with a couple of men-at-arms at his back. He was dressed for hunting, with a hooded gyrfalcon perched on his wrist. Fallow took a couple of startled steps backwards, and Wulfgar found himself having to hop foolishly, one foot still in the rope-loop.

'Wulfgar!'

Had the Atheling come to wish him farewell? It seemed unlikely, and yet he came straight over, without ceremony, leaving his escort at the gate, swinging out of the saddle in one fluid movement, the huge bird still gripping his glove. She gave a great beat of her powerful, silver-grey wings, more than a yard in span, and Wulfgar flinched despite himself.

'I was afraid you might have gone already,' the Atheling said. The stable-lad ran up to hold his gleaming mount, at which Ednoth gazed open-mouthed.

Wulfgar stepped back down from the mounting-block, one hand still on Fallow's reins. He found the Atheling taking his other arm, drawing him aside, speaking fast and low.

'Things are changing so fast, Wuffa, here and in Wessex. You're right at the heart of things here. What do you think is going to happen?'

Wulfgar was taken aback by this friendliness. No one in Mercia called him by his boyhood pet-name of Wuffa, *little wolf-cub*. Not even the Lady – not anymore. What was going on?

'I – I don't know, my Lord. I'm only the secretary.'

'Only! I'll wager you hear everything. Go on. I want to know.' The gyrfalcon gave a sudden shake of her head and another shiver of her wings, setting the bells on her jesses tinkling. The Atheling gazed fondly at her. 'She's eager to be flown.'

Wulfgar was finding it hard to refuse this intimate, smiling pressure. Hoping to deflect the conversation, he, too, stared at the beautiful, ferocious bird. He realised he recognised the hood, with its tuft of colourful feathers.

'Is she yours?' he asked. 'Doesn't she belong to the Lord?'

The Atheling shrugged.

'He has no need of her at the moment. Answer the question, Wuffa.'

Wulfgar swallowed.

'The Lady will take over until the Lord recovers.'

'Recovers? You really think . . . ?' The Atheling let his voice trail away delicately.

'There is precedent. Even if –' he crossed himself hastily '– even if the Lord dies. Mercian history is full of ruling queens.' Astonishingly so, to someone from Wessex.

'Queens regent, yes. But this one's no Mercian, not by birth.' The Atheling shook his head, his glossy dark hair glinting almost chestnut in the sun. 'And it's not as if she's keeping the throne warm for an heir.'

'She's a Mercian now,' Wulfgar said stubbornly.

The Atheling sighed.

'Forget Fleda for a moment.' His voice softened further. 'Would you rather see me or my dear cousin Edward in the high seat of Mercia when you get back?'

Edward, rule Mercia? Wulfgar's heart faltered. When he looked up again the Atheling was looking into his eyes intently.

'I thought so,' he said, smiling, 'How long will you be away? A week? Think about it. Kingdoms have fallen in a day, you know.'

Wulfgar knew that only too well.

'What is it that you want from me, my Lord?' he asked carefully.

The Atheling's dark eyes flickered.

'I would be King of Wessex, if I had my rights. Failing that, I'll have the Lordship of Mercia. And I want your support.' The grip on Wulfgar's elbow tightened. 'I'll need churchmen I can trust. Abbots. Bishops, even. There aren't enough bishops in Mercia.'

An ox-cart laden with hay rumbled through the gateway. Its driver looked towards them and half-rose to bow in his seat.

The Atheling leaned in close enough for Wulfgar to feel the hot tickle of breath on his cheek.

'I need someone to take a message,' he said softly. 'A private one, to friends across the border, in Leicester and Lincoln. You're going there anyway. It's no extra burden.'

Wulfgar looked at his shoes, conscious of a courtyard full of fascinated eyes. The gyrfalcon rustled her feathers and jingled her bells. Fallow snorted and shifted her weight to a different hoof.

'Trust me, Wuffa. *She* does, you know.'

It was no more than the truth, Wulfgar knew that. But was the Lady right to do so? Did her cousin have her best interests at heart, any more than her brother Edward did? Wulfgar felt the world shifting beneath him.

'I'm a good friend to my friends. You know that, Wuffa.'

It was the truth. But he was also known to be a bitter foe to those who opposed him. Wulfgar tightened his grip on the bridle. He felt a sudden overwhelming desire to know what the Lady would think, but there was no time to consult her.

Fate had indeed been very cruel to the Atheling, there was no contesting that point. And he had always been very kind to Wulfgar, even when there had been nothing obvious to gain by that kindness. There was a debt there which Wulfgar would never be able fully to repay.

'*We light the fire at All Hallows.*' The Atheling sounded on the verge of exasperation. 'That is the message you need to deliver. Can you remember that? Find the Jarls. Hakon Grimsson in Leicester, and Toli Hrafnsson in Lincoln.'

Danish names.

'Tell no one else. No one, do you hear me?' He gave Wulfgar's elbow a little shake. 'Only Hakon Grimsson and Toli Hrafnsson. *We light –*'

'*– the fire at All Hallows.*' All Hallows, he thought, that's the first of November. It was more than half the year away. Or did he mean a church dedicated to All Saints, All Hallows? Wulfgar frowned.

The Atheling prompted him: 'The names?'

'Hakon Grimsson in Leicester. Toli . . .'

'Toli Hrafnsson.'

He repeated it without stumbling this time. Hrafnsson. Raven's son, he thought. Something about it chilled him.

Leicester and Lincoln.

Mercian cities, once upon a time . . . with Mercian cathedrals, and Mercian bishops.

Not anymore.

Not for thirty years.

The Atheling smiled at him.

'Good man! I knew I could rely on you.' He turned to go, saluting Ednoth with a friendly clap on the shoulder, wishing them Godspeed as he went. The hooded falcon screamed, a wild, harsh sound that made the hairs rise on Wulfgar's nape.

He noticed Kenelm, still loitering outside the Bishop's bower, watching them shamelessly. Wulfgar, doing his best to ignore the Deacon's curious gaze, climbed back up onto the mounting block. He grabbed his reins and a fistful of Fallow's coarse mane, and heaved himself onto her back, scrabbling with his right foot for the other stirrup. The cobbles looked very far away but at least he had scrambled up without overly embarrassing himself.

'That was the Atheling!' Ednoth said, excitement infusing his words.

'I know,' Wulfgar said absently, still groping for his right stirrup with his foot.

'Athelwald Seiriol!' Ednoth was glowing. 'He should be king in Wessex instead of Edward, my father says. Because he's the son of the old King's elder brother, the one who was king before him.' He turned to look at Wulfgar. 'Do you know him, then?'

Wulfgar nodded, still deep in thought.

'Of course. He's the Lady's cousin. We all grew up together in Winchester, the cathedral oblates like me, and the royal children, and the thanes' sons at the King's school.' So much older than me, away so often, first at weapon-training, then making his name in battle. But always someone to hero-worship. Always someone you wanted to trot along after, even after the old King named Edward as his heir.

Ednoth was bright-eyed, his hangover and his bad temper apparently forgotten.

'Wait till I tell my little brothers!' he exclaimed. 'We saw him before, once, in Bristol. He's famous, you know. In the battle of Farnham, when he was younger than me . . .'

But, as they walked their horses under the gateway and out of the Bishop's courts, Wulfgar wasn't paying heed to Ednoth's cheerful babble. I never said yes, he thought, I never agreed to carry his message. *Light the fire at All Hallows.* What's that supposed to mean? He chewed his underlip. It didn't matter whether he had acquiesced or not, he realised. The Atheling took it for granted that he had: he was stuck with it.

The streets of Worcester were thronging with carts and barrows, flocks of ewes with their lambs, dairywomen with the first cheeses of the season, salt-wagons coming in from Droitwich. The market-day crowd made for slow going, but at last they came out by the east gate. The circuit of the walls was mostly in timber but here along the river-front – so potentially vulnerable to Danish attack – they were reinforcing the revetment in stone. The gate guards recognised Wulfgar, holding the carts back to let them ride through and greeting him in the Lady's name. Despite everything, he was beginning to feel at home in Worcester. He had a role to uphold. People knew him in Worcester, and they respected him, even if respect seemed all too often to ride pillion with resentment.

He realised Ednoth had been asking him something.

'I beg your pardon?'

'The Bishop said you spoke Danish?'

Wulfgar nodded.

'There are a couple of Danish hostages in Winchester. Handed over as part of a peace treaty when they were still little boys. Baptised, of course.' Young devils, he thought. 'I was teaching them to read and picking up some Danish in exchange. It was the old King's idea.' The boys had seen it as a punishment; he hadn't learned as much as he would have liked. And they had thought it funny to teach him obscenities, without telling him the real meaning, until their sniggers had betrayed them. He felt his cheeks grow warm, remembering.

'Go on, then. Say something in Danish.'

Nasty, spiky language. What can I remember?

'They taught me some songs,' he said at last. He cleared his throat, hummed a note: '*Skegg-old, skálm-old, skildir ro klofnir, Vind-old, varg-old* —' He saw the look on Ednoth's face then, and had to laugh.

'Is it rude?' Ednoth sounded hopeful.

You and those Danish ruffians, Wulfgar thought, you'd have had a lovely time together.

'No,' he said. 'It's religious. *Axe-age, sword-age, shields are cloven. Wind-age, wolf-age* . . . About the end of the world. The Last Judgment, though I don't think the Danes call it that.'

'What do they call it, then?'

He frowned, trying to remember.

'The sunset of the gods. Their gods, I mean. False gods. Who will die and not come back.' And we're going into the lands where those unholy powers hold sway, he thought with a shiver. It hadn't really sunk in yet.

'And did they tell you about their sacrifices?' Ednoth asked. 'Do they really hang people to their gods?'

'I'm told they do.'

As chance would have it, they were reaching the edge of the Bishop's jurisdiction. At the crossroads, workmen were busy on ladders, refurbishing the gallows for the new crop of sinners the shire-court would no doubt be reaping after Easter.

'But so do we.'

He gestured at the gallows, that gateway to assured perdition, and his thoughts turned at once to his Lady, thrust so precipitately into Mercia's judgment seat. She had never held the court before – never sent a man to his death. Could she bring herself to do it?

'But that's different.' Ednoth sounded very confident. 'They're criminals.'

'Is it different? Really?' Wulfgar found himself genuinely unsure. 'I suppose so.'

'And do they – the Danes, I mean – do they really do that blood-eagle thing to your ribs? And lungs?' Ednoth sounded enthusiastic. 'You know, what men say they did to King Edmund of the East Angles? Flaying, and then—'

'St Edmund,' Wulfgar said reflexively, longing to change the subject. Wasn't the boy worried? Didn't he care about the risks they would be running? Did he really see this journey as no more than his prescribed penance, irksome rather than dangerous?

'Ednoth,' he asked suddenly, 'why did you decide to come?' Better not to imply that the fists of the Bishop's men were reason enough.

Ednoth was quiet for a moment, an uncharacteristically pensive look on his face.

'You've never been to Sodbury, have you?' Ednoth asked.

Wulfgar shook his head, puzzled.

'My father's a two-hundred-shilling man, you know.' Ednoth's voice was full of pride. 'Our hall stands on the western slope of the Cotswolds. It's the southern tail end of Mercia. You look down over the pasture – those water-meadows your damn Bishop's after – and you can see the River Severn, and the Welsh hills beyond. Wessex is only a couple of miles behind us, and Wales in front. We have to watch ourselves, front and back. But we've held that land from the Kings of the Mercians for five lives of men.'

Only half as long as we've been at Meon, Wulfgar thought, and my father's wergild was twelve hundred shillings. He bit his tongue, though. He didn't want to sound boastful, even if his father had been a king's thane, valued second only to the King himself, and from one of the oldest of the West Saxon noble families.

'This is us fighting back, isn't it?' Ednoth went on. 'This is the start of the new Mercia, rescuing St Oswald? Making us supreme again. I want to be part of it.' His young face had briefly lost its puppyish quality; he looked fierce and proud. 'I'm a true Mercian. And the Lady's my Lady.'

Wulfgar nodded, thoughtful. In some ways, then, they weren't so different, he and Ednoth.

Jolt, *jolt*. Jolt, *jolt*. Jolt, *jolt*. At every lurch, Wulfgar felt the thud of his bones against the wooden frame of his saddle. The layers of woollen padding might as well not have been there. He wasn't looking forward to a week in this saddle. The least St Oswald could do in return was to be waiting for them at the end of the road. St Oswald . . . His thoughts were questing this way and that, hounds on the scent, trying to remember everything he had ever learned about the saint.

'What are you singing?' Ednoth asked.

Wulfgar was startled back into the moment.

'Singing? I wasn't singing, was I? What have I got to sing about?'

'You were. Humming, if you like. Under your breath.'

'Was I?' Wulfgar had to stop and think. 'Oh! Oh . . .'

'What?'

'It was that song about St Oswald's niece,' he said slowly. 'She finds his body on the battlefield and reburies it at Bardney. You must know it.'

But Ednoth shook his head.

'If I do, I've forgotten it. What happens next?'

Wulfgar swallowed.

'She's that Queen of the Mercians who . . .'

'Who what?'

'Who's murdered by her own thanes, when – after her husband dies.'

After that, they rode in silence.

Wulfgar had been trying to ward off his darker fears by keeping pace with the Maundy Thursday liturgy in his head, measuring the time by the angles of sun and shadow. The chrism mass at the cathedral should be over by now, and the Bishop would be washing the feet of the twelve paupers. They'd be celebrating the institution of the Eucharist now, and now they would be ringing the bells for the last time until Sunday. He rubbed the top of his head absently, feeling for the palm-sized shaven circle that should be newly there, and wasn't. He was just imagining the sombre ritual of veiling the crosses, snuffing all the lamps and stripping the altars, preparatory to the great and mournful solemnities of Good Friday when Ednoth broke into his reverie.

'Do you want to hear a riddle?'

He jumped violently.

'What did you say?'

'You'll never guess.' Ednoth grinned. 'I'm long and hard and hairy at one end, and I make maidens weep – who am I?'

Wulfgar remembered this sort of thing all too well from his schooldays.

'An onion?' he hazarded, with ill-concealed distaste.

'What? No . . .' Ednoth made a suggestive gesture. 'Oh, Wulfgar, you're such an innocent.'

Wulfgar sighed. That was the worst thing about those riddles, he remembered belatedly. You couldn't win. If he had given the obvious, shameless answer, Ednoth would only have hooted with laughter and accused him of having a filthy mind. It's the sort of joke my father used to love, he thought. God rest his soul.

CHAPTER EIGHT

Good Friday

They spent the night in a verminous inn at the little hamlet of Stratford, which did little to cheer Wulfgar. He woke at his usual early hour in a small hall, pitch-dark and full of snoring, farting strangers, aching in every muscle and with new flea bites in a band across his ribs from the musty straw. No one else was stirring. He huddled himself into his cloak to contemplate the banked embers of the hearth and pass the time till dawn by saying the prayers and psalms appropriate to *Tenebrae*, the heart-breaking service of the shadows, dedicated to darkness and loss. And then he had perforce to watch Ednoth break his fast with roasted eggs and fresh wheaten bread.

'Have some,' the ale-wife said cheerily, offering him the treen platter.

'I'm fasting.'

'But you're a traveller, like everyone else,' Ednoth joined in, gesturing round the hall. 'Surely you don't have to fast?'

He could see the steam rising from the bread as Ednoth broke the crust apart with his fingers. The moist, white interior smelled deliciously yeasty.

Tight-lipped, Wulfgar said, 'But it's Good Friday.'

'And I'm excommunicated, so I'm doubly exempt.' Ednoth grinned and reached for another small loaf from the heaped platter.

Wulfgar got up and walked out of the inn. Penance, he thought furiously. Penance and fasting and alms-giving. That's what excommunication means. It's not a charter of liberties.

Even another bright day couldn't cure his bad temper. Getting back into the saddle had been agony on his already aching limbs. I should be at home in the cathedral, he thought bitterly. Holding up the cross for the people to venerate. *The royal banners forward go*, he chanted under his breath, *The cross shines forth in mystic glow . . .*

Ednoth had been riding a length or two ahead. Now Wulfgar saw him stiffen. The road dipped here to cross a small stream, and he was reining Starlight in to peer down at the mud of the churned-up track-way.

'What is it?'

Ednoth didn't answer. He had jumped down from the saddle and now he squinted at the soil.

'There's been a large party of horsemen along this way. They joined the road a hundred yards back or so. Not long ago, either.'

'Well, we're drawing close to the Fosse Way,' Wulfgar said, not understanding Ednoth's concern. 'We can expect to meet farmers, and merchants.'

Ednoth snorted.

'*Wulfgar.* Look at the hoof prints.'

Wulfgar slid gingerly out of his saddle. The mess of half-moons meant nothing to him.

'So?'

'Look at the size! And do you see the depth to them? We're not talking pack-ponies here, or farm nags like these beasts we're riding. Those were good horses – really good horses. More than a dozen. Ridden hard, too. Look how they've thrown the mud up.' He gestured with his free hand.

'Are you sure?'

Ednoth gave him a long-suffering look.

'Yes, I'm sure. I wonder who they might be. It looks like they've come up from the south. Wessex, maybe?'

'Do we want to stay on this track, then?'

'Do we have a choice?'

'I just thought we might be better . . .' Wulfgar tailed off, unwilling to give his fears a name.

Ednoth yelped with laughter.

'But that's why I'm here! I'll look after you.'

Wulfgar shied away from his pitying look.

'Wulfgar really isn't a very good name for you, is it? You're more like a mouse, really. I think I'll call you Wulfgar *Mouse*.' He snorted at his own wit. '*Mousegar*.'

'You will not call me Mousegar.'

'Give me a reason not to, then.'

Their grassy track joined the Fosse Way soon after that. The famous high-road stretched ahead, straight and true, as far as the eye could see, a hundred feet across. It led them due north east, all the way to its terminus at Lincoln, the lines of old square stones still breaking the soil in places.

Wulfgar found his mind running after the ancient Mercian estate records he had been archiving all Lent, trying to transpose their dry-as-dust legal phrases onto the lush April landscape unfolding around him. When those tattered leaves of vellum had been issued by long-dead kings of Mercia, the Fosse Way on which they were now riding and Watling Street had formed a great saltire cross, carrying Mercia's lifeblood in the form of merchants and warbands and missionaries. Mercia, the Middle Kingdom, had reached east to the Humber, the Wash, the Thames.

But now only the south-western reaches of the Fosse Way belonged to Mercia, and every frontier was menaced.

Watling Street was the frontier with the Danes.

Wessex was laying claim to both Oxford and London.

The border with Wales was endlessly disputed.

Chester and Bristol were the only surviving Mercian ports, and even they were being slowly strangled by the Danish pirates in the Irish Sea.

For all the spring sunshine around him, Wulfgar found his mind's eye overtaken by darkness. Foes on all fronts, and the Lord on his deathbed. Soon, perhaps, the light of the ancient kingdom of Mercia would be extinguished altogether.

Not if he could help it.

Not if St Oswald came back in triumph to Mercia. Not if the Lady's new church in Gloucester became a great node of pilgrimage. Not if the shield-wall of Mercia could march into battle with St Oswald's reliquary in the vanguard. He squared his shoulders, tightened his abdominal muscles, and sat taller in the saddle.

'*Oof*!'

'What?'

'Cramp! It's my thighs – *ow* – Ednoth, I'm sorry, I'm going to have to walk for a bit.'

He bit his lip, clutching his reins in one hand as he frantically massaged the muscles of his left thigh with the other.

'Could you help me down?'

Ednoth looked at him with what Wulfgar read as contempt but, saying nothing, he swung himself easily to the ground and came to lend him his arm.

Wulfgar bent over for a moment, waiting for the deep muscular torment to subside.

He took a deep breath.

'All right.'

They walked side by side for a while, Ednoth leading both horses, with Wulfgar, suffering in pride as much as in body, flinching at every step and trying to keep to the soft turf rather than the unforgiving stone.

The Fosse Way is proving my *via dolorosa*, he thought. My *via crucis*. A feeble imitation of the real blood-stained path to Calvary and the Cross, to be sure, but it felt right to be on this penitential journey, to be fasting and in pain, this day of all days. He plodded on, trying not to let Ednoth see him wince.

The great road was busy. When his cramp had eased enough for Wulfgar to look around he realised that the traffic had a festive air to it which left him baffled: enormous flocks of sheep herded by cheerful shepherds; plodding ox-carts laden with chattering folk; the odd smiling horseman; bands of barefoot girls with wreaths of blackthorn and violets in their hair, carrying beribboned lambs – and all heading in the same north-easterly direction that he and Ednoth were going. Eventually, indignation tempered with curiosity got the better of him, and he hailed one of the passers-by, a stout, friendly-looking woman clinging onto the side of a crowded cart.

She stared down at him, gape-mouthed.

'Don't you know? St Modwenna? At Offchurch? It's her feast today.'

Shock rendered Wulfgar speechless.

'Are you coming?' she went on blithely. 'Everybody's welcome.'

He found his voice at last.

'But it's Good Friday!'

'Aye, to be sure, and the priests will keep that. But we can't slight our St Modwenna, just because another holy day falls along with hers.' She stared at him as though he were simple. 'She hallows the flocks.' She shook her head now. 'It's the great day for us, young man. Where do you come from, that you don't honour St Modwenna?'

'But, but—' But *nothing* was more important than Good Friday. All other feasts were shunted ahead a few days in the kalendar, or abandoned altogether, if they fell foul of Easter. Nothing but *nothing* outranked Easter.

Especially not some petty little saint of whom he had never even heard.

Was this what the Bishop had meant, when he had said the upland minsters needed sorting out? Wulfgar hadn't understood at the time. Now he was beginning to. In his bafflement and unhappiness, it was a moment before he realised Ednoth was talking to him.

'Oh, Wulfgar, you must know about St Modwenna's milk. My sisters will all be drinking milk tonight and dreaming of the men they're going to marry.'

'That's it,' the woman in the ox-cart called over the rumbling of the solid wheels. 'The lads, too, up this way. Nice, warm dreams.' She gave Ednoth a complicit smile.

Ednoth reached over and prodded his ribs.

'Come on, Wulfgar! Don't look so furtive. Who's the girl you're dreaming about?'

Wulfgar looked fixedly at the road and tightened his grip on Fallow's reins.

'I don't know any girls. Of course I don't. I'm going to be a priest.'

'But priests have women,' Ednoth said. 'Our chaplain at Sodbury has got seven children.'

'Exactly,' Wulfgar said, cheeks burning. 'Village priests. Not bishops.'

'And you're going to be a bishop?' Ednoth sounded incredulous. 'What would you want to do that for?'

It was true, though, Wulfgar thought defensively. All his life, he had been told he was destined for the highest ranks of the Church. And senior clerics were married to their minsters, his uncle, the canon of Winchester, had always told him. His elder brother Wystan had been destined for the land, and the wife and the son. You can do better than that, Wuffa, his uncle used to say. And Wulfgar would look at his father, his libidinous, foul-mouthed father, and thank the Queen of Heaven he didn't have to grow up to be like that. Two wives, and a field-slave for a mistress, and Wulfgar was sure there had been other little by-blows running around in the slaves' quarters, even though Garmund was the only one their father had ever acknowledged.

Ednoth and the woman on the cart were still looking at him.

What was the right answer? *I'd rather dream of a nice, warm cathedral . . .* He didn't want them to laugh at him.

The woman appeared to have given up on him. She leaned precariously over the side of the cart towards Ednoth, her voice cheerful and inquisitive.

'You're coming to the feast, then?' she asked him. 'Have you come far?'

'We're on our way north. We're servants of the Lady.'

'Ednoth!'

But the boy went on regardless, in answer to something else the woman had said.

'Oh, no, we answer to her directly! We're on an important mission—'

'*Ednoth!*'

But he was too late.

'Servants of the Lady? Heading north?' Turning to the old lady sitting on her other side, she bellowed, 'Auntie, these boys can take you home!' She swung back. 'She came down to visit us and the children a few days ago, never misses the chance to see our saint and get some holy milk, but she should get home after the procession, really. It's only as far as Wappenbury.'

She looked from Ednoth to Wulfgar and back again.

'One of you can put her up on your crupper. Look at her. You'll hardly know she's there. Now then, Auntie? These nice young men will see you safe back to Wappenbury after you've had your milk.'

'I want to ride with him.' A twig-like finger emerged from the shroud of finely woven wool to stab at Ednoth. 'Broad shoulders. I do like broad shoulders.'

Ednoth bowed.

'My pleasure, lady.'

'Who's in charge here?' Wulfgar was furious. 'Ednoth, we simply haven't got time—'

'We can ride hard this afternoon. You need to rest, don't you?'

'Yes, but—'

'But what?' Ednoth's smile was wide and knowing. 'Isn't this Christian charity? Doing good deeds. Paying our respects to the saints. Isn't that your job?'

CHAPTER NINE

'I've had an idea.' Ednoth was loosening Starlight's girth, having looped his reins round a tree stump just outside the minster yard, within reach of a patch of new grass.

'Yes?'

The boy straightened up.

'Let's grab St Modwenna instead of going hunting for St Oswald.'

'What?'

But Wulfgar wasn't listening. Through the open minster-gates he could see and hear the celebrations getting under way, along with the babble of excited voices, the bleating of hundreds of sheep, and snatches of song. The yard between the gates and the little wooden church was packed with shepherds and their dogs as well as the teeming flocks.

He hadn't really believed that woman on the ox-cart. They weren't very far yet from the Mercian heartlands. Surely Easter would be properly kept by the mass-priests, if not by the people.

But, looking through the gates, Wulfgar saw no fewer than four gaily clad priests, each with his attendant deacon holding a basin of holy water. They were wading thigh-deep through a sea of grey and brown and black fleece, sprinkling the woolly backs with flicks of their rosemary branches. Those sheep that had already been blessed were being herded briskly into holding pens, and the women were hard at work milking. The roasting pits had been dug and the merchants were setting out the trestles for their stalls: cinnamon and silk ribbons, gilt brooches and pepper. Somewhere out of sight for now, the musicians were tuning up.

'What did you say?'

'Come on! I could run in, wave my sword, knock the priests down, grab the saint's bones! We'll be back on our horses and a mile down the road before anyone's even noticed.' Ednoth looked at Wulfgar's face, shrugged, and grinned. 'I was joking, Wulfgar. Don't be so serious. The sun's shining! Come on, let's go and get our milk.'

'You go.'

On almost any other day of the year, Wulfgar would have been impressed by the show this remote little minster was mustering. Today, every note of the bells grated on his ears. It was all wrong, the colour, the music, the mouth-watering smell of roasting lamb. He looked up at the sky, inanely blue. There should be darkness over the face of the earth. An earthquake. The veil of the Temple rent in twain. *All the world wept: Christ was on the Cross . . .*

He had never felt so alone as he did just then, carping and miserable in the midst of this happy throng.

And Ednoth was still laughing at him.

'Ask St Modwenna for her blessing on our journey, if you really don't want a bride. Maybe she could have a word with St Oswald for us.'

'Don't you tell *me*—'

But the boy was already hurrying through the timber gates to the churchyard, lined with wattle sheep pens to make a temporary arena. As each noisy flock was hallowed, it came through into the pens where the girls were milking industriously. Their mothers were staggering back and forth from pen to table with the pails of milk, and ladling frothing spoonfuls into cups which they then passed out to the crowd.

Wulfgar fumed.

I must speak to the abbot, he thought. I may not be here in an official capacity, but even so I can't believe he lets all this carry on.

Why couldn't they have put it off for a week?

And where had that stupid boy got to?

There Ednoth was, shouldering his way through the throng to a pen hard against the south wall of the nave. He was rewarded by a horn beaker of the pungent milk and a brilliant smile from the pretty girl whose flock he'd chosen.

Wulfgar made his way slowly towards him, thinking, I'll just tell him I'm going to find the abbot.

The great bell of the minster had begun to toll; he could see it swinging dizzily back and forth in its little belfry. The priests and their attendants had disappeared back into the darkness of the church and now they were ready to re-emerge in procession with their saint from the west door. Ednoth was saying something to the girl, begging a kiss, it looked like, but her smiling reply was drowned by the sudden joyful ringing of lesser bells.

The crowd fell back.

A subdeacon came first, upholding a processional cross some eight feet high that shone red-gold as his hair in the sunlight. Then came the boys with their hand-bells, keeping admirable time with the great bell, and the acolytes with their great beeswax candles, flames invisible in the sunlight. Next came the deacons, and then the priests, in matching sets of martyr-red dalmatics and chasubles, followed by the old abbot, beaming with pleasure as he blessed the bystanders. And at last, carried by four laymen, their faces glistening with pride and the warmth of the day, came the little saint.

Her reliquary was wrapped in thickly embroidered silks. There were two young thurifers flanking her, clanking their little bronze incense-burners in time with the bells and scattering puffs of smoke. The bitter sweetness of the incense added another layer to air already ripe with woodsmoke, roasting lamb, milk and sheep-dung; the metallic ringing of the incense-burners chiming with the notes of the minster-bells and sheep-bells, the singing of the clerics and the bleating of a thousand sheep.

On any other day, Wulfgar thought, I'd have to give Offchurch credit for this display, but not today.

He pushed his way towards Ednoth, still absorbed in his misery and rancour. Ednoth looked up, smirking unbearably.

'Where's your milk, Mousegar?'

He wasn't given time to answer.

A single shriek sounded, cut off at once.

A drumming of hooves followed, with wild shouts and a cacophony of screaming.

The crowd went scattering this way and that as a band of riders, metal glinting, came thundering through the gates, two and three abreast.

Wulfgar flung himself back against a pile of wicker hurdles. The horsemen galloped past and wheeled to form a circle around the crowd, hemming in merchants, shepherds and priests alike. A man tried to dodge between two of them only to be felled by a vicious thwack from the butt-end of a spear. Another rider leant low from his saddle to overturn a stall with a crash. They were in a ring around the crowd now, three lined up in the gateway blocking escape, spears bristling.

Wulfgar was numb with terror. He pressed himself further back against the hurdles, his hand feeling for the Bishop's ring on its thong round his neck, making sure no flicker of gold was visible, pleading desperately to the anonymous saint whom it contained.

The sheep were bleating hysterically.

No axes.

From some clearer, cooler part of his mind, the observation came again.

Swords, but no axes.

Who had ever heard of Danes without axes?

'We don't want to hurt anybody, but we will if we have to.' The voice of their leader was cultivated, reasonable, and accustomed to command. A very English voice. A very West Saxon one, in fact.

Wulfgar's hands and feet were growing icy. I'm wrong, he thought frantically.

'Let's start with that, shall we?'

Their leader was the only one in a helmet, with nose-guard and cheek-pieces that shadowed his face and dark beard. He was pointing at the red-headed subdeacon with the gold processional cross, and he sounded as though he was enjoying himself.

The young subdeacon glanced in a panic behind him at one of the priests, who was gesturing *Go on*. The lad shook his head. Wulfgar could see his knuckles whitening as his hands tightened around his treasure.

'Come on,' the helmeted man said. 'Don't try my patience.'

CHAPTER TEN

Wulfgar knew that accent, and those vowels, which sounded so long and lazy and superior to a Mercian ear. It was the cadence of the West Saxon heartlands. To be precise, the chalk valleys east and south of Winchester.

Close to home.

Much, much too close.

And it wasn't only the accent Wulfgar recognised. He knew that voice.

But it couldn't be. The man he was thinking of was Edward's man. What would he be doing here, at an obscure Mercian minster in the wilds of the Leam valley?

Ednoth stirred restlessly at his side.

Wulfgar had completely forgotten his existence for those few minutes of frantic terror. Now, his gaze flickering sideways, he saw Ednoth had his sword at his hip in full view, and his hand had shifted to the hilt.

No, you fool, Wulfgar thought. What did the boy imagine he could gain by forcing a confrontation?

As soon as Ednoth moved, the helmeted man's eyes were fastened on him. He jerked his head at one of the other horsemen. There was the sickening rasp of metal, of sword from sheath.

It was that gesture – not the accent, not the voice, but that arrogant flick of the head – that told Wulfgar his fears were grounded in truth. That helmet masked the man he least wanted to see. The man whom he had been forced all his life to acknowledge as his half-brother. The son of one of his father's field-slaves on the Meon estate. The charity-child who had shared his schooling. Edward's trusted second-in-command.

Garmund Polecat.

Wulfgar's first instinct was to turn away, to shield his appalled gaze with his arm.

But instead he found himself lifting that same arm, a strangely awkward movement, caught halfway between greeting and flinch. Simultaneously, and to his utter horror, his feet took him half a pace forward.

Every eye was on him. He felt dizzy, a strange ringing in his ears.

The helmeted man kicked his horse's flanks and the beast walked obediently forward. Those massive hooves stopped no more than three feet in front of Wulfgar. He had to crane his neck and squint past the horse's head to see the mounted figure outlined against the sun. He felt rather than saw the man's shadowed eyes look him up and down.

'You here, Litter-runt? You, of all people? Well, well.'

Wulfgar's heart plummeted. It was Garmund all right.

'You'll keep your mouth shut if you know what's healthy.'

Wulfgar wondered, in a strangely detached way, whether Garmund really hated him enough to kill him with all Offchurch watching. His voice, when he found it at last, was a croak. 'What are you *doing*? Are you here at Edward's command?'

A shout from one of the mounted men: 'Cut him down, Garmund!' Another yelling, 'Come on, Polecat!'

And Cain talked with Abel his brother; and it came to pass, when they were in the field, that Cain rose up against Abel his brother and slew him . . .

Fratricide. The primal sin.

'Come on,' Wulfgar said, trying to find a little more voice, a little more courage. 'Tell us. Or are you ashamed?'

Garmund lifted his arm, fist clenched.

Wulfgar closed his eyes, bracing himself for the blow. He could feel his shoulders hunching and he tried to pull them down, to keep his breathing slow.

A blackbird singing.

The frantic bleating of the sheep.

And then another voice, right under his nose: 'Shame!'

Still cold with terror, he opened his eyes. Blinking against the sudden glare of the sun, he found the old lady, that fragile little bundle of skin and bone whom out of pity they were to carry home, pushing in front of him. She hobbled forward to grab Garmund's bridle and brandish her blackthorn stick in his face.

'Shame and scandal on you, and yours, and your lord, if any will own you!'

The horse was startled, tossing its great head, but the old lady never flinched.

Garmund had to grab his reins hastily, and he shot an uneasy look at his henchmen.

'Shut up, you old bitch.'

She had her hand on his bridle now, stretching as high as she could reach, and he had to pull the horse's head up and away, leaving her stumbling.

By no means silenced, however.

'Old bitch? You hear that, everybody? To a woman who could be his grandmother, though what a blessing that I'm not!' She drew a deep breath then, and let fly. 'A black curse on you and all your kin, on the womb that bore you and the loins that got you! And may your own seed dry, and your children live to damn your name and leave you unburied when your own lord has hanged you for the ravens.'

'I should cut you down where you stand, you worthless heap of bones, you—'

Garmund's own hand was at his sword-hilt now.

'Oh, go on,' she chirped. 'I've lived long enough, my brave young hero. Look, everyone! In the very presence of the saint. Here's a deed for the poets.'

And Garmund's hand hesitated, his sword half-drawn, and, palpable as the wind changing quarter, the mood in the crowd shifted.

Another flicker of movement now, among the priests. The elderly abbot stepped forward.

'Shame indeed! Shame and blasphemy!'

He lacked the raucous force of Auntie, but in his festival vestments he made up for it in tremulous dignity.

'To rob the saint, on this day of days!' He gestured at the reliquary, still supported aloft by its quaking bearers.

And another voice now, robust and bellowing. The woman who had been in the ox-cart with Auntie: 'Shame, aye, and treason, to threaten the servants of Mercia's Lord!' Heads swivelled. She pushed forward to stand next to Wulfgar and Ednoth. 'These men here answer to him and his Lady.'

Garmund's horse was still betraying the unsettled mood of its rider, sidling, laying its ears flat against its skull.

Garmund laughed. 'The Lord of the Mercians? Worm's meat, or will be in a day or two. As for his rutting bitch of a *wife*—'

Wulfgar tried to close his ears.

Garmund was looking right at him now, his reins bundled in his left hand, twisting sideways to draw his sword. Blade in hand, his voice low, controlled, menacing, he said, 'Crow while you can, Litter-runt. I wouldn't serve your masters.'

Somehow Wulfgar managed to stand his ground.

He is planning to kill me, he thought. He really is. Me and my unlikely allies. A doddery old priest, a grandmother, and this well-meaning woman next to me who has her family waiting for her at home. And Ednoth, and his little shepherdess, and that red-headed subdeacon . . .

He was almost choked by his sudden hot surge of anger. Easy meat, is that what Garmund – and Edward – were thinking of Mercia? Of the good folk of Offchurch? Of him? He was determined, suddenly, not to go down without a fight.

'I love my masters. And I wouldn't serve yours.'

Garmund showed his teeth, white suddenly in his dark beard.

'You don't know what I'm talking about, do you? Mercia's a lost cause, you fool. You should have stayed in Winchester.' His voice was cracking with anger. He looked away from Wulfgar now, raking his eyes across the faces of the hostile crowd.

The world hung in the balance.

And it tipped.

Garmund's raiders, well-armed though they were, were out-numbered twenty to one. Many of the feast-goers had good knives at their belts, and Wulfgar suspected some of the merchants might have better weapons stowed about their stalls.

Garmund's moment had been lost, and he clearly knew it.

He spurred his massive, overfed horse straight at Wulfgar, who threw himself sideways, but not quite in time. Garmund lashed out with his booted foot and caught him a glancing blow on the temple.

Wulfgar's world exploded in black stars.

A pounding shudder of hoof-beats, and they were gone.

It had all happened so quickly. Wulfgar lay where Garmund's kick had sent him, across the stack of hurdles, vomiting bile from his empty stomach. He was vaguely aware of the silence, and then the hubbub of the crowd. He put his fingers to his thumping temple but there was no blood. Giddy, he sat up, and was promptly swamped with nausea.

The place was in an uproar. Ednoth was at the centre of a back-slapping throng. His little shepherdess was clinging to his arm, tears of shock and relief pouring down her cheeks. Wulfgar hauled himself to his feet, legs still shaky, vision blurred, mouth sour. He swallowed but the bile wouldn't go away. At least his bladder hadn't betrayed him. Wiping his mouth with the back of his hand, he walked unsteadily over to Ednoth and the girl.

'The Danes haven't raided here since I was a baby.' Her voice trembled and her eyes were huge in her white face.

They weren't Danes. His head pounded. Hadn't the stupid girl been listening? Didn't she understand anything? Did anyone? From the agitated chatter breaking out around them most people were agreeing with the girl. Danes, Danes, Danes, was all he could hear.

He seemed to be the only person in the crowd who had identified the raiders for what they were, and his first instinct was to blurt out the truth. To get them all to understand what life was going to be like, with Edward's hand on the tiller of the West Saxon kingdom and Garmund his most faithful crewman. He had no doubt that this raid was with Edward's blessing. Now, at last, the whole world might see the perils he had known since his childhood.

But, in the time it took his vision to clear and the nausea to ebb a little, he changed his mind. He felt so weary, and so ashamed at the prospect of having to acknowledge Garmund as his father's son. And Garmund and his bullies had gone. There was no point in getting mired down in explanations.

Now, belatedly, the men of Offchurch were looking to their defences. Some were guarding the gates, others tallying such weapons as they had to hand. A sombre group gathered around the merchant who had been knocked down by a raider's spear-butt; they had turned him over but he wasn't moving and Wulfgar could see a lot of blood on his face. A shocked-looking priest hurried over to him.

The panicky sheep were being corralled again.

An older woman came flurrying across and scooped Ednoth's shepherdess into her arms. She looked over the girl's shoulder at Ednoth, then at Wulfgar.

'Are you all right, my heart?'

'Servants of the Lady? The abbot would like to thank you.'

'We're on urgent business,' Wulfgar said hastily. 'Please, pay him our respects. We have to go.'

Go, back on the road. He felt nausea rise again at the thought. So many childhood journeys back to his dormitory from the palace school in Winchester had been similarly fraught with fear, not knowing where or when the ambush would come, only that it was inevitable.

It was too late to escape the abbot, however; he came hard on the woman's heels, pale as the little shepherdess, babbling about thanks, and honour, and privilege, the miracle of their salvation, the shock of such sacrilege in the very presence of their saint.

What do I say in reply? Wulfgar wondered. He still thought the minster-men of Offchurch deserved a reprimand, celebrating their exuberant, inappropriate festivity on the most sombre day of all the Church's year, but, somehow, putting the abbot straight didn't seem so important now. Perhaps the raid had been a warning, but Wulfgar decided to let the elderly man draw the moral himself.

The other clerics were clustering around them now.

Through his now blinding headache Wulfgar had to grip clammy hands, assure them of the Lady's love, give them the worrying news of her husband's collapse, promise to carry Offchurch's protests of loyalty and their prayers for the Lord's recovery.

And there was still the old lady, patiently waiting for her ride. At least she gave them a sound excuse for getting on the road.

At last, protesting that, no, they couldn't stay the night, or even for the feast, that, yes, they really had to be on their way, they were allowed to walk back out through the gates to where they'd tethered the horses.

Ednoth was adjusting the length of his stirrups, his back to Wulfgar.

'Wulfgar?'

'Hmm?' Wulfgar answered nervously. For perhaps the first time he was grateful that he looked nothing like dark-bearded, broad-shouldered Garmund. He didn't want to acknowledge Garmund, especially not to Ednoth. *A black curse on you and all your kin . . .* The old lady's bitter words were still echoing in his aching skull.

Ednoth's thoughts were on a completely different track, however.

'You stopped me from drawing my sword.'

'Yes . . .' Wulfgar said warily.

'I meant to challenge them. I thought, if I led the way, others would follow me. I was being – I was being foolish, wasn't I?'

Wulfgar turned to look at him, impressed despite himself by the lad's honesty.

'Yes. Brave, but also foolish.'

Ednoth appeared to be giving his full attention to Starlight's girth. His ears were red.

'No, just foolish.' Then, 'I'm sorry I called you Mousegar.'

Wulfgar nodded. The apology was balm to his soul.

'My friends call me Wuffa,' he confided, half against his better judgement, thinking that if Ednoth were to say anything unkind about 'an unlikely wolf-cub' the boy would be going in search of St Oswald on his own.

Ednoth had hunkered down, running an appraising hand over Starlight's legs. He straightened up then, turned, held out his hand.

'I'll do that then. Wuffa. We're shoulder-to-shoulder men now.'

Wulfgar looked at the friendly hand reaching out to him. Still more than a little wary, he hesitated. Shoulder-to-shoulder men, was it? Was he supposed to trust Ednoth now? If the boy had done what he'd intended, Wulfgar thought bitterly, if he'd pulled his sword, they could have all been killed.

But Ednoth grinned at him, waiting, and at last Wulfgar reached out to grasp the offered hand.

'Who was he, anyway, this Polecat?' Ednoth asked. 'Had you come across him before?'

Wulfgar pulled away.

'He's got the right eke-name, hasn't he? Vicious animals, polecats.'

He was painfully aware that he was dodging a proper answer, but the moment in which he could have confessed the Polecat as his kin, if it had ever come, had gone again. 'Let's just hope we don't run into him on the road.'

Ednoth appeared to be thinking.

Wulfgar waited, uneasy.

Eventually, the boy said, 'I've a friend called Edwin at home. We call him Dribbler.'

'And does he?'

'Dribble? Not now. When he was little. But you know how eke-names stick?'

Only too well. *Litter-runt.* Blame Edward and Garmund for that one. They'd tried others. *Cheese-mite. Flea-bite. Sparrow's turd.* But Litter-runt had stuck for some reason. He supposed it could have been worse.

As if he were reading Wulfgar's mind, Ednoth said, 'My dad bought some sheep off a man called Sigebert Fart once.'

Wulfgar had to smile.

CHAPTER ELEVEN

A few miles' steady ride along the mossy stones of the Fosse and they turned west once more to walk the horses down into a pleasant little valley, fringed with oaks just coming into their first bronze leaf. A heavy-winged heron flapped low over their heads as the old lady directed them through the stands of trees to a sturdy huddle of solid wooden buildings, set within rings and banks of massive tree-grown earthworks, topped with timber defences. The wooden palisades were golden and barely weathered, but the ditches they fronted must have been raised against far older enemies than the Danes.

Ednoth wound his horn and a door-ward emerged from a postern. The word of their arrival was shouted back, and suspicion soon turned into welcome as the old lady's son realised whom Ednoth had up on his saddle bow.

'Many thanks,' he said by way of greeting. 'She's a terrible worry to me, gadding about the way she does.'

The old woman swiped at his legs with her stick and he fended her off with one huge hand, both mother and son grinning.

'And you'll stay the night, lads? You'll not get a lot further today, not with this weather coming in.' His round red face creased in a smile, framed by long yellow-grey moustaches.

Wulfgar, surprised by the comment, looked at the sky, but Ednoth nodded his agreement.

The Bishop had told them to hurry, however.

'I'm sorry,' Wulfgar said, 'but we have to be on our way.'

'Where else would you stay tonight, that you'd turn down a place by our hearth, and weather closing in? There's no coldharbour left within a day's ride. Better a good hearth here than a chilly camp under a bush ten miles up the Way.'

It was very tempting. The Bishop hadn't known about Garmund, Wulfgar told himself. Touched, and more grateful that he dared admit, he gave way.

Heremod – their host – ordered his slaves to take the horses round to the stables and bring water for the travellers to wash, and he sat them down on benches outside the west side of his hall, catching the late afternoon sun and out of the wind.

Wulfgar was glad beyond words to be off a horse, and to have the prospect of a comfortable night. Their host was right: the fickle April weather was turning against them. Dark-browed clouds were building up to the north east, and for all the sunlight the breeze had a sharp edge to it.

The old lady insisted on serving them herself, bringing out warm crumpets, new curd cheese, smoked fish, rose-hip pickle and garlic relish, shamelessly picking out the choicest morsels for Ednoth – 'My lovely boy,' she cooed – though she cosseted Wulfgar, too, with a cold camomile poultice for his brutally aching temple.

To his surprise he found his appetite returning and, Ednoth was quite right, he told himself: canon law did say that if they were travelling they were exempt from fasting. It wouldn't help their mission if he fainted from lack of food, and the meal was far better than he would have expected from this comparatively modest household. They feasted and drank sweet mead, and Ednoth, shameless as their hostess, fell fast asleep with his back against the sun-warmed timber and his mouth falling open.

Heremod looked at Ednoth and rolled his eyes upwards.

'Ah, youth! Have you eaten enough?'

Wulfgar nodded carefully, one hand on his poultice.

'Tell me more about these raiders, then.' Their host shook his head. 'Things have been quiet across the borders of late. No real trouble for six, seven, years.' He sighed. 'Too good to last. So, men of Leicester, were they, Wulfgar?'

'Those misbegotten louts?' It was the old lady. 'They were no Danes.' She reached over his shoulder for an empty dish.

Heremod swivelled round. '*Not Danes?*'

'Think I can't tell a Danish voice by now, son? Or, if they were Danes, they had a renegade West Saxon leading them.' She cackled with pleasure. 'Ah, that's made you sit up!'

'Wulfgar, is my mother right?' Heremod's voice had taken on a peculiar urgency.

Wulfgar wondered what to say in reply. He looked into the cup of mead cradled in his hands, swirling the sticky liquid, absently noting the fine quality of the earthenware and the rich greeny-yellow depths of its sun-tinted glaze.

'No.' He closed his eyes, trying to banish the ache behind them. 'I mean, yes. Your mother's quite right. They were men of Wessex.'

'Definitely not Leicester?' There was no mistaking the note of relief. 'Lordless men, then.'

Wulfgar shook his head carefully.

'Well-dressed, well-armed, well-spoken, well-disciplined.' He gave his fears voice. 'I think they must have been the King's men.'

Heremod hissed through his teeth.

'That doesn't bode well. War between Wessex and Mercia, then? With the Danes biding their moment to pick our bones? We've been there before.' He thumped a heavy fist on his table, rattling the dishes and rocking the trestles with the sudden gust of his anger. 'All I want is to be left alone. We trade now with the Danes, you know. Better for us than fighting them ever was. And this is where Mercia ends. Right here. Me.' He banged himself on the chest.

His mother, clearing more dirty dishes, coughed and spat on the grass.

'You, indeed,' she said.

'Now, mother . . .' Heremod's voice had a warning note.

She shook her head.

'Mercia ends with me, boy,' she told him.

Heremod turned back to Wulfgar, rolling his eyes, inviting sympathy.

Wulfgar noted he didn't correct her, though.

'I could show you a Dane called Thorleikr,' Heremod said in a low voice, 'straight off the boat, who's bought land not five miles east from here, hard by Dunchurch. Oh yes,' in response to Wulfgar's curious look, '*bought it*. From a Mercian. No land-grab there. Well over on the English side of Watling Street. But Thorleikr looks across the line to Leicester for lordship. Leicester's a damn sight closer than you might think, and it's getting closer all the time.'

Heremod's eyes flickered along the length of the hall and Wulfgar shifted to follow his gaze. While his host's thatch was new enough still to be yellow, the massive earth-fast timbers, the mainstays of the wall, were singed black, even charred in places. 'You see what I mean?' his host asked.

Wulfgar nodded soberly.

'We've built it up again,' Heremod said. 'Once the carrion crows find your flock they'll never quite give up.' He sighed. 'But I must admit there's law in Leicester now. Good law.'

Wulfgar found himself sitting up.

'You mean, you go to Leicester? Often?' He could hear the echo of the Atheling's voice: *Find Hakon Grimsson in Leicester . . .*

His host offered him a sideways glance.

'How much do I admit to a servant of the Lady's?'

'I've eaten your bread,' Wulfgar protested.

'And, clarnet that I am, I already told you we trade across Watling Street. With what's left to us after we've paid our taxes south. In good English coin that gets harder to find every year.' His eyes flared with anger then. 'I'm as loyal as the next man, mind on. But you tell them south that squeezing us dry here on the border and never letting us have sight of them is no way to wield men's loyalties. What do they expect me to do next time raiders come? Run to *Gloucester*, with mother on my back?' His tone had curdled. 'How much longer do I keep faith with a Lord I never see? You tell him that.' He pushed the mead jug across the table to his guest and sat back, arms folded.

'I'll tell him,' Wulfgar said, sorry for the way the talk had gone, his head hurting more than ever now. He wondered if he would ever have the chance to speak with the Lord of the Mercians again. 'Taxes are even higher in Wessex, you know.' Oh, this headache. He reached unthinking for the mead-jug and his elbow jogged his cup off the table to smash on the cobbles. 'Oh, no!'

It lay under the bench in half a dozen pieces.

'Heremod, I'm so sorry.' He bent to pick up the larger fragments. Far beyond mending. 'I'd just been thinking how lovely it was, and what an honour that you should bring these out for us.' He held the biggest shard up to the last long rays of sunlight, looking at the way the light penetrated the glaze. 'We've nothing so fine at court. The Lady has a fondness for Frankish glass, but—'

However, to Wulfgar's astonishment, Heremod dismissed his apology with a wave of his hand.

'We trade for them in Leicester. We've enough and to spare.' As though to prove the truth of his words, a slave-girl had already come forward with a replacement, just as prettily glazed, and Heremod's mother then filled it with mead that Wulfgar didn't really want, not now. Heremod leaned forward, a light in his eyes. 'Do you think folk in Worcester, or Gloucester, would take a fancy to them?' he asked. 'I can get you plenty. I'll show you.' He dismissed the girl to fetch some more cups with a pat to her rump.

'Winchester, even,' Wulfgar said, nodding. 'My mother would have loved these.' An idea was beginning to glimmer through the fog of his headache. 'Do you know a man in Leicester called Hakon Grimsson?'

Heremod whistled softly.

'Hakon *Toad*? Our – their jarl, you mean? You don't mess about, do you?' His face was shuttered, cautious, now. 'If you want a share of the pottery trade, or anything else in Leicester, you'll have to deal with the Grimssons sooner rather than later. But a bit lower down the ladder might be a happier place to start.'

'I'm sure you're right,' Wulfgar said. 'I'd heard the name, that's all.' He tried to settle his aching rump more comfortably but the bench was too hard.

Heremod looked down at his fingernails, and then up at Wulfgar.

'The Grimssons are old Great Army men. Brothers. Hakon Toad – he's the elder, the Jarl. Ketil Scar, he's the little brother, and a much nastier piece of work. The last I heard from Leicester, a fortnight back, is that Hakon had taken sick. But he runs as tight a ship in Leicester as he ever did.'

Toad? Scar? Hardly reassuring eke-names.

'Are they heathens?'

Heremod had the grace to turn his laugh into a cough.

'Hakon's been baptised. Rumour has it Ketil, too. And Hakon shows his ugly face at church from time to time. Or so I hear. But I wouldn't count on them keeping those promises, or any others.'

Drops of mead were drying, sticky, sunlit, on the cobbles among the shattered fragments of the yellow cup, but the wind had sharp teeth.

Wulfgar had an unsettling vision of a little snarling animal, nipping at his nape. A stoat, maybe. A polecat . . . He pulled his cloak more snugly around his shoulders. It kept the chill wind at bay but not the fears which were racking him.

Why would an Atheling of Wessex call a man like Hakon Grimsson his friend? How *could* he? He can hardly have forgotten what the Great Army did to Wessex. I don't remember, Wulfgar thought, as it was around the time I was born. But the Atheling was – what – seven when Wareham was sacked? And then, Exeter, and Chippenham a couple of years later. Rochester, too, I think. And I know he fought in the battle of Farnham, everyone knows that.

Heremod leaned forward suddenly, elbows on the table, and looked him hard in the eye.

'Wulfgar, you tell your Lady and her Lord this. I'm as loyal a Mercian as I can be. But I won't look to Wessex for lordship. And I'm not alone.'

'You mean . . .'

Heremod shook his head, but Wulfgar could hear his unspoken words. *If Wessex takes Mercia, men like me will turn to the Danes for protection.* He closed his eyes. And where is that going to leave the Lady? Unsupported. Defenceless. Unwanted. An embarrassment to her brother.

He knew the most likely outcome.

The nunnery in Winchester.

Or the knife in the dark.

It's happened often enough before, Heaven knows. Men are ruthless to superfluous queens. He pressed the damp linen pad against his temple. St Oswald, dear St Oswald, come to her aid, he prayed silently. You're in this with us. You need her alive and well and on your side. Pray for her. For me. For all of us.

The girl had brought out half a dozen more cups for him to look at – orange, and pale, creamy yellow, sage green and smoky blue – and was now engaged in sweeping up the broken shards.

'I need to think about it,' Heremod said, defensively. 'Giving you a name in Leicester, I mean. I've got to look after my own interests, after all.' His sweeping gesture took in the scorched timbers of his handsome hall, the raw wood of his fortifications, the outbuildings, the bustling slaves' quarters, the stables and chicken house where a girl scattered grain, and the sheep-dotted fields beyond, noisy with the call and response of lambs and their mothers, all yellow where the long evening light was still slanting in under the gathering slate clouds. 'I don't go looking for trouble, you know. When I was a lad our land was smack in the middle of Mercia. Now we live on the edge.'

Later that night, huddled in his cloak by the banked fire in the hall, Wulfgar, on the brink of sleep, mulled over Heremod's bitter words. Loyalty, he thought. Loyalty is everything. But loyalty to what? Why should men like Heremod stay loyal, pay their taxes and renders, send men to the army, keep the roads and bridges in good repair, if they get nothing in return? He shifted restlessly. Especially if this Hakon has been baptised, and gives fair judgments in his court. He may be just as good a lord, in his way. Perhaps, he told himself, it's not so strange that the Atheling should be reconciled with a Great Army warlord. The old King made peace with some of them, after all. Stood godfather to one, even. He yawned, and tried to settle himself on his other side. The headache was almost gone.

His last conscious thought was, if Hakon's been baptised, there must still be a priest in Leicester. And, if there's a priest, perhaps I can go to Mass on Easter Sunday after all.

CHAPTER TWELVE

Holy Saturday

A steady drizzle of rain was coming down from the north east when they set off. Heremod had said nothing more about Leicester while they were breaking their fast around the fire, and Wulfgar had been wondering whether to ask again. But at the last moment, after the formal leave-taking, he came up to Wulfgar's stirrup and spoke in a rapid mutter.

'You should go to the Wave-Serpent. Ask for Gunnar, that folk call Cat's-Eyes.'

Wulfgar could hardly hear him for his old mother, waving and beaming from the doorway of the hall. 'Come back this way, my lovely boy!' she screeched at Ednoth. 'We'll kill a pig for you!'

Heremod backed away, slapping Fallow on her shaggy rump to get her going.

'Yes, come back this way,' he said, not meeting Wulfgar's eyes. 'Always welcome under my roof.'

'What was that about?' Ednoth asked, as they rode out through the gates. 'Your black eye's coming up nicely, by the way.'

Wulfgar stroked the puffy skin around his eye, wincing as he did so. 'It is a little tender,' he admitted. What had Ednoth asked? 'Oh, Heremod suggested someone to whom we could speak in Leicester. I thought we could plausibly claim to be interested in buying pottery to trade south, like the ware Heremod had on his table. He recommended a man called Gunnar, at the Wave-Serpent – that sounds like an ale-house. And the man's a Dane, by his name.'

But Ednoth seemed to have stopped listening several sentences earlier.

'Did you say *pottery trading?*'

'It's very nice pottery.'

'But I'm not a merchant.' This seemed to have touched Ednoth on a tender spot.

'No, of course not.' Wulfgar tried to mollify him. 'You're a sheep farmer.'

'I am not! I'm a warrior, or I will be. And I refuse to peddle pots and jugs.'

Wulfgar took a deep breath. Keep your temper, he thought, and I'll keep mine. 'But it gives us an excuse for being the far side of Watling Street.'

Ednoth exhaled in frustration.

'We're running from every fight, we're not allowed to tell anyone what we're doing, and now we're pretending to be *pottery—*'

'Ednoth, we're a long way from home, and people are suspicious enough of strangers at the best of times.' He winced at the pleading note in his own voice and tried to speak more firmly. 'We need a reason to be this far east. That's all. We don't want to run any risks, or attract unwanted attention.'

'I want to fight for the Lady.'

Wulfgar, his temper shortened by his headache and a troubled night, shifted round in his saddle to face the boy.

'Ednoth, you are a penitent on a pilgrimage. Try behaving like one. You nearly got us into very serious trouble at Offchurch, not just me but everyone at the feast, including your pink-cheeked little shepherdess. What would have happened to *her* if things had turned nasty? Think of that for a moment.' He turned to look ahead again, basking in the unfamiliar and satisfying pleasure of being in the right and having asserted himself.

Ednoth was silent.

The rain was getting heavier again, and colder, and the wind was rising. Wulfgar stole a glance at Ednoth.

The boy was huddled under his cloak, shoulders hunched and lips tight.

Wulfgar sighed, wrapping his own cloak more tightly around his shoulders, and stared between Fallow's ears. The wind and chilly rain were full in their faces; the valiant little horses put their heads down and plodded on.

If the legions of Rome had ever laid their stone road along here, or Mercian lads on military service had hacked these brambles back within living memory, there was no sign of it. The going was sticky mud that sucked at the horses' hooves, and Wulfgar found it hard work even to hold Fallow steady through the dense tangles of fresh green brambles and briars.

In stark contrast to yesterday they had encountered no other travellers for several miles now, nor passed any inhabited dwellings. This was abandoned land: pasture and plough-land gone back to scrub and weed; the coppices overgrown; the homesteads deserted, their roofs fallen. There were no children herding or playing, no women scrubbing clothes in the streams, no men toiling at the spring sowing. Wulfgar was no farmer, but he could feel the sadness of all this once-good grazing and arable, now inhabited by the brittle ghosts of last year's docks and nettles. Holy Saturday, he thought. Hell is being harrowed. The infernal gates are being broken down, and the patriarchs, the virtuous pagans, the parents of us all, are being set free. But oh, Queen of Heaven, while your Son is liberating Hell, He is absent from this middle-earth of ours, and it feels very empty.

By the time evening had started to draw in, Wulfgar was chilled to the marrow, hands, feet and face numb. Earlier fears of another ambush by Garmund and his men had long been drowned by a more general misery. The greasy felt of his cloak was soaked and stinking like a wet hound. It would take days by a good fire to get it dry, and he could see no prospect of that. Despite their day of dogged riding, they hadn't reached Leicester. They hadn't even reached Watling Street yet.

The horses were exhausted, too; they had barely stopped all day and now they were mud-spattered up to their flanks, dragging their feet, heads down, pulling at the reins and trying to graze at every patch of grass. Wulfgar wondered if Fallow were picking up his own reluctance: the closer they got to the border, the sicker he felt.

Finally, he broke the sulky silence that had endured the whole day.

'We won't make Leicester tonight.' His chilled lips could hardly frame the words.

Ednoth didn't turn his head.

Wulfgar repeated himself, louder, and added 'But, unless we've gone wrong, we can't be far from the crossroads with Watling Street.'

That got the boy's attention.

'So close?'

'Yes,' Wulfgar said, relieved to get a reply. 'We must be. But I thought we'd find a busy highway. Instead, it looks as though no one's been along here for years.'

Ednoth pushed his cloak back and looked around him.

'No, it doesn't. This is just the new spring growth. We've been going due north east all day.'

He still sounds grumpy, Wulfgar thought, but at least he's talking to me again.

'Well, that's a relief.' Wulfgar said pacifically, 'I'm glad you're here, Ednoth. I'm sure I'd get lost on my own.'

'Do you want to hear a riddle?' Ednoth asked in a more cheerful voice.

No, Wulfgar thought, and this is hardly the moment, but I don't want to rub you up the wrong way again.

'Go on, then.'

Ednoth chuckled.

'I am the creature without a bone, and when the cunning maiden strokes me under the cloth, I rise – who am I?'

'Bread dough.' Wulfgar replied wearily. He peered ahead through the mist and thickening dusk, eager to forestall any further jocularity. 'What's that?'

A massive fallen tree lay across their path.

His heart plummeted further.

'We *must* have lost our way. No one would leave that lying across a main road.'

Ednoth jumped down from his saddle and handed Starlight's reins to Wulfgar while he loped along to look.

'But this hasn't just fallen,' he called back after a moment. 'The branches have been trimmed.' He made his way to the other end, and Wulfgar could just make out the words he called back. 'Yes, it's been felled and brought here, not long ago. Look, the axe marks are still fresh, and it's not lying next to a stump.' He sounded puzzled. 'Do you see, the road is much clearer beyond here? We'll probably have to hack a way around this to get past it, though.'

Wulfgar looped Starlight's reins over his saddlebow and walked both horses forward. The boy was quite right. He scuffed his foot against the mud and the moss, and the old stone of the road gleamed wet beneath.

'Why would anybody do that?' He raised his eyes ahead. 'Ednoth, look. That must be Watling Street, there.'

Beyond the fallen tree, the road ran on up the ridge in a tangle of greenery, but only a little way ahead a space that he had taken at first for a small clearing could now be seen to open up left and right. Ragged-winged rooks rose in a sudden flurry of cawing from their nest-building in a stand of elms.

'Come on, let's get going.' He found himself eager to see the legendary boundary-road for himself, now that they were there and they had no choice.

But Ednoth wasn't listening. He had his face lifted to the damp breeze.

'Can you smell woodsmoke?'

Wulfgar shook his head.

The boy still sniffled, pulling a face.

'Woodsmoke, and a dung heap. First sign of life all day! Perhaps there's someone we could find shelter with?' He swung himself back into the saddle.

A horse whinnied, but not one of theirs. There was a trampling in the bushes. And then a clear, carrying voice, shouted: 'State your business.'

They were surrounded by riders, cloaked and hooded. The horses had come out of nowhere, out of mist and shadows, blocking the road ahead and behind.

Garmund.

Wulfgar's mind blanked with terror. He dropped his reins and held up his hands, anxious to appease whatever threat was coming.

No.

It wasn't Garmund.

The riders only numbered half a dozen, and the speaker was a slight, straight-backed figure on a rain-darkened mount.

But it was far too soon to breathe again.

'You heard. State your business.' A gruffer voice this time.

'We're travelling, to Leicester,' Wulfgar stammered. 'Are we on the right road?'

One of the men laughed.

'You're still half a day's ride from Leicester,' the first speaker said. 'This is the High Cross, and we are collecting the tolls.' It was a clear voice, perfect English but with something unfamiliar and musical about the vowels.

'Tolls?' Ednoth said.

Wulfgar tensed, hearing the bluster in his voice.

'Whose tolls? By whose authority?' Ednoth asked.

'My tolls, my rights, my crossroads. Granted to me by authority of Hakon Grimsson Toad, Jarl of Leicester. Are you arguing with me?'

Was it amusement colouring that voice now?

They were clearly outnumbered, and Wulfgar didn't think they were being threatened with violence – or not yet, anyway. He prayed Ednoth wouldn't betray them again with that reckless streak of his.

'We don't contest your right to the tolls,' Wulfgar said, calmer now that he knew he wasn't facing his old enemy. 'Please, let us know how much we owe you,' he said with what he hoped was an appeasing smile.

The leader turned to look at him. A little toss of the head and shrug of the shoulders and the hood fell obediently back. It revealed what Wulfgar had begun to suspect – the leader of this band of brigands was a woman. No more than his own age, Wulfgar guessed. She had been bare-headed beneath the hood, her dark hair tightly braided and coiled. The details of her face were blurred in the dusk, but he was struck by her eyebrows, flaring up and out to left and right, giving her the look of some imperious predator.

And he and Ednoth seemed to be her prey.

She didn't return his smile.

'A man of sense. Good. A shilling from each of you.'

One of the men muttered something below his breath, subsiding into silence when his leader's head snapped round.

'*How* much?' The woman's self-possession seemed only to be feeding Ednoth's outrage. 'We're exempt from tolls. We're on the Lady's business—'

'Ednoth, be quiet.'

But the woman was laughing now.

'No ladies round here but me, little one. Now, where's my money?'

It was a hefty sum, but Wulfgar wasn't about to argue. The coin the Bishop had given them was tucked away deep in his saddlebag, out of reach. He started to dismount. There was an instant response from the horsemen, a stir and a rustle that sounded ominously like the scrape of knives in their sheaths.

He stopped and, unbidden, raised his arms above his head again.

One of the men came forward, urging his horse with his knees and gestured for him to remove his cloak. He unfastened the pin and shrugged it off, letting it slump in a sodden grey mass across the back of his saddle. The horseman ran his hands over Wulfgar's torso front and back, and nodded. Wulfgar swung his right leg wearily over Fallow's rump.

And as he slithered down Ednoth came to the end of his tether.

'Wulfgar, how can you let these people walk all over you? We're still in Mercia, for God's sake—' but he wasn't given the time to finish.

The dark-haired woman jerked her head, and said something fast that Wulfgar didn't catch – something in Danish.

The man who had checked Wulfgar for weapons urged his horse sideways while a second man came up fast from the rear. Ednoth was still looking from one to the other when the first man pushed his horse hard up against Starlight's right flank and got Ednoth's arms pinioned behind his back. The other came in from the left and unbuttoned Ednoth's scabbard from his sword belt, ignoring his outraged yells. It was swiftly done, by expert hands.

He tossed it across to the woman, who caught it neatly, half-drew the sword from its scabbard and examined both blade and hilt critically.

'Good enough.' She handed it back to the man, hilt first.

'That's my grandfather's sword!' Ednoth twisted frantically, slipping in the saddle. Starlight, ears pinned back, looked about to buck. 'Give me back my sword!'

She shook her head.

'Give it to me!' His voice broke with anger.

'I have the right to exact my tolls as I see fit.' She nodded to her man. 'Let him go.'

He looked across: 'Wulfgar? *Wuffa!*'

But Wulfgar hid behind Fallow, busying himself with finding the money. His cold hands fumbled with the knotted strings. A sword could always be replaced. It wasn't worth dying for.

He straightened up just in time to see Ednoth clap his heels to Starlight's flanks and put him at the fallen tree. They cleared it from an almost standing start and vanished up the track. One of the horsemen applauded. Wulfgar thought he was mocking, but the woman nodded in approval.

'*Já*, he can ride, your little friend.' She turned back to her men and said something in Danish.

'Two shillings, I think you said?' Wulfgar's legs were trembling but his voice was steadier than he had hoped. One of the horsemen thudded past him, making him stagger. Was he going after Ednoth? Wulfgar scrabbled for the right money, pulling out a fistful of coins. If I pay quickly, he thought, perhaps they'll just go away, without bloodshed.

And I won't hear her voice again.

He paused, shocked, wondering where that thought had come from.

She had taken off one of her gloves and reached down for the coins. He counted the twenty-four silver pennies into her bare palm, and she nodded and put them away somewhere beneath her cloak as the horseman returned, shaking his head. A sigh of relief escaped Wulfgar, and she eyed him curiously.

'Your business on my road?'

What could he say without betraying his Lady, or the Atheling?

'We're riding to Leicester –' he cleared his throat '– on the recommendation of Heremod of Wappenbury. We have a business proposition for a friend of his.'

'Heremod, eh? Heremod Straddler, he's called in Leicester. One foot each side of the fence.' She sounded thoughtful.

Wulfgar, unsettled by her words and even more so by the musicality of her voice, looked up at her outline, misty and unreadable. The rain fell on his upturned face.

'Good luck, then,' she said, suddenly brisk. 'I hope you've some money left. Heremod has thirsty friends.'

He flushed. Had he been dismissed? He tried to heave himself back onto Fallow, who had been snatching the opportunity for a few mouthfuls of grass. Lacking a mounting block, it took him a few attempts before he was securely in the saddle. His back tingled with the sensation of her amused eyes watching him. He yanked angrily on Fallow's reins, trying to get her away from her grazing, to point her head up the road in Ednoth's wake.

But the dark-haired Danish woman hadn't finished with him yet. When he was safely mounted she beckoned him over. Eventually he persuaded Fallow to obey his dogged tugging.

She leaned over in her saddle towards him.

'A word,' she said softly. 'Teach your little friend to tread more warily. A southron needs to look out in Leicester.'

'A what?'

'Southerner.' She glanced over her shoulder at her men and then turned back to Wulfgar. 'Lucky for him, he travels in wise company. I admire a man who knows when it's a waste of time to fight.' She raised those eloquent eyebrows. 'And I can afford to slacken the rope a little, this time.' She turned back to the men. A little jerk of her head. 'Give him the sword.'

Wulfgar blinked, startled and confused.

No one moved.

She waited for a moment, then pointed at Wulfgar and said something fast and foreign, a new and angry edge to her voice. Whatever she'd said, it didn't go down too well. Voices were raised in guttural protest.

Wulfgar sat in his saddle, feeling like a lump, the ready blood burning his cheeks.

She had to give her order for a third time, and only then, and clearly unwillingly, did the man who held Ednoth's sword give it to Wulfgar.

Blinking in astonishment, he took it, holding it awkwardly across his saddle-bow, unsure how to manage both sword and reins. He thought, I'll have to dismount and strap it up with the saddle-bags. And then get back into the saddle. Again.

He was about to stammer his thanks when she said, 'Safe journey,' and turned her horse's head before she and her men melted back into the shadows as swiftly as they had come.

He was alone.

It was deep twilight now, nearly dark, with the rain falling ever more heavily. Grudgingly obedient, Fallow plodded along and crested the ridge at last. Wulfgar, in the last stages of weariness, barely glanced at Watling Street as he crossed it and rode on, down the gentle slope the other side.

And there was Ednoth, Queen of Heaven be thanked, a pale face in the gloom, waiting a little way away on the other side.

'There you are! Thank you for waiting,' Wulfgar called.

But, when Wulfgar had almost reached him, the boy wrenched his bridle round and kicked Starlight into a canter. The startled Fallow followed the gelding's lead, even when Starlight broke into a gallop.

They were hurtling down a tunnel of overgrown briar and bramble, thorny sprays lashing their faces. Wulfgar closed his eyes for fear of being blinded, his arms round Fallow's neck, not nearly good enough a horseman to cope with this pace for long. Now he began to lurch sideways out of his saddle, a little further with every stride, and gasping at the sudden pain of the elf-shot in his side. He wasn't sure if he was more afraid of staying on, or falling off. He didn't have a choice, as it turned out. Fallow gave one last wild plunge and, slowly but helplessly, he slid over her shoulder, out of his wet saddle, to land sprawling and winded in a patch of mud. The horse cantered off down the path.

Wulfgar lay still for a few moments before he dared ease himself to sitting and feel his arms and legs, neck, collarbones . . . no, nothing broken that he could find. The mud had been soft, at least, saturated with the rain. Dizzy and disoriented, he got to his feet, to find that Fallow's hoofbeats had died away. Now what should he do?

Go on: it was the only possible answer. Go on, on foot, all the way to Leicester. All the way to Bardney, if he had to. I can do it, he thought savagely. I don't need Ednoth, or anyone else, to help me.

It took an age to plod and slither through the mud to the next bend, but when he rounded it, he saw Ednoth through a veil of rain. He was out of his saddle, Starlight's reins looped in one hand and with the other holding Fallow's bridle, stroking her nose and talking to her in a low, soothing voice.

'Ednoth! Thank Heaven!' Wulfgar, relieved despite himself, tried to hobble a little faster. 'I thought I might never catch you up.'

Ednoth ignored him until he was only a few feet away. Then he turned abruptly.

'Don't you know you should never let go of your horse's reins? You're useless.'

'*Me*, useless?' Wulfgar really lost his temper then. 'You're the one who keeps acting like a headstrong fool. You'll get us killed if you don't rein in that temper of yours before we get to Leicester. Anyone would think we were on this road for your pleasure. You have to remember where we are.'

Ednoth was silent.

Wulfgar waited but the boy still said nothing and finally turned away, his shoulders hunched. Starlight put his head down and started tearing at the grass.

Suddenly Wulfgar found his anger fading. He was too cold and wet and weary from constant fear of attack. He didn't want to have to go on alone.

'Ednoth?'

Still no response.

'Shall we look for some shelter?'

No answer. The boy was sulking, and in desperation Wulfgar reverted to the language of childhood.

'Ednoth, *pax*, all right?'

Still no response.

Wulfgar made a conscious effort. Give me strength, he prayed. Queen of Heaven, aid me. St Oswald, guide me and guard me and help me find the right words, or our whole mission will fall apart. He took his courage in both hands and went towards Ednoth. Then he realised to his horror that the boy was sobbing, and he hesitated.

Ednoth muttered something.

'I beg your pardon, I didn't hear what you said.' Wulfgar took a step closer, and then flinched as Ednoth rounded on him violently, his face tear-stained and distorted.

'How can you live with yourself? Coward! The way you just

surrendered – and you let them take my sword. I was only given it just before Lent.' He choked back a sob. 'How could you let that bitch take my sword?'

'I've got your sword,' Wulfgar said.

'What?'

'I've got your sword.'

'Where?'

Wulfgar pointed at Fallow's pack.

Ednoth was over there at once, unbuckling and rummaging. He didn't ask how the sword came to be there, Wulfgar noticed, or even bother to say *thank you*, so caught up was he in his delight at having his treasure restored.

Tired of waiting for an expression of gratitude, Wulfgar said, 'Well, let's find shelter.' His teeth were chattering, and he found himself so exhausted suddenly that he could hardly speak. But shelter proved hard to find. That deserted landscape of patchy scrub and overgrown fields offered little more than spindly clumps of young birch, hazel and hawthorn. None of it would serve to keep the rain off. And the wood was full of green sap and soaking wet, none of which would burn.

Wulfgar, who couldn't stop shivering, was only vaguely aware of Ednoth's frown as he hobbled the horses' legs with rope.

'We've got to get you out of this wind,' he kept saying, and 'Take my cloak, it's lined with lambskins.' Finally he found them a big, old bell-shaped holly. 'Crawl in there.'

Wulfgar was too weary to do anything but obey. In the near-darkness he heard Ednoth scrabbling a space of bare earth among the layers of prickly dead leaves and trying half a dozen times to get a fire going, but the handful of fleece he kept in his fire pouch just flared and died without kindling a blaze. In the end he threw his strike-a-light down on the pile of damp tinder in frustration.

'The Devil's in these twigs.'

Wulfgar was slumped with his back against the narrow trunk of the tree, a ringing in his ears. *I am come into deep waters*, he thought he heard the choir singing. Was it one of the psalms? *The floods run over me.* His teeth rattled uncontrollably, louder in his ears than the rain pattering on the holly leaves all around him.

He found Ednoth had squatted down next to him and held his hand, rubbing it between his palms.

'Wuffa, I'm frightened you've caught a chill, or worse. You shouldn't be this cold.'

Wulfgar felt him chafe his hands for a little longer, and then he was aware of the sodden weight of his cloak being pushed away from him.

'That's not doing you any good.' Ednoth clucked with his tongue as though he were trying to soothe a startled horse. 'Steady there. Steady. At least you're not too wet next to the skin. But we need a fire,' he said. 'The cloaks are too damp. I've got to get you warm somehow.'

Wulfgar sank into the embrace as though into the arms of the mother he hardly remembered, so young he had been when he had last seen her. His shivering slowed, and in the end it stopped. And he fell asleep.

CHAPTER THIRTEEN

Easter Sunday

His mother was in the dream somewhere. He hoped to see her face, the face he couldn't quite recall, but when she turned at last it was the Lady looking at him instead, her face unspeakably sad. Then, 'There you are, Wuffa! At last! I knew you'd come. I've been waiting for you.' The young man rose, his fair face breaking into a smile, his hand reaching out to claim Wulfgar's own . . . He wore a royal helmet. Was he St Oswald? Or Alfred of Wessex, the Lady's father, young and hale as Wulfgar had never known him? It didn't seem to matter, somehow.

The rest of the dream faded into the fog of waking, and when Wulfgar surfaced at last he remembered little more than a sense of deep happiness. A good dream. He rolled over and squinted out between the spiky leaves at new grass, celandines and daisies, all sparkling with dew. The rain had stopped at last. The rising sun gave a liquid gilding to the air, though the shallow valley was full of a lingering mist. Kites were screaming as they circled, invisible and far above.

That strange sense of good cheer stayed with him as he staggered to his feet, realising as his body unfolded that his riding muscles ached no more than the rest of him. His left shoulder was stiff and tender, though, and he remembered the fall of the day before. He guessed there would be a fine bruise forming there to add to the one on his face. What I must look like . . .

What must she have thought of me?

The question took him unawares. He winced slightly at the memory of the cool, appraising gaze of the woman at the crossroads. The encounter still disturbed him.

The previous evening was beginning to come back to Wulfgar in more detail, and he paused and looked down at Ednoth. He kept me warm. He may have saved my life. I remember now. He was holding me, giving me his own warmth, until I went to sleep. What did he call us at Offchurch? *Shoulder-to-shoulder men* . . . Wulfgar reflected on his own folly in imagining that he could get to Bardney and redeem the relics by himself, when he didn't even know enough to shelter from the rain. The Bishop had known what he was doing in choosing this lad to come with him, after all.

Ednoth stretched and groaned, and Wulfgar looked away. The mist was lifting. When he turned back the lad was coming awake, sleepy-eyed and smiling, still hugging his sword in its fleece-lined scabbard close.

'Next time we're caught out on the road at nightfall,' he said between yawns, 'let's stop a bit earlier, and get a proper shelter built.'

'Thank you,' Wulfgar said.

Ednoth shrugged.

'Don't let yourself get chilled like that again. You could have died.' He got up and pushed past Wulfgar to where Fallow and Starlight were tethered.

'The horses could do with a rest,' he said. 'Shelter. A hot mash.' Fallow nuzzled at the boy's hair, whickering.

They looked all right to Wulfgar, sturdy and shaggy and soft-eyed as ever. A bit muddy, perhaps. But he knew so little about horses.

'It's Sunday today, anyway,' Wulfgar said, folding his damp cloak away, and sighing. 'Easter Sunday, and Leicester.' He suppressed a shudder. He had heard too many songs about the fall of Leicester, and the ignominious flight south of its bishop. The Danes of the Great Army had tried to take Leicester, and had failed many times, defeated by those famous walls, before they had at last succeeded. What would he and Ednoth find? If the songs he'd been taught were anything to go by, they would walk into a burnt-out city, black smoke billowing to Heaven, the eyeless corpses of women and children in the streets, glutted crows with bloody beaks, and the godless victors swilling communion wine from stolen chalices.

Smoke still rising after thirty years?

Perhaps not.

A lot must have changed since the Great Army wielded the killing-fields of eastern Mercia, he thought. Heremod said there's law in Leicester now, didn't he?

'Did Heremod say they *are* pagans?'

Was Ednoth reading his mind?

'Not exactly.'

'I've never met a pagan.' Ednoth's brown eyes were eager.

Wulfgar could almost admire his ability to see every threat as a new adventure.

'That'll be something to tell my little brothers,' Ednoth said. 'I play Christians and Pagans with them – it's great fun the way they scream when I get one on the ground and tell him I'm going to cut the blood eagle on his back—'

Wulfgar cut him short.

'I know the sort of thing.' Only too well, he thought, his shoulder blades twitching in memory. Great fun, did he call it? *We're going to flay you alive, and hack your ribs open, and pull your lungs out . . .* It's fun for the bullies, but no one asks the victims what they think.

'I'm looking forward to that ale-house,' Ednoth said. 'What did Heremod say it was called?'

'The Wave-Serpent. It's a Danish word for ship,' he said, remembering some of the songs the hostage boys had taught him, back in Winchester. He wondered what he and Ednoth would find there.

They smelt Leicester long before they saw it. But it wasn't the sickly carrion stench of Wulfgar's imagination. The air had much the same reek as Worcester: damp thatch, hearth-smoke and cooking fires overlying the rotting detritus of the city ditch. Cautious, they reined in their horses some distance from the southern gatehouse.

Leicester's ancient stone walls were every bit as massive as Wulfgar had heard, and greater than any he'd ever seen: their beautifully shaped limestone shone white in the late morning sun, banded with broad stripes of red tile, the old gatehouse still arching over the road. At the city's heart, the tower of the cathedral overlooked the sea of smoke-hung thatch, and at the sight Wulfgar's own heart lifted. Whatever horrors Leicester might contain, he thought suddenly, he could face them as long as he was privileged to make his devotions at the cathedral. Just once.

'Do we just walk in?' The hesitancy was unlike Ednoth. 'Can't we go round?'

'No.'

'Why not?' Ednoth frowned. 'Shouldn't we just press on to Bardney as quickly as we can?'

Wulfgar sighed, his ribs tight with anxiety. Whatever had the Atheling been thinking? He said this business would only take us a week, and look at us, he thought in frustration. Three nights on the road already, and we're barely halfway to Bardney. And I've got to deliver his wretched message to Leicester's Jarl, this Hakon Grimsson, which will slow us down even further.

'We need food,' he told the boy. 'A fire to dry our cloaks. You said yourself that the horses need a rest. I'm probably too late for Mass, but I should go to the cathedral, anyway. Have you got our story straight?'

Ednoth nodded and sighed heavily, rolling his eyes.

'Merchants from the south, looking into the pottery trade,' he recited, sing-song.

The gates stood open and there were no guards. Even so, they rode under the archway warily, looking to right and left. Closely packed timber buildings, many of them workshops, lined the street and huddled close to the great stone walls. They could hear the clang of a blacksmith's hammer – on Easter Sunday! – and Wulfgar felt his nostrils tightening against the acrid stench of a tannery. Ahead of them, the street widened out, and a group of men clustered to one side of what looked like the market square. Wulfgar wondered whether to go over and ask the way through the maze of streets to the cathedral, or the Wave-Serpent, but there was something unwelcoming about the men, the way they were huddled, talking in low voices, glancing over their shoulders.

'Where are we going?' Ednoth still sounded unhappy.

'The cathedral. We've got to start somewhere.'

Down an alleyway to their left, there was a gang of children dodging among the puddles and rubbish, pursuing errant chickens.

'I know, I'll ask one of those young ones.'

'Not the cathedral. It's no good to me, is it? Ask where that ale-house is. Will they speak English?'

'How should I know?' *Where's the Wave-Serpent?* He practised *hvar er* a couple of times under his breath, the foreign sounds uncomfortable on his tongue, then dismounted shakily, and, with as much confidence as he could muster, stopped one bright-looking lad, his dog panting at his feet.

'*Ungr mathr,* um, *hvar er Wave-Serpentinn?*'

Oh, the boy had understood all right.

'Wave-Serpent, *herra?* Outwith walls, till nor-east.' He pointed. 'In Dench town.'

Wulfgar blinked. The words made no sense to him at first. Then he pulled himself together, realisation seeping through.

'Dench – oh, *Danish* town. Right. Thank you. How do we get there?'

The boy pointed back towards the gate.

'Through bar, follow walls till Margaret-kirk, along Gallowtree-gate. Wave-Serpent's gainhand in garth.'

Wulfgar blinked again. It might not be Danish, but it certainly wasn't any variety of English he was familiar with.

'Margaret-kirk? Do you mean the cathedral?' But the boy had been pointing in the opposite direction.

'Nay, nay. Margaret-kirk.' The child grinned. 'It's right by Mam's. I'd put you on right gate myself?' He indicated Wulfgar's saddle hopefully.

'That would be very kind.'

He wasn't sure how to get the boy up on his crupper, but before he knew it the child had scrambled up like a cat.

'Back through bar, first on.' He whistled, and the dog ran up beside.

Wulfgar had the uncomfortable feeling that Ednoth was laughing at him.

They rode back under the double arches of the gate. The horses picked their way through a landscape of stinking ditches and pits, middens and market garden trash, keeping the bulk of the walls on their left. The boy chattered away in his near-incomprehensible dialect but his gestures were clear enough.

'What's your name, young man?' Wulfgar had been wondering if the lad would have an English name or a Danish one. But the answer came as a surprise.

'Kevin, *herra*.'

Kevin? What sort of a name was that? Irish? Wulfgar thought back to the huddled groups of men in the market square, gossiping like so many fishwives.

'What's going on, Kevin?' Wulfgar asked. 'What was everyone talking about?'

'Don't tha ken?' The lad twisted round to stare up at Wulfgar in wide-eyed disbelief. 'Our Jarl's dead. Three days gone. Arval ended at dawn.'

'Jarl? Arval?' Wulfgar found the hair rising on the back of his neck. *Three days?* The Jarl of Leicester must have been dying, maybe even dead already, when the Atheling had entrusted him

118

with the message. He wondered fleetingly how his own Lord was faring, and his Lady, and how he would know if the worst had happened.

The boy stared at him even harder.

'The Jarl. His lyke-wake. Hakon Grimsson, tha ken? Hakon *Toad*.' He said the name slowly and clearly, as though he thought Wulfgar were daft.

Ednoth, riding a few feet away, hadn't been able to hear much of their exchange. 'Can you understand him? What's he saying?'

'I – I'll tell you in a moment.'

Wulfgar was finding it hard to think clearly. I can't take a message to a dead man. What am I going to do? He could see the Atheling's dark, smiling face, feel the warm pressure of his hand on his upper arm. What was he going to say? It's the best possible excuse, he thought. The man's dead and buried. I'm reprieved, from half my burden, at least.

'Kirk's yon,' Kevin said.

Wulfgar hadn't known what to expect from the Danish quarter outside the walls, but it seemed little different from the English town within them: the same sort of mongrel dogs barking; similar children charging headlong through a flurry of squawking geese, with their mothers' voices wrathful in their wake – and *come here and help me*, he thought, sounds much the same in both languages. There were the familiar smells of privy and hearth-fire. He was very aware, however, that heads were turning, curious eyes following the strangers on their horses.

Wulfgar found his voice again.

'So, Kevin, there's a new lord – a new *jarl* – in Leicester now?'

'Now arval's done, *já*. Old Jarl's little brother.'

Wulfgar remembered what Heremod had told him.

'Is that Ketil Scar?'

The boy turned his head away and spat.

'There's Mam, *herra*. Wave-Serpent's down the ginnel. Let me down?'

A sturdy woman stood in a low doorway, arms akimbo. The boy ran towards her, shouting with excitement and pointing at the horses. Wulfgar winced. They were attracting far too much interest.

He told Ednoth what the boy had said.

'Nothing we need worry about, then. We're not here to see the Jarl, are we?' Ednoth was still smirking. 'You should have seen your face when he jumped up into your saddle! Now, where's that ale-house?'

'I would like to go to the church the boy mentioned, first.' His voice was wistful. 'Margaret-kirk. He said it was just here.' Another church, he thought. Not just the cathedral, then. Leicester promised to be full of surprises.

Ednoth looked at the expression on Wulfgar's face and shrugged.

The little church was easy to find, its lime-washed walls dazzling among the cob and timber houses, the shingled roof standing proud of the thatched buildings around it, with a sunlit wooden cross fixed to one gable end. But Margaret-kirk was no new, wooden church for the new Danish settlement: it was as ancient-looking as the city walls, stone and tile exposed in the walls where patches of plaster had flaked and fallen. The door in the west wall stood ajar, luring him in.

He slid down from Fallow and handed her reins to Ednoth.

'I won't be long.'

An alcove by the door held a battered and faded painting, a lamp guttering before it. He could just make out the lineaments of a young woman, one foot resting casually on a terrible fanged serpent. St Margaret. The Martyr of Antioch, so beloved of women in childbirth.

'*St Margaret,*' he whispered, '*pray for me, too . . .*'

The door creaked on its iron hinges. After the bright daylight, the church seemed all fire and darkness. A pair of candles in sconces flanking the door gave off a smoky yellow flame and the reek of tallow. Someone had kindled these lights recently but there was no sign of life now. Wulfgar stepped over the threshold and let the door swing to behind him.

'Hallo?' No more than a whisper; his voice was caught in his throat. He felt his hackles rise.

The building had two cells, the nave in which he stood and the chancel ahead of him, hardly wide enough to contain its altar. A third light, a little oil-lamp, glimmered there, hinting at the solemn presences of the saints painted on the chancel walls. The pungent scent of tallow mingled with damp, and he could see on the walls the tracks of water. A draft had followed him in and sent the flames leaping, starting dizzying shadows. The green-tinged saints danced in the candlelight. He noticed with a shiver that most of them had had their eyes scratched out. Was that the work of the Danes?

'Hallo?'

He took a step towards the chancel, but no one was there. Was this still a church? The blinded saints made him nervous. From force of habit, he bowed to the altar and turned to take his leave.

As he turned, he froze.

Something was emerging from the far side of the altar.

Something dark, shapeless, lurching, shuffling out of the shadows.

Wulfgar took a step backwards and crossed himself, his hand

clutching at last the Bishop's reliquary ring on its thong around his neck.

'*Holy Mary, Queen of Heaven*—'

'Who's that, there? Did I startle you?' came a muffled voice.

And he sagged with relief. The creature was unfolding into something no more than human. Its shapelessness explained itself: a big, burly man, on his hands and knees, retreating bottom-first from where he had been crawling in the narrow gap on the south side of the altar.

He hauled himself to his feet now, turning, coming through the tall, narrow chancel arch.

The flickering light showed deep-set eyes and a badger-striped beard, and a friendly but filthy hand which the stranger rapidly pulled back, rubbed down the side of his tunic, squinted at, and offered again at last.

'Were you looking for me?' he said.

Wulfgar nodded, his heart still in his throat.

'I was putting down a bit of poison for the mice. You wouldn't think they could get up onto the altar but they do. Do they *fly*, think you? And it goes against the grain for me to be offering the holy blood and body of Our Lord on an altar that's no better than a mouse's privy, wouldn't you agree? Today, of all days?'

Wulfgar would, and did, though just then he would have agreed to almost anything.

'Are you the priest here, then?' Wulfgar asked. He scanned the other man for clues. No tonsure, he thought, his lips tightening, and his leggings and short tunic those of a layman. But then, he thought belatedly, I'm in layman's attire, too, and although I should have had my hair cut on Maundy Thursday it's still a shaggy mess for the Resurrection of Our Lord. Who am I to carp?

'I am, in faith,' the big man agreed. 'Father Ronan, at your service. And a Happy Resurrection to you.'

'You too, Father. Oh, you too.' Wulfgar felt a grin of sheer relief tugging at the corners of his mouth. 'Wulfgar of Winchester, at yours.'

'*Winchester?*' The priest had been turning to pick up the lamp from the altar, but now he swung round. 'You're a long way from home.' He stared, his eyes narrowing. 'Forgive me, lad, but I pride myself on a fool-proof nose for a whiff of ordination. Is it a brother in the Church I'm talking to?' He raised the lamp higher and squinted through its rays.

Fear and relief had driven all thought of their cover story from Wulfgar's head.

'Only a subdeacon, I'm afraid,' he admitted.

'A subdeacon, and of Winchester? Not from the *cathedral?*'

Wulfgar nodded.

'But this is miraculous! You can help me celebrate Mass here this afternoon, can't you?'

'This afternoon? I'm not too late?'

Father Ronan grinned.

'What with our late Jarl's arval *and* the feast after midnight mass last night, I don't think most folk will be crawling out of bed until it's gone noon today. It'll be a very humble affair compared to what you'll be used to, but you would raise the tone immeasurably, on this day of days. It's usually just me and my altar boy.'

'Of course.' Wulfgar felt his cheeks warm with pleasure. 'I'd love to.'

'Come with me. Where are you staying? Just arrived? Make the presbytery your home while you're in Leicester. Come and have a bite of food.'

Wulfgar was wanting to ask his own questions, about the church, about its priest, about the Jarl who was dead, about the one who was still alive, but he had to surrender himself up to the spate of welcoming talk while the priest gathered together a few bits and pieces, handed him the poison jar to hold, snuffed the candle out, picked up the lamp, took back the jar and ushered him blinking out of the church and into the daylight.

Ednoth looked long-suffering.

'I thought you said you wouldn't be long?'

Wulfgar turned to the priest.

'My travelling companion,' he said. 'Ednoth of Sodbury. Ednoth, this is Father Ronan.'

Ednoth dismounted and they clasped hands.

'Never tell me you're another subdeacon! I have to tell you, lad, you've not quite the look of one.'

Ednoth was visibly taken aback.

'No.' He sounded puzzled. 'We're merchants from the south. Pottery merchants.' He turned to Wulfgar, frowning, a question forming on his lips.

Wulfgar, embarrassed, spoke very fast.

'Yes, that's quite right. Father, we've a name given us by Heremod of Wappenbury, to help with our trade enquiries. Go to an ale-house called the Wave-Serpent, he said, and ask for a man called Gunnar, Gunnar Cat's-Eyes. Is that anyone you know?'

Now it was Father Ronan's turn to frown.

'Heremod Straddler, is it now? And *Gunnar*? Indeed? Sure, are you now, that that's what Heremod said?'

'Yes.' Wulfgar was puzzled in the face of this rain of questions. 'Why?'

'Oh, no reason.' The priest smiled now. 'And aye, I think I can

124

help you. The Wave-Serpent's no more nor a step away down the ginnel. We can go there after Mass, if you can wait? Let's just bring your horses round; if we tie them up in my garth none will meddle, not if you're my guest-friends.' He took Starlight's bridle and led the way round the south side of the church and into a fenced yard as he spoke.

They unloaded their bags and lifted the saddles off the horses' steaming backs.

Father Ronan filled a couple of leather buckets with water and looked Starlight and Fallow over with a critical eye.

'You'll be resting them today?' he asked them.

Ednoth and Wulfgar glanced at each other. Ednoth nodded.

'Because Sunday is given for beasts as well as men,' Father Ronan said firmly, 'and those two poor brutes look in dire need. The righteous man regards the life of his beast. My stable for them tonight, and my hearth for you. How about it?'

Wulfgar looked at Fallow. Mud-spattered, eyes dull, her head hanging wearily. He felt a creeping sense of guilt. 'We'll be resting.'

The priest nodded in approval.

'Now, give me anything that needs putting away in safe-keeping. Your sword, lad, for one. That's a fine-looking piece of kit, but you don't want to take it into an ale-house in Leicester's Dench town. I'll just clear a little space in here, so I will – I won't keep you more than a moment,' and, his arms full of their gear, he ducked under the low thatch above his door.

Ednoth rounded on Wulfgar.

'You said—'

Wulfgar held up his hands to ward him off.

'I *know*. I'm really sorry. He was so friendly – I spoke out of turn and I gave more away than I meant to. I've been a fool.'

'*Been* a fool? *Are* a fool, more like.' But Ednoth couldn't quite hide his smile.

'I'm sorry, I'm really sorry. But—'

'The horses do need a rest.' Ednoth said. 'What kind of a name is *Father Ronan*, anyway?'

'Irish, I would guess. Isn't there a St Ronan? Why don't you ask him?'

Just then the priest re-emerged.

'Come in, boys, come on in.'

Ednoth waded straight in.

'Are you from Ireland, Father?'

'No, not myself, I'm not.' The priest stirred a pot set on the hearth-stones. 'Leicester born and bred. My mother was an Irishwoman, though. She always claimed kinship with the house of the O'Neill, so, who knows, if I talked to the right folk in Donegal I might find myself an atheling of their blood.' He turned to take a flat loaf out of the crock. 'But I've never found her kin, and the chances are she was only telling me tall stories to keep her spirits up. Come and eat, lads. I'll keep my fast till after Mass, but you two are travelling.' The priest went briskly on, 'So, you say it was Heremod of Wappenbury who recommended the Wave-Serpent? We'll head down there after Mass and drink a toast to our risen Lord.'

'Father –' Wulfgar fingered his chin '– if I'm to serve at the altar • I must shave. I should really get a haircut as well—'

'Winchester standards!' The priest looked amused. 'We've no time to trim your hair for you, but I'll get you some water for your beard if it's bothering you, lad. Can you heat it with hearth-stones? I'd do it myself, but I've an errand to run.'

Ednoth had curled up on a pile of rush pallets and fallen asleep soon after the priest had gone out; Wulfgar had a dark suspicion that the boy looked upon his excommunication as a welcome excuse for skipping Mass, but he found himself glad of the peace and quiet. The last three or four days had been so far outside his former experience, he needed time to catch up with himself, to think and to pray.

Tunic and linen discarded, smooth-chinned at last, Wulfgar was kneeling in the light that came from the low doorway and splashing his bare chest and arms with blissfully welcome warm water when the noonday sunlight darkened. He looked up, startled.

A shadow, outlined in blazing red and gold, moved forward and resolved itself into Father Ronan, holding an armful of cloth that shivered and radiated fragments of sunlight. He held it out to Wulfgar, who scrambled to his feet, eyes widening.

'Careful! It belonged to the cathedral in the old, old days, and it's one of the great treasures of Leicester. I've sworn it'll go back as good as it came. And that's none too good, I should warn you.'

He passed the roll of fabric over to Wulfgar, who unrolled it carefully as he would an old parchment, assessing its length. He tried to hide his delight.

'Well, technically, as a mere subdeacon I should wear the tunicle rather than the deacon's dalmatic—'

'But there's no one but thee and me will know the difference.' The priest winked.

'It's beautiful, Father. Thank you.' He looked up. 'Whose is it?'

'It belonged to the last canon of the cathedral.' He jerked his head back in the direction of the walled city just as a nearby bell started ringing. 'His widow keeps it now. Come on, lad, time to busk ourselves.'

Wulfgar was still tying the last of the faded side-ribbons on his

127

borrowed finery when Father Ronan said, 'When are you going to pay your respects to Ketil Scar, our new Jarl? He doesn't miss much, you know. He'll be waiting for you to come.'

Wulfgar looked down at his travel-stained shoes, a lump in his throat.

'Will you not trust me?' Father Ronan asked. 'Tell me why you've come to Leicester? If it really is the pottery trade, then Ketil's your man, you know.'

Wulfgar was silent. Father Ronan waited a moment, then 'Ach, come along then,' he said.

The sweet-voiced bell was still being rung as they processed round to the west door of his little church with as much ceremony as the two of them could muster. The bell hung in the branches of a rowan growing by the door, and a lad of around ten yanked its rope back and forth with glee. He looked familiar.

'Kevin,' Father Ronan muttered sideways at Wulfgar, 'my altar boy.'

'We've met.'

When the boy saw them, he gave the bell one last clang, waved at Wulfgar with his free hand, and fell in behind.

Father Ronan had been too modest about his Latin. Rusty, he might be, but unlike Diddlebury there were no unintended heresies here. Wulfgar was shocked, though, by what the priest had dignified by calling his books: tattered and greasy pamphlets, with whole quires missing.

When I get home, Wulfgar vowed silently, I'll raid my secret store of perfect vellum and find the time to make him a proper lectionary. I'll get it to him somehow.

He was even more shocked by the old mead-horn substituting for the sacred chalice.

But the little church was packed to overflowing.

The west door had been left open so that the people crowded outside could hear the Easter Mass, and the sunlight came slantwise into the church in a long golden shaft full of dust. As Wulfgar moved around the cramped chancel, he was only dimly aware of the congregation, but as Father Ronan was giving the blessing he realised there was one figure who had repeatedly caught his eye: a fox-haired man in a russet tunic, ears and throat glinting with gold. He stood leaning against the wall just inside the doorway, arms folded, never kneeling – as far as Wulfgar could see – or bowing his head, never crossing himself, never parting his lips in prayer.

He meant to ask Father Ronan who the man was, but after Mass, Wulfgar found himself swept up by the priest's energy: 'Let me just wash *those* – and put *that* away – and get *that* bag – kick that boy of yours, would you? We'll need something to eat.' After broth and bread he wiped his hand over his beard and said, 'Now, boys, the Wave-Serpent? Faith, it's early yet but we'll likely find it buzzing. Everyone wants to know what's going to happen, now our new Jarl's got his hands on the reins.'

Wulfgar's heart was still back in the little church.

'Where did you get that wonderful incense? Like roses.'

'It's good, isn't it?' The priest smiled wryly. 'Danish traders bring it from Byzantium. It isn't even that expensive, here.'

Wulfgar nodded, wide-eyed. Greek incense cost more than most English minsters could afford. Perhaps he could take some home.

Father Ronan chuckled at the look on his face.

'It's astonishing what you can get, if you don't mind haggling with heathens. They say the Archbishop of York wipes his arse with silk.'

Wulfgar managed a smile.

The shadows were lengthening. Wulfgar, still humming the Alleluia, and a bleary Ednoth followed Father Ronan down a narrow muddy alleyway.

Father Ronan stopped abruptly in a small yard, two sides of which were closed in by a low building. The priest shouldered the door open and they followed in his wake. The Wave-Serpent proved to be a hive of little rooms, one leading from another, lit by torches and smoky braziers, the beams low enough for both Father Ronan and Ednoth to have to duck at times. The place was heaving, voices raised, and Wulfgar smelt the same tension that he had scented in the market-place earlier. They went on, following the priest, past knots of men jabbering at one another in Danish and English alike, until at last they came to a room where great barrels rested on their sides. A pot-boy crouched before one, filling a jug.

'Wave-Serpent?' Ednoth muttered in Wulfgar's ear. 'Beehive, more like.'

Father Ronan pushed his way through.

The ale-wife, a gaudily-dressed, tight-mouthed woman, was standing over the boy, her hands on her hips. 'I can't leave this place for a minute—', they heard her saying but she looked round then, and Wulfgar saw her face soften as she spotted the priest. 'Like a bad penny, you are, Father Ronan,' she said. 'The usual?'

It was the woman from the Watling Street crossroads.

CHAPTER FOURTEEN

He wouldn't have known her by sight, not at once, but Wulfgar recognised her as soon as she spoke. No one could mistake that voice, throaty as a ring-dove's, somehow clear and husky at once. When she looked beyond Father Ronan's shoulder their eyes met and held. She nodded slowly, raising those swooping eyebrows. A flush crept up from Wulfgar's neck, invisible, he hoped, in that warm dim light. He broke his gaze at last to turn to Ednoth. Perhaps the boy would not recognise her; perhaps he would remember no more than a blur of hood and cloak, veiled in rain.

Some hope. Ednoth's hackles were rising even as Wulfgar turned, and, looking back to the woman, Wulfgar saw her mouth begin to twitch.

Then Father Ronan said, 'Gunnvor, my soul, these lads have come a long, long way, from the deep south of the Angle-law, just to find you. Wulfgar, Ednoth, you said you were looking for Gunnvor, called Cat's-Eyes, of the Wave-Serpent? Well, here she is.'

Gunnvor, Wulfgar thought, shocked. Not Gunnar, but Gunnvor.

'That can't be right,' Ednoth said loudly. 'We're looking for a man. Not her.'

'Ah, so Heremod Straddler names *me* as his friend, does he? Well, that's worth knowing.' She laughed, low in her throat. 'I did warn you he has some thirsty friends.'

Wulfgar, still startled, thought back to his parting with their host at Wappenbury, and Heremod standing at his stirrup leather, muttering a name. Both Gunnvor and Gunnar were so alien to an English ear; he could easily have misheard.

'What are you all drinking?' she asked. 'Father Ronan, the heather ale for you?'

'Tell them to bring a jug and a loaf, and come sit with us,' he said. 'Oh, and some of that sorrel cheese, lass.'

Wulfgar glanced at Ednoth again. His face had flushed dark red. Wulfgar touched his arm.

'Come on.'

Father Ronan was already working his way back through the crowd to the main room, where, at his approach, a couple of men rose from one of the tables: 'Just keeping it warm for you, Father!'

The priest laid his bag down and they all squeezed round. Wulfgar looked back to see Gunnvor Cat's-Eyes coming towards their table followed by the pot-boy, who laboured with a brimming pitcher and four cups. The light was brighter in here, with a good hearth-fire in the middle of the room, and it was the first chance he'd had to see her properly. Still unveiled – not as much as a token triangle of linen to scarf her hair. Not too tall, but she carried herself like a queen, holding her small head high on a long neck that made Wulfgar think of the spike of a lily. Her face was beautifully modelled, with a small, firm chin and high cheekbones, giving her eyes a truly feline slant. But any impression of delicacy was countered by her high-bridged, eagle's nose and those predatory brows, as well as her imperious manner.

She was dressed like an empress, too: thick black braids piled up the back of her head; silver trinkets tucked in among the braids and glinting at her ears; gold embroidered at the neck and wrists of her green tunic; more silver in the brooches of looped wire pinned to her shoulders; bright keys jingling at her waist; and a sleeveless overdress of some lush red fabric that shimmered as she waved at the pot-boy to put his burden down.

He'd thought her gaudy at first sight. But gaudy implied cheap. In the better light of the fire he realised that sumptuous was a better word. Even his Lady rarely dressed with such splendour. What was this woman doing presiding over a common ale-house?

Father Ronan beamed with delight.

'Cat's-Eyes, my love, this is Wulfgar, a subdeacon of the true Kirk and trained at Winchester Cathedral, no less. What a treat for me, on this Easter Sunday. And Ednoth, of Sodbury.'

Ednoth looked fixedly at the table.

Gunnvor glanced at him and raised her eyebrows, then caught Wulfgar's stare and returned it, unsmiling, giving nothing away. He was the first to blink.

'Any room for me on this end of the bench?' she said.

He realised in a sudden panic that she meant to squeeze in next to him, and shuffled up as far away from her as he could. She sat down in a rustle of skirts and put her elbows on the table, pushing her green linen sleeves back, showing the smooth skin of her forearms.

'Let's have our drink, then.' She raised her eyebrows at Wulfgar.

'Welcome to Leicester, Wulfgar of Winchester. And what might a subdeacon be, anyway?'

He had opened his mouth to stammer something when Father Ronan cut in.

'Gunnvor, my soul, it's an honourable and noble stage on the journey to the priesthood. Now, enough babble.' He raised his cup, '*Christ is risen!*'

'*Indeed, He is risen,*' Wulfgar answered happily, and drank deeply, but he couldn't help noticing that Gunnvor Cat's-Eyes didn't join in the toasts until they drank to long life, health and happiness. She was the first to slam her cup down again on the table and lean back, wiping her mouth with the back of her hand. Firelight shimmered over the crisp red fabric she wore tight across her breasts and swathed around her hips, and Wulfgar realised, now that he could examine it at such close quarters, that it was *silk*.

Yards of it.

And not just any silk.

He took a quick, shocked breath. A red as deep as wine, thick-woven with peacocks and eagles. And such a *breadth* of silk – he'd only ever seen the like in the richest West Saxon minsters, for altar-hangings, vestments, palls for reliquaries . . . In Mercia, no woman but the Lady sported more silk than would trim a tunic. He stared; he couldn't help himself. Where had she got it from, this ale-wife, this toll-collector, this – whatever she was? From some Greek merchant? Or, his jaw tightening, had it indeed once formed part of a church's dowry? Plundered . . . He realised then that he had been scanning her up and down with fascination and he dragged his gaze away, face hot.

'What's the news?' Father Ronan asked.

She quirked her eyebrows at that.

'I should be asking you. It was past midday when I got home from my crossroads.'

Father Ronan frowned.

'So that's where you've been. Ketil noticed you weren't at the wake, you know.'

'You know how I feel about Ketil.' Gunnvor shrugged elaborately. 'I couldn't stand seeing him peacocking about like that before Hakon was cold, that's all.'

'Really, lass? That's really all?'

She nodded, tight-lipped. Father Ronan gave her a long look before sighing and turning to Wulfgar.

'You two must have come along the Great Road. Did you meet any trouble?'

'Trouble?' he stammered, thinking of Garmund.

Gunnvor chuckled.

'No trouble they couldn't handle.' She raised her eyebrows at Wulfgar again. 'Though I did need to assert myself at times.'

The encounter at the crossroads came vividly back to him as he blushed yet again: his sense of the shifts and eddies of power, of Gunnvor wresting control, retrieving Ednoth's sword, from her sullen and reluctant men by sheer effort of will. She reminded Wulfgar of his Lady, facing down the Bishop, trying to break in Mercia's stubborn thanes, although the comparison felt almost blasphemous.

'We're very ignorant about Leicester and your ways,' he said diffidently. 'We gather Jarl Hakon has just died?'

Gunnvor and Father Ronan glanced at each other.

'I buried him two days ago,' said Father Ronan, 'in my little boneyard at St Margaret's. If you'd told me thirty years ago that *that* was going to happen!' He coughed with what might have been laughter and took a long pull at his cup. 'Him receiving the last rites, meek as a mouse – confession, viaticum, unction and all – and me, the Grimssons' tame priest, to provide them.' He shook his head. 'Well, never mind that. Hakon Toad and his gang from Hordaland snapped Leicester up when Mercia fell apart, thirty years ago, and he'd been sitting on it ever since. Not a sparrow fell but he knew about it.' Father Ronan raised his cup in tribute. 'And now he's dead, God rest him.'

'His gods won't,' Gunnvor said.

Father Ronan shot her a glance, refilling his brightly-glazed cup.

'You shouldn't say that. He was very good to you,' he said mildly, 'and he made a good death.'

'Straw death.' She saw the puzzled frown on Wulfgar's face. 'What warrior cares to die in his bed? He can't go home to the hall of the Spear.'

'Hakon died a good Christian,' Father Ronan said firmly.

'That's what you think.'

This time the priest ignored her retort.

'And his little brother's taken over,' he said, 'and straight away he's stirring up the mud at the bottom of the pond.'

'What kind of a man is Ketil?' Wulfgar asked. 'Is he a good Christian, too?'

Again, that wary glance. Father Ronan pursed his lips.

'Ambitious. Wants to call himself King in Leicester, as that old war-wolf Knut is wanting to do in York.'

Wulfgar didn't like the sound of that. He tilted his cup for more ale. It was good, strong, flavoured with an unfamiliar mix of herbs. He wondered what the Lady would need to know.

'Should the Mercian levies be putting a new edge on their weapons? Is it that kind of ambition?'

Gunnvor shook her head.

'It would be a good time, now, with your Lord bedridden. But Ketil needs to make his own grip strong, first. There are a lot of people here who don't like him. If he succeeds, then, *já*, go home and tell them to get the whetstones out.' She set her cup down on the scarred wood. 'Now, why were you looking for me? We could have saved time, back there on the Great Road.'

How did she know about the Old Boar's illness? *News runs fast; ill news fastest.* But, he supposed, she must hear everything, if she held the right to the crossroads.

'Heremod showed us the pottery that's brought in from these parts. Lovely stuff, bright glazes, like this.' He held out his cup. 'I said I could find a market for it in the south, and he said we should talk to you.'

'And Gunnvor's the one to talk to,' Father Ronan agreed, 'for a broad-minded subdeacon who wants to branch out into ceramics.' The priest met Wulfgar's eyes then, and smiled, his head lightly to one side, looking curious, inviting confidences.

Wulfgar wanted to change the subject.

'Is it difficult being the only priest in this part of the world?'

Father Ronan caught his eye, seemed about to say something, and then shrugged.

'Is it easy anywhere?' He ran his hand through his wiry grizzled hair, leaving it standing up in a crest like a lapwing's. 'I baptise the babies, say the Mass, and hold the hands of the dying.' His voice had taken on a resigned tinge. 'I can't get books, I have to bumble through half the liturgy from memory. I did have a grand gilt chalice and paten, once, but they were stolen. So I consecrate the blood of Our Lord in that old mead-horn – and I saw you raise your eyebrows! This isn't Winchester, you know.'

Wulfgar nodded, slowly assimilating everything the priest had said. No, this wasn't Winchester. It wasn't even Worcester. He remembered the parlous state of affairs at Offchurch and – where was it the Bishop had showed him that letter from? Diddlebury, that was it. Just be grateful there's a priest here at all, he told himself, and all the more so for one with a real sense of vocation.

'What's it like once you get north of here?' he asked.

The priest eyed him sideways.

'I can answer that one better if you tell me where you're headed.'

How much did he need to know? Wulfgar wondered.

'Lincoln, for example,' he said, a sudden catch in his throat. He glanced at Ednoth to see whether the boy had heard, but he showed no sign of listening, still scowling at the table, picking with his nail at a loose splinter.

Father Ronan frowned.

Gunnvor broke in: 'Oh, Lincoln's not as bad as some people make out. Though if it's pottery you're truly chasing you'll do better heading due east of here, not north east. It's Stamford you want. That's where—' She clearly had more to say but Father Ronan cut across her words.

'Enough for the moment. Pleasure before business.' He unfastened the toggles on his bag as he spoke.

Gunnvor snapped her fingers for another jug.

'Later,' she murmured in Wulfgar's ear. 'And I'll let you know my commission.'

Wulfgar nodded, only half-attending. He was too troubled by what they had said – and what they hadn't said – about Lincoln. He was even more troubled by Ednoth's silence. The boy hadn't uttered a word since they had sat down. Now he was still fiddling at that bit of wood at the edge of the table, seemingly giving it his whole mind, and drinking steadily.

But Wulfgar's worries were dispelled like darkness by sunrise at the sight of the instrument that Father Ronan was unveiling from her beaver-skin lining. Old, old wood smooth as glass, with silver-gilt plaques in the shape of eagles' heads to left and right, her bridge of amber, every curve honed and polished where a dozen generations of men had caressed her. A true long-harp to sit on your knee and hold to your heart like a lover.

Wulfgar caught his breath. He could hear his uncle's voice sternly quoting canon law at him: *a cleric must not sing in taverns in the manner of a common glee-man . . .* and a tavern full of heathens, at that! But the priest's harp was filling him with an overpowering desire.

Father Ronan looked over at him and the corners of his mouth tugged into a smile.

'Flotsam from the world before the Flood,' he said enigmatically. 'Maple, willow and limewood.'

Wulfgar nodded, only half-understanding. There was clearly a story here, but now was not the time to ask. The appearance of the harp had been greeted with raucous approval by the other drinkers, and the benches were already being hauled round for a makeshift arena.

'Come on, Father,' someone yelled, 'Give us "The Cuckoo Song".'

But the priest was taking his time, tuning each string with the aid of a little bronze key, and he just nodded and went on smiling.

Wulfgar wondered what one might sing for this audience. St

139

Andrew, perhaps, and his mission to the cannibals? Or one of the greats, the songs of doomed heroes, of love and gold and the darkness at the heart of things? He sat up, all eager attention. But when Father Ronan finally finished tuning, a sparkle in his eyes, it was the first request that was rewarded: a song of such startling vulgarity about a promiscuous young wife that Wulfgar didn't know where to look. It was the sort of song that Wulfgar's own father would have loved, though. God rest his blemished soul, but my father would have fitted right in with this crowd, Wulfgar thought, he would have been pounding the table and singing along; I can just hear him bellowing *Kukkuk* along with Father Ronan in the chorus.

But it was no fitting song for a priest. Wulfgar, who had been longing with a passion to try out that glorious harp himself, was now quite sure it would be wrong.

But no one was watching, he realised with a shock. No one who was going to carry spiteful tales back to his uncle, that upright canon of Winchester, anyway. Queen of Heaven, forgive me, he thought, but Winchester is a very long way away.

When Father Ronan had finished, Wulfgar half-stretched out his hand despite the nagging voice of conscience, but Gunnvor Cat's-Eyes was too quick for him. As she leaned across him to grasp the harp, her clothes gave off a sharp, spicy scent. Cinnamon, he thought, nostrils quivering. Pepper. She shifted away from him to the bench-end and turned sideways slightly to make room, retuning the harp quickly, as though she played it often.

'New one,' she said shortly. 'I heard it from one of my men.'

Her song was in Danish; Wulfgar could only catch scraps of the meaning. Her singing had the same husky, crooning quality as her speech. He frowned, watching her mouth while she sang, trying

to make what sense he could from her words. *Swan-feathers* . . .
Whiter arms . . . Something about girls – *the maidens yearned* – or
were they swans? Flying away . . . and a man left lamenting his
unbearable loss.

'You don't like it?'

He blinked. The spell was over and she was staring back at
him.

'Or you don't like my voice?' There was a challenge there.

'No, I do, I really do. Both. I'd like to hear it again. I only—'

'Your turn,' and she shoved the harp straight at his chest.

He clutched at it helplessly.

'I really shouldn't—'

'Come on, Wulfgar, don't be a Caedmon.' Father Ronan
grinned. This was another kind of challenge, one Wulfgar found
more familiar.

He sat up.

'I have no intention of being a Caedmon,' he said indignantly,
'unless you mean *after* the angel gave him the miraculous gift of
song?' But what about singing 'Caedmon's Dream'? His thoughts
ran for a moment after the tale of the Whitby cowherd, miserably
exiling himself evening after evening from the cheerful gatherings
in the feast-hall, until that miraculous night when a heavenly
visitor had awarded him not only an angelic voice but also a song
to sing . . .

He realised a thick, grizzled eyebrow was being raised.

'Cocky, aren't we, lad? Let's hear you, then. No hymns, mind,
not for this audience.'

Cocky? Aren't you confusing me with Ednoth? But the priest
was offering him the harp now, and he gave it his full attention.
It nestled thrillingly into his left arm's embrace. He held out his

other hand for the tuning key. It was topped with a little bronze figure of a stag, burnished almost to gold, old as the harp herself. He plucked at the strings experimentally, retuned them a little. Nothing too long. Something that they might not have heard. He didn't want to break the spell Gunnvor had cast.

And, swimming up out of nowhere, he remembered scraps of a song his mother used to sing. Not remotely suitable for someone who wanted to be a bishop, or even for a subdeacon, but it responded to something plaintive in Gunnvor's lament, something that had touched his core.

'When it was rainy weather,
And I, weeping, sat . . .
Wulf, my Wulf,
Why did you come so seldom?
Easily parted, what was never joined –
Our song together.'

He drew his fingers across the strings with a last plangent little flourish, like tears.

There was a moment's silence. And then that roar of approval, the pounding of fists on the table, that warmed his heart like little else. He looked across at Gunnvor, a challenge in his own eyes now.

She nodded.

'*Já*, so there's more to you than meets the eye. He –' she jerked her chin at Ednoth '– can ride and you can sing.'

'Sentimental twaddle,' Father Ronan said, but he said it with a smile.

'Me now.'

Ednoth hauled himself to his feet. It was the first time he'd spoken since they'd sat down. Wulfgar offered the harp to him across the table but he brushed it aside with a rough gesture that had Wulfgar clutching the instrument protectively.

'You don't need a harp, not for what I'm going to sing.' He swayed slightly, still scowling, and leaned forward to brace himself with one hand on the edge of the table, half-turning to include the whole room.

'Hey!
We've heard and we've told of the battles of old
when we first won this land as of right
but the greatest of all was that wonderful brawl
men know as Edington fight.'

The room had fallen silent again, but there was a different quality to it now. Wulfgar's warm glow was evaporating like dew in the sun.

One verse of 'The Battle of Edington' should be quite enough in present company, he thought. More than enough. He cleared his throat.

But Ednoth was already raising his voice and swinging into the chorus. In Winchester, even in Worcester, everyone in the room would have joined him. Here in Leicester, the silence was growing ominous.

'Edington! Edington! Fed the wolf from sun to sun!
Edington! Edington! Made the Danish buggers run!'

He was still singing alone, but his stride wasn't thrown for a moment.

'By the Wessex White Horse those sons of old whores,
Guthrum and Halfdan and—'
Crash!

One of the benches had gone over. Wulfgar squinted into the smoke and glow to see a massive figure staggering towards them. It looked as though Ednoth had got his fight at last.

'My father fell in Guthrum's service!' the big Dane bellowed. He had already pulled back a fist to swing.

Ednoth's head went up, nostrils flaring, a fierce joy in his face.

Father Ronan shoved the harp and its bag at Wulfgar and forced his bulk out round the end of the table.

'Steady on, lads, we're all family under this roof. That battle was a lifetime ago, Alfred and Guthrum are both in their graves—'

'Not your business, Father,' the Dane said, never taking his eyes from Ednoth.

'Oh, I think you'll find it is,' Father Ronan responded amiably. He was between the two of them now, and they were circling him, trying to get at each other.

'Come on, Englishman,' said the Dane. 'Hiding behind a priest? Typical of you people.'

Ednoth roared with frustration and lunged, shouldering the priest out of the way. They grappled and swayed, and Wulfgar saw to his horror that they were coming his way. Hugging the harp to his breast he wormed down from the bench, his only thought to save the harp – and himself – from harm. He crawled under the table, onto his hands and knees on the sticky packed earth of the floor.

The racket of swearing and shouting was deafening. A confused forest of legs wove and stumbled back and forth, a crash and a yell and a flurry of sparks as someone fell into the fire. Wulfgar hoped it would be the Dane, the man whose father had fought against Alfred of Wessex at Edington, but then he glimpsed him still on his feet, a solid lump of a man, a good decade older than Ednoth.

Ednoth was never going to win this fight. Wulfgar began a frantic squirm out from under, desperate to stop the madness somehow. And then, just as he was emerging, there came a gut-wrenching groan and the thud of a body falling, and an uproar of voices.

Wulfgar went cold from top to toe and fell flat again, squinnying out through the trestles, wondering despairingly who had drawn his knife, and whose the corpse would be.

CHAPTER FIFTEEN

Before Wulfgar could crawl out from under the table, the door from the courtyard burst open. The ale-house was crowded suddenly with men with lanterns and sticks. They came piling in, three or four of them, their swaying lanterns bringing a little more light. A pause, and then a fifth man came slowly stepping over the threshold. And the room, at loggerheads only a moment before, was united in silence.

Father Ronan stepped forward, his hands spread in pacifying mode.

'My Lord Ketil! You honour us! No trouble here. Just a little – lively – political debate between friends.'

To his disbelief, through the legs of the bench, Wulfgar saw the former combatants beyond the priest, on the far side of the room: Ednoth grinning, the big Dane feeling his windpipe and swallowing, but both apparently otherwise unhurt. Wulfgar wondered for a moment about worming his way out now, making himself known to Ketil as the priest had recommended, but something stopped him.

The sound of one person's footsteps.

Coming towards the centre of the room, crunching on shards of pottery, stopping by their table. His shins were inches from Wulfgar's nose. All Wulfgar could see of Leicester's new Jarl was his kid leather boots, the fringed and braided hem of his tunic, the fine gilding and the filigree chape of the leather scabbard swinging at his hip. He moved stiffly, as if his joints troubled him. But Wulfgar could also see the others falling back, hear their silence, and smell their fear.

When Ketil spoke it was in Danish, his tone quiet, conversational.

'Gunnvor Bolladottir? *Far thú hingath til mín.*' A harsh, slow, guttural voice, with a thickness about the tongue. Wulfgar had to strain his ears, and all his knowledge of Danish, to make any sense of it.

A rustle of silk. Gunnvor's voice. *'Herra.' My Lord.* He could see her feet, neat in silver-buttoned leather, as she curtsied.

'Look at you, dressed for a bridal, not an arval. Angling for another man already, and my brother but three days in the ground?' An ostentatious sigh. 'Fighting over you, were they? I should have known you would forget him so soon.'

'I have not forgotten, *herra.*' Gunnvor's voice, low as it was, was bell-clear in comparison.

'Really? No? But they tell me, Bolladottir, that you are any man's now, for the asking.'

'Not quite, *herra.* I'm not yours.'

No Danish was needed to interpret the sound that came next – the sharp *smack* of a blow. Wulfgar, appalled, saw her feet stagger at the impact. But she didn't fall – she recovered her stance quickly while Ketil was still talking.

'Who are these *utlendingar* I've had word of? Do you know anything?'

Outlanders?

Us?

There was a pause. Then Gunnvor spoke, clearly and deliberately.

'Nothing, *herra.*'

'You hear anything, you tell me. Understand? I want to talk to them.'

'I understand, *herra.*'

'Be sure you do.'

Wulfgar saw Ketil's well-shod heels turn, his guards jostling to follow. He'd still not seen the man's face.

The door closed.

There was a long moment of silence.

Gunnvor's voice broke the spell: 'What are you staring at, you fools? You, sweep that up.' The pot-boy appeared with a besom and began clearing away fragments of pottery.

Wulfgar crawled out at last.

'Comfortable, under my nice table?'

He turned. Gunnvor watched him, arms folded across her silk-swathed breasts. The right side of her face was marked with red, angry against the cream of her skin, and, in the centre a bleeding cut, right on the cheekbone.

'I – are you all right?' He stared, horrified.

She put the back of her wrist up to her face and wiped the trickle of blood away.

'He's a vain man, our Ketil. He likes his rings big.'

'I – I was protecting Father Ronan's harp.'

'Better protect it then.' She turned away.

He bent to retrieve it. When he straightened up he saw, to his surprise, that the big Dane had invited Ednoth over to his table. The two of them were acting out their battle: Ednoth miming the upthrust of a vicious elbow into the other man's throat, and the Dane cheerfully following up with an exaggerated staggering fall into the arms of his friends – a whole rough easy mindless world of men from which Wulfgar felt profoundly shut out. And it was only then that he realised just how drunk they all were.

Father Ronan put a hand on his shoulder. He saw Wulfgar's frown.

'I have you to thank for looking after Uhtsang. The harp. It's her name.'

Wulfgar nodded, thinking it over. It was a good name. *Uhtsang*. Matins. Or the dawn chorus, perhaps.

'Did you name her?' he asked, as he gave the harp into the priest's arms.

'Not I. I'll give you the story some other time.' He tucked the harp away safely, then turned back to Wulfgar. 'Now,' the priest murmured, 'I want you to tell me the real reason you two have landed in Leicester.'

Wulfgar pulled back sharply and looked at him, startled.

The priest just grinned.

'I've whittled down my list of possibilities.' He ticked them off on his fingers: 'Now, are you subdeacons, smugglers, slave-dealers, swords for hire or spies? Tell me, go on – then we can decide how much you need to tell Ketil Scar when you pay your respects to him tomorrow.'

Wulfgar, sick of a sudden at the prospect of facing Ketil, opened his lips to say *pottery merchants* but the lying syllables wouldn't come out, not in the face of that knowing and patient gaze. He glanced across to Ednoth, but there would be no support coming from that newly cheerful quarter.

The priest's eyes followed Wulfgar's, and he smiled.

'Boys,' he said, shaking his head as he tucked the harp into her bag.

That sympathetic one word was enough. Wulfgar felt a great urge to unburden himself to this understanding man but he could not. A tidal wave of exhaustion washed over him. It must have shown in his face.

'Later then,' the priest said. 'Let's get you to bed. I'll come back for yon lad.'

Wulfgar began to haul himself to his feet, muffling a yawn, looking at Gunnvor. He wanted to say goodbye, to thank her for her hospitality, to ask forgiveness on Ednoth's behalf for the trouble they'd brought her.

I can't approve of her, he thought wearily, but she's been very kind. He half-wished he were really interested in dealing in pottery, so that they could have that later conversation she'd promised him.

But she wasn't looking at him.

He followed her gaze.

The fox-haired man he'd noticed in the congregation at St Margaret's was making his way towards them.

'Orm Ormsson, as I live and breathe,' he heard her saying. She sounded none too pleased.

'Gunnvor Cat's-Eyes.' He lifted her hand to his lips and paused, looking at the smear of blood on the back and then the gash on her cheekbone. 'Did you meet someone with sharper claws, little cat?'

She ignored his question.

'May I join you?' His accent came from the same stable as

Gunnvor's but much stronger, a sing-song that sounded to Wulfgar as disarmingly comic as the man's name.

'Can I stop you?'

He crowded in on the end of the bench, blocking Wulfgar in, reaching for the jug. His smell was sweet, musky, foreign. He rattled with more gold than Wulfgar had ever seen on a single human being: several rings in each ear, numerous chains and beads and pendants at his throat, chunky braids of solid silver at each wrist. A toy-like axe, its blade no longer than a handspan and inlaid with exotic gold curlicues, hung from his studded belt.

'You're a stranger in Leicester, these days,' Gunnvor said, sitting down and snapping her fingers for another jug.

Father Ronan caught Wulfgar's eye: '*Soon*,' he mouthed.

Orm Ormsson grinned, toothy but no warmth.

'The Miklagard run. Over-wintered there.'

'*Constantinople*,' Father Ronan muttered.

Wulfgar nodded, impressed despite himself. He had thought Worcester to Bardney was a long journey. Another yawn overtook him. Whatever this Orm person wants, he thought, I hope it isn't going to take too long. I can hear that pile of pallets in the corner of the presbytery calling my name.

'Grikkland, is it?' Gunnvor said. 'Don't I remember you bragging about some palace-quality silk you could get me? Something about a *friendship* with one of the imperial officials?'

He shrugged.

'He proved less friendly than I had hoped.' He looked across the table at Father Ronan. 'You might say a prayer for his soul – he was a Christian.'

'Did I see you in church this afternoon?' the priest asked.

'You did. Surprised, were you?' Another grin from Orm Ormsson, revealing small, sharp teeth.

'Nothing much surprises me nowadays,' Father Ronan said.

'Well, I hoped I might learn something.'

'And were your hopes fulfilled?'

'Not by what I heard from you.' Orm Ormsson frowned, leaning forward on his elbows, his foxy hair falling forward. 'There's a lot of things about the Christians I don't understand.'

'I know that feeling,' Father Ronan said, unsmiling. 'What were you after learning?'

Orm Ormsson fingered the largest of the gold hoops through his right ear.

'Saints. Shiny, shiny boxes, full of dead bones. What's all that about?'

Wulfgar froze, his cup halfway to his mouth. Orm Ormsson wasn't sounding remotely comic now.

Gunnvor took a long pull of her beer.

Father Ronan looked thoughtful, his grizzled eyebrows furrowing.

'Well, Orm, unlike you – and me – the saints are folk of heroic virtue. When they die, their souls go straight home to God—'

Orm looked sceptical.

'*Já, já*, if you say so. I'm not so bothered with their souls. What about their bones?'

'I was coming to their bones,' Father Ronan said mildly. 'The soul is only half what makes a person. Soul and body come back together, transfigured, at the end of time. And so that power resides in saints' bodies, as well.'

Orm leaned back, eyebrows raised.

'Hear me out,' the priest said. 'And anything which has been part of a saint, owned by a saint, even touched by a saint, can invoke that virtue. A relic is like a – a bell you can ring, to get the saint's ear. And the saints plead for us to God, if they choose.'

Orm had already started shaking his head while the priest was still speaking. 'But what is so special about their bones? What do they *look* like, out of their boxes?'

'I've told you.'

'You trying to hide something from me?' Orm asked, raising his eyebrows.

'Why are you, of all people, worrying about the Christians' little gods?' Gunnvor asked.

'She only does it to annoy us,' Father Ronan muttered. 'She knows perfectly well that the saints aren't gods.'

Wulfgar was concentrating so hard on Orm that he barely heard him.

Now the trader was shrugging and rolling his eyes. 'What do you think, Cat's-Eyes? There's money in it. You want to hear a riddle I heard in Lincoln?'

'Go on,' Father Ronan said.

'When is a dead man a better bargain than a live one?'

'And the answer?' Wulfgar asked, his throat tight, not sure he wanted to hear it.

Orm turned and looked at him for the first time.

'Hello, Englishman,' he said. 'I saw you in church, too. Very pretty, all in red and gold. The answer, Englishman, is "when he's a saint". A dead saint is worth more than a live slave, they say. Than ten live slaves, even pretty ones, if it's a good saint. Even a little tiny bit of him.' He crooked his little finger and waggled it. 'Even without his shiny box.' He took another long swig of beer.

Wulfgar felt sick. He forced himself to ask, 'Do you mean there's a market for relics among the Danes?'

'Why does he call us Danes, this little *Englis-mathr*?' Orm asked, addressing Gunnvor.

She shrugged.

'They all do, in England. Perhaps they've never heard of Norway.'

Father Ronan was stroking his beard, looking thoughtful.

'I suppose,' he said, 'that from your point of view, relics are the perfect article of trade. All their worth is in the eye of the beholder.'

'*Exactly.*' Orm rubbed his hands. 'To me, nasty old bones – pick them up anywhere. To you, a saint. Play my counters right, flog bits of St Ásvald north of Tees and south of Watling Street. Sit back and tally my profit and watch the minsters squabble.' He finished his drink and stood up, axe swinging, strings of pendants jingling.

Ásvald, Wulfgar thought, frowning. It sounded familiar. Too familiar . . .

'Orm . . .' It was Gunnvor, her voice holding a note of genuine menace.

'*Já*, Cat's-Eyes. I know. The silk.'

'Palace-quality?'

'Palace-quality, but of course. For you, only the best. Straight from the emperor's *ergasteri* and dyed with the purple.'

Gunnvor snorted at his departing figure.

'He better keep his word. He owes me so much money, I'm going to have to do something about it one of these days.'

Father Ronan and Wulfgar were silent.

She looked from face to face.

'Nothing too nasty, you understand. Nothing that a few weeks' bed rest won't cure. He's had it coming for a long time, and my boys are gentler than some.'

But Wulfgar could barely hear her. Some dark angel had him in a stranglehold, one arm crushing his windpipe, the other gripping his ribs, great black wings blocking his eyes and thrashing his ears, breathing out cold. He had no power to resist. Only dimly did he become aware of the priest's hand on his arm.

'Wulfgar, are you all right?'

He couldn't find an answer.

'What is it? Come on, man, you look as though you've seen a ghost.'

He still felt as though he were being choked. Somewhere the voice of reason was still urging caution, but something else – something stronger than reason – prompted him to tell the truth. He stuttered, '*St Oswald.*'

The priest shook his arm gently.

'What about St Oswald? Something Ormsson said? Come on, Wulfgar.'

Slowly the dark angel was letting go. The red-tinged blackness began to fade from his eyes and he saw the fire-lit room again, the table, the priest's concerned face. I've been wasting time, he thought desperately. Far too much time. He took a deep breath. If he had to trust someone, then why not this straightforward priest? He seemed an honest man enough, for all his crowd-pleasing bawdy. Closing his ears to the little voice of doubt still nagging at him, Wulfgar said softly, 'Bardney. We're going to Bardney. We're looking for St Oswald.'

It was Gunnvor who spoke first – Wulfgar had almost forgotten she was there and he looked at her in shock.

'Eirik's land?' She sounded stunned. 'Eirik the Spider? That Bardney? You're crazy. Ronan, tell this little subdeacon of yours he's crazy.' She folded her arms.

Wulfgar looked over at the priest, who sat very still. Eventually he stirred, like a man waking from sleep.

'Is it indeed *that* Bardney you mean? Eirik's Bardney?'

Wulfgar nodded, feeling miserable. It was too late to keep silent now.

'We had word that the bones are still there. The Lady – she needs the relics for her new church in Gloucester.' He swallowed, still trying to pick up the threads of his thoughts. 'The Lord – as you've heard – he's desperately ill. We all need a miracle. A sign that God's not turned his back on Mercia for the last time.'

Father Ronan cleared his throat and breathed in deeply through his nose. Then he said, 'Eirik's a dangerous man, so he is.'

'We've got the name of someone who knows where the bones are buried.' Orm's words came back to him with terrible clarity. 'It was supposed to be a secret. The Bishop of Worcester didn't think anyone else was party to it.' He put his head in his hands. 'And now I come here and find St Oswald is ale-house gossip.' Their reaction to the name of Bardney was only slowly sinking in. 'Is it really so dangerous?'

Gunnvor and the priest exchanged glances. She shrugged.

'Have you always lived in Winchester?' Father Ronan asked.

Wulfgar nodded, puzzled, and said, 'I was born on my father's estates in Meon – we're less than a day's ride from Winchester. And then I was sent to Winchester, to my uncle at the cathedral, when I was very—'

But the priest was riding over him, thinking along some tangent of his own. His eyes had gone very dark.

'Wulfgar, my friend – can I call you my friend?'

Wulfgar nodded.

'With all due respect, you're not taking this seriously enough.' He snorted. 'Men like Ketil, Hakon, what they love is wealth. They'll do almost anything for it.'

Gunnvor was nodding her agreement.

'Listen to the man,' she said. 'It could be my own father he's talking about. Never missed an opportunity to turn a profit.'

'Are you talking about him, or yourself, lass?' Father Ronan chuckled dryly. 'Your father wasn't as greedy as some, rest his soul.'

She looked thoughtful. 'Not as ruthless, maybe. But every bit as greedy.'

Father Ronan shrugged. 'Aye, and that's why they call you the richest woman in the Five Boroughs.' He turned back to Wulfgar. 'But even Ketil has standards. Men like him, they don't want to lose face. Eirik – Eirik is another matter. There's no appealing to *his* sense of honour.'

Gunnvor was shaking her head in agreement. 'And you're thinking of walking into the Spider's web and taking something precious from him?' She drummed her fingers on the table. 'I don't know him well but I know him well enough. Gore-crow – comes in after a fight to strip the bones. Took Bardney in payment of a debt.' She bared her teeth then, an odd glint in her eye. 'He's had it these ten years, although I've heard his wife runs it. You'll be a popular man if you rob Eirik, but I doubt you'll be a long-lived one.'

Wulfgar felt a chill run up his backbone.

'He's a slave-dealer, the Bishop told me.'

'*Já,*' she said, nodding, 'and on the grand scale. He trades in Dublin as well as Lincoln, and somewhere in the Northern Isles

– Hoy, maybe? Hrossey?' She shrugged at Wulfgar's blank face. 'He sits in Lincoln most of the winter. He's little Toli Silkbeard's man now old Hrafn's dead.'

'And Orm?' Wulfgar was finding it hard to voice his thoughts. 'Does he – I mean, should I –' he glanced across the room at Ednoth '– should we worry about him? Should I take him seriously?'

Gunnvor and Father Ronan exchanged another glance.

Father Ronan nodded. 'If Orm's on the scent, yes. Worry. He doesn't let much stand between him and a bargain.'

Gunnvor snorted. 'Nothing less than an imperial official in Miklagard, anyway.'

Wulfgar put his head in his hands.

'I knew we should be hurrying. We didn't think . . . we've been four days on the road already.'

'Four – from *Worcester*? Oh, Wulfgar, Wulfgar.' Father Ronan shook his head. Then, 'I'm coming with you,' he said. He laughed, deep in his beard, but Wulfgar didn't think he was amused. 'Don't look so shocked, lad. You, nesh as you are, and that gawmless boy, doing this on your own?'

Wulfgar felt an uprush of indignation. I might admit privately to myself that I'm a lost lamb here in the Danelands, he thought, but is it really so obvious to other people, too?

The priest looked over at Ednoth, knocking back drink for drink with his new friends, and shook his head, smiling.

'What was he thinking, yon Bishop? No, I'll come with you. Now Easter's over, no one will fret if I'm away for a day or two.' He cracked his knuckles. 'Faith, it'll be a penance for me, scrub a few grease-spots off my soul. I've an old horse and an older sword to put at St Oswald's service.'

A priest with a sword?

'Father, we can't ask that of you—'

The priest looked amused.

'Oh, I think you can. Don't forget, my lad, I'm a Mercian, too. St Oswald's one of mine. And Eirik and I go a long way back'

'I never knew that,' Gunnvor said, her head on one side.

Father Ronan shook his head at her.

'There's a lot you still don't know about me, girl. Me and the Spider, we crossed blades in Dublin, a lifetime ago. And I've still a score or two to settle.' He stood up, shouldering his harp bag. 'Come on. The more I think about what Ormsson said, the more worried I get.'

Wulfgar, still weighed down by doubt and anxiety, was trying to chew the indigestible lumps of information that had been tossed his way. He didn't like any of what he had been hearing.

'You don't think St Oswald was just the first saint that came to mind? Orm never mentioned Bardney, after all—'

Gunnvor snorted. 'Come to *mind*? What mind? Ormsson doesn't have a mind. And he knows less than I do about saints.' She rubbed her hands together. 'Maybe I'll come with you, too. I could check no one's been pilfering from my Lincoln warehouse while I'm about it. I've not been there all winter. And,' her voice hardened, 'I don't fancy keeping company with Ketil, not in his present mood.'

Wulfgar's eyes darted to the cut on her cheekbone. He took her point, but nonetheless he found himself blurting, 'Come with us? Is that a good idea?' Quailing at the sardonic look she gave him, he ploughed on, 'I mean – I only meant – it's supposed to be a secret. The more we are, the harder it'll be . . .' He subsided into silence. Now that his indignation was waning, he could admit to himself how truly grateful he was for Father Ronan's offer. A priest, and a Mercian, too – he understood what was at stake, and his help would be invaluable. But this woman – this Gunnvor Cat's-Eyes – coming as well? A Dane, he thought, and no daughter of the Church. My enemy.

Father Ronan frowned. 'St Oswald's remembered in Leicester, of course, but I've certainly never talked to Orm about him. And I can't think where else he might have picked up the name, unless there are rumours coming out of Bardney. Unless, maybe, someone's been singing him that old song?'

Wulfgar looked up, briefly distracted.

'Song?'

'"St Oswald's Tree"?'

Wulfgar shook his head.

'The raven – his tame raven – gathering the fragments of his body, after the battle?'

He shook his head again.

'Ach, Wulfgar, I can't believe you don't know it! I'll teach it to you, sometime.' Father Ronan jerked his head towards the door. 'But this – Orm, I mean – is bad news. Never mind paying your respects to Ketil. We'll leave at first light.'

CHAPTER SIXTEEN

Easter Monday

It was long before first light, though, when Wulfgar felt Father Ronan's hand shaking his shoulder. He sat up and tried to make sense of what the priest was saying.

'Do you want to walk down to the cathedral with me? I can't let you leave Leicester thinking my poor little St Margaret's is the only kirk we have.' He reached out a hand and pulled Wulfgar to his feet. 'I've got to take your borrowed glory back before the world wakes, or my name will be mud. Besides, it's all the Easter horse-racing and football today, and if we leave things too late we'll never get away.'

Wulfgar struggled into his tunic and carefully bundled up the fragile red silk vestment, and the two clerics went quietly through the tangled lanes of the Danish settlement, and under the great gate in the walls, to where the cathedral sat at the heart of the city.

The cold air worked its little miracle on Wulfgar's aching skull as they walked through the streets of the English town, where people were just beginning to stir.

'Where does Ketil have his hall?' he asked, trying to sound as though he didn't care. 'Will we be going anywhere near?'

Father Ronan shook his head.

'We'll be steering well clear – you don't want him to catch wind of your being here, not now that you're leaving without greeting him.' He jerked a thumb to the north west. 'He lies yonder. When Hakon took over Leicester, the Grimssons built themselves a longhouse, outside the walls, handy for the river.'

Still talking, they came through the gateway into the cathedral yard.

Wulfgar stopped in his tracks.

Leicester Cathedral. Even in the grey half-light he could see how beautiful the towering building was – or had been. It had been made of golden stone and russet tile, with a broad frieze of carved leaves and flowers around the outside of the building and a fine stone cross standing before the west door.

But the paint and plaster on the cross were faded and chipped, holes gouged where its gems had been hacked out; the cobbles around the door were matted with new chickweed and goose-grass, and the dried clumps of last year's weed crop still disfigured the sagging roof. The surround of every window was smoke-blackened still, even after more than thirty years.

Father Ronan took one look at Wulfgar's face.

'Go in, why don't you? I'll take this back and come to find you.'

The great door creaked on rusty iron hinges, letting Wulfgar through into darkness. There was just enough light outside to show where the small, high windows were, and more came trickling in through the roof where tiles had fallen.

Just enough light to show how lovely it once had been, this cavernous shell of scorched and falling plaster. Wulfgar thought at first that he was alone, but there were rushlights burning at makeshift shrines around the walls and as his eyes made sense of the gloom he became aware of the occasional shadowy, kneeling figure. He lit a gift of his own from a light already burning at a shrine too murky to identify. It didn't matter; he was making his offering to Mary, Queen of Heaven, and her Risen Son, St Oswald, St Modwenna, St Margaret, the nameless saint of the Bishop's ring, lying against his breast-bone.

St Oswald . . .

King and Martyr.

When you were alive, he thought, the heathen Mercians were your enemies. You were slain fighting against them. And your death changed everything. The son of the king who killed you was the founder of the Bardney shrine.

Mercia never looked back, until this last generation.

That's the sort of power you had, for over two hundred winters.

St Oswald, we need you now.

He was still hoping for a sign.

But all he got in return for his little, guttering light was silence and an overpowering sense of sadness.

The words of the psalmist came back to him unbidden: *Your foes have made uproar in your house of prayer . . .*

He didn't realise he had been singing aloud until he heard a second voice at his shoulder . . . *Their axes have battered the wood of its doors . . .* It was Father Ronan. And together, quietly, they sang the whole psalm: *Oh God, they have set your sanctuary on fire . . . Do not forget the clamour of your foes, the daily growing uproar of your foes.*

Their eyes met.

'I never hoped to meet anyone like you here,' Wulfgar said.

'Me? I was brought up in this church. My father was one of the canons. And my mother was one of his slaves.' Father Ronan turned then and walked away, and after a moment's hesitation Wulfgar followed.

'Look,' the priest said, 'This was where the shrine of St Cuthwin used to stand. Our first Bishop, two hundred and fifty years gone.' He pointed at a battered block of stone, the remains of painted carving just visible, shattered where metal fittings had been hacked out.

Wulfgar thought he could make out what had once been an angel. There was no sign of the reliquary.

'This is where Uhtsang came from.'

'Your harp?'

Father Ronan nodded.

'Bishop Cuthwin's relics. It was one of my jobs to dust them, as a lad. Nobody played her, ever. It used to drive me distracted, her hanging up there, long gone out of tune, the wood thirsty and the silver dull. You could see that she would be the sweetest singer, and I was learning on a dreadful old thing.'

'So you stole her, from the saint?'

'No!' The priest's note of outrage rang true. He lowered his voice. 'Not that I didn't think of it. I was only a little lad, mind. I still had to learn better. But I didn't steal her, for all that. I just prayed to St Cuthwin to let me have her, for about ten years.' He sighed.

'*So*—'

'*So* – so, it was after Hakon and Ketil and their army . . . had arrived, and the Bishop had fled. I wandered into the cathedral after the row had died down a bit, and Uhtsang was gone. The shrine had been smashed, and everything they hadn't taken, they'd burned. And they'd burned the books. The ashes were still hot.

I poked around and found a few scorched pages, but there was nothing much left worth the saving . . . well, the power and mystery are still here.'

Wulfgar could only nod.

'But the glory had gone. And the harp.' The priest shook his head. 'It was as though someone had gralloched me with a hunting knife. I wandered out of the kirk-garth still clutching those bits of charred vellum.' He smiled then, but without pleasure. 'Well, you'll always find people ready to make money out of an army, and the ale-houses were open. Some of them, anyway. I went into the nearest, and there was a Danish soldier with Uhtsang on his knee. He didn't know what he'd got, he was all ready to prise off her trinkets and burn the rest.'

Wulfgar remembered those silver-gilt birds with their fierce garnet eyes, and he felt a shiver of something close to grief.

'So, I offered to buy her, and I ended up winning her at dice. He wasn't a bad man,' Father Ronan said. 'He was a good loser, anyhow. Some of the lads with him would have had me down the alley and taken the harp back with a few of my teeth for good measure, but he wouldn't let them.'

'The saint wanted you to have his harp after all,' Wulfgar said.

'But at that price?' Father Ronan looked down at the scorched and battered tiles and shook his head again. 'Be careful what you ask the saints for, Wulfgar. Come on, let's quit this blackened sepulchre.'

They found Ednoth stirring, just emerging from the cave of his hangover. Father Ronan gave him a bucket of water and told him to get on with it.

'You boys haven't exactly been going as though the hounds of Hell are on your heels, have you? It's a matter of another fifty miles to Bardney. Let's be getting out of town before everyone's up and going to the football.'

The sun was lifting clear of the hills to their right.

'Now, let's ride hard,' Father Ronan said. 'I'll be having no more of your nesh excuses.'

There was no sign of Gunnvor as they rode a looping road around the outside of Leicester's walls to pick up the Fosse Way once again. Wulfgar told himself he was relieved, tried to ignore a nagging twinge of disappointment, to stop glancing half-hopefully over his shoulder.

They stopped mid-afternoon to let the horses breathe, at a crossroads where half a dozen green mounds slept in the sun.

Wulfgar swung down out of his saddle to have a closer look.

Father Ronan followed him.

'Old kings.'

'Heathen kings,' Wulfgar said sadly. 'Gone under the hills, into the dark.'

Father Ronan murmured something in Latin: a snatch of prayer.

'Do you pray for the damned?' Wulfgar asked, not able to stop himself.

The priest was silent for a moment, looking up at the great green barrows.

'I heard a story once,' he said. 'It's the last day, and all our middle-earth has been rolled up like a scroll and thrown on the fire, and Our Lord is waiting at the gates of Heaven, with St Peter, welcoming in the dead. And in we all come, the saints and the kings, monks and priests and ploughmen, fighting-men and nuns and dairywomen. And then the sinners, the liars and cheats, the adulterers and oath-breakers, the weak and the forgetful – don't make that face, Wulfgar. Hear me out. And then come the heathens, the sackers of churches, and those who never heard the Holy Name. And still Our Lord waits, looking out over the falling darkness. And St Peter can't think who might be yet to come. So he asks, "Lord, for whom are you waiting now?" And Our Lord says, "For Judas, Peter. For Judas."'

Ednoth was waiting for them at the roadside.

'You wouldn't catch me going up there.' He shuddered, and crossed his fingers. 'My father knew a man once who went poking into a mound.'

'And what happened to him?' Father Ronan asked.

'My father wouldn't say.'

Wulfgar looked at the late daffodils nodding on the shadowed north side of the mounds, and the one big black crow stalking among them, hunting for worms.

It was a beautiful story that Father Ronan had told; he only wished he could believe it.

CHAPTER SEVENTEEN

'What frontier?' Ednoth asked, in response to something Father Ronan had shouted.

'The Trent,' the priest said, gathering his reins in one hand in order to point towards the river with the other. 'We're moving from the lands that answer to Leicester into those that look to young Silkbeard.'

There was that name again: Silkbeard, whom Gunnvor had described as Eirik the Spider's lord.

'Tell us more,' Wulfgar called, trying to sound no more than casually curious. 'About this Silkbeard, I mean.'

'No love lost there! Our old jarl, Hakon the Toad and Silkbeard's father, Hrafn, were rivals in the bad old days when the Great Army was still in the ascendancy. When the Army divided, Hrafn threw in his lot with the northern troops, the men who took York. So Lincoln still looks north to York and hates Leicester, even though Hrafn's six months dead, and Hakon Toad's dead now, too.'

'Slow down!' Wulfgar was getting lost in the maze of strange names and unfamiliar politics. 'Do you mean Silkbeard rules Lincoln? I thought Lincoln was held by someone called Toli Hrafnsson?' It was the name the Atheling had given him. He felt guilty just speaking it aloud.

'That's right. That's the man. Little Toli Silkbeard. Hard to think of him in charge of Lincoln.' Father Ronan laughed. 'He was knee-high to a handworm when I last saw him.'

'Is there a church in Lincoln now?'

The priest looked at him. Wulfgar found his gaze hard to fathom.

'No, lad,' he said, after a pause, 'there's no church in Lincoln. Not at all, not now.' He reined in. 'And there she is.'

A distant escarpment had come into view. Even at this distance, buildings could be seen crowning the ridge, though a haze of hearth-smoke smudged the details.

'We'll be there before dark.'

'Why are we going to Lincoln? We want Bardney,' Ednoth said. 'Why waste time?'

Wulfgar looked at the distant city and felt the hair prickle on the back of his neck. He shook his head.

'We need to go to Lincoln,' he said. 'We can't just walk into Bardney and ask to see the reeve. We need to find out if Eirik is there, see if we can get hold of the relics in secret, that sort of thing . . .' And I have to deliver the Atheling's message to 'little Toli', he added silently. Somehow the diminutive failed to reassure.

'Wuffa—' Ednoth began, but Father Ronan was already nodding in agreement.

'You're right,' Father Ronan said. We need to sniff around.

169

Cautiously, mind. It's a rough place, Lincoln. It may be early in the season but there'll be a few ships in from the Baltic run, and we don't want to tangle with that lot. They'll have been sitting on their hands all winter and spoiling for a bit of excitement.' He looked hard at Ednoth. 'You don't want to tweak the wrong tail there, lad.'

Lincoln was unlike any place Wulfgar had ever seen. The prospect had deceived him: the old city, whose buildings they'd seen on top of the ridge from miles away, was a ghost town now. That was where the cathedral had been, and the royal palace, both within the Romans' walls. That was the town that the Lord of the Mercians and his Bishop had known as children. Long burnt and left desolate, and up a precipitous rocky slope; Father Ronan told them it was nothing now but a haunt for rats and owls and the restless dead.

Life in Lincoln these days centred on the foot of the slope, the priest said, on the river Witham and its ford, where the water had cut a steep gash through the hills and opened up into a wide inland harbour. Once across the Bray ford, they dismounted and led their horses through the bustle of a market packing up for the night.

Looking to right and left, Wulfgar thought, how different this feels from Leicester. Leicester seems like somewhere for Danes who want to settle, and become Englishmen. Lincoln's for those just passing through. Its ale-houses, warehouses and strand-market echoed with babble in half the tongues of the world, mixing with the cries of a thousand gulls. He overheard Irish and Frankish as well as Danish coming from the merchant crews and their ships with tented awnings, and more languages beside those he recognised. Some English, but not much. Even so, he thought, no one should notice us here, not unless we try very hard to draw attention to ourselves.

He wondered how he was going to deliver his message to Toli Silkbeard without doing exactly that.

They got themselves settled in the outer courtyard of an inn Father Ronan knew, with the horses unloaded and safely tethered.

'We may not have earned a rest,' Father Ronan said, 'but the nags have.'

Wulfgar could only think of one thing, here in the enemy's citadel.

'Tell us more about Toli Silkbeard.'

'*Silkiskegg*?' Father Ronan snorted, before glancing around warily. 'Well, never call him that, for a start. Not to his face, any road. Nor where his men might hear.'

'Why not?' This, slightly truculent, from Ednoth.

'Well,' Father Ronan said, looking amused, but Wulfgar noticed he spoke more softly than usual. 'Skegg – it means beard, you know? But it's also slang for a Danish axe. You must have seen one? No? You *have* led a quiet life, Wuffa. Those flared edges their war-axes have, they call them "beards".'

'Oh,' Wulfgar said. 'Yes, I see. Orm Ormsson had a little one at his belt.' He couldn't remember asking the priest to call him Wuffa, but he found he was pleased rather than offended.

'Orm who?' Ednoth looked baffled.

'The Danish trader,' Wulfgar said. 'I did tell you.'

'Oh, yes, I remember now. But I still don't understand what's wrong with *Silkiskegg*?' Ednoth said.

'Silk-Axe,' Wulfgar said. 'Not exactly flattering.'

Father Ronan nodded. 'It's only because he's so young, mind,' he said. 'Hasn't had much chance to blood his axe.'

Wulfgar swallowed. 'And his hall?' he asked. 'That's here in Lincoln?'

'Aye, in Silver Street where his father set up thirty years ago, where else?' Father Ronan peered at Wulfgar, curious. 'Don't fret, lad. We'll be shaking the dust of Lincoln off our feet before young Toli sniffs us out. Lincoln's not like Leicester, it's full of strangers. We shouldn't be noticed by anyone, let alone the Jarl.'

Another night, Wulfgar thought, pulling his cloak round him and curling up on the straw-packed pallet. Another strange hearth and a new gang of fleas to get acquainted with. He slept, but badly, and woke far too early, the inn still dark apart from the glowing of the banked hearth and no sound outside but blackbird song.

He turned over restlessly. Easter Tuesday today. *Tuesday*, and we're not even in Bardney yet. Yes, it's only six miles away, but who knows what obstacles we may yet encounter. The Atheling had sounded as though he knew his way around the Danish lands, Wulfgar thought miserably, but he must have been bluffing. How could he ever have told us this mission would only take a week?

He rolled over and tried to make himself comfortable, but it was a waste of effort. He found himself counting on his fingers, tallying days and miles, over and over.

The Atheling must have been reckoning they would cover more than thirty miles every day, he concluded to his perturbation. But that was far more than their little mounts could manage. And he must also have assumed that Wulfgar and Ednoth would meet the reeve – what was his name . . . Thorvald – with the relics straight away, and be turning right round, and galloping thirty miles a day back again.

Either the Atheling had been wildly optimistic, or he had been mad.

Or – and Wulfgar sat bolt upright then, his mind racing – what if he had intended to mislead them? If a week went by, and

Ednoth and he hadn't returned – and Gloucester's further still, he thought frantically, *another* thirty miles . . .

It could easily take them two weeks to get back with the relics. Two weeks, or more.

Anything might have happened by then. The Lord could have died . . .

Or he could be dead already.

Dying or dead, the Lady would be in despair, waiting for Wulfgar's return, her expectations and hopes raised by the Atheling's breezy prediction – which he would probably be repeating by the hour – waiting and waiting, and more anxious, more vulnerable, more easily preyed on, with every day that passed.

A great wash of fury flooded through his veins.

I'm buying his time for him.

No wonder the Atheling had been so eager to back the Bishop's plan, and to send Wulfgar off into the wilds. The Lady and the Bishop would be safely distracted with their hopes over the relics, while he made his bid for power . . .

And I even agreed to be the Atheling's errand-boy. What a gullible fool I am, Wulfgar thought despairingly.

Why had he ever thought he could play this game? He was no politician. He should have stayed in Wessex, he thought, even if he had ended up teaching farmers' sons like Ednoth their *abecedarium* in some backwoods minster.

He bit his lip. Did he really mean it? Give up everything he had been trained to do, destined for since birth? Abandon the thrill of working at the heart of the court, among the rich and great? Relinquish the hopes of a cathedral or at least a great minster of his own?

And then, for the first time, he thought, if this mission were to fail, he might have to, willy-nilly. No one would be very pleased to see him come empty-handed back to Mercia. Especially not the Lady.

No one – except perhaps Athelwald Seiriol, Atheling of Wessex.

There was no hope of getting back to sleep now. He pushed his cloak away and levered himself to his feet, then shuffled his way between the sleeping figures, brushing bits of straw from his clothes as he went, feeling his way with his feet, nervous of treading on someone's hand or leg. He needed a quiet place to interrogate the hubbub in his head.

If the Atheling had really wanted the relics back in a week, he would have gone himself.

Or sent one of his bodyguard.

Someone like Garmund, Wulfgar reflected bitterly. Garmund would go thundering up the road, grab the relics, whack a few people on the head for good measure, and be back in plenty of time.

And then, tight-lipped with humiliation, he thought, perhaps the Atheling chose me because he knew I would fail.

Once he was out in the courtyard, the stable offered itself to him in the first grey light. He let himself in, leaving the door ajar and taking care not to wake the ostler or the horse-boy, and went over to where Fallow was tethered in the gloom, between Starlight and Father Ronan's black gelding. Fallow whickered softly in recognition, and for the first time he noticed with appreciation the moleskin sheen of her nose and the gentle, slightly anxious gleam in her eye. He scooped up a handful of oats, offering them to her carefully flat-palmed. She shook her fringe out of her eyes and snuffled them up, damp and tickly. He patted her neck with his free hand. 'Oh, Fallow. I feel such a fool. You don't care though, do you? You still trust me.'

He wasn't sure how long he stayed there, leaning against Fallow's warm bulk, but he became slowly aware of voices, cooking smells, seeping silvery light. He didn't want to face Ednoth or Ronan just yet, and he turned out of the stable and through the inn's gatehouse, into the street outside. The inn was set back from the river, and he turned that way, drawn by the shrieking of the gulls. The great pool was full of trading ships among which dozens of swans swam, searching for scraps. Something in the arrogant, fastidious way they carried their heads reminded him of Gunnvor. The merchants had drawn up their boats on the shelving mud and were setting out their stalls, shouting cheerfully at one another as they carried baskets and barrels and bales up from their vessels.

Wulfgar noticed amber necklaces, and exquisitely polished stone cups and bowls, bronze lamps in styles he didn't recognise, and silver or tin brooches to suit every taste and pocket. There was a food market, too: local farmers coming in with their carts and selling from the cart-tail. He stopped at one to buy a fresh curd cheese to eat there and then: moist and rich and sweet, he could almost taste the spring grass the sheep had been eating.

His head was still buzzing, his angry thoughts half-directed at himself and half at the Atheling. It was time to be getting back though: Ednoth and Ronan would be waking up and wondering where he had got to, and, although he was still confused as well as furious and humiliated, one thing was quite clear to him.

The Bishop's story is true: St Oswald needs me; and Mercia needs St Oswald.

What was it Ednoth had said? *This is us fighting back. This is the start of the new Mercia* . . . Thousands of other people would feel the same way.

If we bring St Oswald home to Gloucester as soon as we can, he thought, I've done my duty. This isn't about me. I've got to forget about being angry, and about being a failure, and just find the relics, and take them to the Lady, as quickly as possible.

His heart pounded. He pressed the palms of his hands together, and forced himself to breathe deeply.

He found he had walked the whole length of the market and, as he turned round, he wondered whether there was anything worth knowing to be gleaned from the stall-holders. Some of them might well know Eirik the Spider.

Wulfgar had averted his eyes from the slave-merchants' stalls as he came past the first time. It's one thing, what we do in Wessex, he thought, taking a family on your own land into bond to save them from famine. That's people you know, people who already work for you. But stealing people from their homes and selling them overseas? How can that be justified?

And so *young*, so many of them quite little children. He frowned. They can't all be orphans, can they? Many of them looked no more than seven or eight years old, little groups of them huddled close together. And lots of young women. He didn't want to think about how they had got there, or their probable future. As he drew closer he could see the slaves had no choice but to huddle; they were roped or, in one or two cases, chained. He wondered if they were local or whether merchants had brought them in from further afield. He felt a terrible squeamishness about going closer. There was nothing he could do to help them, and he couldn't bear the dull hopelessness in their young faces.

It occurred to Wulfgar with a pang that maybe he hadn't had

such a bad time after all, when he had been their age. Yes, Edward and Garmund had tormented him. But he had been safe, really. Not only at Meon, when his mother had still been alive, but even after he had been despatched to Winchester. There had always been someone looking out for him.

Why do I find it so hard to admit that I was privileged, cosseted even? That there was nothing special about the hard times I had? Just a different throw of the dice, a different strand in Fate's weaving, and I could have been here, tied by the ankle, staring at the dust. If I were here under different circumstances, I'd buy one, free him, take him home . . . But which one? There are so many.

He watched a buyer examining one young woman, pinching her arm and her thigh, getting her to open her mouth to let him check her teeth. Wulfgar burned with indignation on her behalf, but apart from a sullen expression she made no protest.

How could men like this Eirik the Spider do what they did?

At that question, he turned back to his immediate problem. Being in the market was too good an opportunity to waste. He should wander over to one of the slave-traders, pretend to be a buyer himself, make an idle comment – *Eirik usually has a good stock* – and ask, *where is he to be found today?*

But what if he asked his questions of Eirik himself, without knowing it?

Ever more jittery, he drifted in the direction of the slave-stalls, pretending interest in this and that. The place was getting crowded now, pedlars looking for bargains to take round the hinterland of Lindsey; housewives wanting the fresh chalky cheeses and the cabbages with the dew still on them. As he pushed past one scrap-metal stall, Wulfgar looked idly over the goods on offer, and froze.

To the untutored glance it would have looked like a small red box, sparsely set with metal. Wulfgar's trained eye saw it at once for what it was.

A gospel book.

A single gospel, its leather binding tooled with a cross whose arms were set with silver. They would have held cabochon glass or gems once, but those had been long lost from fittings which gaped sadly as toothless gums.

He reached out his hand.

But someone else got there first.

The stall-holder, a dark-haired, burly man, had swooped down, and now he held it just beyond arm's reach.

'I'm afraid that's sold,' he said in English. 'Sorry. My mistake.'

Wulfgar found his voice.

'If I could just have a look?' He wiped his damp, sticky hand against his tunic and held it out.

'If it's silver you want, perhaps I could interest you in this wire? I'll give you the same price. There's more here than you've got there, and it's already refined.'

'Refined?'

'Melted down. Burned. Whatever you call it.' He grinned. 'I'm no silversmith.'

Wulfgar was still holding out his hand.

'Just a look?'

The man shrugged.

'Go on, then. But it is sold.'

Wulfgar took the book into his hands, shivering slightly. This was a book to be enthroned as the Son of God, not haggled over or fingered by hands still smelling of cheese. *I've never touched a gospel book before, not with my bare hand . . .* The leather was calfskin, supple still to the touch, embossed over a design made,

178

Wulfgar guessed, by gluing thin string to the boards beneath. He touched the inlaid silver cross lightly, noting the depth of the cavity at its centre and guessing that this had once held a relic. The back had a winding pattern, a muddle of knotwork to the uninitiated, but Wulfgar could pick out the overlapping crosses hidden in the intersections and interstices.

He opened it.

As he had thought, a single gospel.

St John: *IN PRINCIPIO . . . In the beginning was the Word . . .* The flawless curves of the deceptively simple script marked it as the work of a scribe as skilful as the binder, writing long ago: eight lives of men, he guessed, or more. He wished he could write as beautifully as that, but these were skills that had been lost, somewhere along the road.

It was a gospel book fit for a bishop.

Or a king.

St Oswald could have owned this, Wulfgar realised. It was old enough, and more than beautiful enough . . .

Refined, the man had said. *Melted down. Burned.* Someone could buy this wonderful book? Someone could buy it for its *silver*?

'I have to have this,' he said. He hadn't meant to speak his thoughts aloud, but once he had started he couldn't stop. 'How much?' He couldn't buy a slave, but he could redeem God's Word.

'I've sold it already, I tell you.' The man glanced around, furtively. 'He promised me five shillings, in English coin.'

Wulfgar felt a gust of hope.

'So he's not paid you yet? I'll give you ten.' It was the Bishop's money, not his. Half of their travelling expenses – significantly more than half of what was left to them. He told himself the Bishop would understand.

179

'But it's my good name, and he's a good customer, a regular,' the man said. He put his head on one side, wheedling. 'Surely that's worth a bit?'

'Fifteen,' Wulfgar said, reckless in his lust. He wasn't even sure there was that much left in the Bishop's bag. 'I'll have to go back and get it.'

The trader frowned.

'But the other one, he might come back—'

'Let me take this with me – I could leave you my cloak, my belt-knife—'

But the trader was shaking his head.

'Do I look born yesterday?'

And a new voice, tinged with foreignness, said, 'Got my goods there?'

Wulfgar turned.

'Did you buy this? Can I buy it from you?'

The newcomer's eyes narrowed. He was another big man, older, a conical hat trimmed with fur on his head, a fur-lined cloak and leather boots.

'Why? What's it worth to you? There's not much silver in it.'

'But it's a *book*. No, *the* book! St John's gospel, and it's so old, and it's so beautiful—' Wulfgar stopped.

The fur-hatted man was laughing, laughing so hard he had to bend forward, laughing so that he wheezed, tears squeezing themselves out of his eyes. His red, slab-cheeked face was turning purple. The stall-holder, nervous, was joining in.

Wulfgar held on to his treasure.

'You could have the binding,' he said, though it cost him a pang. 'I could just keep the pages.'

Wulfgar thought at first that the fur-hatted man wasn't

listening, so caught up was he in his mirth, but when he finally finished wiping his eyes, he said, 'It just gets better and better. Christians – don't you love them? I haven't had a laugh like that for years. No, my boy, it's got my name on it. Hand it over and I'll pay the man.'

'No,' Wulfgar said. 'You're not being fair.'

Fur Hat reached out a meaty hand and tried to grab the little volume.

Wulfgar turned away, shielding it with his body, and found himself being hauled backwards by the neck of his tunic. He staggered a couple of steps away from the stall, still clinging to the book. Fur Hat came for him. He ducked his head, shoved the little gospel down the front of his undershirt, and blundered away.

The stall-holder shouted now.

Wulfgar heard 'Help!' and 'Thief!' behind him. He looked frantically up and down the rows of stalls, trying to remember the way back to the inn and that bag of redeeming silver. He had every intention of paying for his prize. But a crowd was already beginning to gather, blocking his view.

'What's going on?'

'Get the port-reeve!'

'Thief!'

And as he turned to run he felt a heavy hand on his shoulder.

Fur Hat?

No.

'What's going on?' asked a commanding voice, loud above the racket. Fifty people were trying to answer at once. The stall-holder and Fur Hat were both talking to the port-reeve, jabbering and pointing at Wulfgar.

'What have you got there?'

Wulfgar looked down to see a corner of the book still poking out from the neck of his tunic.

'Is that your property?'

Was there hope here? Wulfgar twisted, trying to see the face of the man who was holding him. Fifty winters or so, grey-haired with a greasy felt hat crammed on anyhow. Pouchy, tired eyes. English, by his voice. He didn't look that strong but his hold was remorseless. And he had two watchmen at his back.

'*Yes*! At least, I want to buy it – at a fair price—'

He found himself at the centre of a circle of faces, some excited, others hostile.

The port-reeve let go his grip and looked hard at Wulfgar's face. The watchmen moved in.

'I've not seen you before,' the port-reeve said.

Fur Hat and the stall-holder both started talking again, expostulating in Danish so rapid that Wulfgar couldn't understand a tenth of it, but he recognised some of the more appallingly obscene epithets his Danish pupils had thought it funny to teach him: *nithing*, Fur Hat was calling him, and *ragr*, jabbing an index finger in his direction. He felt his face growing hot, humiliation stoking his fury.

'You wanted to *burn* it!' he shouted. He was afraid he was going to start crying. 'I won't let you. I won't!' He cuddled the little book against his breast.

The port-reeve shook his head.

'Let me see what you've got. A book, is it? Come on, hand it over.' He held out a hand, coaxing, his tone of voice one you might use to a child. 'Come on.'

Wulfgar looked wildly around him.

'Come on, son. There's nowhere to run to. Give the book to me.'

Deeply unwilling, slowly, using both hands, Wulfgar proffered the little gospel.

The port-reeve took it, respectful, in both hands.

'I'll have to hold on to this,' he said, stowing it away in a pocket tied somewhere under his baggy tunic. Fur Hat and the stallholder both raised their voices in protest but he quelled them with a look. 'Evidence.' He turned back to Wulfgar. 'And you're under arrest.'

Wulfgar's heart sank. What had he done now? This was a disaster.

'That's more like it!' The stall-holder pushed his face into Wulfgar's. 'That'll teach you, mucking me around like that.'

'*Da*,' said Fur Hat. 'Take him to Toli. Teach him a lesson.'

'I'm not wasting Toli's time with a petty thief like this. He doesn't quite look the full shilling, anyway. I'll have him cool his heels in the watch-house for a few days.'

'What about my property?' said Fur Hat.

'*Your* property?' said the stall-holder.

'You'll get it back when I've had a look at it, and decided its value. Come on, you. Show's over,' he shouted to the crowd. 'Nothing to see.' He had Wulfgar's arm twisted behind his back in that remorseless grip, one hand on his elbow, the other on his wrist. It was agonising. 'You're coming with me.'

Wulfgar was thinking frantically. He simply couldn't be locked up for a few days, it was out of the question, but what were his alternatives? He didn't know anything about the laws in Lincoln: in Winchester they could justifiably charge him with breach of the peace as well as theft. He started totting up the amount of the potential fine and groaned inwardly. This could eat a long way into Thorvald's five pounds, never mind the travel expenses.

Damn Fur Hat, he thought vindictively. God *damn* him. And that little book, still only inches from him, might as well have been a thousand miles away.

But it's my own stupid fault. I castigated Ednoth for being foolish and headstrong, and now look at me. I should have just shut up and done what I was told to do. What I was told to do . . .

He swallowed.

'Take me to Toli.'

CHAPTER EIGHTEEN

The port-reeve sounded startled. 'What?'

'Take me to your Jarl, Toli Hrafnsson,' Wulfgar repeated, in Danish this time and then in English. 'I deserve a proper hearing. Take me to Toli.'

'Are you mad?' The port-reeve never paused in his steady pace, but Wulfgar did, dragging his heels and twisting against the hands that held his arm so firmly. The port-reeve pushed at him. 'Come on, son, don't make this hard for us. You don't look like a trouble-maker.'

'Take me to Toli. You can't call me a thief and lock me up just because –' he jerked his head back in the direction of the stall '– *they* say so.'

'You damn well look like a thief, running off with something you hadn't paid for.'

'It was a misunderstanding. Take me to Toli. I want a fair hearing. I know my rights.' He hoped he sounded more confident than he felt.

'A *fair hearing*?' The port-reeve cleared his throat. 'Oh, you're within your rights, but if it were me I'd rather have a couple of days peace and quiet in the lock-up than face Toli.' He sighed then. 'Much rather. Are you sure? This way then.' His grip had never slackened.

They were changing direction, plunging into the muddle of streets behind the harbour. Wulfgar's heart thumped, his thoughts a jumble. How, for Heaven's sake, had he ended up here, begging to do the very last thing he wanted to do? But, no, he amended, not the very last thing. That would be going back to the Lady empty-handed. But in order to get the relics of St Oswald for her, he had to find a way out of the current trouble. The Atheling's message was the one stake he had to play in this game.

But, he wondered, did he have to give Toli Silkbeard the Atheling's real message? He had such dark suspicions now.

My Lord Seiriol, he thought, what are you planning? I'm so afraid it's not in the Lady's interests, even though she's your cousin, and you claim to love her, too.

So, what to to do? Tell Toli Silkbeard something else, something anodyne, meaningless, misleading.

And then Wulfgar thought of the Atheling's anger when he eventually found out. And he would find out, in the end, and Wulfgar the scholar could hardly claim to have forgotten those few, simple words. He didn't want the Atheling as an enemy – about that, he had no doubts – and his heart quailed even further.

All the while, the port-reeve was shoving him through the mire of the streets, the watchmen in front of them forcing a way through the curious townsfolk. Wulfgar struggled to keep up with the pace, stumbling and getting splatters of mud up his leggings, red-faced, ragged of breath. It was not at all how he wanted to present himself in front of this unknown Jarl. They were fast approaching a big stockade with massive iron-bound gates and guards to right and left.

'Wait here.'

The guards were very close, and armed with spears, standing under the bare branches of a towering ash-tree.

Wulfgar waited.

The port-reeve had a muttered word with one of the men, who nodded and turned to slip through the wicket gate, which stood ajar. The same guard came out again moments later and gave a brief nod.

The port-reeve turned back to Wulfgar, with a cheerless smile on his tired, pouchy face.

'Your lucky day, son. He's up and he's broken his fast. Last chance to change your mind?'

Wulfgar shook his head.

'Like I said,' the port-reeve said to the guard, 'more than a few pennies short of his full shilling. In we go, then.'

The smoke stung Wulfgar's eyes. The Jarl of Lincoln's hall was smaller than the Bishop of Worcester's but he still had to squint deep into the reeky murk. Half a dozen dark figures were standing round the hearth-place where a fire was blazing. Wulfgar wondered which of them was Toli Silkbeard.

The guard behind him said something in Danish.

He caught, '*Englis-mathr*' and '*Thjófr*'.

Englishman, he thought. Thief.

The port-reeve's off-hand manner had evaporated. He bowed to the group of men, suddenly diffident, deferential, as he began to explain what had happened. One of them cut him off with an abrupt gesture.

'Let me see him.'

Could this blond stripling really be the terrible Toli Silkbeard? He looked even younger than Ednoth, but from the way the port-reeve was twisting his hat in his hands, it had to be him.

Father Ronan had said he was young, Wulfgar remembered. I thought he'd be dark, Hrafnsson, the Raven's son, but he's fair as thistledown, fresh as a girl but for that shimmer of beard. He remembered Ronan's explanation of the lad's eke-name. *Never call him* Silkiskegg, *not to his face . . .* He realised that none of the Lincoln men had used it when speaking of their Jarl.

One of the guards shoved Wulfgar in the small of his back, and he staggered forward almost to Toli's feet.

'On your knees, thief,' the guard said.

'So, who is this little thief?' Toli spoke over his head. 'And what has he stolen, so early in the morning? Shall I hang him?'

'You're the law, *herra.*'

Toli preened.

Wulfgar swallowed. He looked up to left and right, and saw only amused faces.

'My Lord—' he began.

The port-reeve turned on him.

'Who said you could speak, thief?' He shoved his hat under one arm and foraged for the pocket under his tunic, eventually bringing out the little gospel-book. 'This, my Lord, is what he stole.'

Wulfgar watched the little book pass into Toli's hands with a despairing pang. The Holy Word in the hands of a heathen. He longed to speak but he didn't dare interrupt again, not yet.

Toli turned it over, frowning.

'Ah, *silver.*' He looked up at Wulfgar. 'Is this what you wanted, thief? Do you still want it? Here.' He held it out, smiling.

188

Wulfgar, hardly believing his luck, reached out. His fingertips had just brushed the calfskin binding when Toli snatched it away, still smiling.

'Come and get it, then!'

And, with no other warning, he tossed it at one of his companions.

Wulfgar stumbled to his feet. The man caught it in one hand as Wulfgar lunged, and threw it back-handed to another. They were laughing now, surrounding him, shoving him with one hand, throwing the book with the other. Faster and faster the little book flew, with Wulfgar, dizzy and distracted, turning on the spot to follow its path, always too late to reach out for it as it winged past him. It was the sort of game he was familiar with from his childhood, but now the stakes were all too high. Toli's men feinted left then right, jeering and cat-calling, tossed it back and forth over the fire, skimming it lower and lower through the flames.

Wulfgar, heart-sick, stopped trying in the end. He stood, head bowed, at the centre of their merriment, waiting until they tired of their sport and dreading the prospect of their next game. He thought instead of Pilate's soldiers mocking the Saviour, a crown of thorns, a purple robe, a reed. Queen of Heaven, get me out of this alive, he prayed. Why had he come here? The port-reeve had been right: Wulfgar should have gone with him quietly to the watch-house.

At long last, Toli, too, tired of the game. He reached out a lazy hand and plucked the little gospel-book from the air.

'Silver,' he said again. 'I suppose someone should weigh it and find out how much it's worth before I hang you, thief.' He tugged a little knife from his belt and, holding the book in his left hand, began prising at the fittings.

'I am no thief, my Lord!' Wulfgar's voice came out high, ragged, on the edge of breaking. 'But an errand-bearer, from Wessex.'

And Toli stopped, the absolute stillness of a hunting cat, the moment before it pounces. The background hum of voices fell silent.

'What errand?'

'I need to speak with you in private, my Lord.'

And Toli Silkbeard laughed.

'Very well, little thief. This had better be good.' He put his knife away again. 'Come with me.'

He sat down at the high table, gesturing his men to the other end of the hall. A waiting woman approached but she, too, was dismissed.

Wulfgar stood with his back to the hall. He could feel the whispers and giggles as prickles on his nape. The little gospel sat on the table between them.

'Well?' Toli tapped his fingers on the board, glanced at Wulfgar, and then looked down the length of the hall. 'I'm waiting. Show me you're telling the truth.'

Wulfgar's lips felt numb. He swallowed twice, watching Toli's impatience mount, those restless, tapping fingers.

'I've a word for you, my Lord,' he managed to say. 'A word from Athelwald Seiriol of Wessex. From the Atheling.'

The tapping stopped.

Toli's eyes came to meet Wulfgar's.

'Do you?'

His eyes stayed on Wulfgar's for a long-drawn, searching moment.

'Do you indeed? *Athalvald inn hungrathr*, we call him up here. So, tell me. What's this word from my sharp-set friend?'

Sharp-set. Hungry. *Athelwald the Hungry* . . . It suited him.

Wulfgar thought back to the bishop's stable-yard in Worcester, the Atheling's hand warm and firm on his shoulder, his soft, persuasive words. *Take a message to my friends* . . .

'We light the fire at All Hallows,' Wulfgar whispered.

It was done.

There was a long, long silence. Toli Silkbeard stared at the table, but Wulfgar thought he wasn't seeing it. His lips moved as if he were praying – to his heathen powers, Wulfgar thought, flinching – or tallying something. What would he be counting? Soldiers? Weapons?

Wulfgar observed him closely. Now that the threat of the wolf-pack was beginning to withdraw, and his heart beating less wildly, he was able to look at this boy. Toli's sparse beard was almost invisible except where its cropped strands caught the flickering light of lamp and fire. He had hair fine as gossamer, a soft red mouth, eyelashes and brows so light they too almost vanished against his smooth skin. He looked so very young, his pale eyes pink-rimmed, misleadingly like those of a new lamb.

'So,' he said at last, and again, '*So*. He gives me half a year.' He seemed to be looking through Wulfgar to some distant prospect, his eyes flickering in tiny movements. Then he asked, 'Who else gets this message?'

The Atheling had said nothing of whether Lincoln and Leicester were to know about each other. But Wulfgar had hesitated too long now, to say nothing.

'Hakon Grimsson, but—'

'He's dead.' So he knew that too. 'Who else? Ketil Scar?'

He shook his head.

'So I'm the first.' Toli smiled at that. 'And Stamford? Nottingham?'

Wulfgar shook his head again.

'Derby?'

Where? Wulfgar wondered.

Toli Silkbeard saw Wulfgar's frown, and laughed.

'Northworthy, you'd call it. On the Derwent. No? What about York?'

'I don't know, my Lord.'

Wulfgar was feeling ever more inadequate in the face of these relentless queries.

'I was only told to take the message to you and Hakon Grimsson,' he said desperately, 'but the Atheling might have a dozen other errand-boys.' He hadn't thought of that before, but as he said it he realised the truth of his words. He had no idea how widely this net was being cast.

Toli Silkbeard stood up then and took a few restless paces, back and forth behind the high table.

'York would be good. There's power there!' He shook the stray lock out of his eyes. 'And if it's just me and Leicester? Well, why not? My father was daggers-drawn with Hakon, but that's no reason why I shouldn't stand shoulder to shoulder with Ketil. I'm one of the players now.' He was thinking aloud.

Wulfgar pulled himself back into the shadows. He was still cold with fear, not knowing what remark might provoke another cruel game.

'Ha!'

Wulfgar jumped, and flinched when Toli turned to him, but the boy who had played cruel cat and mouse with him had vanished. Instead Wulfgar found himself being ushered round the table to sit at the Jarl's side, with Toli clapping him on the shoulder and beckoning the servant to pour wine for them both.

192

'The old men, eh? How they squat on our lives. Look at me: my father six months dead and I can still feel him tugging on the bit. I expect yours is the same?' He smiled, waiting for a response, and despite himself, despite everything, Wulfgar found himself being charmed, smiling back. They were drinking from chased silver cups, and the wine was sweet.

His father? That broad, loud king's thane, with his bluff persona of good cheer hiding a cold-eyed, ruthless ambition? Wulfgar had the sudden, unwelcome realisation that his father would have been proud of Garmund at Offchurch. He would have said, *That's the way to treat the damned Mercians, keep them on their toes, show them who's wielding the sword these days.* It had been the luckiest day of his life when they had given him into the care of his mother's brother at the cathedral. Wulfgar realised then that he hadn't just been homesick for Winchester; he was missing the tough, scholarly old man to whom he had been apprenticed, whose voice he could hear so often in his head. Tugging on the bit? It was a good way of putting it.

'For me it was always my uncle, my Lord,' he answered at last, with a lump in his throat, 'but, yes, I know what you mean.'

'Uncles, fathers!' Toli waved a hand. 'Well, I'm free now, to rule my own roost.'

'You speak such good English,' Wulfgar said curiously.

Toli laughed.

'Why shouldn't I? I was born here. My mother, my wet-nurse, my first girl, all Lincoln women.' His face grew serious again. 'Does your Lord want an answer?'

'He's not my Lord,' Wulfgar blurted before he could think better of it. 'But no, he didn't say anything about wanting an answer.'

'Not your Lord?' Toli Silkbeard looked at him, curious. 'Do you know what this message means?'

Wulfgar shook his head. He realised, through the warm, honeyed mist of wine, that he didn't want to know.

'Will you take word back to him?'

Wulfgar nodded a yes, sensing that this boy would not take a flat refusal well.

'Tell him . . .' Toli drummed his fingers on the table. 'Tell him that I received you graciously, that I listened to the message with interest, and that I will see what I can do. If he hears nothing more from me then, yes, let it be All Hallows. And I will wait for further word.'

Wulfgar repeated it verbatim, not understanding anything, and Toli Silkbeard nodded, satisfied.

Then he looked at Wulfgar, head on one side.

'Why are you doing this, and you a man of Wessex? What has he promised you?'

'Nothing.' Nothing but words.

Toli Silkbeard widened his eyes.

'*Nothing?* We reward our men better than that here, I can tell you.' His voice was suddenly kind. 'What do you need? Silver? Money?'

Wulfgar shook his head.

'I'm not a paid messenger, my Lord.'

'A bed for the night? A girl? I've got some new ones. Pretty.'

Wulfgar, blushing, shook his head again.

Toli picked up the little book.

'This?'

It's not yours to give, Wulfgar thought, with a surge of bitterness. Toli held it out to him, though. Wulfgar clasped his hands

194

together and concentrated on the feeling of interlocking fingers, gripping ever more tightly until his hands began to prickle and throb.

Toli frowned at him curiously.

'You'd steal it, but you won't take it as a gift?' He began to pull his hand back.

What would Toli do with that glorious little book? Strip off the silver and throw the goatskin and vellum on his midden? Wulfgar's fingers slowly uncurled and with a will of their own reached out. The little book nestled into his grasp like a child into his mother's bosom.

'I'm not a thief, my Lord,' he said softly. 'I didn't steal it. It was a misunderstanding in the market. The stall-holder will need paying.'

'Yes, yes. I'll have someone sort it out. More wine for my new friend!'

It was still too early in the morning for Wulfgar to be happy drinking so deeply. He shook his head.

Toli Silkbeard put an arm around his shoulders.

'Just a drop. Seal our friendship. There's really nothing more I can do for you?'

Rueful, Wulfgar thought – for the first time since he had set eyes on the little gospel-book – of the real object of his quest. *Bardney.* Had his lips moved?

Toli was on to him at once.

'What?'

Lulled, flattered, tipsy, he blurted it out: 'Bardney. I'd like some news of Bardney.'

'Bardney? Is that all? That's easy enough.' Toli Silkbeard raised his voice. 'Eirik? Come here, will you?'

And one of the group of lounging figures by the door detached himself and began to stalk the length of the hall towards the high table.

Wulfgar scrambled to keep ahead of his panic. It only took a few heartbeats for the newcomer to move into their lamplight.

'*Herra?*'

A long grey wolf-spider of a man, tall and stringy and lantern-jawed. Not one of the group of flashy lads who had teased Wulfgar earlier; it was hard to imagine this man teasing anyone. Alone among the men in the hall, he wore no jewellery, had no ornaments on his belt, no gold or silver braid trimming on his tunic of undyed grey wool. At first sight, he didn't look as though he were trying to impress, or intimidate, anyone. Even so, Wulfgar did not like the way the man looked at him, eyeing him up as if he was putting a price on his head. And not thinking he'd get a good one, at that.

'English, please, Eirik. This man is a good servant of some southern friends of ours, and he has travelled a long way to bring me important news. And in turn he asks for news of Bardney.' Toli Silkbeard clapped Wulfgar on the shoulder and withdrew his arm. 'Go on, ask him.'

'Bardney? What do you want with Bardney?' Eirik's voice was flat, devoid of expression, thick with strange consonants. *Vot do you vant . . .*

Wulfgar swallowed.

'Oh, nothing, just old family associations . . . the saint, you know . . . I was wondering if the church is still there?' He could have bitten his tongue off, he was so angry with himself and his blabbing.

'Kirk? *Já*, it is still there.'

196

'Eirik and his family use it as their hall, don't you?' Toli Silkbeard said encouragingly.

Eirik turned to him and said something rapid and angry in Danish.

Toli Silkbeard laughed.

'Did you catch that?' he asked Wulfgar.

Wulfgar shook his head. Something about Bardney . . .

'"Between my wife and the mosquitoes, why would I ever want to go to Bardney?"' Toli Silkbeard translated, and laughed. 'My Eirik is an important man with business that takes him far and wide; the backwaters of the Lindsey fen are the least of his concerns, I can tell you. Have you learned what you wanted?'

Wulfgar nodded, mute. He was afraid now of opening his mouth for fear of what else might emerge.

Eirik looked at him suspiciously.

'And there's nothing else we can do for you?' Toli Silkbeard asked.

Wulfgar thought, he's getting suspicious, too. But he just wanted to be out of there.

'I need to get back to my friends,' he said.

Toli Silkbeard looked hard at Wulfgar, shaking his head. His colourless locks were tied away from his face by a band of dark fabric interwoven with gold, but one thick strand had worked free. He brushed it out of his eyes and grinned.

'I don't know what to make of you, Englishman. Do you have a name?'

'Wulfgar,' he said. He thought it better not to mention Winchester.

Toli Silkbeard put out his hand.

'Wulfgar. *Ulfgeir*, eh? Is that right? Spear of the Wolf?'

If he makes a joke about my name, Wulfgar thought, I'll, I'll – what, exactly?

But he didn't.

Warm in the lamplight, red lips smiling, Toli Silkbeard said, 'Ulfgeir the Lordless, friend of *Athalvald inn hungrathr* and friend of mine, you are always welcome in my courts.'

On his way out, the little book clutched to his heart, Wulfgar stole another look at Eirik, only to find he himself was still being watched from those deep-set sockets. Wulfgar was frightened to the marrow. But it was the Atheling's message that was lodging now in his conscience like a fishbone in his throat. He wondered what on earth the Atheling was planning for All Hallows, and what it was that his own bearing of the message had set in motion. What had Toli Silkbeard called the Atheling? Athelwald the Hungry? Oh yes, it suited him all right.

CHAPTER NINETEEN

Wulfgar made his way out through the gates of Toli Silkbeard's outer stockade, elated to have escaped with his prize and his skin intact, but rendered slightly hysterical by his encounter with the young Jarl, and more than a little drunk. What was he going to say to the other two? How was he going to explain the little gospel-book, which he was still clasping to his breast like a lover? The morning had vanished somehow; the sun was high now over the bustling streets. He was disoriented; when the port-reeve had brought him on that forced march through the streets he had paid no attention to their route. But Silver Street ran obliquely downhill, and down seemed the most likely way back to the harbour.

He wanted to avoid the market. The last thing he needed was another run-in with that aggrieved stall-holder, especially as he didn't trust Toli to honour the debt. Or worse, another encounter with Fur Hat. But every path he tried seemed to lead that way. He ended up turning uphill again in a great curve that took him west, almost all the way back to the ford where the Fosse Way came into the town, before dropping him back down to the riverside. The ford was bustling with traffic.

Among the ox-carts and the mules, something about the way one grey horse lifted her feet high out of the water, and the spear-straight back of her hooded rider, caught Wulfgar's eye. The horse-woman was no more than a couple of dozen yards away when she turned her horse's head, shortening her reins as she did so and shrugging her hood back onto her shoulders to reveal her unveiled hair. It was a gesture he'd seen before, and committed to memory.

Without thinking, he hailed her.

'Gunnvor Bolladottir!'

Their eyes met.

She raised her eyebrows and trotted up the last few yards to his side, little bronze bells tinkling against the red leather of her harness. A couple of horsemen followed her a discreet length behind.

'Ha! The saint-hunter! I thought I might have to hunt for you all the way to Bardney.'

'Ssh!' He glanced around. 'No, we stayed here last night.'

'Ronan must have ridden you hard.' She leant down from her saddle and offered him a hand. 'Come up on my pommel?'

He blushed furiously and shook his head.

'I'll walk.'

'Then I'll walk with you.' She jumped down from the saddle in a flurry of skirts. 'What are you hiding?' She put out her hand and touched his hand where he still clutched the little book under his tunic.

He flinched away from her.

'Something – something to show Father Ronan.' His treasure had been mocked enough for one morning.

She shrugged.

'Any luck in finding your man with the bones? What was he called? Thorvald?'

'No, not yet, unless Ednoth and Father Ronan have had more luck.' He felt hot under the collar, but she wasn't even looking at him. Some of the traders along the foreshore were trying to get her attention, calling her by name, and she raised a hand in greeting.

'Not buying, not today, lads!'

They were almost at the inn now, and Gunnvor looked approving.

'Best wine in Lincoln. Trust a priest.'

Wulfgar wondered what he would say to Ednoth and Father Ronan, but there was no sign of them. Gunnvor left her men to oversee the stabling of her silver-grey mare next to Fallow. Wulfgar noticed with a pang that his poor little Fallow looked stumpier and squatter than ever in that elegant company.

'Come in with me?'

They were hardly through the door, however, when they heard Father Ronan roaring in the yard.

'I know that mare! Gunnvor Bolladottir! What the hell are you doing in Lincoln? Whom did curiosity kill? Eh, lass? Answer me that!'

She turned back out through the door, and Wulfgar followed helplessly.

'And why shouldn't I be in Lincoln? I've a house here, business interests here – as you know full well.' She shrugged. 'I thought you would be pleased to see me?' From another woman it might have sounded flirtatious. She quirked her eyebrows. 'I might even be useful.'

'Have you been looking for Thorvald, Father?' Wulfgar was anxious to deflect any questions about his own absence.

'Putting word about,' Father Ronan said. 'Luck may be with us. Someone thought your man was in town to see Eirik – we're told Eirik's in attendance on Toli Silkbeard at the moment, so we've been stepping softly. The last thing we want is it getting back to him that outlanders have been asking questions about Bardney and his reeve. But if word reaches Thorvald he'll know to come here.'

Wulfgar swallowed uneasily, afraid that he might confess to having met Eirik the Spider already. He had to learn to control his tongue.

'Shall we have something to eat?' he asked quickly. 'Before we go on looking?'

Father Ronan grinned and pointed to Ednoth sitting on a bench in the yard.

'Your lad here has been talking about nothing but food since sunrise.'

They sat in the courtyard eating barley-bread and bean broth and more soft new cheese. Father Ronan borrowed a table game-board from the ale-wife and started teaching Ednoth how they played in Leicester.

'But this way anyone who starts on King's Side is going to win,' Ednoth complained. 'It's not fair.'

Father Ronan caught Wulfgar's eye, inviting laughter.

'But how like life! No, you see, if you start King's Side—' He began rearranging the counters.

'Was someone asking for me?'

They all turned and saw a slight, russet-clad figure, hesitating by their bench.

'The ale-wife said –' he frowned, looking from face to face '–

202

she said someone was asking—'

Father Ronan rose to his feet

'Is it yourself? Thorvald, Reeve of Bardney? Here's a sweet piece of luck! Put the game away, lad.'

Thorvald looked to be in his late twenties, already greying, with weathered skin and tired, blood-tinged eyes. Wulfgar offered him his hand but the newcomer didn't take it.

'How do I know you are who you say you are?' he said. He looked from face to face, a muscle jumping in his cheek. One of his front teeth was badly chipped.

Wulfgar groped down the neck of his tunic and pulled out the Bishop's ring. Unknotting the thong he slipped it off and passed it across to Thorvald.

'The Bishop of Worcester gave me this a week ago. He told me you'd recognise it.'

Father Ronan whistled.

'Now there's a pretty thing.'

Thorvald turned it over in his hands.

'Yes, he's right. I remember this on his finger.' His eyes met Wulfgar's and he passed the ring back to him.

Wulfgar was about to put it away, when Father Ronan asked, 'May I . . . ? Is it . . . ?'

Wulfgar nodded.

The priest closed his eyes and pressed it to his lips before passing it back.

But Gunnvor reached out a hand.

'A pretty thing, indeed,' she said.

Reluctant, Wulfgar let her take it. She lifted it to her mouth and for a moment he thought he'd been misjudging her. But, no, she was baring sharp, white teeth, ready to bite.

He snatched it back.

'Just assaying the gold,' she said, ingenuous.

'Stop teasing him, woman,' Father Ronan said.

Retying the thong with more knots than it really needed, Wulfgar said to Thorvald, 'Do we trust each other then?'

'What choice do we have?' He glanced around the courtyard and out through the gateway towards the wharf. 'Go in, shall we? You never know who'll tattle, and the Spider's in Lincoln at the moment.'

Wulfgar bit his tongue.

They ducked under the reed-thatch, away from the wind and prying eyes. Thorvald was acting like a horse who smells smoke, nostrils flared, the whites of his eyes showing startled in the gloom. That muscle in his cheek jumped more quickly than ever. He found them a dark corner, away from the barrels and the hearth.

'I wasn't expecting . . . I don't know what I was expecting.'

'Take your time, man,' Father Ronan said. 'You've kept this secret a long time; it can wait a little longer if it needs to.'

He shook his head.

'But it can't. Ever since I told the Bishop—' It was warm and stuffy inside the inn but he had kept his cloak on and his hood half up around his head.

Curious, Wulfgar asked, 'When did you tell the Bishop?'

'A while ago.' His face drew in. 'She – Eirik's wife – sent me down till London at ploughing-time, on business. And I heard that the Bishop was there. I went to see him, in his muckle great house by the river?'

Wulfgar frowned, nodding.

'The Bishop leases a lot of the waterfront there,' He said. 'But

204

this must mean he knew about St Oswald's survival for – what? Something like two months? – before he decided to act.' He shook his head in disbelief.

'Two months of tenterhooks for me,' said Thorvald.

The memory of Eirik's skull-face hovered before Wulfgar's eyes. He thought of being Eirik's man, being subject to the Spider's will day in and day out, and he shuddered.

Thorvald caught his eye and nodded. There was a moment's silence. Then he said, 'If you're going to trust me, I'd maybe best tell you how I know where the saint's hidden.'

There was a general murmur of agreement.

He closed his eyes and pressed his hands together for a moment; Wulfgar thought he might be praying.

Then Thorvald took a deep breath.

'The minster of Bardney died in a single night some thirty years ago. The way my mother told it, we were rich, some three hundred folk – lay and learned – serving our saints. We'd heard there was a lot of bother around, but we're almost an island, cut off by fen, and we thought we were safe. Then the Great Army came.'

He fell silent briefly, and when he spoke again the words came tumbling out. His accent was getting thicker; Wulfgar had to grab each word as it came.

'My grandfa' set the wake over the saints' shrines; that night he was doing it himself. He must have told me the tale a hundred times. They came by water, on a night with no moon. They surrounded the stockade and fired it in a dozen places at once. They broke in and fired the thatch on the out-buildings. They waited by the doors and ran our people through as they came running out—' He broke off again. 'I wasn't there, you know. I wasn't born. But it feels . . .'

'I know how it feels,' Father Ronan said. 'We understand. Go on.'

Thorvald shrugged.

'There's not much more to tell. They got to the kirk last – it's in the middle, in a garth of its own. My grandfa' was no gawby. He'd heard the screams and smelt the reek. He got the shrine open and took the inner kist out. Three foot long, and made of wood. He'd have to stow it in the gainest place. Another of his jobs was to make the graves. He'd buried one of the brothers only the last week. The earth he'd back-filled the grave with was still claggy.'

'You'd have us credit none of the raiders noticed the grave had been disturbed?' Father Ronan asked. 'I don't doubt your tale, but . . .'

Thorvald shrugged again.

'It was dark. My grandfa' said we were like swans who wouldn't leave their clutch, we were giving them all the trouble we could. And there was loot everywhere. They didn't have to go digging for it. And by sun-up they'd gone.' He closed his eyes. 'Abbey and outbuildings burned, stock they hadn't rounded up slaughtered. My grandfather counted two hundred corpses, men, women and beasts. The shrines were smashed and ransacked, and about fifty folk unaccounted for. The oblate boys had been taken, and the young servants, male and female.'

'But your mother and your grandfather survived?' Ronan was frowning.

The reeve nodded.

'After he'd buried the saint grandfa' grabbed Mam and rolled with her under a thorndyke on the edge of the bone-garth, clapped a hand over her mouth, and they stayed there till it was all over.

206

She was na but a bairn then. Not a hero's doing, maybe, but they lived, didn't he?'

'Hero enough for me,' Father Ronan said.

'So where are the relics now?' Ednoth said. He looked Thorvald up and down as if he thought the little man might have the bones stowed under his cloak.

'Who are you? I know he comes from the Bishop,' jerking his head at Wulfgar, 'but who are the rest of you? Who's *she*?'

The reeve was so nervous that Wulfgar was astonished he'd ever had the courage to approach the Bishop.

'We're all your friends,' Wulfgar said. 'Ednoth's here to help me. Ronan's a priest, and a Mercian, and . . .' He ground to a halt.

'And me?' Gunnvor's eyes were gleaming with a mischievous light.

Yes, Wulfgar thought. What about you? Why are you here? Fair questions, but he didn't dare to ask them, and he wasn't sure he would like the answers.

Gunnvor looked at Thorvald now. 'You really don't know who I am? Gunnvor Bolladottir?'

He shook his head.

She shrugged, amused. 'You must spend a lot of time mired in your fenny fastness, Reeve of Bardney.'

Wulfgar felt it was time to change the subject. Father Ronan had brought the saddle-bags in, and Wulfgar opened one up and brought out the Bishop's bag of silver.

'Here's your money, if that makes you feel any better.'

'It's not just the money,' Thorvald answered, peering into the bag. He looked up at Wulfgar, gnawing his lip. 'Five pounds, yes, he promised me, but also safe conduct for me and my family, and a place on Worcester lands.'

'Safe conduct? Family? Land?' Wulfgar could feel his jaw dropping. 'The Bishop never said . . .'

'That's what the Bishop said to me.' Thorvald's thin face was set. 'Think on – why did I tell him now about my saint? My *son*. Having a son.'

Wulfgar nodded.

'Then that's what we'll do.' He hoped he sounded as though he knew what he was talking about. In his short encounter with Eirik he had learned everything he needed about why Thorvald wanted to raise his boy far away from Bardney.

'Do you mean we'll be fleeing Eirik with a pack of bairns bealing and yammering?' Gunnvor asked.

'Who's this *we*?' Father Ronan asked her.

'As if you could do it without my help,' she said, lifting her chin defiantly.

Thorvald had folded his arms across his chest.

'I'm asking no more nor less than what the Bishop promised me. There are only two. Bairns, I mean. Small ones. We'll see they're kept quiet.'

Gunnvor snorted.

'You'd better. You're not wanting us to rescue your old mother as well?'

He shook his head. 'Mam's been gone these three years. It's only my wife and my bairns.' He weighed the bag of silver in one hand, chewing the inside of his cheek, and then he handed it back to Wulfgar. 'You hold it safe for me. I trust you if you're the Bishop's man.'

Wulfgar about to protest but in truth he was deeply moved. He stowed the bag away.

'What do we do now?' Wulfgar asked. He found Thorvald was

still looking at him, and realised that he was the one making the decisions.

He cleared his throat. 'Can you bring the relics to us here?'

Thorvald shook his head at that. 'It's not a job for a man alone. Two to dig and one to stand watch, at least.'

The others were still waiting.

'So, we have to come to Bardney,' Wulfgar said. 'All of us, I suppose.' He tried to think. The smoke was making his eyes water. 'Road or river?'

Thorvald was still shaking his head. 'Too many people around. Even Eirik, maybe.' He bit his lip and thought. 'You'll have to come through the fen. There are causeways. Do you have horses?' At Wulfgar's nod, he said, 'Leave as soon as you can, by the muckle south road. It climbs south of the river. Once you're on top, there's a track east that takes you three miles across the heath.' He paused to see if they were taking in his words. 'Follow it right till the fen-edge, look for the sheep-cots. That's best. My wife and bairns are there already, for the lambing. Leave the horses there. Wait there while the moon rises and I'll meet you and guide you across.' He stood up, swathing himself in his cloak.

'Wait a minute, Thorvald,' Ronan said. 'What's your wife's name?'

'Leoba.' An Englishwoman, then. Or at least a woman with an English name. Wulfgar had a hundred more things to ask him.

A sudden flurry of activity over by the main door made Thorvald look up and flinch back at once into the corner, jerking his hood further over his face.

It was Toli Silkbeard.

And his men.

And Eirik the Spider.

Wulfgar's first thought was that they were after him.

And the second, hard on the heels of the first, was that they were looking for Thorvald.

But they weren't. Of course they weren't. What was the point of being rich and young and well-dressed if you couldn't strut and crow on your own little dung-heap?

Silkbeard and his friends came barging in, scabbards swinging and cloaks swirling, shouting for wine. And then he saw Gunnvor.

'Gunnvor Bolladottir! By the Spear, why didn't you let me know you were honouring my town?'

They were coming straight over.

Gunnvor rose at once and went to forestall them, putting on a good show of eagerness. 'Toli Hrafnsson! *Herra!* We only arrived today. What's new? Who's in town?' This was another new Gunnvor, sparkly, demure, resting her hand delicately on Silkbeard's arm, looking up at him from under her lashes. He was evidently dazzled. Wulfgar felt the rustle of rough cloth against his arm and half-glimpsed a shadow slipping past him. It was Thorvald, hood up, dodging along the wall to the door, unnoticed by anyone but Wulfgar while the ale-wife and her slaves were fluttering round Toli Silkbeard and the half-dozen men he'd brought with him like moths round a candle.

Silkbeard seated himself on the one bench with a back to it, pulling Gunnvor down to sit on his left, pointing Eirik to a place on his right, and disposing the rest around him on low stools. Wulfgar's party were all being drawn into the circle. He saw Silkbeard nod at Ronan, acknowledging him but with none of the warmth with which he'd greeted Gunnvor. He was asking her for news from Leicester: who was out, who in.

She laughed. 'Still buzzing like bees in a toppled hive. Ketil's flexing his muscles, calling in favours. He's confirmed my grant of the High Cross south of Leicester.'

Wulfgar noticed she said nothing about Ketil slapping her face, though the little red welt was still visible.

'And adding to your fortune?' Silkbeard said. He put his hand on her knee and Wulfgar saw her stiffen.

She doesn't like that, he thought. He felt an unfamiliar, protective rage blaze through his veins, but it was damped too quickly by fear as Silkbeard caught his eye and smiled, before turning to the whole room.

'Richest woman in all the Five Boroughs and still she wants more.' His tone invited their laughter. 'Richest, and prettiest.'

'Toli Hrafnsson,' Gunnvor said. 'Let me present my friends. You know Father Ronan – this is Wulfgar of Winchester—'

But Toli, who had been nodding impatiently, interrupted her. 'So, Gunnvor Bolladottir, now that Hakon's dead, who's the lucky man? Ketil? Or am I in with a chance?'

Her mouth twisted. It might have been a smile. 'Oh, I'm past the age for that, Toli Hrafnsson. Better ask who my heirs are.'

Silkbeard looked round the company, still inviting their mockery. 'Listen to her! Ripe as summer berries, she is, and the nonsense that comes out of her mouth.'

Gunnvor raised her eyebrows. 'I might ask you the same, Toli Hrafnsson. Look at you, Jarl of all Lincoln for a whole winter and not even one wife yet?'

Silkbeard laughed.

'Buy a cow, when milk's mine for the taking?' He went on stroking her knee. 'It would depend on what the wife brought with her, of course.' He glanced over at Wulfgar then. 'Ulfgeir! When you said "your friends", I didn't know you meant Gunnvor

Bolladottir. I'd have come straight down with you if I'd known she was here.'

Thank my guardian angel I didn't know she was coming, then, Wulfgar thought. He said something in response, he had no idea what.

Silkbeard snapped his fingers for wine, and in the bustle Father Ronan leaned over, tickling Wulfgar's ear with his whiskers.'Your friends?' he said meaningly. 'Have you been hobnobbing with Toli? You've got some explaining to do, my lad.'

Wulfgar nodded, unable to meet the priest's eyes.

Ednoth stared at him, too, a furrow deepening between his brows.

Wulfgar looked away.

And now Silkbeard was shouting at him: 'Ulfgeir the Lordless! I want to know you better. Are all your friends so interesting?' He snapped his fingers again and gestured to the ale-wife, and Wulfgar found his cup was being filled.

'Drink, Ulfgeir! Swear friendship with me!'

Wulfgar knocked cups with the Jarl and drank, but he couldn't hold Silkbeard's gaze; he found his eyes flickering past, looking into the shadows for Thorvald. No sign of him, but then he couldn't see much beyond the firelight. He hoped the fragile little man had managed to slip out.

Eirik was looking at Father Ronan, something unfathomable in his eyes.

'Still wasting your breath preaching, priest?' he asked.

'You should come along to my Margaret-kirk, next time you're down in Leicester,' Father Ronan said easily. 'I had your friend Orm Ormsson in my flock on Sunday, setting you all a good example.'

Eirik hawked and spat into the straw.

'Christianity,' he said with great deliberation, 'is a faith for thralls. And fools.'

Wulfgar felt his stomach twisting.

But Father Ronan only smiled.

'Yes,' he said, 'my friend. That's just what it is.'

'Ormsson is no fool.' Eirik stared at Ronan, expressionless. 'Impulsive, maybe. But no fool.'

Wulfgar stood up, his knees shaky. He was tipsier than he'd realised.

'Where's the, um . . .' He wanted to say *necessarium* – the need-house.

But the attentive ale-wife knew what he meant.

'Skitter-house, *herra*? Through that doorway, in the garth.'

He stumbled out. The sky was still light but the little backyard with its high walls lay in shadow. He nearly fell over the snoring pig and in steadying himself put his hand into a stand of nettles and swore. The pit had wattle hurdles around it and a wooden seat. He fumbled with his belt and got his leggings down, his guts twisting painfully now. But all to no avail. He sat there in the stench, listening to his belly gripe and gurgle and the pig snorting and rootling in the midden, watching the sunset-tinted clouds move across the sky and wondering how he could face his friends. He thought, I can't go back in there and explain when I don't know what I've done. Perhaps I could just stay out here, find a refuge with the safe, friendly pig. Like St Frideswide, he thought. Didn't she work as a swineherd for three years to avoid the unwanted attentions of a wealthy man who wanted to marry her? I can't see Gunnvor Cat's-Eyes doing that, he thought, and snorted aloud.

In the end, it was Ronan who came out looking for him.

Wulfgar scrambled unsteadily to his feet.

Ronan stood by the inn door, silent, waiting.

When Wulfgar had finished tying his leggings, the priest said, 'More secrets, Wuffa? Or am I talking to *Ulfgeir*?'

'I only met him for the first time this morning,' Wulfgar said.

'Toli?'

'Who else?'

Ronan shrugged.

'Perhaps it's no business of mine, even though I've come along on this escapade solely with the aim of helping you.'

Wulfgar felt a blush start. He looked down.

'I'm a good listener, though,' the priest went on. 'If you need me. And discreet. It comes with the job.'

The pig was on its feet now and snuffling around Wulfgar's legs, and he bent to give it a scratch behind its hairy ears. He longed to tell Ronan everything, but he was prevented by a forceful memory of the Atheling: Wulfgar could sense him now, looming over him, gripping his elbow, saying, *Tell no one else. No one, do you hear me?*

'We need to go,' Ronan said. 'Now. If Eirik is here, dancing attendance on Toli Silkbeard, then at least he won't be at Bardney. And if we go now, we'll be there for Thorvald at moonrise. God knows, that poor little man and his saint have been kept waiting long enough.'

The only way out of the yard was through the hall.

As Wulfgar ducked to go in, Father Ronan put his arm out to block the other man's path.

'Be warned. These are dangerous men.'

His hand still on the door curtain, Wulfgar said, 'Silkbeard has been very kind to me.' Silkbeard had liked him, he thought, had trusted him. Wulfgar sensed no danger, not from that quarter, anyway. He allowed himself a little spurt of anger. 'You and the Spider seem to be old friends.'

Father Ronan pressed his lips together for a moment. 'I told you we'd met. Eirik and I, we've had our disagreements over these many years. I don't know what game you're playing, Wuffa. But remember, no man can serve two masters. I hope you know what you're doing.'

Not as devoutly as Wulfgar did himself.

CHAPTER TWENTY

Ednoth saw them come in and he stood up. Wulfgar could see at
once it was going to be hard for Gunnvor to extricate herself,
however. Toli Silkbeard was still paying her that over-flattering
attention, turning frequently from his men to speak to her in a
low voice, resting his hand on her arm or her thigh. Wulfgar
wondered whether Toli would notice him going and bid him
farewell, but Lincoln's Jarl was wholly caught up in his banter with
Gunnvor.

Eirik the Spider saw him, though. His face didn't change but
Wulfgar could feel those hollow-socketed eyes following his
progress all the way around the hall. He glanced back when they
got to the door into the main courtyard to find Eirik was still
watching him, his body twisted round, one elbow resting on the
back of the bench.

As soon as the three of them were outside, Wulfgar said, 'What
about Gunnvor? We can't just abandon her.'

'Who wants *her* to come?' Ednoth asked.

Ronan shook his head, smiling wryly. 'If any woman can look after herself in that company, it's Cat's-Eyes.' He saw Wulfgar still hesitated. 'Leave it, Wuffa. She knows what she's doing. Silkbeard won't leave while she's there, and Eirik can't leave while Silkbeard's there.'

Wulfgar took the point.

The ostler helped them saddle and pack the horses. Within moments they were riding out the way they'd come, but instead of bearing south west for the Fosse Way again, they took another road, just as old, just as straight, once they had splashed across the ford in accordance with Thorvald's instructions. The new road took them due south, and they climbed the far side of Lincoln's steep river valley and up onto open heathland. *Ermin Street*: the name drifted up from some long-forgotten charter. But they didn't keep to the great road for long. As the sun westered, casting their shadows far to their left, Ronan steered his sturdy little beast off on a track that led away from the heathland and down through groves of lime just coming into leaf.

The track wound slowly but steadily downwards; Wulfgar was surprised when he looked back briefly and realised how steeply the heathland rose behind them. Darkness was drawing in more quickly here in its eastern lee. His skin prickled in a chill and rising wind that came to meet them face on, and he took one hand off Fallow's reins to tug his cloak more closely about him.

Ronan had stopped.

Wulfgar caught up with him, and asked, 'Do you know where you're going?'

'Following my nose,' Ronan said thoughtfully. 'There isn't that much room to farm along this edge of the fen, and we've done as Thorvald said. We should be close.'

They were; a few more twists of the track, the trees thinning, and Ronan reined in again, holding up his hand.

Ednoth nodded.

'What?' Wulfgar asked.

'Barnyard fowl,' Father Ronan said.

'Lambs,' Ednoth added.

The yard was fenced with a high ring of bundles of dead thorn, with a single entrance. Ducks and chickens scattered, raucous in their displeasure, from under the horses' hooves. There was one low building, reed-thatched, with smoke trickling out where it could, a dung heap to the left and a lambing pen to the right. A mule was tied to a stump. There was a young woman coming out of the hut, a child of three or four clinging to her skirts. She saw the men riding through the gap in the thorn-hedge and stopped dead, then glanced wildly to left and right. There was nowhere to run. She fell to her knees. The little girl at her side began to scream.

Ronan reined in sharply and gestured to the other two to do the same. He handed his reins to Ednoth and swung down out of the saddle. He raised his empty hands. Without taking a step towards the woman, he said, softly, 'Leoba. Your husband sent us. Thorvald. Your husband. It's all right. I'm a priest. No one here is going to hurt you or yours.'

Slowly she got back to her feet, hushing the child.

'Who are you?' Her voice trembled.

'We've come from the Bishop of Worcester,' Ronan said. 'Everything's going to be all right.'

She looked at him long and hard, and then did the same for Ednoth and for Wulfgar. Her little girl was still crying, clinging to her legs.

'Thank God,' she said. And again, 'Thank God.'

She was shaking uncontrollably now, her arms cupped about her body, and Wulfgar realised she was holding another child in there, a very young one, pouched against her breast in a fold of cloth.

Thorvald's son.

Father Ronan looked up at the sky. 'Why do we have to live in a world where strangers mean trouble?' he asked.

Wulfgar didn't think he expected an answer.

There was nothing to do then but wait.

Leoba had some pottage simmering over the hearth: more oats and much less meat than Wulfgar was used to, but warm and welcome all the same. There was just the one wooden bowl, which they passed around, squatting on their haunches to keep their heads below the blue smoke that hung in loops and skeins below the thatch.

Their hostess said little, but Wulfgar found himself watching her every move. She thrummed like a plucked harp-string. Much younger than Thorvald, closer to Ednoth's age. A dark girl with fine eyes, but her looks were marred by her thinness and the same harried air as her husband. She was like some marsh-wading bird, all drab plumage and bright eyes, dunlin or sandpiper. Both children stayed almost invisible, the little girl hiding in the folds of Leoba's skirts and the baby tucked into her bodice, suckling, its fingers toying with a twisted silver ring that hung from a loop of blue yarn around her neck. Wulfgar caught a glimpse of blue-veined breast and moist, pink nipple as the baby quested, eyes closed and open-mouthed, and he looked away. An orphan lamb lay crying faintly in a basket.

After they'd eaten, Wulfgar got up and stretched and went outside to a late evening full of birdsong and the robust bleating of those new lambs who still had their mothers. He was finding the waiting hard. The lambing pens were right on the edge of the dry land. Beyond the thorn-hedge, hazel scrub quickly gave way to swampy-looking meadow thick with pink cuckoo-flower, and beyond that the reed-beds began. The wind was bitter, carrying the smell of damp and decay. The marsh looked mild enough in the afterglow of the sunset, but his flesh prickled at the thought of going down there in darkness. Three cormorants sat on a dead tree drying their inky wings, and a noisy arrow of greylags went over, low enough for Wulfgar to hear the beat and whistle of the wind in their flight-feathers. His eyes followed them flying high towards the fen, but even as he watched the geese banked and turned and flew over his head, circling the enclosure and crying as they flew, their wings catching the last of the light.

'That's bad luck.' Ronan had come out to join him. 'Or so my mother would have said.'

Wulfgar glimpsed a flurry of movement from the corner of his eye. Leoba, standing just behind them with the baby in the crook of her arm, had crossed herself at Ronan's words.

'Are you really taking us from here?'she asked quietly.

Wulfgar nodded.

'The Spider's a bad master. He and his, they can't tell a freeman from a thrall.' She lifted her eyes to Wulfgar's. 'Thorvald and me, we're old Bardney folk. Our kin served the monks before Eirik and his like ever came. But they don't see we're here along of the place. Eirik thinks we're his. He thinks our bairns will be his to do as he wants with, when they're old enough.'

She had all their attention.

'And what would he do with them, when they're old enough?' Ronan said lightly.

'What he's done with others. Sell over the western sea.'

'Dublin?'

'Aye, happen.'

Ronan was silent a moment. Then he said, 'We'll get you away.'

'You're a priest,' she said.

He nodded. 'Margaret-kirk, in Leicester.'

'Would you christen my bairns? And me?'

'Now?'

She shook her head. 'In your kirk. Done right, not here.'

'Done right,' he said. 'We might even find you some godparents.'

Ednoth had been busy unsaddling all three horses and rubbing them down with wisps of grass, and now he ran his hand up and down their legs. He got to his feet and came over.

'I think Fallow's got a splint, Father.' He was speaking to Ronan but his tone was accusing and Wulfgar knew the words were intended for him. He didn't know what to say; he wasn't even sure what Ednoth meant, or how he could have prevented it.

Father Ronan sighed.

'Let's have a look.'

When he had felt Fallow's front legs he nodded.

'All this way on hard roads, no great surprise there.'

Now Ednoth did look at Wulfgar.

'She must have been lame all day. But you're such a rotten horseman, you wouldn't notice, would you, *Ulfgeir*?'

Wulfgar found himself wishing Ednoth would just shout at him. He could deal with that. He thought, oh, damn it. I *like* that horse. She's looked after me better than I've looked after her.

'*Steady*,' said Ronan. 'It could have happened to either of your two nags, neither in the best condition, ridden day after day.'

'Cold poultices,' Leoba said. 'I'll see to them. She should rest but there's little we can do there.'

'You know about horses?' Ednoth asked.

'I know mules,' she said, thrusting the baby at Wulfgar. 'Take this, he likes to play with it.' She pulled the loop of wool with its silver ring over her head and pushed it into his hand.

He'd never held such a young child before. It – no, *he* – was astonishingly light. Not knowing where to put the baby, he tried to copy Leoba's stance, holding the swathed bundle against his shoulder. It felt as though there were a conspiracy against him, to make him look a fool. He wanted to explain everything to Ednoth but he didn't know where to start.

'Can I help?' he asked Ronan.

The priest looked down at the baby and raised his eyebrows.

'I think you've got your hands full.'

Leoba had found rags and comfrey and water, and she and Ednoth occupied themselves with Fallow's legs, followed every-where by the solemn, thumb-sucking little girl.

Ronan brought out his sword and began to sharpen it with long, slow strokes of a little whetstone, which he took from a leather pocket that hung at his belt.

Wulfgar was left with the baby, who looked at him with bright, round eyes, small pink hands clutching at his tunic, the swaddling-cloth stale with old milk. Wulfgar remembered again the son born last autumn to his brother's house, and he dangled the silver ring in front of the baby to see if he liked it. He did, reaching out and gurgling. Wulfgar hunkered down over the little thing in the lee of the hedge, dangling the ring, careful that the baby didn't scratch himself on the sharp, protruding end of the silver wire.

Ronan looked across and smiled.

'Have you children?' he asked Wulfgar.

He shook his head.

'Little brothers?'

Wulfgar flinched involuntarily. Ronan doesn't know about Garmund, he reminded himself. 'All my siblings are older than me,' he said carefully. 'Wystan's the eldest. He's inherited our father's estates near Winchester. He's got a new son, but I haven't seen the child yet. And my sister – she's older than me, too.' No need to go into further detail.

Father Ronan nodded.

'Wife?'

'No.'

The baby let a dribble of milk emerge from a corner of its mouth. Wulfgar found himself profoundly moved by the child's smallness, his trusting way of clutching a finger in his tiny fist. Why did everyone keep asking him about getting married? He tried to find an honest answer.

'I serve the Lady now. Maybe, if I found a woman to match *her*, one day . . .' This conversation was making him uncomfortable. 'You?'

Ronan snorted. 'Kevin. My altar-boy, remember? At least, his mother's always claimed he's my getting, and I've no reason to doubt her. He's a good boy. I'm happy to train him up to fill my shoes.' He shrugged. 'Wife? Not for a long time.'

Wulfgar ruminated on this. It seemed an over-casual arrangement, even for a priest without ambition. I'm in this man's debt, he thought, I'm in no position to judge him. He forced himself to voice the nagging thought at the back of his mind. 'I thought, perhaps, you and Gunnvor . . . You seem so easy with each other.'

'Our lovely Gunnvor.' Ronan shook his head.

Wulfgar frowned at him, concerned at the edge of bitterness in the priest's voice.

Ronan cocked an eyebrow at him. 'You feel it too, don't you? Ach, she's got the elf-sheen on her, all right. And she likes men to acknowledge it. And – be warned, subdeacon – she likes a challenge. But—' Father Ronan pressed his lips together as though preventing his thought from becoming speech. At last he said, 'She's a law to herself, our Gunnvor. I did suggest I could look after her, a few years back when her father died, but she's not such a fool as I am.' He pulled out a bit of well-worn leather and started polishing the sword-blade. 'Her father was one of Hakon Toad's house-carls. Came over from Norway to join the Summer Army as a stripling, thirty years since. Hoarded a fair fortune.' He paused. Wulfgar waited, his hands gripping each other. At last the priest went on, 'Hard man, Bolli was, with just the one soft spot. She was his only child. He adored her. So did Hakon. His pearl of great price, our old Jarl called her.'

'No,' Wulfgar said.

'No?'

'She's not a pearl. She's more like – oh, I don't know, carnelian. Or jasper. Something streaked with dark red, with fire—'

Father Ronan gave him a sharp look. 'Easy, lad. That's as may be. Anyway, Bolli died, oh, five, six, years ago?' He eased his blade back into the fleece of its scabbard. 'So how does a lass that age, with not a soul to call kin this side of the North Sea, hang on to her father's fortune?'

Wulfgar's mind blanked.

'She doesn't,' he said.

The baby mewed and squawked, and he shifted it to the other arm.

'*She* did. You might have thought she looked like a doe-faun among wolves back there in the ale-house, but don't be fooled. Sharpest teeth in the pack.' There was a note of sadness there that Wulfgar had not heard from him before. 'Her father bequeathed her into Hakon's protection, and the Toad was only too happy to oblige. He may be in his grave, too, now but he throws a long shadow. And Ketil would like to pick up what his brother had to let drop, but she's not so sure. Not so sure at all. You've seen his temper.'

'You're saying Hakon never married her?' Wulfgar felt as though the earth had shuddered beneath him. That exquisite, fastidious woman had been kept by a man known as the Toad?

Father Ronan snorted. 'She didn't marry him, you mean.' He rubbed his hands together. 'Cold out here, isn't it? Don't mind me. Cat's-Eyes has the right to use all the weapons God gives her, God knows. But these things have a way of turning in the hand, to bite the wielder, not the foe. That's all.' He cocked his head and frowned eastwards. 'I hope that's Thorvald. I've had enough surprises for one day.'

It was. Punctual to his time, the moon in the east just beginning to lift free of the reeds, he was leading a mule, burdened by what turned out to be three spades and a couple of digging sticks bundled up in sacking, and a lantern. As he came through the gap in the thorn-hedge, the little girl left her mother's skirts for the first time and hurtled towards him with shouts of 'Dadda! Dadda!' He dropped the bridle and scooped her up just as she was about to go headlong – and then he pivoted on his heel, nearly overbalancing in his turn, to stare up the slope.

Then they all heard it: the thud of hoof-beats, coming from the darkening west.

Wulfgar scrambled awkwardly to his feet, the increasingly restless baby under one arm. Ednoth scrambled for his sword while Father Ronan hefted his own newly whetted blade. For a long moment it was sickeningly reminiscent of Offchurch.

'One horse only,' Ronan said, after a moment.

Ednoth, alert now, nodded.

The galloping horse came into view, a dark shadow in the dusk. Wulfgar heard Ronan's blade loosening in its scabbard.

And then they breathed again. It was Gunnvor Cat's-Eyes, almost kneeling on her saddle, riding her grey mare headlong down the track. She swung herself down before the horse had skidded to a halt and stood there looking at them, holding the snorting mare by the bridle.

'I should have known. I should have known.' Wulfgar, still queasy with nerves, looked behind her for the signs of pursuit. 'Is Eirik close behind you?'

She wasn't even out of breath.

'No one's after me.' She stifled a laugh. 'Not like that, anyroad. I didn't want to miss the fun, that's all. Or have to be poking about in the fen after you, in the dark.' Now she wrestled with the buckles of her saddle. Wulfgar noticed she'd taken those little bells off the harness. 'I've been hearing all about you from Toli. *Ulfgeir the Mysterious.* You are a deep one, aren't you?'

Their eyes met, and then hers dropped to the baby in his arms.

'Yours?'

He thought he heard mockery in her voice.

'Mine,' Leoba said firmly, relieving Wulfgar of him and tucking him back into that fold of her outer dress.

Wulfgar took a step or two closer to Gunnvor.

'What did Toli Silkbeard say about me?' He badly needed to know.

She lowered the saddle onto the ground and looped her mare's reins to a post before replying. 'He said, "My, what soft hands the man has".'

Their eyes met and he saw her mouth twitch.

He recoiled, stung. 'They're not that soft!' He turned them palm upwards, offered them to her. 'Look, I've got calluses from playing my harp.'

She reached out a hand and stroked across his fingertips and over his palm with unexpected gentleness. 'So you have.'

'Why did you come after us?' he said. His palm tingled, the nerves set on fire.

She pulled a silver pin from her hair and plunged it back in to recapture an errant braid.

'I don't like Eirik the Spider, and I despise his master. I'd like to see them bested.' Her face was alight with mischief suddenly. 'And I do like a gamble. Though I must say –' and her eyes ranged from Wulfgar to Father Ronan to Ednoth and back to Wulfgar '– I usually prefer better odds.'

'Mind your manners, lass.' Father Ronan's gaze was still directed up the track. 'You're sure you've not been followed? It was daft of you to come straight here.'

Her face turned scornful.

'They'd just broached a kilderkin of southern wine. They'll not be budging, not in the dark.'

Thorvald was holding his little girl by the hand. 'We'll have to go by foot across the causeway. We can't chance the horses – too heavy, too much noise. When we get back, we'll be six, and the two bairns, four horses and the mule. The bairns can go in the mule's panniers.'

'How will you keep their mouths shut?' Gunnvor asked.

Leoba took the little girl's other hand and pulled her gently away from her father. To Gunnvor's question, she said, 'Enough honey beer and they'll keep quiet, never you mind.' She looked heavenwards for a moment, then took a deep breath. 'We never thought we'd see this day come. We'd been wanting to flit for so long. Tor and me. We'd been talking and talking about how our holy man might get us free, and no word came from your Bishop. And then when we heard yon man was coming back we thought we'd left it too late—'

Thorvald made a chopping gesture with his hand.

'Have you not told them?' Leoba asked him. 'You're a fool, Tor.'

'What man?' Father Ronan's voice was full of weariness.

'Don't listen to the woman, Father,' Thorvald said, 'she doesn't know what she's about. Never can hold her tongue.'

Father Ronan ignored him. He spoke urgently now to Leoba.

'What man? What is he not telling us?'

Wulfgar thought he knew, and said, 'Orm Ormsson.'

But Leoba shook her head. She bent down and hoisted up the little girl, settling her against her left hip like something very precious, a shield, a harp. She spoke into the child's hair.

'No, no, I know *him*. Everyone knows *him*. This was a southron. A stranger from the English lands. Spoke like *you*,' she said to Wulfgar, suddenly. 'Came very courteous last Yuletide, talked to Eirik's wife. Word was, he said, there might be a great treasure of the Christians somewhere about her land. Something no use to her but for which his master would pay. She said she had to think about it. He said he would be back.'

'And who is he? Who's his master?' Wulfgar found his hackles were prickling. There was a long pause, filled with the crying of lambs.

'His master, I don't know,' she said, 'but I heard *his* name, or the name he went by.'

Wulfgar waited on her words, terribly afraid of what he might be going to hear.

'He called himself Garmund. Garmund Polecat.'

Wulfgar bit his tongue.

Ednoth swung round, swearing violently, flinging the bridle he'd been holding to the ground.

'You *fool*, woman.' Thorvald said. Even in the near-darkness the fury was visible on his face.

Leoba buried her face briefly in the child's wispy hair. Then she looked up at him and said passionately, 'Word gets out, Tor. Everyone in the island knew he had come, and why. Folk have been gabbing, even if none else but you knows right where our saint lies. You know they have.'

Wulfgar knew, even if Thorvald was claiming not to. *When is a dead man a better bargain than a live one?* Others beside Orm Ormsson could guess the answer to that riddle. His temple had started throbbing again as though Garmund's boot had only just made contact.

'What? Did you think we wouldn't come to Bardney if we foresaw trouble?' he said to Thorvald. 'Would we have come this far if that was the case?' Yes, and probably not, he answered himself, silently. And, sixteen, was it, or seventeen, men Garmund had with him at Offchurch? Mounted and armed.

'But why should we let this fret at us?' Gunnvor asked. 'He isn't here now, is he?'

At that, Leoba and Wulfgar both began to speak. She stopped at once and looked at him.

Sighing, he said, 'We met him on the road, with a big armed band. Coming up from the south. And, yes, I'd guess coming here, though I don't know how quickly so large a gang would be travelling. I've cause to think he's King Edward's man.'

Wulfgar looked at Leoba then.

'They were expected soon,' she said. 'Today, maybe. Maybe there now.'

'They don't know where the saint lies,' Thorvald said. 'Only I know that for sure. But the bone-garth's not so great that they won't find him in the end.'

CHAPTER TWENTY-ONE

Thorvald told them to keep their mouths shut while they crossed the marsh.

'Sound travels far in fen. And there are always a few folk around at night this time of year, netting for eels and the like. A man in a boat could get back to Bardney and rouse the hunt and we'd never know till they were on us. Follow me, tread where I tread, never you leave the causeway.'

He had gained confidence, now that the time had come to be doing. He handed out the tools, passing them into groping hands. The last glimmer of the daylight had left the western sky and the bats were hunting over the reeds.

They'd never have found their way through the marshes without a man who'd grown up treading those wetlands. For all that, Thorvald took them slowly, pondering every few moments.

'How do you know the way?' Ednoth asked him. 'Especially in the dark?'

He paused and pointed.

'There are markers. See?'

Willow wands, no more than waist-height, staked into the causeway, slender and hard to see, some fallen, many of the others sprouting new growth.

'I need to come by and make new ones,' he said. Then he laughed. 'Someone else's business now, I reckon.'

The causeway itself was little more than packed reed bundles, added to through life after life of men. With each step Wulfgar found his feet sinking and the water welling up around, and into, his shoes; he had kept them well-greased but long before they got to the far side he was sodden up to the knees and stinking. In some parts the way was more mud than reed, a mud that sucked hungrily at their feet, splashing and squelching. At certain points on the track, Wulfgar thought they might as well throw caution to the wind and shout, 'Eirik, the thieves are on their way!' But Eirik was in Lincoln, he hoped, and prayed.

The rising moon, low and gibbous in the eastern sky, was giving just enough light to cast shadows. More shadows moved to the left and right, dazzling dark and flashes of silver, and splashes not made by men. The hair was prickling on the back of Wulfgar's neck, but no one else showed any sign of being afraid. So he told himself it was otters, or beavers, or merely moorhens, and kept on plodding, dogged in Father Ronan's wake. Muscles he thought he'd tamed with a week on horseback were waking up and turning vicious. Neither land nor water: this was no place for men.

They had no idea how long it was taking, but the moon was already high when at last, almost too slowly to be noticed, the ground began to slope upwards and to dry out. The causeway went on rising until there was a drop the height of a man either side, down into the marsh below. Wulfgar became aware of dim massive shapes ahead of them, and his nostrils prickled at new scents, not bog and rot now but smoke and midden. Thorvald had stopped, and now he held out his arms to draw them into a tight little group.

'We're at the outer bank,' he breathed. 'But we can't enter here – we'd need to go too nigh the main door of the hall, and past the kitchen. We need to go right round.' His arm described an arc. 'Don't fall in the dyke,' and he turned and moved on in the direction he'd indicated.

The mood was changing, being so close. Wulfgar's heart buzzed in his breast to think of the saint only yards away. Surely he must be on their side, having let them come this far unscathed. St Oswald wanted to be delivered. The moon was on their right now, blocked by the great earth ditch and bank that curved ahead to the north and east, and they followed its line. Out of the moonlight they were invisible, even to each other. Thorvald stepped out briskly, too fast for Wulfgar over the tussocky ground and he kept stumbling.

Ronan grabbed his elbow. 'All right?' he breathed.

Wulfgar nodded, forgetting the priest couldn't see the gesture, and nearly walked into Thorvald, who'd stopped again. The reeve pressed Wulfgar's shoulder, meaning for him and the others to squat down in the lee of the bank, and spoke under his breath. 'Coming this way, from the north, we come through the orchard and then into the old bone-garth of the monastery. Tread carefully there, it's full of haunts. After-gangers. Souls of the unchristened dead. We've all seen things.'

'But we have to go there?' Ednoth sounded jumpy.

Thorvald's shrug was audible. 'That's where the saint lies.'

Wulfgar's hand groped after the Bishop's ring for comfort.

'I know where my grandfather said he is,' the reeve went on, 'but it's hard by the wall of the old kirk, and inside the old kirk is where they'll all be tonight. If your man, your King's man, is here, that's where he'll be.'

Wulfgar nodded, digesting his warning, resisting the urge to say *Not my King*. Not his man, either. But Wulfgar's father's son, for all that. My half-brother, he thought, and one day I'll have to face up to the truth of that. He shivered.

Thorvald gestured that it was safe for them to go on.

There was a way over the ditch and through the bank, a sudden powerful whiff of pig, and then they were among the silvery apple trees. The night was heavy with the scent of new blossom. Dry twigs cracked under their feet and they slowed, easing their feet to the ground.

Gunnvor, her skirts kilted around her knees, moved quickest and quietest, and the others caught up to find Thorvald exchanging urgent whispers with her at the gate.

The moon sent his angled pale beams across the rough ground beyond. Wulfgar could see the remains of crosses, both stone and wood, the latter half-rotted, most of them slanting where grave-fill had slumped and no one had cared in thirty years to pull them straight again. Beyond loomed the dark bulk of the church.

Leicester's battered cathedral was still holy ground, thought Wulfgar.

Lincoln's church was gone beyond recall.

And here, at Bardney?

The great minster stood, walled and roofed yet, and the row of small arched windows along the north wall, just below the roof line, flickered with a deceptively friendly light. So it must have looked when the Mercians' Lord came here as a boy; when St

Oswald lay wrapped in damask and gold behind the high altar, the goal of pilgrims in their thousands; when Thorvald's kin were honoured minster-men. Wulfgar half-thought to hear the strains of the *Nunc dimittis* from the windows, but instead the fitful wind brought the faint sound of men's voices, punctuated by the odd burst of raucous laughter.

His jaw tightened. It was all too easy to credit that Garmund's men had overtaken them, somewhere on the road, when their attention had been elsewhere.

St Oswald couldn't choose Garmund and Edward over the Lady and me, could he? he wondered. *What can the West Saxons offer him that we can't?*

The answers came in on the wind. *Security. Power. Peace.*

Oh Lord, he thought in desperation, *now lettest thou thy servant depart in peace . . .*

Ednoth tugged at his sleeve. The other two were already following Thorvald, picking their way gingerly between the dip and hummocks of the graves. Wulfgar followed, carefully treading between the crosses and stones. The grass grew wild and untended, but there were little worn paths through the grass, and at the foot of some of the crosses he saw little cups and pots, offerings to the dead, their liquid contents gleaming in the moonlight.

He was very cautious where he put his feet.

Thorvald led them to a spot in the angle where the wide nave abutted the narrower chancel. The little windows were a good twelve feet above their heads, but they hunched away from them all the same. Out in the churchyard the cheerful sounds from the hall could be clearly heard but here up against the wall they were muffled.

Ronan took Wulfgar's arm and pointed down the length of the nave wall.

'No door on this side,' he muttered. 'Be thankful for small mercies.'

Thorvald had hunkered down in the corner and the others gathered round him.

'Here, my grandfa' always said. No more nor two paces from the wall.'

They looked down at the grass. If Thorvald was right, they were standing on the very spot. Wulfgar stepped back, nervous of sacrilege, and then smiled at his scruples. St Oswald was hardly going to mind an intruder, not now, not after thirty years of neglect. He felt a sudden thrill of confidence, hardly dampened by his awareness of so many enemies separated from them by only a couple of feet of rubble, lime and rough-cast.

'Give me the lantern,' Wulfgar whispered.

Thorvald passed it across and he opened its door a crack, just enough to let a yellow sliver of light gutter out, hardly bright enough to match the moonlight. He let the glimmer of light play over the grass and thought he could indeed make out a hollow. The spring grass was still short: another couple of weeks and their task would have been much harder. He closed the lantern and looked up to see Ronan nodding.

'Start at each end?' Ronan asked. 'He shouldn't be down too deep. He was buried in a hurry, remember.'

Wulfgar wasn't likely to forget.

Gunnvor was already squatting at one end and levering up squares of turf with her belt-knife, clearing the ground for Thorvald's spade. Ednoth and Ronan were picking up the other spades.

Wulfgar was left with a digging stick, and the middle. He tore the grass away with his hands before levering up clods of earth. Once they got down below the grass roots the earth was loose, soft, free of stones. They worked in silence, other than the scrape and thud of digging. The wind was picking up, and suddenly it gusted full in their faces, with a sharp scent of the far-distant sea. Wulfgar had a sudden vision of the same place, of standing sheltered as he was now by the comforting wall of the church, but instead of moonlight the grave-yard was lit by an orange glow that sent the shadows leaping. From somewhere near at hand there came the crackle of burning thatch, and screaming, and even nearer there was the same sound he could hear now, the urgent scrape of a spade . . . He blinked and shivered, breathed deeply, and brought himself back to the work in hand.

They were well hidden by the north-east angle of the nave, and slowly they began to relax. The piles of earth grew, with Ednoth and Gunnvor wielding their tools most vigorously.

'Slow down,' Wulfgar hissed. 'We don't want to do any damage.'

Thorvald had stopped digging; he was standing upright a few feet away, looking this way and that. Wulfgar caught the repeated silver glint of moonlight in his eyes as his head moved.

Gunnvor snorted.

Wulfgar could almost hear her rolling her eyes, but she did as he had asked.

He put his digging stick to one side and started using his hands. His soft hands.

Worms wriggled away from his probing fingers. He was elbow deep now, and he wriggled round to lie on his belly, the easier to reach into the hole. But a clink from the iron edging of one of the spades had him scrambling to his feet and grabbing for the lantern.

'It might be just a stone,' Ednoth said.

'Not many stones in this soil.' Ronan, on his knees, reached down and pulled out a massive, earth-encrusted lump. He gave it a shake, and then began pulling the clods of soil away with his fingers.

Wulfgar angled the lantern, breathing down the priest's neck. His ribs felt painfully tight. Beneath the dirt, patches of smooth surface began to appear, brown in the candlelight.

A skull.

And Wulfgar sagged with disappointment, turning away to find Gunnvor frowning at him.

'Not the saint,' he said. 'Not his head, it can't be. His head shouldn't be here. It ought to be in Chester-le-Street.'

'Christians. You're all crazy,' Gunnvor said.

'But St Oswald was buried in a grave, wasn't he?' Ednoth asked.

Wulfgar just stared at him.

'I mean, there was somebody already in it,' Ednoth continued. 'It was somebody's grave. Perhaps we've found the somebody?' And he turned back to the pit.

Wulfgar set the lantern down and followed.

Ednoth was right. The saint had not been alone and forsaken, the last thirty years. He had been given refuge by this nameless brother of Bardney. For all he knew their bones were irretrievably mixed together, but better surely to take this unknown man too rather than to leave a toe-bone of the saint behind.

A surge of gratitude to St Oswald's unknown host drove out Wulfgar's disappointment and he began to scrabble in the dirt again with greater zeal. There were more bones coming up now. Thorvald had brought a couple of sacks and Wulfgar scooped up hands full of dirt and ran his fingers through them, feeling for the smallest bones, before putting all his discoveries into the sack.

Then, leaning back into the hole and reaching for the next wormy handful, his fingertips encountered a new sensation. Something flat and softish, but with a different softness from the soil. Friable, damp, yet splintery. A surface rough and smooth at once.

'Give me the lantern,' he said again. He tilted its feeble light into the hole, but there was nothing to see. He reached in again, head and shoulders in the hole, stretching his arms to their limits.

The surface extended to left and right. He groped for an edge. The others had stopped digging. He could feel that they were watching him, although he must have been all but invisible. He tried to ignore them, closed his ears to the sounds of the night and let his fingers make sense of what he was feeling.

St Oswald, are you there? Speak to me.

'It's wood. I think it's a box. It feels rotten. We won't get it out in one piece.' He struggled back out of the hole and let Ronan and Ednoth move in.

'Be careful,' he said in agony. They were clearing the earth of the top of the box, then digging down either side of it. There were still more bones coming up and Wulfgar gathered what he could.

'Get your spade underneath,' Ronan said to Ednoth.

Wulfgar stood up again, keeping out of the way of their spades, and held the lantern high.

'Lever,' he went on. '*Gently!*' But too late. With a crack that split the night, the box shattered in a fountain of mud and splinters. They froze.

'Close the light,' Thorvald hissed. Wulfgar swung the little door shut. Was it his imagination, or had the hubbub from the hall fallen quiet? It was a while since he'd remembered to listen for it.

His heart clattered in his chest, loud enough to alert the dead around them. They waited a long, long time.

Nothing.

Wulfgar dropped to his knees and started reaching in after the bits of wood from the grave. No one else moved. There were four or five large fragments, flat pieces of plank. Glancing around, he opened the lantern again. The candle had guttered down almost to nothing but it flared again then, enough for him to make out that, scored into the rotten mud-clotted boards, there had been runes and haloed faces. He couldn't read the words or name the saints; the wood crumbled away even as he held it, but he had seen enough.

'It's him,' he said, his breath tight. He was sure of it, as sure as though the saint had reached up and grasped him by the hand.

The lantern died.

'Come on,' Thorvald said, 'let's get out of here.'

Wulfgar scooped up a precious armful of bone, wood and soil and shovelled them all together into the sack. Ronan and Gunnvor joined in his trawling through the dirt, searching for more bones.

They were all working frantically now, even Thorvald, who had overcome his anxiety enough at least to get down on his knees and help.

Then Wulfgar froze.

As Ednoth reached past him, Thorvald grabbed his arm.

'Did you hear that?'

They all stopped then. Thorvald flattened himself into the grass. Wulfgar found himself immobilised by terror, and Gunnvor had to drag him back against the wall, into the corner made by the nave meeting the chancel. The long, swinging yellow light of a lantern, not theirs, was coming from beyond the west end of the church, sending predatory shadows across the grass. Suddenly the corners of the churchyard were full of threatening movement.

They've got us surrounded, he thought, but then realised he could only hear two voices, dim over the rushing of the blood in his ears.

The first voice said something, but he missed what.

'We'll come back in daylight,' said the second voice.

Garmund.

As at Offchurch, Wulfgar would have known him anywhere. He was no more than thirty feet away and voices carried on the cool night air.

'But I just want to get an idea of the lie of the land. Are you sure he's here?'

'Here, if anywhere,' came the answer.

To Wulfgar's surprise, the other voice, clear now, was female. She had the flat, deliberate vowels of north of Humber. She gave a little barking cough, like a sheep's cough.

'You can't give me a better idea?' Garmund asked. 'It's a big area, a lot of graves.'

'It's here Bardney folk say is haunted.' Wulfgar could hear the shrug in her voice. 'I know nowt about all this myself. And I still don't see why you need a particular set of old bones. One dead man's much like another, surely. If they're not your kin.'

'Not this one.' Garmund's voice was smooth, soothing. 'My masters will pay well, very well, if I can bring them the bones, and proof. Without proof, I don't know how much more I can promise you.'

'Well, you're welcome to look. You'll have to pay me for the looking, mind. And I want it done and filled in before any word gets back to my man. I'll not have him knowing about this.'

It's the Spider's wife, thought Wulfgar. It has to be.

The light started moving again. They were coming around the north-west corner of the church, into the burial ground. They must have been looking around them; the light flung this way and that. Suddenly it darted up along the side of the nave. Wulfgar could see Father Ronan crouched in the grave, back-lit. He closed his eyes and waited for the end.

Her voice came again, pettish of a sudden.

'It's damp out here.'

'Just a moment,' Garmund said 'What's that?'

'No. No good you making my fortune if I catch my death first.'

'Let me take you back inside, then.'

Wulfgar opened his eyes again. But the light was still there, sending the shadows fleeing. Garmund wasn't to be distracted so easily. At last, though, it dwindled and vanished.

A pig snuffled and grunted from somewhere on the far side of the churchyard.

'May I have my hand back?' Gunnvor's whisper was amused. Wulfgar hadn't even realised he had grabbed it. The reflection of two tiny moons danced in her eyes.

'Sorry.'

He got back down on his knees.

'Have we got everything?' Father Ronan asked.

'I think so,' Wulfgar said, breathing deeply. 'Should we back-fill the grave?' He reached after a spade.

'*No!*' Thorvald sounded in agony. 'Don't you understand? That was *her*. She'll kill us out of hand. She's as bad as he is.'

'We've got all we can,' Gunnvor said, very definite.

'How do you know?' Wulfgar said.

White teeth flashed in the moonlight.

242

'See in the dark, can't I? They don't call me Cat's-Eyes for nothing. Let's pack it up and go.'

When they had sorted out their booty, it came to three loads of heavy damp sacking, full of soil, and flaking wood, and bones. Wulfgar took one, and Father Ronan and Ednoth shouldered the others. Wulfgar worried aloud about the tools and lantern but Thorvald hissed to leave them.

He was halfway across the graveyard. Wulfgar was sick and dizzy with relief; he still couldn't believe they'd got away with it.

Fast-moving clouds were running like wolf-packs over the face of the waning moon. It took them what felt like a long time to stumble over the graves and through the wildly tilting crosses of the churchyard, and then the densely growing apple trees. Shadows moved in corners. All the tales Wulfgar had ever heard of the creatures, dead and alive, that haunted barrow-fields and bone-yards were coming back to haunt him now. He tripped and stumbled half a dozen times before they achieved the outer bank, but he held on to his share of the saint somehow. Ronan and Ednoth were a dozen paces ahead of him, muttering about something in anxious voices. In an effort to drive away his fears, Wulfgar forced himself to think about the reception he would get in Gloucester, of the joy on the Lady's face, of the songs that could be made to celebrate this moment.

CHAPTER TWENTY-TWO

There was no warning. The onslaught seemed to come from all sides at once.

In the dark, Wulfgar couldn't see how many they were. He stood there on the causeway like a stock of wood, dumb and panicking. Father Ronan and Ednoth had let their bundles fall: he could see they had their swords out and were fighting back to back. Wulfgar couldn't see Thorvald anywhere. Someone barged into him and he caught the glint of moonlight on a knife blade, but he lost his footing and, still hugging his precious sack, he half-slid, half-fell six feet down the side of the causeway to land rump-first in mud and shallow water. He looked up to see shadows and grappling figures above him. *Who were they?* It was all still strangely silent apart from the clash of blades, the thump of blows, the odd grunt and gasp for breath.

Then there was someone slithering down next to him, hissing, 'Stand up and put that sack down.'

He clutched his bundle to him for dear life.

'*Drop it!*'

Strong hands were pulling at it.

He fought for a frantic moment, before he realised they belonged to Gunnvor. Far too slowly, he did as he was told. As he stood again, he felt her move close to him, almost within the folds of his cloak. Was she afraid? Did she expect him to protect her? He could smell that aura of spices she always seemed to carry with her. He felt a sudden tugging at his waist, and then her warm, dry hand grabbed his and pushed something into it. His nerveless fingers recognised the hilt of his own belt-knife.

'Follow me. Climb. Now.'

He hauled himself after her up the muddy slope. Now he could see Ronan, further along the causeway, black against the moon-bright clouds, fighting two knife-wielding men at once – fighting far too competently for a priest, and Wulfgar, distracted, wondered where and how he had come by his sword-skills.

Then he turned, jumping at a grunt, and realised Ednoth was only feet from them, hard-pressed, being driven back towards them by a half-glimpsed assailant with a long knife in each hand. The lad swung his sword with great force, but even Wulfgar could see there was more power than finesse in his use of it, and he was gasping for breath, great ragged gulps of air. Ednoth had finally got the adventure he craved, and it looked as though it might well kill him.

Oh, Queen of Heaven, Wulfgar thought desperately, what do I do now? I've a knife in my hand and a friend in desperate need.

But, even as Wulfgar dithered at his prayers, Gunnvor launched herself at Ednoth's assailant from behind, her blade in her right hand. Wulfgar saw her twine her fingers in his hair and yank his head back. He turned away in horror.

As he turned he stumbled over another body hunched at his feet. Numb, he bent to heave it over, convinced it would be Thorvald. Or Garmund, heaven help him. But it was a face Wulfgar had never seen before, thin, long-nosed, clean-shaven. There was dark blood everywhere, sticky and strong-smelling, on the man's chest, on Wulfgar's hands now. Who had killed him?

Ednoth and Gunnvor were running down to join Ronan.

Where *was* Thorvald? And then he heard a shout.

He looked around wildly.

It came again, from the marsh below the far side of the causeway.

Wulfgar ran across.

Thorvald and another man were grappling frantically. The stranger had a long knife. Thorvald was showing astonishing strength for such a slight man, holding the stranger's wrists high above his head. He looked to be unarmed.

Thorvald had more to fight for than any of them. But he was not winning. Wulfgar could see his feet skidding under him as he was being forced away from the drier ground. He flung himself headlong down the slope, heedless of the risk of impaling himself on the blade he was still holding.

Thorvald saw him.

'Wulfgar!' he yelled.

But the moment's inattention was enough. The stranger kicked out at Thorvald's kneecap and his leg betrayed him, crumpling him backwards into the mud, his opponent on top of him. And the stranger shouted, 'Men of Wessex, to me! To me!'

Wulfgar half-heard the words but they made no sense to him in his feverish state. He hurled himself across the half-a-dozen paces of ground and jabbed his knife down into the stranger's back.

It went in, deep, astonishingly easy. He heaved it out and stabbed once more. This time it stuck. He had to jerk it out, and then he stabbed again, over and over and over. He kept seeing Leoba's strained young face, and that of her tiny, helpless baby.

'Wulfgar. *Wuffa*.' A hand fastened on his shoulder. 'You can stop now.'

The voice came from very far away. It took a while for the sense to filter through into his mind. When it did he went cold. The hand holding the knife loosened its grip as all his sinews disobeyed him. He staggered a few paces away from the body of the man he had been butchering, fell to his knees, and was sick. But, on another plane, he was clear, cold and hard as the moon now sailing free above. This is not the time, that part of him said. It was that part which won. He struggled to his feet and went back to where Ronan was turning the man over.

That answered his first question.

It was not Garmund.

'Is he dead?' And a third question he hardly dared ask. 'Was he a West Saxon?'

'Oh, yes.' Father Ronan's tone was one of bleak satisfaction. 'And a very dead one at that. Well done, Wulfgar.'

Wulfgar crossed himself slowly. He thought, I am a man of the cloister. Dealing death is not my profession. I have vowed never to hunt animals, not so much as a bird, and now I have killed a fellow human being, the pinnacle of God's creation. He looked in disbelief at his belt-knife where it lay in the mud, and at his bloody hands.

'Shit, shit, shit,' said Father Ronan, looking at Thorvald. The little reeve lay curled on his side. Ronan moved across and turned him over, gentle as a mother. The remorseless moonlight showed gouts of blood black across his chest and, more ominous, more blood oozing from the corner of his mouth.

'Surely we shouldn't move him,' Wulfgar said.

'But what choice do we have?' Ronan looked up, back in the direction of Bardney. 'We didn't kill them all. I missed my stroke, as luck would have it, and my man escaped. And from what you said earlier, there'll be plenty more to come.'

'Sixteen, when we met Garmund at Offchurch.'

Ronan crossed himself. 'And we've only dealt with four. And there will be Bardney men to reinforce them. What do we do? Leave him to die? Or take him and chance it?'

Put like that there was no choice. Wulfgar helped Ronan cradle Thorvald and supported the priest as he staggered to his feet.

'Can you manage?'

'Ach, he's no more burden than an empty basket.'

There was a slithering from behind. They both jumped out of their skin. But it was only Ednoth, sliding down the bank.

'Put your sword back in its sheath,' Father Ronan said, 'before you do yourself some damage.'

'There are three men dead up there! I killed one, and Gunnvor—' Slowly he took in the tableau in front of him. 'Oh.'

Wulfgar could see Gunnvor's dark outline against the moonlight on the bank above them. There was a moment's silence.

'Well done, lad,' Father Ronan said. 'No point in waiting for their friends, though. The man I let get by me will be raising the cry by now. Let's see if we can find our way across that stinking marsh without a guide. Pick up your knife, Wuffa.'

Wulfgar looked at it in revulsion.

'I don't want it any longer.'

'That's as may be. But you might need it.'

They let Gunnvor go first. She was the lightest on her feet and still claiming to be able to see in the dark. Ronan followed with Thorvald across his shoulders. Wulfgar squelched along a pace or two behind him. He had two sacks of bones to carry now and he could feel the difference they made, his feet sinking far more deeply into the mud than they had on the way out.

Always assuming Gunnvor was bringing them the right road.

He was keeping at bay the truth of what he'd just done, bringing the power of every prayer he knew to bear on the limp body in Ronan's embrace. Thorvald looked unconscious, but every so often a deep rattling moan escaped him and more blood bubbled at his mouth. Ednoth brought up the rear, his sword back in its scabbard now to allow him to carry the third trophy-sack, turning often to look and listen along the near-invisible path behind.

It seemed that Gunnvor had been paying close attention when Wulfgar had asked Thorvald how he knew the way, for she brought them slow but sure-footed all the way back to the lambing pens. As she went, Wulfgar saw her pull up each of the willow staves and cast it aside.

She saw him watching her, and her teeth glinted in the moonlight. 'No point in helping our pursuers.'

Moonlight shivered and broke on the water. As they drew nearer, and the ground became drier under their feet, his thoughts were caught up less with thoughts of pursuit, more with the picture of Leoba, innocent ahead of them, waiting for her husband to come home.

Thorvald was still alive when they got back to the lambing pens. Ronan laid him down inside the thorn-hedge just as Leoba came out through the hut's low doorway. She took in the scene at a glance.

'He's dead.' Her voice was flat.

'Dying,' Ronan corrected her gently.

She came over and looked down at him for a moment, and then knelt. Just as she did so another great bubbling groan came out of him and a new rush of blood poured over his chin.

'Lung wound, then,' the girl said. 'He'll not have long.' She turned to Ronan. 'Will you see he goes like a Christian?'

'Has he been baptised?'

She shrugged and turned her head away.

Wulfgar couldn't bear it any longer. Pushing Ednoth out of the way, he got down on his knees the other side of Thorvald and picked up his arm, moving down to find his hand.

'Thorvald, don't move. Don't try to speak. But if you can, squeeze my hand.' The secretary looked intently at the dying man's face. Did he dream it, or had those thin, hard fingers fluttered butterfly-like in his? 'Thorvald, do you believe that God is Father, Son and Holy Ghost? Do you believe Christ died for you?' Wulfgar thought, I killed to save this man, and now his life is draining out before my eyes. I can't let his soul go, too.

Thorvald coughed once more, and even in the moonlight they could see how bright the blood was.

'Thorvald, if you can hear me, answer. Squeeze my hand, God damn it.'

And he did. No doubt about the pressure this time. Wulfgar's eyes blurred. He looked up at Ronan. 'He said yes. He said yes.'

Ronan had to bless the dying man with his left hand as his right hand was supporting Thorvald's head. He said rapidly, 'Thorvald. You died a hero in the service of your saint. The angels stand waiting, rejoicing with St Oswald, to lead you through the gates of paradise.' His voice was steady but Wulfgar could see there were tears running down his face.

Wulfgar pressed Thorvald's hand but this time there was no response.

'He's going,' he said.

'Then, Thorvald, I absolve you from all your sins by the powers vested in me, I absolve you in the name of Holy Peter, who guards those gates, who has the power to bind and loose.' The priest spat on his thumb and made the sign of the cross on Thorvald's forehead, his eyes, over his breast. As he was doing so a little guttural noise escaped from Thorvald's mouth. Then he went limp, his hand slipping from Wulfgar's.

Wulfgar bit hard on his lip.

When he looked up, he saw Gunnvor hunkered next to him.

'I tried to save him,' he said. 'I killed that other man to save him. I thought I had saved him.' He couldn't stop shaking.

'I know,' she said gently. She reached over to close the dead man's eyes and used the cuff of her sleeve to wipe away the blood from his mouth. 'Wulfgar, I know. Here.' She helped him to his feet, her hand steady below his elbow.

He thought of that moonlit vision he had had of her, back on the causeway, with those same strong, warm hands ready to yank back the head of a fellow human being and jab a knife-tip into his exposed throat.

The moon was low in the west now, occluded with dirty rags of cloud. With that, and with the chill and exhaustion that had come over them all, there was no going further until they had a few hours' sleep.

'We should be safe enough,' Ronan said out of the darkness. 'Safe till dawn, at least. We should sleep out here, though, where the first light will wake us.'

Wulfgar shivered at the mere thought of sleeping in the hut;

Garmund's men could catch them there like cornered rats. He sat down heavily next to his sacks of earth and bone. Ednoth sat down next to him and yawned luxuriously.

'I should clean my sword,' he said. There was a note of intense satisfaction in the boy's voice.

Four men dead back there, Wulfgar thought, and one here, and I'm the only one who seems to care. He put out a hand to grasp the rough, damp, lumpy bulk of the sack beside him. Thorvald died for these trophies, he thought. Are they conceivably worth that sacrifice? He put his head in his hands. He couldn't resolve these riddles.

'Wulfgar?'

He looked up. The dim bulk looming over him had to be Ronan.

'Wuffa,' the priest said, 'I'm sorry to ask anything more of you. If we can, we should sort out the bones now. We can rest until first light but then we have to be on our way at once. We can't load these sacks onto the horses, not as they are.'

Ronan was right. The sacks were sodden and the sacking itself was beginning to give way. Wulfgar squatted down beside the priest, only a few feet from Thorvald's body, and they started work once more. Wulfgar plunged in his hands, scooped up fistfuls of the dirt, rubbed his fingers through it, over and over again. He was reminded, in a strange, sideways fashion, of his mother making pastry. The repetitive action was deeply soothing.

'Do you remember?' he said to Ronan. 'Bede writes that the very soil from the spot where Oswald fell could cure the sick.'

Ronan paused for a moment, sitting back on his heels and knuckling his lower back.

'Faith, I do indeed,' he said, 'but Thorvald's not sick, lad. He's dead. Very, very dead.'

Leoba came out of the hut with a fresh sack, and when Wulfgar found any bones, however tiny, he put them into the new one. It seemed that none of them could sleep, but Gunnvor.

Ednoth, too, came to help. He didn't say anything but Wulfgar found some comfort in the way that he settled down to work at his side.

'We did well back there,' Ronan said. 'They weren't expecting us to be so well-armed, maybe. And they had surprise on their side. But I shouldn't have let that man get by me.'

'I killed a man,' Wulfgar said. It was all he could think about.

'You were trying to save Thorvald. But you know that, lad.' Ronan sat back on his heels and looked at him. 'I'll hear your confession when we get time.'

Wulfgar nodded his gratitude. The lump in his throat stopped him speaking.

Those bits of spongy carved wood went into the sack as well, and something else, a little plaque that felt like metal, that must have been scooped up with the coffin. There was some kind of embossed design on it and Wulfgar wanted to have a closer look but the night was too dark, the moon wrapped in ragged clouds and no paling yet in the eastern sky. They worked as fast as they could by starlight, using their fingers as much as their eyes.

'That's it.' Wulfgar stood and stretched. Ednoth picked up the sack and weighed it at arm's length.

'Much better,' he said.

'Can Fallow manage it?' Wulfgar asked him. 'I – I would like her to carry the bones, if she can.'

'She'll have to,' Ednoth said, and then, 'I'll put your other saddlebags up on Starlight, with mine, if you want. Spread the load a bit.'

It felt like a truce, and Wulfgar was glad.

The longest day of my life is over, he thought. I must go to sleep.

But his mind was racing, his thoughts a chaotic jumble of impressions and anxieties. He still couldn't really believe Garmund was here at Bardney. Even though Leoba had warned them. Even after Garmund's men had attacked them.

Offchurch, he thought. Now that might have been your own idea, Garmund Polecat. But not this. No, not Bardney. Not St Oswald. He could sense the long arm of King Edward in this.

How in the name of Heaven had they heard about the relics in Winchester?

Ale-house gossip, he guessed wearily. Like that mocking, red-headed trader who had drunk with them in the Wave-Serpent. He couldn't remember the man's name.

Garmund's never going to give up, he thought, even if he doesn't know it's me who's beaten him to the prize. Yet. Doesn't know yet.

If he learned *that* . . . Wulfgar shivered and pulled his cloak more closely around his shoulders, rolling down a long slope into sleep.

CHAPTER TWENTY-THREE

When he woke, after a brief and fitful doze, everyone else was asleep. The stars were fading and the waning moon was dropping in the west. *Uht,* he thought, like *Uhtsang,* the light before the true light. Like St John the Baptist . . . the light that shows the way to the sunrise . . . Where am I? Still half-asleep, he stretched, head aching, face stiff and every muscle protesting, and looked around, wondering what had woken him. Birdsong, perhaps.

Ednoth lay face down, his head on his arms and his arms on his scabbard. Leoba was curled around her children like a cat with kittens, her face grubby with old tear-stains. And last night's events came rushing back to him on a flood-tide of grief.

Father Ronan looked as if he had tried to keep watch through the night: he had sat up with his back against the wall of the hut but he, too, had nodded off. Wulfgar shook his head. The priest would have a stiff neck when he woke, in this damp breeze. He was covered, face and hands and tunic, in dried blood.

Wulfgar looked down at his own tunic then and shuddered in

horror. And the tightness on his face was more blood, caked and crumbly. He picked at his stubbly cheek and looked at his fingers in revulsion. Thorvald's blood on his hands, and the blood of the man he himself had killed, engrained in every faint crease and whorl of his hands. That none of it was his own proved small consolation.

Gunnvor, now – where *was* Gunnvor? It was quite light enough to see that there was no sign of her. And, as he looked around, he saw that the sack of bones, which had been by his head as he slept, had also vanished.

The shock hit like a drench of icy water. Aghast, he shot to his feet. Then he saw that her grey mare was still hobbled with the other horses. Gunnvor wouldn't have left her horse, surely. At the very least she couldn't have got far on foot. But – that must mean she had headed back through the marsh, back towards Bardney.

Some pre-arranged interview with horrible Eirik?

Were they even now haggling over the market price of the saint?

Finding it hard to breathe, he picked his way back down towards the fen-edge, trying to retrace their steps of the night before. The water was screened by thickets of gold-dusted goat-willow dotted about with rowan and alder, and there were wreaths of white mist rising from the reeds. A dauntless wren bobbed and sang on a willow branch, so close that he could see the lining of its beak, all pink and gold.

And there she was, crouched at the water's edge.

His panic subsided but he still felt an unreasoning anger as he walked down towards her. He wasn't stalking her on purpose but his footsteps must have been soundless because she didn't hear him, though the wren flew off. It was a chilly morning, but Gunnvor didn't look as though she was bothered by the cold.

She'd taken off her over-dresses, leaving them in a gaudy pile on the bank, and she was hunkered down at the water's edge wearing only her open-necked linen under-shift, kilted up to her thighs, with the sleeves pushed high above her elbows. She did the same thing over and over, twisting to reach for something, leaning forward to her hands in the water, then putting whatever she had been holding down to her right. Wulfgar frowned. There was something pale and gleaming in her hand. He could hear her singing under her breath.

The hairs rose on the back of his neck. Seeing her like that had a dream-like quality, but he had never dreamed in this kind of detail. Her forearms and throat were stained by the sun, but her upper arms and her thighs were white as ivory, her breasts round as apples, white as the flesh of the sour-sweet apples from his father's orchard . . .

He put a shaking hand to his forehead to find the skin damp. He felt dizzy, hot and confused in a way he'd long told himself he'd outgrown, that belonged to the muddle of adolescence. But she moved him so profoundly, this forthright, unpredictable woman.

I've always claimed the Lady has all my devotion, he thought. But, oh, Queen of Heaven, I'm coming to see that my love for her is hardly different from my dedication to You.

He swallowed painfully. Loving the Lady was so familiar, so safe, so hopeless. Here and now, by contrast, every beat of his thudding heart said *danger*. But he couldn't tear his eyes away. He had no idea how long he had been standing there. She was so very beautiful.

He realised with a sudden uprush of shame that he was spying on her. He pulled back. But she stood now, turning, bending forward. Her already diaphanous linen was splashed with water to distracting effect. Had she seen him, heard him breathing? She reached for the protection of her long green tunic, still singing softly in her throat. He pressed himself back into the scrubby goat-willows. The trees were barely coming into leaf, and she'd see him if she bothered to look through the reeds. But she was covered now, and, relieved and emboldened, he moved out into full view.

'Wuffa!' She didn't sound startled. Glad, if anything.

He stepped forward.

'What on earth are you doing?' he asked. 'You're all wet. You'll catch cold.'

'Come here,' she said. 'Let me wash your face.'

Still hardly knowing what he was doing, he went down to join her, and she dipped the cuff of her tunic in the water and scrubbed hard at his face. He could feel her breath on his cheek. When the dried blood got wet it smelled fresh again, and a wave of nausea heaved over him, making for an uneasy mixture of queasiness and desire. He asked again

'What have you been doing?' he asked again.

'Sorting your bones.'

'*What?*'

She looked very pleased with herself, almost girlish, and, for once, unguarded. She knelt again now, rinsing the blood out of her sleeve, but she turned her face up to him.

'Look. We must have found the right grave. There are two different people here.' She moved to one side and gestured at two piles of bones.

Frowning and fascinated, Wulfgar came closer to kneel at her side and have a better look.

'See? This person, *já?*' It was the pile topped by the skull. 'He didn't die so very long ago. Thirty years, did you say? That could be right. The joints even have some sinews still attached. And the bones are quite light in colour.' She offered him a femur.

He nodded, tight-lipped, but didn't touch it.

'Now these –' she moved on to the second pile and found the matching bone '– *these* are old. See? And the bones are dark brown, very smooth.'

'Polished,' Wulfgar said, his voice cracking as he reached for it. 'Venerated. Where did you learn so much about bones?' He thought of devoted hands for over two hundred years, caressing these bones, bearing them in procession, wrapping them in eastern silks; of the lips of pilgrims, abbots and kings, pressed to them, murmuring in prayer, whispering to them all their hopes and dreams and fears. If he hadn't already been kneeling he would have knelt then.

St Oswald, he thought, you are here, you are really here, in my hands. He felt the tears rising as he pressed his lips to the silky brown bone. Oh, my dear, dear Lord and Saint. Pray for the Lady, pray for all Mercia, oh, pray for us.

It hadn't taken a miracle to know the saint when they met him, only common sense. Gunnvor's common sense. The practical abilities of a woman, a heathen and a Dane. But perhaps that was the miracle.

Trying to mask his emotion, he asked, 'What about the fragments of the reliquary?'

'Those bits of old wood? Here. I didn't want them to get wet. They're so fragile already.'

Wulfgar nodded.

'We'd better get back. The others will be wondering where we are.' He started pulling bones from both piles with the aim of getting them into Gunnvor's sack. His hands were still shaking.

'You're taking the other one too?' she asked in surprise.

Wulfgar nodded again. 'He's guarded the saint for us for thirty years. The least we can do is thank him. I'll see he's reburied with all ceremony when we get him home.'

'I have more sacks,' she said. 'Keep them separate?'

They started sorting and packing. Gleaming ribs, the strange, flanged discs of vertebrae – so many ribs! so many vertebrae! – a pair of shapes like angel's wings that Wulfgar puzzled over until he realised they were the saint's hip-bones. The little lumpy bones that had made up his feet. It was a profoundly intimate process.

As they worked side by side in silence, Wulfgar felt an extraordinary sense of contentment stealing through him. He could have wished the moment to go on for ever.

But, all too soon, St Oswald had been reduced to a neat package, as long as a femur and wide as a hip-bone. He should be wrapped in finest white linen, Wulfgar thought, in silk as fine as moonbeams, in the softest lambswool worsted . . . That length of ragged sacking would have to do for the meantime.

The other, the Bardney monk, made for a bulkier, ungainly pile, his lower jaw still attached to the skull, his pelvis articulated. Wulfgar wrapped the fragments of frail wood in yet another piece of sacking; he longed to puzzle over their arcana but it would have to wait.

Gunnvor was kilting up her green skirt, but she paused just as they were bending to pick up their burdens and return up the bank.

'Wuffa?'

'Mmm?'

'Aren't you going to say thank you?'

'To the monk of Bardney?' He looked at the bulkier of the two sacks. 'We're taking him with us, aren't we? He must know how grateful we are. We'll bury him in the minster-yard—'

'Not to your bony friend there.' Her voice had grown acerbic. 'Thank you to me, I mean.'

He straightened at that, and flushed.

'You shouldn't have taken the relics off to wash them without asking me. You shouldn't—'

'What?' She looked up at him. Her eyes were bright, but that old mocking tone had come back into her voice.

His flush deepened.

'Never mind.' It was the memory of her body, the thin wet linen barely shielding her, so soft and white and vulnerable, and so close to the saint's bones. Too close. And singing, as well. It hadn't seemed right.

She looked down at the parcels. 'All this bother for a bit of charnel. Who was this Oswald, anyway, that you price him so highly?'

'Saint. Martyr. King.'

She shrugged. 'Words.'

He was silent for a moment. His heart was full of things he wanted to make clear to her. And what's my faith worth, he thought, if I can't even explain to this woman why St Oswald could be the saving of Mercia?

'I—' he gestured in frustration. 'Oh, it would be so much easier if I had my harp.'

She raised her eyebrows, and he thought for a wonderful moment that she was about to smile. Instead, glancing at the wet bank behind her, she settled down on her haunches.

'Go on. I'll imagine the harp.'

'Right. Yes.' Feeling wrong-footed, he cleared his throat. 'Well.

This is the one my uncle taught me. *Listen! Oswald the noble,*
Northumbria's king, was wise and worthy in wielding his kingdom . . .'
He started off down the well-trodden path, chanting the words at
first, but as the story drew him in he began to sing them properly,
his left hand beating time against his thigh:

> *'Hard to the heathen*   *hostile against him;*
> *Mild to his own folk,*   *merciful and fair;*
> *To orphans and widows*   *always a guardian.*
> *He first founded,*   *fair in God's eyes,*
> *Lindisfarne*   *loveliest of monasteries,*
> *Brought from Iona*   *the first Bishop,*
> *Aidan, Christ's darling . . .'*

The tale unfolded like a rich tapestry: battles the warp; miracles
the weft. He felt as though he were an actor in the tale, kneeling
with Oswald's still-heathen soldiery before the wooden cross the
saint had raised at Heavenfield . . . Victory after victory, and then
the turning of the tide, the last great battle against Penda of
Mercia . . .

> *Hateful heathen*   *hard oppressed him,*
> *Penda the pagan,*   *the promise-breaker.*
> *He perished at last*   *at Penda's hand.*
> *'God send salvation*   *to their souls,'*
> *Oswald the faultless*   *cried as he fell.*
> *Merciless Mercians*   *martyred the king,*
> *Hacked off his head*   *and his noble hands,*
> *Set them on high*   *as a horrible sign . . .*

He bit down hard on his lower lip and blinked furiously.

His body they buried   on the battlefield,
A nameless pit   the noble one received . . .

It was no good. His voice was wobbling too much to carry on.

'Sorry,' he said. 'Sorry.'

'But what happened next?' Her eyes were shining, and her lips were slightly parted.

He knuckled his eyes.

'His hearth-men rescued his head and his arms from Penda's scaffold and took them back. North of Humber. They're still there.'

She frowned.

'And it was the Mercians who killed him?'

'Penda, who killed him, was Mercia's last heathen king. It wasn't many years later that St Oswald's niece married a Christian king of Mercia. Penda's son, as it happened. She had her uncle's body exhumed from the battlefield and taken to Bardney. It's all in the song.' He looked down and saw the bags at his feet as though for the first time. 'And now he's here. In our care.' He felt the blood drain from his face, heard the ringing of distant bells in his ears. He stumbled.

'Careful, there.' Gunnvor was his side, supporting his elbow. 'You need to sit down . . .'

He nodded, still dizzy. 'Thank you,' he said at last, and in saying the words he found that he meant them with all his heart. 'Oh, Gunnvor. Thank you so much, for everything.'

Her eyes found his then, and for once there was no mockery in them.

'Wulfgar of Winchester, you are welcome,' she said, shaking her head. 'I've never met anyone like you.'

CHAPTER TWENTY-FOUR

They stood there in the pearly light, looking at each other. Wulfgar started to say something, but she held up her hand. He was almost glad; he was so far out of his depth.

But she wasn't looking at him any longer. Her head had jerked round, to look eastward, over the marsh.

Then he heard it, too. Too steady to be the splashing of water-birds. A rhythmic creak underlying it. They strained to hear, a brief moment that felt as though it was lasting for ever. Splash, and creak, and splash, and creak . . .

'It might just be night fishermen, going home,' he whispered.

'It *might*.' She was still listening. 'And then again—' She turned on her heel, and pelted back up towards the lambing hut.

Wulfgar, taken aback, waited a moment or two longer, long enough to see emerge from the mist two big, flat-bottomed punts of the sort that fowlers used, each poled by a man standing at the back, riding low in the water because they were laden with more men. Many more. The mist came down again, the spell was broken. He hurtled after her, all three sacks of bones and wood clutched in his arms.

By the time Wulfgar reached the thorn-hedge, he was yelling fit to crack his throat: 'Get out! Get out of the yard.'

Leoba had been swaddling her sleepy children; now she was stuffing them into a shallow, wide-mouthed pannier as if she were readying ducklings for market. Ronan grabbed the pannier from her and lashed it to the back of the mule before swinging round and drawing his sword. He slapped Ednoth on the shoulder and at once the two of them, blades out, were heading for the gap in the hedge, shouldering past Wulfgar. Gunnvor, who had headed straight for her grey mare, was vaulting onto her back and pulling the reins up short, wheeling the horse.

'Get on the mule,' Wulfgar shouted at Leoba.

She stared at him for a moment before hauling herself onto the mule's wooden saddle.

'Go! *Go!*'

There was shouting from the marsh. He looked round. The punts were grounding in the mud, men jumping out. They were running. More shouting.

'Come on, lad!' Ronan shouted. He and Ednoth were blocking the way up the slope, or trying to.

Wulfgar could see only one end to this story. He tried to think, his heart pounding so hard it shook all his ribs. What was really important here? No time to think things through.

'Go!' he shouted again at Leoba. 'Go, with the children!' And then, 'No, wait!' He grabbed the slim, bundled sack of the saint's smooth, ancient bones and thrust them up into Leoba's arms.

And Gunnvor was there on the other side, grabbing for the mule's bridle, ramming her heels into the grey mare's flanks.

'*Já*, we'll see you in the Wave-Serpent.'

Leoba had gone white, but she nodded, tucking the swaddled bulk of the relics into that useful fold of her dress as though it was another baby. Then she picked up her own reins and drummed the startled mule with her own heels, and the two women were away up the track.

Had their attackers seen them?

Wulfgar was still staring after them when his arms were grabbed from behind. Other men were disarming Ednoth and Ronan, with humiliating efficiency. Ten armed men in the enemy party, Wulfgar found himself tallying, against a priest, a sub-deacon, an untried boy. And Thorvald's body, lying unnoticed under the pile of brushwood some thoughtful person – Ronan, he thought, it will have been Ronan – had stacked to keep the foxes at bay.

Once they had been rounded up and put under guard, the other men started piling up their goods, stacking the saddlebags in the punts.

It was only then that Wulfgar realised: their orders have been changed since last night. This time, they must have been told not to hurt us. Or, not more than they can help.

Why not? he wondered, at a loss. Last night they meant to kill. And now they've got a grudge. We killed, how many, last night? Four?

His eyes flickered again to where Thorvald's body lay in the lee of the hedge. Why don't they just kill the rest of us? If it's the relics they're after, he thought, they must know we've got them.

But no. Once their attackers were confident they had everything that might be part of their baggage, the prisoners were rounded up and prodded towards the boats. Their hands weren't even tied.

And no one fought back, once they'd been disarmed. Even Ednoth could see they had been outnumbered.

Wulfgar had assumed their captors were southerners but their voices had Thorvald's accent, so broad Wulfgar could hardly follow their speech, such as it was. They didn't talk much. They had their orders, and they were sticking to them.

When everyone was aboard and their stuff was shipped, the punts rode even lower in the water. Wulfgar thought then, *of course*, they have to be Bardney men. How would West Saxon strangers find their way through this wilderness of reeds? The marsh was no cheerier a place in the growing day than it had been by moonlight.

For the first time he found himself wondering how old Ronan was. The priest's skin looked even greyer than the dawn light warranted and there were dark blotches beneath his eyes. As the boats creaked and splashed their way through the reeds, Wulfgar felt a growing sense of detachment. It was as though it were all happening to somebody else, someone he'd heard about in an old song.

They were all going to die, and soon.

But his own job was done.

Leoba was safe, and the children. And Gunnvor.

And St Oswald.

As safe as I could have made them, he thought sadly. But I would so have liked to know what happens next . . . His heartbeat reminded him of the pounding of the horse's hooves, thudding away up the track – they're *safe*, they're *safe*, they're *safe*. They must be, he told himself. They must have got away. Over and over, the same tune, keeping time with the soft liquid sound of the boat as it was poled through the shallow water.

The boats travelled far more quickly than Thorvald and Wulfgar and the others had the night before, squelching on foot through the dark. The earth banks and thatched roofs of Bardney were before them again all too soon, silhouetted against the rising sun. As soon as the prows of the punts sank into the mud of the bank, they were hustled out and up the path that led to the main door of the old church. The interior was dark, reeky. They were stopped just inside the door, their captors crowding in hard on their heels. The smoke was eye-watering.

A cackle broke the silence. A woman's laughter. Then, 'You mean to tell me, *this* is your band of warriors?' The laughter broke out again, ending in a fit of coughing.

'It can't be.' A man's voice, his accent West Saxon, sullen in disbelief. 'We were outnumbered. Armed men. Not – not *these*.'

Wulfgar could see more clearly now, in the dim glow of the banked central hearth, the only source of light other than the doorway and the high small windows. There was no sign of Garmund. A woman of forty or so, a shawl around her head and shoulders, was standing a few feet in front of them, with a man at her side. He was muddy, blood-stained, unshaven.

'The one that got away,' Father Ronan breathed in Wulfgar's ear. 'Damn him.'

The woman looked each of them up and down in turn. Her face was set in hard planes, though the beauty that had been there once was still visible in the well-modelled cheekbones and the long line of her neck. She turned to shout at someone at the back of the hall. 'Where's that southron? I want him.'

'Still out on the hunt, lady.' Another servant came forward, wiping her hands on her apron. 'He and his party went north, up the roadway.'

'Send after him. Keep these under guard until he gets here.' She pushed past them.

'Keep them in here, shall we?' Their guards sounded at a loss.

'Why not? Don't touch their kit. Don't touch them, unless they try to run. It's all to wait for *him*. That's what he said.'

So they waited.

Prickly with nerves at first, moment by moment expecting disaster, it was clear by the time the sun had moved round to shine into the doorway that this was going to be a long wait. At first the three of them were kept standing, huddled together, but by midday their four guards had relaxed enough to allow them to sit and doze, backs against the wall; to eat a little dry bread; to be taken one at a time outside to relieve themselves. If they tried to talk, though, there was a rough command and the butt-end of a spear thrust menacingly in their direction. But no one tried with any conviction. Ronan slumped against the wall, eyes closed. Ednoth, white-faced, twisted the leather strap of his now useless sword-belt, back and forth, over and over. The sunlight inched across the floor as though the whole building were a giant mass-dial, waiting for the hour of Garmund's return.

Wulfgar had all the time he wanted, now, to look around the inside of the Spider's hall. Smoke-darkened plaster, tiled floor. Chickens wandering in from the sunny courtyard. Woven hangings along the walls, telling alien tales, with unreadable figures in dull reds, blues and greens. Flies buzzing in the rafters. No fragment remaining of an altar, or a shrine, but scars in the tiles marked where they once had stood. Without those, would he have known it had ever been a church? He squinted at the space above the south door where he would once have expected to see the image of St Oswald.

And he was there. Wulfgar had to cup his hands around his eyes to block out the light, but when he did so he could make out two faded, painted figures: a king to the left, a bishop to the right. The king was armed with sword and shield, and at first he thought the bishop too was carrying a shield. But, no, it was a great platter.

And then Wulfgar remembered how Oswald had broken up the silver dish he was eating from and given it to the poor at his gate, and how Aidan of Lindisfarne had praised him for it, holding up the king's right hand: *May this arm never wither!*

And it never had. Even now (men said) that right arm – enshrined in silver at Bamburgh in the distant north – had never lost its freshness.

He took a deep breath. My Lord and Saint, he thought. You were so valiant in life, fighting so hard to bring light in the darkness, to create holy spaces in which men might talk with God. And in death you were so foully treated, your body torn apart by pagans on the battlefield, and then your bones forced into hiding here at Bardney. And now – oh, my Lord, what have I done? Given you into the care of a couple of unbaptised women and sent you off . . .

But you're *safe*, he thought. And they're *safe*. He heard again the thud of hooves in his memory, fading away as Gunnvor and Leoba, with her children and her precious bundle of bones, had galloped up the hill. Had anyone followed them? He hadn't seen anyone go after them. Their captors had had no horses, after all.

If they had been allowed to talk, he would have liked to share some of the stories of St Oswald with Ednoth and Ronan. And he still longed to hear that song about St Oswald and his raven, the one that Ronan had mentioned. But their guards were bad-tempered, and Ednoth, like Ronan, had nodded off now. Wulfgar himself had never felt so tired, and yet so far from sleep. He daydreamed instead, spinning visions of a Bardney reborn, clerics returning – maybe even monks, one day, if true monks ever came back to the English kingdoms – and himself masterminding a glorious ceremony of cleansing and reconsecration, bringing the light back to the dark places . . .

It was a long, long dreary day.

As the light through the door began to slope from the west towards the chancel, the Spider's wife started coming back, snapping at her slaves, striding in for no apparent reason, as abruptly turning and going out again into the yard. By the time, at last, they heard the noise of men and horses in the yard, her feverish impatience was testing everyone's nerves to breaking point. The doorway darkened.

'I hear you've some good news for me?'

Those smooth tones had to belong to Garmund, though the newcomer was no more than a bulky shape against the light in the doorway. Wulfgar sat up straighter.

'These are what you want,' the woman said. 'My men brought them. Do you want them killed?' She gestured at her men. 'Get them on their feet.'

Garmund took a step or two into the hall.

'What's the hurry?' He looked at Wulfgar, a disbelieving smile breaking across his strong, dark features. 'Well, well, well.' He turned back to the Spider's wife. 'I'd like to know what they can tell us, first. If they've not got what I want, they can tell us where they've stashed it.'

'*First*, my money. Or you're not going anywhere.'

His smile widened. He spread his hands. 'Of course. A moment.'

He stepped back outside and could be heard giving orders. When he returned, he said, 'Three of my men dead. One of yours. This is turning into an expensive game. But I'll pay you what I promised, all the same.'

A man came in then, carrying a sturdy leather bag in each hand and handed them to Garmund.

'Thirty pounds.' He hefted the bags, which gave forth a faint, inviting jingle. 'Seven thousand, two hundred silver pennies. Fresh from the mint, with the king's name on every one. I've tallied them. Do you want to?'

'You promised me fifty.'

Fifty pounds. It was a fortune, and not a small one. Wulfgar thought bitterly of the five pounds his own cheese-paring masters had offered to poor Thorvald.

'And you'll get the other twenty, lady. But I've not got them with me. You know I'm not authorised to hand over the rest till we've got the relics home and the bishop's given them his seal of approval. Those were our terms. Don't you trust me?' He was still smiling, teeth white in his beard. He chinked the bags again. 'You should know by now you can trust me.'

Where have I heard that sort of intimate, coaxing tone before, lately? Wulfgar wondered. Oh yes, I know – the Atheling's voice, a long week ago in Worcester. *Bishops, even. There aren't enough bishops in Mercia.* I should never have let the Atheling beguile me, any more than the Spider's wife should be putting her faith in Garmund now.

But the Spider's wife seemed cannier than Wulfgar, unwilling to take Garmund's word for anything. She received the proffered bags warily, one at a time, weighing each one in her hands and frowning. 'Bring me a blanket.' She emptied the first one of its clinking contents and did a quick reckoning of the coins, biting a few, holding others up to the light for scrutiny, a disconcerting mixture of scruple and haste.

'Aye, that'll do, to be going on with,' she allowed at last. 'I'm guessing you'll find your bones in their baggage. They're muddy enough.' She coughed again.

'Haven't you *looked*?' Garmund's voice cracked, showing impatience for the first time. 'You've had all damn day.'

She shrugged.

'I don't know what to look for, you told me that. I've not touched them, or their gear. Just like you said.'

Garmund, tight-lipped, looked first down at the pile of silver, and then over at the stacked saddle-bags, and finally at Wulfgar. Their eyes met, and locked.

'You,' he said. 'Get me the relics. Come on, I'm in a hurry. You've either got them with you or you've hidden them somewhere.'

Wulfgar felt a hard coal of slow-burning anger ignite in his belly. *So that's why we haven't been killed, yet: Garmund thinks we might have had time to hide the relics somewhere, in the night, out in the marsh. He doesn't want to kill us before he's made absolutely sure of getting his filthy hands on them.*

'Relics?' he said to Garmund.

'St Oswald. I know you've got him. I saw that dirty great hole you left in the churchyard.' He jerked his head at the bags. 'I'm not grubbing through your stinking flea-ridden linen. You do it.'

Ednoth made a strangled noise.

Garmund shot him a glance.

'I've seen you before,' Garmund said, 'and you didn't impress me then, either.'

'Why should I do what you say?' Wulfgar asked. It was as

though they were taking up their positions for an old, old dance. Who was going to be the first to crack, to go running to the grown-ups? *Fleda, Garmund hit me . . .*

'Because I'll kill you if you don't.'

'But you made out you were ettling to kill them anyway,' the Spider's wife said.

Garmund smiled again.

'I thought they might be more dangerous than this. But once we've got the relics we could let them go. What do you think? They look harmless enough to me.' He flashed a contemptuous smile at Wulfgar.

'Kill them,' she said, stubborn as ever. 'Tip them in the marsh. Who's to know? I want them got rid of. I don't want word getting back to my man.'

Garmund turned to Wulfgar again.

'Go on, Wuffa. I'm getting bored with this. Get me the relics.'

The onslaught of so many eyes came as a physical shock.

'*Wuffa?*' Ronan said in disbelief.

'You know this man?' The Spider's wife sounded equally taken aback, setting the empty money-bag back down. Her gaze flicked from Garmund to Wulfgar and back again, narrowing with sudden suspicion.

Garmund, smiling, said, 'What's the matter, Wuffa? Embarrassed?'

This is my chance, Wulfgar thought. Yes, you great bully, I am embarrassed. But not for the reasons you think. Not because your mother was one of my father's field-slaves. But because you're a cruel, power-hungry, self-seeking sycophant. He opened his mouth to say as much, but he was too late.

'I'll tell you, then,' Garmund said, 'since he's too mealy mouthed. I'm his brother.'

'*Brother?*' Ronan mouthed at Wulfgar.

'You might have told me, at Offchurch.' Ednoth's tone was savage, as if he had encountered betrayal.

'Yes, what *were* you doing at Offchurch, Wuffa?' Garmund asked. 'Other than spoiling my fun? I thought you'd grown out of that, Litter-runt, but you're still at it. Get the relics, and I'll let you go.'

'Do it yourself, why don't you?' But he muttered it below his breath, and he knew the answer: Garmund doesn't want to go on his knees like a slave, rummaging through our bags in the sight of his men. If he can force me to do it, why, so much the better. And let's give him a little credit – he might not want to risk touching the relics with those corrupted hands of his. We went to the same school, after all; he knows those cautionary tales of men struck down by saints they've insulted, in the midst of their strutting and bragging, just as well as I do.

He took a deep breath.

What on earth do I do now? St Oswald, come to our aid . . . But the formal phrases appropriate to prayer were driven out of his head at the sight of Garmund's knowing smirk. St Oswald, he thought wildly, please help me. Or he'll kill me. And the others. He really will, this time. No one will ever know what he did, or what happened to us.

St Oswald, I've seen you into safety. Now it's your turn.

And he knew what to do, then, as though the saint had breathed in his ear.

Lifting the bulkier of the rolls of sacking with as much reverence as he could muster, he got to his feet, his soul welling over with a profound gratitude to the saint. Now all hung on how thoroughly Garmund had been briefed, what he expected to see . . .

He reached in, half-pulled out a femur, and said, 'Here.'

'What?'

Louder: 'Here you are!'

'Give them to me.'

'*Bones?*' the Spider's wife said in disbelief. 'All this for *bones?*'

Wulfgar tried to hand Garmund the sack but he flinched away. 'You show me.'

Wulfgar held it out to him, and he looked inside.

'More bones,' Garmund said then. 'All right. They look old, right enough. But where's your proof?'

'Proof?' Wulfgar poured outrage into his voice. 'You're looking for the bones of a saint. I give you the bones we were taking from his grave. What more could you possibly want?' Wulfgar took a step towards him.

Garmund held up a warning hand.

'Watch it,' he said. 'King Edward wants proof, I'm going to bring him proof.'

'For the sake of God, Garmund, I'm not armed. Look at me. I'm trying to help you. I'll give you everything we've got.'

Garmund narrowed his eyes.

'Don't you dare hold out on me.'

Putting the sack down gently, Wulfgar got down on the tiles and brought out the tenderly wrapped fragments of wood.

'Look at these. These were found with the bones.'

Garmund stood over him, watching him lift out the incised scraps of coffin. 'Read them to me.'

'I can't.'

'What do you mean? You're the *scholar*, aren't you?' Garmund loaded the word with contempt. 'Of course you can.'

Wulfgar sighed. *Wuffa, do my Latin for me or I'll break your arm . . .*

276

'No, I can't, not just like that. Look how damaged the wood is. I can't read them, not without a lot of work. But the Bishop of Winchester's scholars will be able to. Ask my uncle.'

'Your uncle?' Garmund spat.

'I know he never approved of you being taught at the King's school.' Wulfgar sighed profoundly. 'But he'd be glad to help with something as marvellous as this.' Still kneeling, he closed his eyes. 'Proof doesn't get better. From here, you'll have to fall back on faith. Just as we've had to. These are the bones we were planning to take to Gloucester. But I suppose St Oswald would rather be in Winchester, for some reason best known to him and God.' The bitterness in his voice sounded convincing even to himself. 'What's Edward going to do with him? Put him in the big new church he's said to be planning?'

'That's none of your business, Litter-runt.' Garmund showed his teeth. 'Well, if this is the best you can do . . .' He nodded to one of his men, who picked up the two sacks gingerly and took them out into the bright courtyard.

'Be careful!'

'Oh, we will be, runt. My career depends on those bags.'

I've done it, Wulfgar thought. He looked round at the others. Ednoth gaped at him, truculent and outraged. Ronan was shaking his head sadly and staring at the floor. Wulfgar wished there was some way of explaining what he had done straight away. He knew that Ronan and Ednoth thought he had given the saint to Garmund, but there was no help for it: they would have to go on thinking it for some time to come.

'You've got what you want.' The Spider's wife sounded agitated. 'Go now. Get out. You're right, I'll find a use for these.' She gestured at her prisoners.

Wulfgar looked up at her, still on his knees.

'He promised he'd let us go.'

Garmund raised his hands, smiling, placatory. 'As you say, my part is done. Kill them if you like, what do I care?' He turned and bellowed through the open door, 'Get the horses ready!' Then, 'I take my leave of you, dearest lady.' The rest of his men had gone out before him. He bowed mockingly. 'Goodbye, Wuffa.'

There was the welcome clatter of many hooves on cobbles from outside. Just let Garmund get clear, Wulfgar thought. Once he was away from Bardney they could bribe their way out, or blag, or fight. If they could get weapons. They could give the Spider's wife the Bishop's silver. Thorvald's silver. She seemed to like silver. Just let him go away, Wulfgar prayed. Bear with me, St Oswald.

Garmund had left the doorway. A jingling of harness and the creak of saddles. The sound of horsemen riding out.

A long, long silence in their wake.

Wulfgar looked up again at the painted image of St Oswald in the semi-circular space above the door.

My Lord and King, he prayed. Thank you. We're working on this together, we're getting there at last, he thought.

If the saint could see Leoba safe to Leicester, Wulfgar could meet him there and they could both get home. He started to rise to his feet.

The Spider's wife frowned at him.

'Don't think you're going anywhere.'

'But Garmund said—' Wulfgar began.

'He's gone, hasn't he? And he's not master round here. I am.'

'If it's Dublin you're thinking of,' Ronan said, 'I can tell you this much: you won't recoup the cost of shipping my sorry carcass.'

'Not you, old man, no. But *him –*' she jerked her chin at Ednoth '– he'd be worth it. I'm not holding my breath to see the rest of my money. I'm guessing I've been bilked by that smooth-talking southron. I'll have to make it up somehow.'

CHAPTER TWENTY-FIVE

Wulfgar glanced at Ednoth and saw how pale he was, his freckles standing out, his jaw tense and the muscles in his neck strained. He's terrified, Wulfgar thought suddenly. For the first time on this whole sorry jaunt he's realised the danger we've walked into.

And he's killed someone for the first time, too.

It's not just me.

Their eyes met, and Wulfgar smiled, trying to put all the sympathy he felt into his face.

Ednoth lunged to his feet.

'You – you bastard!'

'*What?*'

'Traitor. You and that – yes, I can believe he's your brother. You and smelly-arse Polecat. What a pair.'

'Steady, boys,' Father Ronan said.

The Spider's wife was still talking, ignoring their confrontation.

'You're in league, aren't you, you and him?' Ednoth shouted.

'Never trust a West Saxon, I should have known. I should have known.'

Mouth closed, Wulfgar shook his head violently, trying to catch the lad's eye again.

What can I say, he wondered, while the Spider's wife can overhear us?

But the boy wasn't prepared to listen to anything he might have to say.

'And you, too, Father! How could you let him give away our saint?' He swung back to Wulfgar. 'It was all a plot – a plot to get the bones to Winchester – wasn't it? After all that we've done?' His eyes narrowed. 'Thorvald – did you really try to save him? Or kill him? And I've lost my sword. And God only knows what's going to happen to *us* now—' Ednoth fell silent at last as a grim-faced man swung a spear-butt at him. It missed, but he slumped back in his corner, levelling one last look of hatred and misery at Wulfgar before folding his arms on his knees and resting his head on them.

'Thorvald?' The Spider's wife was listening now. 'What has Thorvald to do with this?' She went to the door, shouted to summon a slave, gave orders, turned in the doorway. 'Where is Thorvald?'

'Where you and yours can't get at him,' Father Ronan said.

She bared her teeth.

'He's our thrall. Was he working for you? Are you telling me he's dead?'

Ronan crossed himself. 'May he rest in peace. But not your thrall, and not your husband's. Your people here are free men and women of Bardney.'

She seemed to find something funny in that.

'Freedom in Bardney? There's no freedom anywhere Eirik wields the rod.' She turned back into the hall and stared down at the rug with its treasure-trove of coins. 'You,' she said to Ronan, 'you think you're so clever. Do some work for once. You bag my silver again and stow it in my kist.' She gestured at a small leather-covered chest that stood on the inside of the west wall and began fumbling with the keys at her belt. Ronan, meekly obedient, scooped up the rug, gathering stray coins, as she opened the lid of the chest and kicked the money bags towards him.

'Help me, Wuffa. Let's do a bag each.'

The Spider's wife nodded. 'Get on with it.'

Wulfgar shuffled across. He had never seen such a pile of money in his life. He peered curiously at the first one he picked up. Deorwald's workshop – the Winchester moneyer's name was there for him to read, but he thought he would have known the old man's craftsmanship anyway by the beautiful cutting of the tiny letters. He turned it over and tilted it to read the name circling round the rim with a pang. EDWARDUS REX. *New-minted, indeed*. Edward had wasted no time.

The coin was snatched from his hand.

'Stop laiking about.'

It was a slow job, the Spider's wife watching like a cat at a mouse-hole to see that not a single gleaming disc went astray. She stood over them the whole time, her hands knotted and clenching.

'What are you so afraid of?' Ronan asked, almost gently.

The Spider's wife made a noise; it sounded almost like a whimper, and Wulfgar looked up at her, startled. Her shawl had fallen back, revealing a flash of metal at her long throat.

'That's a thrall ring, for all its silver,' Father Ronan said slowly.

She looked at him with hatred.

'My wedding ring,' she said.

Ronan had filled his bag. He stood up, holding it out to the Spider's wife, who snatched it from him with both hands. 'Come with us, lady,' he said. He put his hand on his heart. 'Bring your silver. Come away with us.'

Her eyes had widened. Wuffa watched in fascination.

'Come back to the faith of your parents,' Ronan said,

'My parents?' She laughed, a brittle sound that tailed away into coughing. 'Who was it sold me to Eirik, think you?' she said, when she had got her breath back. Her mouth twisted. 'May well be I'm not staying here. But I'll put no faith in the word of Christians, either. You'd kill me for the silver.'

'Lady, lady!' A young woman ran into the hall, her face wild, too short of breath to do more than point a frantic arm out into the courtyard.

The sound of horses outside.

A voice shouting a harsh command in Danish.

In Danish.

Her head swivelled from side to side, eyes wide like a doe at bay. She snatched at the other bag of silver, the one Wulfgar was holding up to her, but he hadn't fastened the draw-string and it up-ended. A shower of coins slid from its mouth, flickering like fish-scales in the shaft of sunlight, ringing sweetly as they tumbled onto the flagged floor.

'*Help me,*' she said.

The doorway darkened. Wulfgar looked towards it, hoping for the first time in his life to see Garmund.

A lanky, angular figure, his hair backlit grey.

Eirik.

He looked slowly around him, eyes adjusting to the smoky

gloom. His eyes lingered, squinting, on each small group, as he tallied the unexpected scene. Ednoth sitting in the corner, still resting his head on his folded arms. Their guards. Ronan, standing, holding an obviously heavy bag. Wulfgar, still kneeling by the rug, empty-handed. The woman scrabbling on the floor for a small fortune in silver.

There were no shouts, no angry questions. Eirik just stood there, waiting, until they all had seen him, had stopped what they were doing, until he had their full attention. And even then the silence stretched on and on.

'What's that?' he asked his wife at last in his guttural, lifeless tone. He pointed accusingly at the scattering of silver and the tumbled rug. 'Stand up. Who were those men riding out on my road?'

She was silent.

His eyes narrowed as he acknowledged Ronan, and he looked around the group again, nodding.

'You,' he said, pointing. 'Friend of Silkbeard. You stand up too.'

He means *me*, Wulfgar realised.

'What is all this? What are you doing here?'

'What are *you* doing here?' his wife asked. 'You never come here. Never.'

'People are talking in Lincoln,' he said. 'Saying there is a great treasure hid at Bardney, and Eirik the Spider is a fool not to know about it. A bigger fool to trust his wife.' He spat onto the tiles. 'Nobody calls me a fool.' He took another step towards them. 'Then yesterday this one –' he indicated Wulfgar again '– starts asking questions. *Bardney, Bardney, Bardney.* So I decided I would come and see. And what do I find? Strangers on the road, and – not strangers – in my house.'

There was a long silence.

'You have been cheating me, haven't you?' Eirik said.

She shook her head, speechless.

He sucked his teeth.

'I should have known.'

Extemporising frantically, Wulfgar said, 'Those men you saw on the road, they've taken your treasure.'

'What?'

Encouraged by Eirik's response, Wulfgar spread his hands.

'They stole it from the churchyard. We were too late.' He looked at Ronan: *support me here.* But the big priest was silent. He went on, scrabbling after words with a sense of digging his own grave. 'We were after the treasure, but we've only just got here. We found those men already here, they'd been digging in the graveyard, and when – when they saw us they jumped on their horses and rode away. The hole they left was empty, and their saddle-bags looked full, so we assumed—' Where is my eloquence when we need it? 'I can show you the hole,' he said, desperate.

Eirik's head swung round to find one of the men who had been guarding them. 'Search their bags.' It didn't take him long, up-ending and stirring with his foot. He found the Bishop's silver, and handed it to Eirik.

'Glad now I didn't bring my harp?' Ronan muttered.

Wulfgar nodded, only too aware of the Bishop's ring and his little gospel of St John, both lying warm and secret against his breast.

'*See*,' Wulfgar said, wishing someone else would join in his storytelling. How had he ended up being the only spokesman of their little party? 'We haven't got it. We're telling you the truth.'

Eirik looked up from inspecting the two little bags of coins from Wulfgar's saddle-bag.

'You have not got it here. So? You might have hidden it.' He looked at the floor. 'And what was she doing? Whose silver is that?'

Wulfgar cleared his throat.

'Um, well, we brought that silver, hoping to buy the treasure, but your wife was just telling us that unfortunately she can't help us, because we're too late.' Hollow, hollow, hollow.

Eirik looked out at him from those deep eye-sockets.

'Then why is she putting it in her own kist?'

'Well, perhaps she was going to keep it,' Wulfgar conceded. 'But she's innocent of anything else, and so are we. We've all been tricked, by those men – those thieves – on the road.' Go *after* them, he thought desperately.

'Who were those men?' Eirik asked.

'Wessex,' Wulfgar said shortly. 'Silkbeard's enemies, and ours.'

Eirik was silent a moment. Then he said, 'And this famous treasure? What is it?'

His wife began to laugh. The laughter went on and on, more like sobbing all the time.

Eirik looked around helplessly.

'Make her stop. Stop her.'

But the woman brought herself back under control without help. Wiping her eyes and coughing, she said, 'Bones. Old bones. That's what all this is about.'

'Bones?'

She nodded.

'But what about the gold?' Eirik's eyes narrowed. 'People in Lincoln have been saying gold.'

'Just bones,' his wife repeated. 'Dry old bones you'd not insult a dog with. And these men here have offered me – *us* – silver for them. Who's the fool now?'

'How much silver is here?'

'Thirty pounds. For old bones! Thirty pounds and—' She pressed her lips tight.

And then one of the guards spoke very quietly to Eirik, in Danish. His tone was tentative, even apologetic, his eyes flickering constantly over to the Spider's wife. Wulfgar strained to hear, a terrible cold fear growing in his belly, but the man's voice was little more than a murmur in Eirik's ear.

He finished, and stood back. Eirik nodded, his face a mask. His wife looked half-furious, half-terrified.

Ronan stirred then.

'We've nothing of yours, Spider. You've got the silver, and lost nothing that you value.'

Nothing but your reeve, Wulfgar thought. He looked down at his hands. Thorvald's blood was still clogged thick under his fingernails.

'You're lying to me,' Eirik said again. 'If what my man tells me is true, those riders on the road have your bones, but you did the digging. And he tells me this is *their* money. If you wanted to buy my treasure, then where is *your* money?' He turned to Wulfgar. 'And whose blood is that? He tells me, my reeve is dead. Have you killed him?' Eirik sounded frustrated, almost peevish. 'Enough. This has gone on long enough. Take off your ring.'

Wulfgar blinked, hand at his collar. How had the Spider known about the Bishop's ring? But Eirik's attention had moved on.

His wife had known exactly what he meant. Her hands had gone to her own throat, gripping the thick silver ring as though for protection. Earlier Wulfgar had thought he had seen the traces of beauty in her face, but there was none there now. Her skin had gone the colour of curdled milk and there were beads of sweat on her upper lip. Wulfgar felt a sudden, unexpected pang of pity for this woman, who had been a child once. Free once, too, he thought.

'Take it off,' Eirik repeated. Slowly, as though some external force were compelling her, his wife dragged at the ends of the metal, and, slowly, obedient to her white-knuckled grip, the silver wire bent apart. She pulled it from her neck, leaving a red mark behind.

'Drop it.'

It clanged on the flag-stones.

'Nobody cheats me,' Eirik said, almost lightly, 'but especially not my wife.' He nodded to the men in the doorway, and said something in Danish.

Wulfgar blinked. Had he understood Eirik properly?

The Spider's wife had been standing as if frozen, but now she looked wildly from one side to the other.

'*Nei!* I—'

But they were bundling her out of the door as if she were a ewe brought unwilling to her shearing. The sunlight sent long, thrashing shadows across the threshold, and then the doorway was empty and still. There was a brief silence, and then a wild, frantic scream, agony on the ears, ending in a splutter and choke, and silence again.

Eirik walked to the doorway and paused, looking out, blocking any view from inside. He stood there for a long time. Eventually he said something in Danish.

Wulfgar didn't understand, and wasn't sure he wanted to. But Ronan stirred at the words.

'*No*. Give her a clean burial. The marsh is for unfaithful wives.'

Eirik turned.

'And what is this called? *Faith*?' His gesture took in their little party, the rug, the spilled silver. He sucked his teeth again. 'Better she had been bedding another man.'

Wulfgar was finding it impossible to breathe. The casual way in which this man had given his orders, the readiness with which his servants had committed the horror, somehow all the worse for happening out of sight. Over and over his imagination painted in the missing details, too easy after the violence he had witnessed – no, be honest – the violence he had partaken of, last night. He closed his eyes. That long white throat bared in the evening light, the head dragged back, the knife . . . and the life-blood, soaking into her ill-kept cobblestones.

He blinked, and swallowed, and tried to pray for her. The Spider's wife. She must have done something in her life that merited redemption. She must have suffered . . .

He'd never even learnt her name.

CHAPTER TWENTY-SIX

One of Eirik's men hovered in the doorway.

'*Já?*'

Wulfgar tried to follow, but could make nothing of it. He looked in hope at Ronan, who had drawn his breath in sharply.

'What?'

'They've gone to bury her. In the bone-garth. In the hole we dug last night.' He crossed himself, and Wulfgar followed suit. 'Dear Christ, Wulfgar, I hope our saint is worth it. There's a mort of blood been shed over this.'

It was all supposed to have been so easy. Go to Bardney. Get the relics. Go home.

'Is this Toli's law, Spider?' Ronan asked. 'You can kill your own wife without cause, without trial?'

Eirik spat into the rushes.

'You can kill your own thrall, priest. Any law allows that.'

Wulfgar found a ghost of a voice.

'Not in Wessex,' he said. 'And not in Mercia.'

'And you can kill the thief found with your goods in his hand.' Eirik nodded at them, his face almost happy. 'That's good Army-law. And we still have Army-law in Lincoln.' He turned to the four men in the doorway. 'Them, now.' He jerked his head at Wulfgar. 'Him first.'

'I told Toli where we were going,' Ronan said evenly. 'He'll want to know if you've seen us.'

Eirik bared his teeth in a parody of a smile.

'I haven't seen you. Nobody has seen you.'

Ronan smiled. 'But we have a meeting planned, Silkbeard and I.'

'Now I know you're lying, *prestr*,' Eirik said again. 'I was there when you left Toli. You said nothing to him. What would Toli plan with *you*?'

'Can you be sure? Would he tell you all his plans?'

'Toli doesn't know you came here,' Eirik said, but he sounded less happy.

'You've profited by thirty pounds of best Wessex silver,' Ronan said. 'We've got nothing of yours, not *in our hand* or anywhere else. What kind of thieves does that make us?'

'What about me?' Wulfgar said, 'I'm Toli's *friend*. You saw us swear friendship, you just said as much!'

Eirik shrugged.

'Toli swears and forswears as it suits him.' He walked over to Wulfgar and looked into his eyes. 'You want to risk it? You want to go back to Toli and see how he values you, compared to me?'

Wulfgar found himself flinching at the proximity of that gaunt, greyish face. Yes, it was easy to believe that Eirik was telling the truth.

But it had worked last time – *Take me to Toli*, he'd said, and escaped scot-free – and what alternative did they have?

'You want good law?' Ronan said. 'Then respect Toli's law, Eirik. You need to take us to Toli. Charge us in public.'

Eirik turned. 'I should have had you killed twenty years ago in Dublin.'

Ronan grinned. 'As you found then, I don't kill so easy.'

Eirik jerked his head. 'Tie them up. They want to go to Toli. Let them. I want to see them regret it.'

The three of them had their hands tied behind their back and were shoved up onto scrawny, dull-eyed mules, a rope tying ankle to ankle under the girth. Wulfgar thought with a sudden pang of his Fallow, abandoned at the lambing pens all day. She'd been tethered near plenty of grass, hadn't she? Would she need water? How long before someone found her, and Starlight, and Ronan's black Dub? One of Eirik's men had a massive coil of rope in his hands, and Wulfgar watched him lash it behind his saddle. There was a dark puddle on the cobblestones at the horse's feet, and Wulfgar suddenly recognised it for what was. The flies helped him to understand. He flinched, and looked away.

They made a strange cavalcade, Eirik riding in front with a couple of armed men and a third bringing up the rear. Wulfgar thought – prayed – that Lincoln could be no more than an hour's ride, because this was agony. Although the mules went at no more than a shambling plod, he was lurched from side to side at every pace, his thighs clenched around the mule's ribs, the knobs of its backbone digging into his groin. His bound hands scrabbled behind his back but there was not so much as the hem of a saddle-cloth to cling to. If I do fall, I'll get tangled up with the mule's hooves, and it'll tread on me. I mustn't fall. Think of something else. The coil of rope tied to the guard's saddle caught his eye again, and the thought flashed across his mind: *that's for hanging us.* And, if Lincoln's no more than an hour away, then does that mean my death is only an hour away? Toli wouldn't hang a man he'd sworn friendship with, surely? He wouldn't hang a *priest* . . .

He glanced across at Ednoth: stiff and furious and, it seemed to Wulfgar, terribly vulnerable.

'Ronan,' he hissed.

'Eh?'

'What's Army-law?'

'For outlanders like us? No court. No right to plead. We live or die on Toli's say-so.'

'No *court*?'

And then, Wulfgar thought, why am I surprised?

'Shut up, there.'

They were splashing across the Bray ford by early evening. Heads turned, and a few people jeered. Boys picked up handfuls of muck to throw, with results that clearly satisfied them. Tied as they were, there was no chance of ducking the shower of filth without risking falling off.

'And that would make the brats even happier,' Ronan muttered.

Eirik did nothing to discourage the whoops and catcalls. Ednoth's cheeks were fiery, but Wulfgar found he was past caring. It was only mud and dung. No stones. Or not yet.

Eirik and his men made them dismount outside the stockade in Silver Street and they staggered, still tied and hobbled, through the gate, encouraged by spear-butts and kicks. The gate closed behind them, shutting out the jeering urchins.

'*Jarl Toli?*'

'*Já, herra.*'

The guard turned to go inside, not to the hall as Wulfgar had expected but a small private bower set to one side.

'*Herra*, the Jarl is not well. Can it wait?'

But a tousled, fair-haired figure stood in the doorway, rubbing his eyes, wearing only his fine linen shirt and woollen leggings.

'I'm nursing my hangover, that's all. What is it, my Eirik?'

Eirik jerked his head.

'These,' he said in English. 'Thieves. Murderers. Found in my hall. I want you to give them to me, Jarl of Lincoln.'

Toli half-turned and called something over his shoulder. Moments later a sleepy-looking girl emerged from the bower with a basin of water and a linen towel. Toli splashed his face and dried himself vigorously enough to raise red marks on his fair skin.

'Bring me some ale and a tunic,' he said, handing her the towel. He yawned and stretched. 'Let's start again. What did you say?'

'Thieves. Murderers. Caught on my land. I want their heads.'

Toli paused, tunic in his hands, and looked past Eirik for the first time.

'Ah,' he said. '*Ulfgeir*, my friend, you seem to be making a habit of being arrested. Do you *want* to be a martyr?'

Eirik broke into Danish then, a rapid but passionless monologue.

Bardney . . . Wulfgar heard. *Treasure . . . thieves.*

Toli let Eirik talk himself out, nodding from time to time.

'And what was this treasure?' Toli's eyes were gleaming. 'Did they find it? Is there a share for your Lord?'

Eirik's voice was tinged with contempt.

'Bones. One of their holy men. But such things are worth a lot of silver. And they killed my reeve. I have witnesses.'

Toli swung round.

'So, *Ulfgeir*, my Eirik says you and your friends are thieves. And liars. And murderers. But you're also my sworn friend. So I'll give you a chance to plead.'

Wulfgar found his voice wobbling shamefully.

'Jarl Toli – my Lord – my friend – we didn't kill the reeve, Thorvald. That was someone else, not one of us. And – and you can't steal a saint. Nobody owns him. If he comes with you, it's because he chooses to come. I'm no more a thief than I ever was—'

Ronan shook his head. 'Be quiet, Wuffa. Toli of Lincoln,' he said to the Jarl, 'whatever we may have done, it's immaterial. We're not your men. We're not your problem.'

Toli smiled. 'You're quite right. Yes, I could send you back to Leicester, to Ketil Scar, but would you really thank me for it?'

'Do you know what this man did?' It was Ednoth, hoarse with anger, gesturing at Eirik with his bound hands. 'He killed his wife. Killed her like a pig. Put him on trial, if you like.'

Toli shrugged.

'I never meddle in other men's marriages.' He took the cup of ale from the girl and downed a long draught. 'Ah, that's better! Now, let me see. Of course, I want to make my Eirik happy. To be sure, I don't want to distress *Athalvald inn hungrathr*.' He nodded at Wulfgar. 'But I expect I can make it up to him, come All Hallows.' Wulfgar was finding it hard to reconcile that sweet, boyish face with the words coming from his mouth. 'What will you do with them, my Eirik?'

'Hang them. The ash.'

Toli held out his cup for a refill.

'Will the big branch take three?' he asked.

Eirik's lips were tight-pressed, white with satisfaction.

'It has before. And I have rope.'

'*Toli*,' Wulfgar hardly recognised his own voice. 'You swore—' He broke off. We're going to *die. I'm* going to die, unconfessed, with the blood of the man I killed still under my nails.

He swallowed, newly aware of the pulse fluttering in his throat, the air in his windpipe, the stiff, tired bones of his neck. He hunched his shoulders and bowed his head, trying to shield the soft places under his chin. That rope, he thought wildly, that very rope I can see coiled over there – that's the rope which is going to kill me. They'll throw it over that big branch of the ash tree and make me stand while they loop a running noose over my head and pull it tight, and then they'll go behind me and they'll pull. They'll haul on the other end and lift me off the ground. It'll be slow, very slow, choking . . . sometimes they pull on your knees to make it quicker, but it's never very quick . . . 'Toli, *herra*, you swore to be my *friend*.' He could hear the shameful, pleading note in his voice.

'The dead have no friends,' Eirik said, satisfaction in his voice.

Toli shrugged, and smiled. 'The law should be above friendship, *Ulfgeir*. What choice do I have, as Jarl of Lincoln, but to uphold the law?'

And a new voice said, 'Sell them to me.'

They all swung round to stare at the gate. As he turned, Wulfgar tripped over the rope that hobbled his ankles and fell hard on the cobbles, his tail-bone bruised. With his hands tied, he couldn't get up again. He found himself gazing up at a grey horse, with a splendidly dressed rider. Her upright figure was swathed in a soft black cloak trimmed with wide braids in blue and purple, the white fox fur around her throat skewered through its empty eye-sockets with a silver pin, which could have done double service as a dagger. The evening light flashed fire from the trinkets pinned in the great plaits and coils of her dark hair. Another couple of horsemen were riding in behind her.

She urged her horse forward a pace or two.

'Name your price, Spider.'

Wulfgar felt a wild surge of hope.

Eirik hawked and spat.

'Too late, Bolladottir. They are already dead.'

She raised an eyebrow at that.

'What use are they, dead? That's not like you, Spider. Not your style. When is a dead man a better bargain than a live one, eh?' She glanced at Wulfgar, still lying on the dirty cobbles. 'Jarl of Lincoln, do you hang men on hearsay?'

Toli grinned up at her, pushing that errant lock of hair out of his eyes.

'My Eirik brings more silver into Lincoln than any ten other traders. I want to keep him happy.'

Gunnvor gathered up her reins in one hand and swung easily out of the saddle. Handing the reins to one of the men who had ridden in with her, she walked up to Toli, her skirts brushing Wulfgar as she went by, giving no sign that she had even noticed him. He saw how Toli stood straighter at her approach.

'Toli, my Jarl,' she said as she put her hand on his arm and looked up at him through those rook-feather lashes, 'don't you want to make *me* happy? What do *I* bring you?'

Watching Toli's expression, Wulfgar thought, look at him, the poor fool. When she's close to him, he can't think about anything else. And then, with a sudden twist somewhere in his chest, he thought, *I know exactly how he feels.*

Without turning away from Gunnvor, Toli said, 'Eirik, what's your price?' The courtyard had fallen silent, but for the clucking of a chicken who was pecking her way around the mules' hooves.

'I want them hanged.' Eirik stared at Toli, but the Jarl's attention was all elsewhere now.

He's like a butterfly, Wulfgar thought, a cruel, young butterfly.

All shimmer and dash, taking what he wants from a flower and then moving on as soon as he gets bored.

And he gets bored very quickly.

Toli had covered Gunnvor's hand with his but he let it drop then.

'And *I* want them sold. To Bolladottir, if she's offering. It's just as good a judgment in law.'

'Your father—'

And Toli turned round.

'My *father?*' He flung the half-full cup of ale down on the cobbles to smash and splatter at Eirik's feet. 'Never tell me what my father would have done. My father is dead, thank Spear and Hammer.' His fair skin had flushed deep red; Wulfgar could almost see the steam coming from his nostrils. 'You're a good servant to me, my Eirik, and I've been thinking of you as a good friend. My friends don't remind me about my father, or make comparisons.'

Eirik's eyes were as flat as ever, but he had taken a step backwards. There were shards of clay and splashes of ale on the greasy leather of his shoes.

'I will not forget this, Toli Hrafnsson.'

'Put a price on them, my Spider. Or do you want me to give them to Bolladottir freely, as a gift?' He took Gunnvor's hand again. 'A tribute to her beauty.'

They are both beautiful, Wulfgar found himself thinking in a jealous agony, he so fair, and she so dark.

I am inches away from dying, he realised then, and all I can think about is a woman's face. A woman's body. He closed his eyes briefly. How he had got here? *Our Lady, Queen of Heaven, forgive me.*

'Do you want me to go on trading out of Lincoln, *herra*?' Eirik asked. He made the title sound like an insult.

Gunnvor reached in her turn for Toli's other hand, lifting his fingers to caress the soft white fur that encircled her throat.

'Shall I give the Spider *twice* the market price, my Jarl?' she asked.

Wulfgar saw in disbelief that Ronan had started to chuckle. 'You've lost this one, Spider!' he said. 'Think on, the dead *do* have friends after all.'

Eirik's fingers were clenching like claws, his whole body trembling. 'Next time, *prestr*, next time.' He inhaled deeply through his nose, looking first at Toli, then Gunnvor, and then at his three captives. He breathed out then. His deep-set eyes had narrowed; he looked as though he was making some complex calculation. At last he nodded, very slowly. 'As you say, *herra*. Twice the market price.' Eirik walked over to Wulfgar and prodded his buttocks with the toe of his shoe. 'Get up.'

'I – I can't.'

'You can.'

He knew Toli and Gunnvor were both watching him. Burning with humiliation, Wulfgar heaved himself onto his side, and somehow got from there up on to his knees. But he couldn't bring a foot forward to lever himself up to standing: the rope hobbling his ankles was too short. Trying to stand just threatened to pitch him forward onto his nose.

Gunnvor summoned one of her men with a jerk of her head. He dismounted and was at her side.

'Untie him,' she commanded.

'They're mine, Bolladottir,' Eirik said.

'For now, Spider.'

With one ankle now freed, Wulfgar stood up, still stumbling and awkward, hands still bound, the rope trailing from the other ankle.

Eirik walked up to him.

'Stand with them,' he told Wulfgar.

Wulfgar shuffled into line.

Eirik walked up and down, looking at all three of them. Eirik had frightened Wulfgar before, but he found the slave-dealer even more frightening now. He had changed, somehow sharper, more at home in his skin. There was something altogether inhuman in the way he was sizing them up. Wulfgar thought, he can't see me for whom I am; he can't see human souls as anything but a commodity. This must have been what Gunnvor and Father Ronan meant, he realised, when they had said there was no appealing to Eirik's sense of honour. The slave-dealer didn't have one. He didn't care what other people think. He wasn't aware that other people *did* think.

Eirik reached out a hand.

Wulfgar flinched away, but there was no escaping that probing hand, its grip relentless as a blacksmith's tongs, assessing the muscles of his upper arm and shoulder.

'Teeth,' Eirik commanded, grabbing Wulfgar by the chops and digging his fingers into his cheeks. Wulfgar had thought he had plumbed the depths of shame already, but, as he opened his mouth to let the Spider assess his molars, he realised he had done no more than paddle in the shallows. Eirik pushed his mouth closed, gave him a shove, and said, 'Run.'

Wulfgar stared at him.

'From here to the ash and back.' Eirik flicked a hand at him. 'Hurry. I want to check your wind.'

Gunnvor had been looking up at Toli, seemingly giving him all her attention, but at that she said, 'Eirik, that's not needed.'

'Market price,' Eirik said. He bared his teeth.

Toli nodded.

So Wulfgar did as he was told, his hands still bound, shambling and stumbling over the trailing ankle-rope and the cobbles in the gathering dusk, desperate not to fall again. He wished Gunnvor wasn't there to see it. He turned at the tree and came limping back. Now what? But that turned out to be the end of it, for him, though he had to watch first Ronan, then Ednoth, go through the same ordeals.

Finally Eirik nodded, pointed at Ednoth, and said, 'For him, thirty øre. For the priest, twenty. That one, five.'

Five øre? Wulfgar wasn't sure of the exchange rate, but could Ednoth really be worth six times what he was?

Gunnvor shook her head.

'The old man isn't worth so much.'

'Hey!' Ronan exclaimed. 'Watch it, Bolladottir!'

'Broad back, like a bear,' Eirik said, sucking his teeth. 'He might not last long, but he should work well while you have him.' He stared at her. 'You want I should take them down to the river and find another buyer?'

Toli laughed. 'And so little for *Ulfgeir?*' he said. 'You hear that, *Ulfgeir?* Five øre! Look, he's blushing!'

'Soft hands.' Eirik shrugged. 'Too much pride. Those ones turn to the wall and die – I have seen it often enough.'

He and Gunnvor stared at each other.

Toli grinned.

'Go on, my Eirik. Say fifteen for the priest and ten for *Ulfgeir.*'

Eirik shrugged.

'She can pay more for him and less for the priest if she wants. The market price is still forty-five øre for the lot. So, ninety.'

'Eighty,' Gunnvor said instantly.

'No, no, Bolladottir.' Toli put an arm round her waist and pulled her against him, laughing. 'This isn't a game. Eirik wants them hanged. The least we can do is give him a fair price.' He grinned at Eirik. 'I'll even forgo the Jarl's tithe. Just this once.'

Gunnvor nodded then, all wide-eyed acquiescence, soft-faced, smiling up at him and pulling away at the same time.

'I'll do as you say, Toli my Jarl, though it cuts me to the quick.' She waved a lordly hand at one of her horsemen, who dismounted and brought a bag of silver over. 'It's hack-silver,' she said.

'Scales,' Toli commanded. 'And torches.'

And then it was all a twilight blur of bonds being cut and Toli weighing out fragments of shining metal from Gunnvor's bag, with Eirik hanging over the pans of the scales and sucking his teeth, and Gunnvor holding Toli's arm and fluttering her eye-lashes and vowing that his scales were out of true.

One of Eirik's men tied the bags of silver to the saddle-bow of Eirik's horse. Eirik turned back to where Wulfgar stood watching. His long-fingered hand came out and grabbed Wulfgar by the chin again, and he leaned in close, with a carrion gust of breath, and said, 'I do not know why, friend of Toli, but you are the one who makes me angry.'

Wulfgar tried to pull away but Eirik's grip was remorseless as winter.

'I am letting you go now, to please the Jarl of Lincoln. But if I catch you again, be warned. I will kill you.' Only then did he let go.

'You'll have to learn to run faster, *Ulfgeir!*' Toli called.

'Kill another's thrall, Spider?' Gunnvor said. 'What kind of law is that? If you want a bit of fun, go kill your own.'

Wulfgar's heart hammered. It was all he could do not be sick at the man's proximity. Only when Eirik, and his three men, and their mule-train, had all ridden out through Toli's gates into the dusk of Silver Street did he find that he could breathe anything like evenly.

Toli put out a hand and caught Gunnvor's arm though her cloak.

'Stay and drink with me, Bolladottir.'

'Another day, my Jarl.' She stroked Toli's cheek with the back of her hand and smiled tenderly. Wulfgar had to look away. *She's never yet smiled at me.* 'I want to take my new purchases home and wash them.'

'I've made you happy, Bolladottir. Now it's my turn.'

She gave the Jarl a long, steady look. His face was unsmiling now and he held her gaze for a long time. In the end she bowed her head.

'As my Jarl commands.'

'Before dinner?' Ronan muttered. 'And with a hangover? Oh, what I would give to be young again.'

Wulfgar turned away.

CHAPTER TWENTY-SEVEN

The three men were settling themselves around the hearth in Gunnvor's Lincoln house, adjoining her locked and barred warehouse by the river. Her old housekeeper brought fresh barley-cakes and new butter, and ladled out helpings of a rich, peppery broth. Wulfgar was dizzy with hunger, but for all that he found the food sticking in his throat. *Drink with me*, Toli Silkbeard had said, but that wasn't what he had meant, was it? Not at all, not the way he had been looking at her.

'Well?'

Wulfgar looked up from his pit of misery to find Ednoth glaring at him from a few inches away, his face still pale and set.

'Yes?'

'You gave away our saint.'

Wulfgar, caught unawares and with his mouth full, shook his head furiously, and tried to swallow.

'What do you mean, shaking your head like that?' Ednoth got to his feet. 'I saw you. You gave him to that man. *Your brother.*'

Still gulping, Wulfgar said, 'No, Ednoth, I didn't. I gave Garmund the other one, the monk of Bardney.'

Ednoth stared for a moment.

'I don't believe you. Where's our saint then?'

Wulfgar swallowed the last few morsels, and then said, 'He's with Leoba.' How, he wondered, could this possibly be the evening of the same day? A dozen lifetimes had come and gone, surely, since he had thrust that little bundle of bones into her arms at dawn.

'Oh, well done,' Ronan said softly. 'Well done, Wuffa.'

'But where's Leoba?' Ednoth still sounded aggrieved.

A voice said, 'I gave her some silver and sent her and the brats on to Leicester, to the Wave-Serpent.'

Their heads turned. Gunnvor stood in the dark doorway. None of them had noticed her pull the door-curtain aside. She showed her teeth.

'I must say, you boys are running up quite a tab. And, what's more, I've sent one of my thralls to the lambing pens at Hanworth to collect your horses.' She came into the firelight, shrugging her hood back and unpinning her cloak as she came.

Wulfgar found himself scrutinising her face for evidence of what she had been doing, but she still retained her cool, creamy air, every silver pin and trinket in its proper place as far as he could make out.

'Another of your thralls, you mean.' Ronan's tone had an acerbic edge to it.

'No, just the one.' She pulled the white fox fur from around her throat and came to sit down next to the priest on the edge of the sleeping platform heaped with lambskins. 'This is cosy. Give me some of that bread, Wuffa.'

'Another thrall besides *us*,' the priest said, and a snatch of conversation drifted back into Wulfgar's mind: the shadowy, scorched splendour of Leicester's cathedral, and Father Ronan saying, *And my mother was one of his slaves . . .*

Small wonder then that Ronan had seemed so attuned to Leoba's fears about thraldom and the risk of her children being sold.

Ednoth was still looking for something to do with his anger. He stood up abruptly.

'But what was your brother doing at Bardney, hey, if you didn't tell him? And how in the name of Hell do you know Silkbeard? Because he knew you.' He loomed over Wulfgar now, balling his fists. 'You've been lying to us.'

Wulfgar put his head in his hands and stared at the black mounds and orange caves of charcoal glowing in the hearth. 'Oh, Ednoth. Think about it. If that had been your father's son, at Offchurch, would you have confessed it to the world?' He glanced up at the lad then but Ednoth wasn't ready to help him, not yet. 'Garmund's my father's son, yes, and King Edward's man. I have no idea how they learned about St Oswald in Winchester, but it was nothing to do with me.' He sighed. 'Rumours must have been flying for months.' He passed a hand over his eyes, gritty and stinging with hearth-smoke and weariness. 'Maybe it was Thorvald's fault, blabbing to all and sundry.'

'We can hardly ask him the truth of it now,' Ronan said, 'but Leoba might tell us, if we ask her gently.'

Wulfgar gave him a grateful smile.

'As for Toli Silkbeard –' the name was sticking fast in Wulfgar's craw and he had to swallow hard '– it was the Atheling. You remember, Ednoth, when we were leaving Worcester?'

Ednoth nodded, his eyes still narrowed with suspicion.

'He asked me to take Silkbeard his regards. That's all.' Wulfgar crossed his arms over his breast and hugged his half-truths behind them.

'This Atheling you talk about – who is he, exactly?' Ronan was looking troubled.

'*The* Atheling!' Ednoth said. 'Athelwald Seiriol – everyone knows him! Oh, well, if he asked you, you couldn't say no.' He sat down again.

Wulfgar remembered how dazzled the lad had been by the Atheling's attention, back in the Bishop's yard in Worcester. How long ago it seemed.

'Ach, so that's the man you mean,' Ronan said thoughtfully. 'Athelwald the Hungry, they call him up here. He's been seen in Leicester. Friendly with the Grimssons. And now you tell me he's on nodding terms with little Silkbeard, too.' Ronan drew his grizzled brows together. 'Would he have had greetings for anyone else east of Watling Street, now?'

Wulfgar could hear the Atheling's voice: *We light the fire at All Hallows . . . Tell no one else.* The air in Gunnvor's little hall was warm and close, but the words went through his mind like winter wind hissing through a dry thorn-hedge. He shook his head, painfully conscious of his duplicity. He leaned forward, and said softly, 'Father, when we have a moment, would you shrive me?'

Ronan nodded.

Gunnvor rubbed her hands together, brisk and cheerful.

'Now I've bought you all,' she said, 'what am I going to do with you?'

Ronan turned to her, a new heartiness in his voice that didn't quite ring true.

307

'Free us, Bolladottir, if you know what's good for you.'

'*Já, prestr*? I was minded to mark you with my thrall-brand.'

'That's not funny, Bolladottir.'

'Why, you think I'm joking?' She looked amused. 'I've paid Eirik very good money for you three.'

'You didn't pay good money for me,' Wulfgar said, trying to make light of it. 'I was quite cheap.' *Five øre.* It still rankled.

'Ah, I've got me the best bargain with you, *Ulfgeir*,' she said, her voice still mocking. She sat opposite him, and he squinted at her through the hearth-smoke. 'An oaf like Eirik doesn't appreciate the finer things in life the way I do. I think I'll keep you to sit at my feet and teach me English love-songs of a winter evening.'

Stay here? he thought. With her? Surely she was teasing him. Memories rose unbidden: the swell of her breasts, the curve of her hips, defined by her damp linen shift. The dawn light. The song of the wren. Her strong, capable hands, sorting the bones. Some memories, he thought, will stay with me for ever, whether I want them to or not.

There was a subdued knock at the door. Gunnvor rose and had a muttered conversation.

'The horses were gone,' she said, turning back to the room.

'All of them? Dub, too?' Ronan asked.

'I'm sorry.'

'Damnation,' the priest said. 'I love that beast.'

'But I've got these for you.' She nodded at her man, who came in and showed them what he held: two swords.

'That's mine!' Ednoth's delight was unabashed, the last of his bad mood put to flight. 'How did you get my sword?'

She showed her teeth.

'Eirik still wants to keep Toli sweet.'

Wulfgar had a worrying thought about the vanished horses.

'Gunnvor, could anyone have followed you and Leoba, when you rode away? On our horses, I mean.'

'I didn't see anybody.' She sat down again, next to Wulfgar this time, looking thoughtful. 'We came back here. I gave her some food and a little silver and sent her down the Fosse, with my name as a surety. And then –' she glanced at him with amusement '– I heard a rumour that you might be needing me in Silver Street.' She gazed into the fire for a moment. '*Nej*, no one came after us. Maybe your horses have been taken to Bardney.' She gave him another sideways glance, her eyes sparkling. 'Shall I go back to Toli and wheedle for the horses, too?'

'*No*,' he said and stood up, stumbling away from her, his back to the room, appalled by the violence of his response.

'Don't you understand, Bolladottir?' Ronan said, his voice savage. 'He thinks you've been tumbling Toli.'

There was a long silence. Wulfgar stared unseeing at a row of bags of dried herbs hanging from a beam.

He heard a rustling behind him, but he didn't turn. A hand rested on his arm, and he jerked it away.

'Wuffa,' she said. 'Listen to me, will you?' His shoulders tensed, as though in anticipation of a blow. 'Little Toli might want to bed me, * já*? But that's nothing compared to his lust for my father's silver. Only I know where Bolli buried it, you see.' She pulled at his arm. 'Look at me.' This time, still reluctant and angry, he obeyed her. Her beautifully modelled face was stern and proud, and as serious as he had ever seen it. 'I may not be your idea of a noble and virtuous lady—' He opened his mouth to interrupt, but she stopped him, pressing his mouth closed with her fingertips. Her eyes were fierce. 'Do me the courtesy of listening, for once. My father earned his fortune on the whale-roads, sure, going a-viking up and down your coasts, and fighting your kings, and I'm proud of him, do you hear?' She lifted her chin, the hearth-light sparking fiery flashes from her silver hairpins, and took her hand away. 'No, Wulfgar, I've no ancient English, Christian lineage behind me. I wasn't brought up to weave and spin and bake and brew and run a great household.' He blinked at her, rubbing his own fingers over his lips, dazed. 'But,' she said, 'I still will not throw myself away on trash like little Toli Silkbeard. Do you hear me?'

Wulfgar felt furious shame, hot and cold in turn, flushing through his veins. It might have been less agonising if Ednoth and Ronan hadn't been there as witnesses. He felt as though his world was tumbling around him. He fell to his knees.

'My lady,' he said, 'I'm so sorry.'

He felt her fingertips on his head, stroking his hair.

'Stand up,' she said.

He obeyed slowly. When he was on his feet, she clasped her face in his hands and held his gaze. He felt as though she were surveying every last murky corner of his soul; it was a struggle not to turn his head away.

'What beautiful eyes you have,' she said at last. She leant forward and kissed him lightly on the forehead, between the brows.

'Gunnvor, I—'

She was already turning away from him and clapping her hands.

'Nonna!' Her old house-keeper emerged from behind the curtain, and Gunnvor rattled off a string of orders in Danish, *a feather-bed, a warm stone, lambskins*, before turning back to her new purchases. 'You sleep here. It's plenty warm enough.'

'Keeping the creature-comforts for yourself, eh, lass?' Ronan raised an eyebrow.

'I'll let my old Nonna share my bed. She earns her keep, unlike some of my other thralls.' She wrapped her arms around her ribs and gave a little shiver, though the room was stifling. 'How any of you could think I'd bed Toli...' Her voice brisker, she went on, 'If you boys can't sleep, then you can spend the night working out how to pay me back.'

'And what to do tomorrow,' Ronan said.

'Ah, tomorrow.'

Wulfgar said, 'We've got to ride to Leicester and find the saint.' His eyes widened in realisation. 'But we've no horses. We must find horses. We must get the relics back at once.'

'Nonna, find me a tally-stick,' Gunnvor said. 'I'll sort out horses, Wuffa. Just add it to your bill.'

Ronan put his hand on Wulfgar's shoulder.

'Easy, lad. With any luck we'll overtake Leoba on the road. They'll not be going fast, her and the bairns. And if not on the road we'll find her safe at the Wave-Serpent.' He looked hard at Wulfgar's face. 'Don't let your dreams bother you. We're on the homeward run now.'

CHAPTER TWENTY-EIGHT

'Come on, lad.' The priest was sitting himself down on the end of the sleeping platform where Ednoth was still snoring, and he gestured to the floorboards before him. Gunnvor had not yet emerged from her curtained alcove but old Nonna was bustling around, readying their bags and cooking their breakfast bannocks. 'It's hardly hallowed ground, but it will have to serve.'

'Forgive me, Father, for I have sinned.' Wulfgar stopped, his tongue of a sudden too big for his mouth.

The priest had to prompt him.

'What are your sins, my son?'

He took a deep breath.

'I have – I have – Father, I killed a man. I stabbed him in the back.' His lips were quivering of a sudden. 'I murdered him.'

'Was this for personal gain, my son? Or for hatred of the man?' Ronan's voice was gentle, the measured, impersonal tones of the worldly-wise confessor who has heard it all before.

'Oh, no, Father. I didn't even know his name.' He clenched his hands together to stop them shaking. Those killer's hands. Putting it all into words was making it so present to him again.

'And the man you killed, would he have done you the same favour?'

Wulfgar thought back to that dark, muddy nightmare at Bardney.

'Yes, Father. I think he would.'

The priest cleared his throat.

'My son,' he said, 'the secular law would call your actions justified. Not murder. Not even manslaughter. But I am not the secular law. You have done a most serious thing in the eyes of God. Every man is His handiwork; no man is to be thrown away.'

Wulfgar nodded. The floorboards swam before his eyes.

'Father, what is my penance?'

'Is there nothing else on your conscience, my child?'

Wulfgar closed his eyes. Wasn't that enough? But the silence grew, and grew. Outside he could hear an early blackbird piping up. He opened his eyes again and focused on the worn, well-dubbined leather of Father Ronan's shoes. The familiar rhythm of the confessional began to reassert itself. What are my sins? Anger, yes. Pride, sloth, envy, yes. Lust, yes. A yoke of guilt and sorrow began to press down on his shoulders.

'I have lost my temper several times.' The next admission was harder. 'I have been thinking about a woman. With bodily desire.'

'Indeed,' Father Ronan said dryly.

Wulfgar didn't dare look up.

'Pride,' he said next, with relief. 'The relics. I've been thinking about bringing them to the Lady. How she'll praise me. The songs men will make about it. Me carrying St Oswald through the streets of Gloucester, both of us in purple and gold . . .' It was such a beautiful vision, so hard to relinquish. 'I keep thinking it's all about me.'

'And it's not, my son.' Father Ronan's voice was very gentle.

'No, Father. And that's not all.' He braced himself to confront the hardest admission of all. 'I have failed to tell the truth.' *Tell no one*, the Atheling had said. *Tell no one else*. But telling a priest was like telling no one. The confessional was sacred and sealed, and his soul was at stake. He licked his lips nervously. 'No, I mean, I *lied*. I lied to you, Father. The Atheling gave me more than greetings. For Toli Silkbeard, and for Hakon Grimsson.'

'Just Hakon? Not Ketil, then?' There was a new edge to Ronan's voice.

Wulfgar shook his head.

'And it's heavy on your conscience?' the priest went on.

'I don't know what it means,' Wulfgar cried. Ednoth lifted his head sleepily. He lowered his voice. 'He wants the high-seat of Mercia. But I can't believe he would do anything that might hurt the Lady.'

'What is the message?' Ronan asked.

Wulfgar's whisper was almost too faint to be heard: '*We light the fire at All Hallows.*'

'Riddle upon riddle. Would yon hungry Atheling's belly be satisfied with Mercia, think you?'

'I don't know.' He thought back to the Atheling's dark, vivid, contained face. 'I doubt it, somehow.' He looked up at Ronan. The priest frowned, preoccupied. 'Father, my confession?' Their talk seemed to have travelled a long way from his sins. Ednoth sat up and yawned loudly, and Wulfgar wanted to get to the end.

Ronan blinked, and cleared his throat.

'When you get home, dedicate three masses to Thorvald's

memory. For the man you slew, a year of bread and water every Friday. For the other sins, three Paternosters every day for a month.' He got to his feet.

'But what about my absolution?' Wulfgar asked, baffled.

Ronan sighed.

'It's the poor priest you must be thinking me.' He sketched a cross. '*Ego te absolvo*. Go and sin no more. Try not to stab anyone, at least.'

What was the likelihood of that? I'm going home, Wulfgar thought, where I'm safe. He'd never need or want to kill a man again, of that much he was certain. High time he said his goodbyes to Lincoln. Back to Leicester, meet Leoba and the children, and then ride hard as they could for home. He couldn't wait.

Gunnvor had lent Ednoth one of her own horses – 'I trust you, I've seen you ride' – and had borrowed others of lesser breeding. Wulfgar found himself on an old slug, who proved impossible to goad into more than a trot, shuffling his hooves and for ever drifting back to plod in the others' wake.

After ten miles or so he woke from a half-doze to find the other three far down the road ahead of him, and his own horse at a standstill, tearing up mouthfuls of grass. Yanking on the reins and belabouring the beast's ribs with his heels achieved nothing. In the end he slid down from the saddle, meaning to grab the halter and see if dragging might work where riding had failed.

He staggered slightly as his feet hit the ground, and as he was righting himself he heard a faint sound. He thought at first it was the cry of an unfamiliar bird, or perhaps an owl by day, and he crossed himself against ill-luck.

But then the sound came again.

There was no house in sight, not so much a shieling, but the sound was unmistakably that of a baby's cry, coming from somewhere close at hand. The others had ridden out of sight, and he was frozen by indecision – perhaps it was just some travelling woman and her child, and she had understandably made herself scarce when she had seen men on horseback riding towards her. He tugged again on the old hack's bridle and succeeded this time in getting it to relinquish the succulent grass.

Then the cry came again, a dull, tired grizzle. Wulfgar didn't know much about babies, but this one sounded very young and very unhappy. Surely it wouldn't make that appalling sound if it was with its mother? The crying seemed to be coming from a tangled stand of hawthorn and hazel.

No harm in going to see.

He hauled on the bridle again and the sulky horse fell in behind him as they walked through the grass, starred with white and yellow flowers. Celandines, he thought. Daisies. The swallows will be back soon. Somewhere invisible above him a lark was pouring out its praise-song at Heaven's threshold. But it was the crying that drew him on.

He was so intent on the sound that he failed to notice where he put his feet, and he stumbled heavily over something that tangled his feet, only just saving himself from falling on the damp grass.

A basket. No, a straw pannier. He'd caught his foot in one of the handles. The sort of capacious, saggy old thing that would sit very well on a mule's flank, full of apples, or leeks, or carrots, to take to market. But this one was empty, apart from a crumpled length of dirty, ragged sack-cloth that trailed from its mouth. Without even noticing he let the horse's bridle and reins slip from his fingers as he bent to pick the sack-cloth up. But it too was quite empty – except – what was this?

Wedged into a corner.

His fingers scrabbled at the tiny object and brought it before his eyes.

Smooth, brown bone.

The back of his neck and shoulders crawled with a spidery sensation. He longed to doubt the evidence of his eyes and fingers, but he couldn't. This was the sacking that had held St Oswald's bones, the very bundle that he had thrust into Leoba's arms.

So, where was Leoba?

And where were the relics?

Had she stopped – to feed the children, or to clean them, or whatever you did with children – and dropped the bundle? Let the pannier fall off, without noticing? Where were the other bones, then?

What a fool he had been, to expect an unbaptised girl to know their value.

That crying was getting on his nerves. Why didn't she come out of the bushes? She must have recognised him by now.

He held the one little toe-bone tight in his left fist as he searched, turning the pannier over with his foot, but there were no more bones underneath it, none lying in the grass round about. He searched in circles, moving further and further away from the pannier.

'Wuffa?' It was Ronan, calling to him from the road. 'What on earth are you doing?'

He couldn't find his voice, his distress was so great; he just stood there, his lips quivering, a terrible cold seeping through his body.

Ronan was riding towards him now.

'I told the others I'd come back and round you up, lad. Do you need a sheepdog, lad? Hey? What's wrong?' He swung out of the saddle, leaving his mount to fend for itself, and ran towards Wulfgar. 'Christ and all His angels, lad, what are you doing? What's happened?'

Wulfgar, still voiceless, held out his hand. Ronan took him by the wrist and pried his fingers away from the little bone in his palm. He stared and crossed himself. 'Is this what I think it is?'

Wulfgar nodded, and pointed wordlessly towards the thicket.

Ronan frowned at him, and then he, too, heard that faltering grizzle.

'Oh, dearest God, what's that? Come on, Wuffa!'

Wulfgar let the priest run ahead, and had to force himself to go stumbling in his wake. Whatever there was to see, he wanted Ronan to see it first.

When he rounded the thicket, frothy with blossom, he found Ronan on his knees. There was a bundle of cloth, which the priest first tugged at, and then leaned forward to turn it over.

'Oh, no,' Wulfgar said. 'No.' He tried to look away but he had already seen. It was the little girl. Thorvald's little girl. He crossed himself in despair.

Ronan stood up, shaking his head, and walked a few more paces into the thicket.

Blinded by sudden tears, turning the little bone over and over in his fingers, Wulfgar followed him.

The cry was loud now. Leoba lay on her side. Wulfgar had seen her sleeping like that, only yesterday morning, curled around her children, keeping them warm and safe. He didn't think she was sleeping now – the side of her head was a great clotted mass of blood – but she was still curled around the baby. Ronan bent down and drew the furious, red-faced bundle out of the pouched front of her dress.

Wulfgar held out his arms and Ronan passed him the bundled child. It was damp and it stank, but he held it close.

'Hush,' he said. What did mothers say? 'Husha husha husha.' He walked up and down. The baby went on screaming.

Ronan stood up, looking around the little hollow where Leoba lay; now bending over her again, lifting her body with great care and looking underneath. He said something.

'Sorry?'

Ronan raised his voice over the baby's cries.

'She's not been here that long. Her hands are cold, but there's no dew on her for all the grass is so wet.' He knelt again. 'Forgive me, lass,' as he insinuated his hand into the folds of her dress. 'Aye, her belly's warm yet.'

Wulfgar didn't want to hear any of this. He looked back to the road to see Ednoth and Gunnvor riding towards them. Ronan walked back and forth, searching around the pannier.

'What are you two doing?' Ednoth shouted. 'Come on! Do you want to hear a riddle?'

Ronan called something to him then, and Ednoth stiffened. He jumped down from his saddle and joined the search, looking closely at the grass. They conferred. Wulfgar looked at Gunnvor. Her creamy skin had gone chalk-white, her lips bluish. He watched her knuckles whiten as she gripped the reins. He thought she might faint and fall from the saddle, but even as he took a step towards her she took a deep breath and sat straighter.

'Do you know anything about babies?' He was pleased to hear how normal he sounded.

'They need cleaning,' she said. 'I can smell it from here.' She took another deep breath and lifted her head. 'She was under my protection. I didn't think I needed to send a man with her.' She closed her eyes. 'My name should have been enough.'

Ednoth had picked up the pannier and the roll of sacking, and he came over to them then.

'Only two sets of hoof prints,' he said. 'Coming separately, and leaving together.' There was a wobble in his voice.

Wulfgar held the little bundle of howling baby against his heart.

'It's hungry,' he said. He kept seeing Thorvald bringing the mule down to the lambing pens, and the little girl leaving her mother's skirts and running towards him with that happy shout of 'Dadda!' Less than two days ago, and now all three of them were dead, and it was his fault. The baby's screams were reaching an unbearable level. He clutched it tightly to him.

'Give it here,' Ednoth said. He looked at Wulfgar's face. 'I've got little brothers and sisters. You can have it back when I've cleaned it.'

Ronan came over then, his step heavy and slow.

'Both of them, one blow to the head.' He looked at Wulfgar. 'They didn't suffer long.'

Wulfgar could feel his lips trembling.

'Why did he have to kill the little girl?'

'Why did he have to kill either of them?' Ronan shook his head. 'The way they've fallen, I'm guessing he killed the little girl first. It wouldn't be hard. A hammer could have done it, or the back of an axe. Even a stone. And only one horse, so I'm thinking it was a man alone. And he's not far ahead of us.'

Ednoth looked up from where he was wiping the baby's bottom with a handful of leaves and grass.

'Then let's get after him.'

CHAPTER TWENTY-NINE

It had been a hasty burial, horribly reminiscent of Thorvald's: dry branches and a few squares of turf, hacked out with their belt-knives and laid over the bodies of mother and daughter, both looking so small now. The crows and foxes would find little difficulty breaching those barriers.

Father Ronan said a brief prayer.

Wulfgar found himself unable to join him. All he could hear was the voice in his head, shouting – no, screaming – at St Oswald: *They died for you. They would have been baptised if they had had any say. Why didn't you help them? You're famous for your care of the widow and orphan. Where were you? You've got to help them now.* He clutched the little bone convulsively in his hand.

The baby was asleep now, exhausted and lulled by the easy rhythm of the horse. Wulfgar had rigged up a kind of sling for it to rest against his shoulder. Ednoth had shown him how, when it started fussing, to hold it at arm's length and bare its scrawny little bottom. Gunnvor had produced dried apple from a bag, and he had chewed it into a mush and poked it into the toothless mouth. Some of it had gone down.

'Will it die, too?' Wulfgar asked.

Gunnvor had shrugged.

'Probably.' Then, 'Don't look at me like that! What do I know about babies?'

They rode close together now. Even Wulfgar's horse was behaving itself, as if picking up their powerful sense of purpose. There were no hoof prints visible on the road, but Ednoth scouted the verges, on the look out for any sign that two mounts had left the road, and he had found none.

'It won't be Eirik himself,' Ronan said. 'But it could be one of his men.'

'It's not Eirik,' Ednoth said. 'If it were, he'd be heading back to Lincoln, or cutting across to Bardney. Not going on the Leicester road. My money's on Garmund.'

Not Garmund. Wulfgar shook his head. Garmund wouldn't kill a girl not yet four years old. Wouldn't smash a young mother's skull. Wouldn't. Please. I don't want it to be Garmund.

Ronan was shaking his head, too. 'But if it's Garmund, why is he alone?'

'One of *his* men, then,' Ednoth said.

'Could be.' The priest sucked his teeth. 'Heading for a meeting place on the Fosse somewhere. We need to look out – we could find ourselves outnumbered again.'

'Couldn't it just be some horse-thief?' Wulfgar's voice shook. 'Mule-thief, I mean.'

'Faith, an ordinary thief wouldn't have killed them,' Father Ronan said. 'Robbed them, aye, but where would be the need to kill? And no ordinary thief would have been interested in the bones. Chances are this is someone we've come across before.'

'There was no need to kill.' Gunnvor sounded bitter. 'We're looking for someone who likes killing.'

'No shortage of candidates round these parts, then.' Father Ronan sighed. 'Sorry, Wuffa, but it keeps coming back to Garmund. How did he get called Polecat?'

'Have you ever seen a chicken-roost when a polecat's been in?' Ednoth asked. 'They kill a dozen for every one they eat.'

Wulfgar felt their words on his skin like blows. For the first time in his life he felt the need to defend Garmund. 'He had a tame polecat, a little one, when he was a boy. That's why he's called Polecat.' Then the creature had bitten him, Wulfgar remembered, and escaped. 'Yes, all right, it could have been Garmund!' He found he was shaking. 'But how would he know Leoba had St Oswald with her?'

'They had met before, remember?' Father Ronan said slowly. 'The first time he came to Bardney. Maybe he recognised her, got talking to her, she let something slip—'

'She wouldn't give him the bones,' Ednoth chimed in, 'there was a struggle . . .'

The pictures were horribly clear. Wulfgar put his free hand up to fend them off.

'That still doesn't explain why he's doing this alone,' said Gunnvor.

Wulfgar felt ridiculously grateful.

'Come up with a better idea then,' Ednoth said.

Silence.

They rode on late into the night, stopping only once to buy a leather bottle full of milk from a farmwife, and finally camping off the road when exhaustion forced them. The occasional pile of dung had been the only sign that another rider might be a few hours ahead of them and, even so, as Ednoth muttered to Ronan, there was no guarantee that the dung had been left by the beasts they were seeking.

Wulfgar couldn't sleep, disturbed by the butting and whimpering of the baby he carried next to his chest. He dipped a rag in milk and let it suck that, or his little finger, and watched the slow greying of the sky. The others woke after a few hours' rest. Leicester was only a dozen miles off.

'Do we need to stop in Leicester?' Ronan asked, rolling his shoulders and yawning.

'We?' Ednoth paused in buckling his sword-belt.

'Oh, I'll keep with you a few miles past Leicester,' Ronan said.

Gunnvor seemed about to speak, then closed her mouth again. Ronan raised an eyebrow.

'It's wonderful of you to want to help—' Wulfgar said to her.

'Help?' she said. 'You think I care about your bag of bones? Those two were under my hand. We'll find their killer.'

Wulfgar looked at her face, pale in the dawn, the set of her mouth and the faint line between her brows, and he was reminded again of a hawk, its cruel beak and remorseless yellow eyes. He was glad someone else was her quarry.

'What about the baby?' Ronan leaned over and turned the fold of Wulfgar's cloak away from his shoulder. Owlish little eyes gazed back at him. 'You're doing a grand job, Wuffa, but he needs a wet-nurse.'

Wulfgar pulled away. 'I brought the trouble to his house. He's my responsibility.'

'So find him a foster mother in Leicester,' Gunnvor said.

Mulish, Wulfgar shook his head.

'He'll die, you know,' Ronan said.

'We'll need to go into Leicester anyway,' Gunnvor said, 'to ask about a man with a horse and a mule.' She looked at Wulfgar then. 'And a bag of bones.'

They met a farmer driving his ox-cart up from Leicester, and grilled him for news. He'd seen no one who might be the murderer they sought. But, Ketil was away, he told them: 'Aye, off with great pomp last night. Ganging the round of the out-lands that answer to the Jarl.'

'Taking men's oaths?' Ronan asked.

'Taking their taxes, forbye.' He spat.

Leicester looked welcoming and familiar to Wulfgar this time, the great roof of its cathedral a reminder – even with its thatch of weeds – that they were coming back into a world he understood, a world that recognised his status and his talents. Even more welcoming, now that he knew Ketil was out of town. They left the horses to be fed and watered and curried in the yard at the Wave-Serpent.

'Leave the baby with Kevin's mother while we're here,' Ronan had said. He pointed out the house. 'My altar-boy, remember?'

And your son, Wulfgar thought. But he no longer felt in any position to judge the priest's short-comings.

'She loves children,' Ronan went on. 'Tell her I sent you – she'll do anything for me.'

And, indeed, the plump, dark woman had glowed with delight when Wulfgar explained his errand.

'Grand to have a little one to cuddle again, even if it's only for a day or so,' she said, pulling the child's swaddling bands aside, 'and such a handsome boy, too. What's your name, my little lovely?'

Although she had cooed her words to the baby, she seemed to expect Wulfgar to answer.

'Do they have names, this small?'

She shook her head at him, amused.

'What was his father's name, then?'

Wulfgar shook his head in turn. *Thorvald*, may he rest in peace, is no fitting name for a child in my care.

'Well, I have to call him something.' She kissed the baby on the top of its wispy head.

He thought wildly. Every name he came up with seemed too much of a burden for this tiny scrap.

'His name is . . . is Electus.' The Chosen One. I have chosen this child.

'Splendid,' Father Ronan said briskly. 'We'll baptise him this afternoon, and then we'll press on, if we don't find our quarry here.'

'Taking that poor baby with you?' Kevin's mother sounded outraged. 'Then let me pack up some clean tail-clouts, and a flask of milk at least.'

While they had been talking, Gunnvor had vanished into the depths of the Wave-Serpent. Emerging now through its door, she said, 'I'm sending everyone out to ask questions.'

But the people of the houses round the Wave-Serpent appeared to be far more interested in Gunnvor, and what she had been doing, than in some putative stranger, possibly accompanied by a horse, a mule and a mysterious lumpy sack. Wulfgar intercepted a lot of curious glances, and he overheard her name, and Hakon's and Ketil's, over and over in the mouths of the passers-by, and the women standing in the low doors of their houses. He and Ednoth were also the focus of much interest, sidelong stares and jerking of heads and muttering of *utlendingar*. It was making him nervous.

And, in the event, Gunnvor's enquiries led nowhere.

'He can't have stopped here. We need to be getting on.'

They only waited for the christening. Kevin's mother and Wulfgar stood as godparents. Wulfgar's hand shook, holding the candle on the baby's behalf, watching the wax drip onto the packed earth floor of St Margaret's, listening to the oaths he was swearing. *Do you abjure the Enemy? And all his works? And all his empty promises? I do, I do, I do.*

But I can't even keep these vows for myself, he thought in despair, so how can I make them for you, little soul?

His eyes swam, blurring the candle flame into a huge cloud of light. Father Ronan refused to skimp the ceremony, for all their need to hurry. Flame and salt and water and oil all played their part, and when Wulfgar took the baby into his arms at the end of the ceremony, he felt another small fragment of his burden lift.

I'm stuck with you now, little soul.

Closer than blood.

I'm all your family now.

CHAPTER THIRTY

Gunnvor's presence, disturbing as Wulfgar might find it, was making their journey so much easier. For all the excited, salacious muttering and the sidelong glances from her neighbours, she was someone who mattered in Leicester and along the upper reaches of the Fosse Way. She had brought two of her men with her, and they all felt safer for the silent company of her well-armed shadows. Wulfgar was all too aware that he and Ednoth would have been penniless and horse-less now, without her.

And, without her desire for revenge, there would have been no pursuing the man who had killed Thorvald's wife and daughter, and stolen the bones.

A man who seemed to have vanished like morning mist in sunlight. They asked everyone they met as they rode steadily south west; no one had seen any man who answered to that description. They spent the night at the house at High Cross where Gunnvor's toll-collector lived, and the morning found them riding back down to Heremod's estate at Wappenbury.

One little week, Wulfgar thought. We left here last Saturday, and now it's Saturday again. Easter Saturday. How can it only be a week since we sat outside his hall in the sunshine, talking about pots, with his mother feeding us on those excellent crumpets? Look at me, I'm not the same person. I've got a murder on my conscience, and a baby in the crook of my arm, and one tiny toe-bone of St Oswald's tucked away in a bag round my neck, with the Gospel of St John, and I'm at least a thousand years older.

'We'll ask Heremod if he's heard anything,' Ednoth said, interrupting his thoughts.

'The trail's cold.' Ronan sounded glum. 'You must have missed his tracks, where he went off the road.'

'Not unless he really tried to hide his tracks, I didn't. And why would he do that? He doesn't know we're after him. If it's Garmund –' Ednoth looked hard at Wulfgar '– or one of his men, he'll be going to Winchester, won't he? And this is the fastest road.'

'We'll ask for news,' Gunnvor said, 'but if there's no news we won't stop here.'

Wulfgar found he was looking forward with relief to seeing Heremod again; his bluff, good-humoured face and easy hospitality were a pleasant prospect, but the thought of being back on land loyal to Mercia was even more attractive. At the thought of the Lady and her Lord, he heard again that distant little wolf-howl of *failure*, and hugged the sleeping child closer against his heart. How on earth was he going to tell them that he was coming home – not exactly empty-handed – but without the treasure for which he had been sent?

And would it still be *them*?

No, he thought, I have to assume the Lord's still alive. Someone would have told us if there was any really big news; if he had died, or Edward had invaded, or some disloyal thane had staged a coup we would have heard *something*. He held onto that thought like a talisman.

And there's nothing I can do, he admitted. No more than I am doing, anyway.

They were onto Heremod's land now. Ploughmen and sowers in the fields, flocks of sheep in the meadows with gangs of rowdy lambs playing follow-my-leader and king-of-the-hill in the evening sunshine. Nothing seemed to have changed.

Ednoth wound his horn at the gates of the stockade and Heremod's reeve came out to usher them through.

Wulfgar blinked in confusion. The courtyard, so peaceful when he had last seen it, was a turmoil of bustle and disorder. One flank of the byre was stacked with barrels of butter and mounds of fresh cheese; there were straw-packed baskets of eggs, sides of smoked bacon, tuns of ale in one corner, big jars of honeycomb in another. The reeve had to cut short his words of welcome to relieve a man of a bundle of tally sticks while shouting something about killing chickens to a harassed-looking slave-girl.

He turned back to them.

'Come out of the gateway, would you? There's an ox-cart needing in.'

Still mounted, they shuffled their horses to one side to allow the cart, groaning with cords of fire-wood, to come through.

'What's going on?' Ednoth hissed.

'Is that who I think it is? My boys!'

Heremod's mother stood in the doorway of the hall. She nodded a greeting to Father Ronan and Gunnvor as, helped by her stick, she came picking her way through the mountains of provisions that stood between them. Ednoth slipped easily down from his saddle and held out his hands to her.

'Are you well, Auntie?'

'My lovely boy! You came back!' Her dim eyes shifted from him to Wulfgar and back again. 'Both of you! I wish I could offer you a better welcome.'

'We're looking for a man, Auntie,' Ednoth said. 'We think he's on his own—'

'Aye, and a man's looking for you.'

'Wulfgar!'

They all turned then. Another ox-cart came jolting through the gates, with Heremod at the reins. He jumped down to them, handing the reins to his reeve. Wulfgar slid out of the saddle onto the unforgiving cobbles to clasp the extended hand in both of his.

'Heremod! It's good to see you. And to be back in Mercia!'

Heremod beamed between those long yellow-grey moustaches.

'Good to see you, too, boys.' He saw Gunnvor then, and he made a deep bow. 'Gunnvor Bolladottir! So, you found each other! Honoured to have you here. And you, Father. What a pleasure!' He clapped his hands. 'A drink for my friends!'

'This looks to be a busy time for your house, Heremod,' Wulfgar said. 'We won't intrude—'

'Intrude? Nothing of the sort. I insist you stay. Let me feed you, at the very least.' His eyes flickered from face to face, and he turned suddenly to look behind him, out through the gates. 'It's an honour,' he said again, swinging back again with his broad smile, 'and I want to know everything about what you've been doing. Come in here, it's warmer than the hall.'

Relinquishing their horses into the care of his stables, they followed him into the small bower across the yard from the hall, and let him order bowls of warm water, and towels, and oatcakes, curd cheese and mead. His eyes went wide at the sight of the baby, but he said nothing, letting his mother summon a slave-girl with a cup of warm milk.

'We need news, Heremod,' Ronan said. 'We're hunting a man who's travelling alone, with a horse and a mule. We think he's heading south, in a hurry – probably too much of a hurry to stop more than he must. Have you had any word of a man like that, in the last day or two?'

'Now . . .' Heremod smoothed his moustaches with finger and thumb. 'Not *seen* anyone like that, not myself, but it seems to ring a bell – I'll ask, how's that? Someone here must have mentioned something to me, and I'll try and find out who.' He sounded agitated. 'You stay here, and my reeve will see to your needs. Make sure he takes some ale to your men, my lady.' He had already taken a pace backwards, his hands spread wide as though to keep them where they were.

'Tell them to be on their way, boy.'

Wulfgar, startled by her words, saw that the old woman had a grim look on her face.

'Now, Mother!' Heremod's tone took on a note of outrage. 'I'll allow we're busy, but there's no excuse for being inhospitable. You come with me, there's a problem with the saltfish.' He pushed her out before him.

Wulfgar plunged his hands into the wooden bowl of warm water and reached for the linen towel he was being offered.

'Ah, that's better. My fingers go all tingly when I've been holding the reins for a while, and carrying the baby doesn't make things any easier . . .' He tailed off at the look on Gunnvor's face.

'I thought we weren't stopping,' she said.

'Well, just while Heremod sees if he can track down the rumour—'

'I don't believe in that rumour. I don't like this.'

'But these are our friends,' Ednoth said. 'We helped Auntie on the way up here. Heremod's looking after us.' He grinned. 'And I don't know about you, but I'm starving.'

'It'll be dark soon,' Wulfgar said. 'Do we really want to head off into the night?'

'We'll stay to eat, at least,' Father Ronan said. 'Heremod may have news for us by then.'

'Who put you in charge?' Her voice was icy. 'Do I need to remind you that you are still my thralls?'

The slave-girl kneeling in front of Wulfgar dropped the wooden bowl of water she held. It rolled noisily away over the floorboards, a lake of water spreading around their feet. Gunnvor pulled her skirts away from the puddle with an impatient gesture.

'I'm sorry, I'm so sorry,' the girl gabbled, mopping with her small towel. They all backed away from the puddle as another slave hurried up with a broom.

'In law, yes,' Father Ronan said 'but surely you won't make a point of it?'

'I will if I have to.' She turned away to look towards the door.

'Ah, Cat's-Eyes, haven't I done you a good turn now and then, over the years?'

'And you'll redeem them all now, will you?'

He reached out to take her hand. 'If that's the fee, Cat's-Eyes.'

'*Don't touch me!*' She snatched her hand away as she whirled to face him, her other hand to her mouth as though she was surprising even herself by her vehemence. She breathed deeply through her nostrils, her head back, as she struggled to master her temper. At last she said, 'Why is the old lady telling us to go? And Straddler so eager for us to stay?'

Wulfgar had forgotten Heremod's eke-name till Gunnvor reminded him.

Ednoth shrugged. 'Old people are funny sometimes.'

'Cat's-Eyes, face it,' said Father Ronan, 'we may never find this man. And Wuffa's loss is greater than yours. We'll hear what Heremod has to say, stay the night here, and we'll make our farewells to Wuffa and Ednoth tomorrow, eh? Let them go south. And I'll take you home.'

Her breathing was still irregular, and her eyes were shining. Wulfgar realised to his astonishment that she was trying not to cry. It was all he could do not to reach out a hand to comfort her, but he was afraid of what she might say if he did.

'Home?' she said eventually. 'With Hakon dead? With Ketil master? Do you really think there's a home for me in Leicester now? But I'll do as you say, *prestr*. What choice do I have, really?' Her lips pressed together, she started pulling off her gloves. 'Bring me some more water. Make sure it's properly hot. And don't spill it this time.' The girls scurried off to her do her bidding. She handed her gloves to Wulfgar. 'Look after these for me.'

The gloves were warm from her hands. He held them tight while she unfastened the massive silver ring-brooch that kept her cloak together now. Tendrils of thick black hair had come loose during the ride, and when she had repinned the cloak-brooch she began twisting them back into place, strong, shapely hands busy plaiting and pinning. The water arrived and she rinsed and dried her hands before summoning a cup of mead with a terse gesture.

She pulled a face. 'This can't be his best.' Her eyes met Wulfgar's. 'What are you staring at?'

Colour flooded his face.

Horns sounded outside.

'What the—?' Father Ronan swivelled to face the door of the bower.

Wulfgar could see over the priest's shoulder. Both the great gates into Heremod's courtyard were being opened. A brace of outriders, still winding their horns, came first. Then a man with a banner, unfurling in the sunset breeze to show a grotesque mask surrounded with wild snake-like patterns. Then half a dozen armed men, hooves clattering on the cobblestones. They parted to draw up, three to a side, flanking the doorway, allowing two more horsemen to enter. These carried torches, and Wulfgar had to admire the ease with which they wielded the reins and kept the horses obedient while holding their flaming brands aloft. They wheeled and flanked in their turn, and the gateway stood empty.

A long heartbeat.

And then a final rider entered, on a magnificent black horse whose gilded harness glittered in sunset and torch-light. He was hooded and cloaked, his face in shadow. Wulfgar heard Gunnvor's sharp intake of breath without understanding it.

Heremod walked forward.

'My Lord,' he said, his voice cracking. 'Welcome to Wappenbury.'

The hooded rider swung down from his saddle, staggering a little as he landed. He came two or three paces towards Heremod and stopped. Heremod, bowing deeply, went to meet him, and knelt at his feet. The rider extended one heavily ringed hand, and Wulfgar frowned. There was something nagging at his memory, but he would have sworn he had never seen this man before. Then Father Ronan growled something deep behind his beard, and Wulfgar watched, riveted in growing disbelief, as Heremod swore life and love and heart and hand to the service of Ketil Grimsson Scar.

CHAPTER THIRTY-ONE

'So,' Ronan said, 'the wind's from that quarter.'

'I don't understand,' Wulfgar said. He looked from Ronan to Gunnvor, and then back out into the courtyard. 'Heremod said he was loyal to the Lord and Lady of Mercia. He told me so himself—'

'Shh!' Gunnvor batted at him with the back of her hand as if he were a pestilent fly. Her face had taken on a pinched look, giving Wulfgar a sudden premonition of how she would look as an old woman. He turned back to the courtyard. Ketil took his hand from Heremod's head, stepping back, extending his hands again to lift Heremod to his feet, embracing him and kissing him on each cheek.

Wulfgar could feel a muscle jumping in his own cheek.

'I don't understand,' he said again.

Now Heremod stepped back, saying something, gesturing towards the bower. Wulfgar took a step backwards, stumbling against Ednoth. Ketil clapped Heremod on the shoulder, and ushered his host towards the door in the long side of his own hall, past the benches where Heremod had seated Wulfgar and Ednoth as his guests, a long week since. They went inside.

'Now do you see why Heremod wanted us to stay?' Gunnvor's voice could have curdled milk.

Ronan shook his head. 'This is my fault. I should have insisted you boys go to greet Ketil before we left for Lincoln. I know you meant no insult, but he's so damn touchy.'

It was dark in the courtyard now, except for the flare of torches. More of Ketil's entourage were coming in, carts and men on foot as well as more horses and mules. The reeve bustled about, shouting orders at all and sundry.

'Can't we slip away?' Ednoth asked. 'The gates are open. No one will notice, in all this racket.'

'No,' Wulfgar said, 'Father Ronan's right. We should have spoken to Ketil before. And now he'll know from Heremod that we're here with Father Ronan and – and Gunnvor, and they've got to go back to Leicester and face him, no matter what we do . . .' He swallowed.

Gunnvor raised her eyebrows at Ednoth.

'Ah, little one, I'm with you,' she said, 'but I think we're too late.'

The shadowy figure in the doorway jerked his head.

'Is this a dinner invitation,' Wulfgar asked, 'or a warrant for our arrest?'

Father Ronan shrugged.

'There's only one way to find out.' He held up a hand, 'Yes, yes, I'm taking off my sword.' He began to unbuckle. 'Do the same, lad. Don't argue.'

The four of them went out of the bower door.

Wulfgar was aware of men moving in to escort them on either side. The hall door gaped like a mouth, ready to swallow. Inside it was crowded, a great fire blazing on the hearth. Hands gripped his shoulders and he was forced onto his knees. A quick sideways glance showed him that Ednoth was getting the same treatment. He couldn't see Ronan, or Gunnvor.

Ketil was seated in Heremod's great carved chair, which had been moved to the side of the hearth. One side of his face and body was illuminated by the jumping orange light, the other half in deep purple shadow. He looked hard at each of them, and nodded. There was a long moment's silence.

Ketil Scar was well-named. At some point, a long time ago, someone had tried to take his face off, with a sword or maybe an axe. Not the kind of wound many men survive. The tissue had healed shiny in the firelight, puckered and warped, squeezing one eye to a slit, halving his nose and giving his mouth a permanent curl of contempt. His hood was pushed back now, revealing hair close-cropped as if to assert that he disdained to hide his mutilation. His beard grew thickly, but not over the fault-line of the scar. A face with which to frighten small children. It certainly frightened Wulfgar.

Ketil took his time about acknowledging them, long enough for Wulfgar to take in the lustre of bullion at his ears, neck and shoulder, the beautifully cured wolfskin jerkin, even the thread count of his fine wadmal leggings. His knees were only a foot or two away from Wulfgar's face.

Ketil said something then, in Danish. Fast and guttural, and Wulfgar hadn't understood a word. And this, too, came as a shock. He had started to think that all Danes could speak perfectly adequate English. And to preen himself, just a little, on having understood so much of the Danish that he had heard on this journey.

At last he dared look up at Ketil again, to find the Jarl staring back at him, the firelight sending shadows leaping diabolically across his twisted face. After an eternity, Ketil lifted his head and pointed at somebody standing behind them.

'*Thu. Prestr.*'

There was a quick, muttered exchange. 'The Grimssons' tame priest', hadn't Father Ronan once called himself? Before Wulfgar could think too much about this, he found Ketil staring at him again. This time he spoke very slowly, and very loudly, but whether through terror, or Wulfgar's poor Danish, or the impediment caused by the thick scar tissue around Ketil's mouth, Wulfgar found himself incapable of responding. He blinked and looked at Ronan in desperation.

'I was hurt,' Ronan translated smoothly, 'to hear that two visitors from the Lord of Mercia's court had passed through my capital without coming to pay me their respects. I am not a hasty man. I did not get where I am today by being hasty. But I would like an explanation for this breach of protocol. Such secrecy suggests underhand motives. Spies? Assassins? Give me a good reason why I shouldn't have you executed out of hand.'

Elaborate, formal, courteous language. Wulfgar had understood just enough of what Ketil said to know that Ronan was translating with scrupulous accuracy.

I'll have to reply in the same mode, he thought. I hope I can.

'Please – please accept our heartfelt apologies, Jarl of Leicester. We were in a hurry on our way through. We had every intention of calling on you now, on our homeward journey.' The conventions called for a gift, some rich token. But what?

Ketil answered at length, and then leaned forward, scowling, hands on knees, eyes fixed on Wulfgar. Waiting.

Ronan translated again: 'So you consider it acceptable to commit acts of trespass, to disdain my hospitality, to arouse my suspicions, to come to me only when cornered like rats in a barn, and *then* to tell me to my face that you were going to come to me of your own free will? Is this kind of effrontery acceptable to the Lord of the Mercians? If so, manners must be cruder among the Mercians than they are with us.'

Wulfgar didn't dare look up at that face again and he focused on the hands instead. Crooked and battered; swollen flesh around the massive rings.

Wulfgar put his hand to his heart, preparing to grovel and scrape and apologise elaborately for coming to this man's court uninvited and empty-handed, and, as he did so, he felt the outlines of the Bishop's ring beneath his tunic.

Perfect.

He started picking at the knot.

How in the name of Heaven was he going to explain this to the Bishop when he got back?

But there was no time to agonise over the propriety of it, or to get worked up about what the Bishop might say.

Survival was the challenge here.

'As a token of our love,' he stammered, 'please accept this ring.'

The knot was proving stubborn, and his nails kept skidding off it.

Ronan translated and fell silent.

Wulfgar tried at last to snap the thong, failed, and had to pick at the hard little knot for another eternity. Ketil didn't move and Wulfgar found himself sweating under his gaze.

Finally it came undone. He slid the ring off the end and offered it in his cupped hands.

He waited, head bowed, not daring to look up. He was getting pins and needles in his left foot. The men were silent. The fire crackled and spat. Finally he felt Ketil's horny-skinned fingers scraping in his palm. Wulfgar tried not to sag with relief. Ketil leaned over towards the fire, turned the ring over, and squinted at it with his good eye. And now he spoke in thick but clear English.

'Nice. Good gold.' He picked at the setting of the red stone with his thumbnail. 'Out of Miklagard? Jasper, is it?'

'Carnelian, I think,' Wulfgar said, nonplussed.

Ketil still squinted at the ring. He nodded without looking up.

'*Já*, good enough.' He tried to force it over a knuckle and failed, but he had a thong of his own round his neck and it was now his turn to fiddle with knots. Wulfgar watched him adding the ring to his jingling collection.

Blessed Mary, ever Virgin, he thought, all the Angels and Saints, forgive me. I don't know whose relic I've given into the keeping of this monstrous man, but you do. Forgive me, he prayed. Use it as a channel into his heart. I'm sorry, Queen of Heaven. I'm so sorry.

The Bishop, on the other hand, would be wanting more than an apology.

Ketil looked up.

'The priest tells me you have an errand to me.'

Wulfgar gaped.

'Do I have to say it again?'

Wulfgar turned to look up at Ronan. The priest gazed into the fire. Wulfgar struggled up from his knees.

'Father Ronan?'

'Am I wrong?' Ketil asked.

'Father Ronan!' Wulfgar muttered in outrage. 'I told you that under the seal of the confessional! And—' *the message wasn't for Ketil, it was for Hakon.* He bit his tongue.

Ronan shook his head.

'I have not broken the seal,' he said quietly. He looked hard at Wulfgar. 'Not yet, at least. Are you going to make me break it, or will you tell the man?'

Wulfgar was giddy with shock. The secrets of the confessional were beyond sacred.

'I—' Wulfgar stopped. But he had no choice now, did he? He would have to give Ketil the Atheling's message. He couldn't let Ronan throw his own soul away, giving out the secrets of his confession. Treachery, he thought blackly, treachery everywhere. The sin of Judas.

And then he thought: the Atheling's message – what does it *mean?* Is it, *Do nothing till All Hallows?* That's what it sounds like.

Because, if so, that gives Mercia six months' grace. Six months' warning. Half a year to drill the levies and sharpen the spear-blades. And for the Lady (and the Lord? Please, dear God, *and the Lord*) to come up here, let the borderers renew their vows, remember how much they love them, and how much they owe them. Otherwise, what are we left with?

Ketil poaching the petty thanes along the border. Men like this damned Heremod: I should have seen it coming, when I heard him called the Straddler.

Toli Silkbeard and the Atheling in cahoots, plotting Heaven knows what, and pouncing when we're looking the other way.

Maybe I did the right thing after all, he thought, with a wild flash of hope, in giving the message to Toli.

And then he wondered, could this be what Ronan is praying for? *Give Mercia time.*

When I get home, I can give the Lady every detail of what's happened, what I've seen and heard, and with whom I've talked. Whether the Atheling likes it or not.

He swallowed.

'My Lord – *Jarl* – of Leicester, Father Ronan is right. I bring you a private message.'

'Private?' The Jarl held out his hand.

'It's not a written message, my Lord.'

Ketil Scar could *read?*

Ketil gestured for Wulfgar to rise and come a little way towards the dais end of the hall.

'The message?' he said softly, after a dozen paces separated them from the nearest of the fascinated bystanders.

Wulfgar bit down hard on his lower lip to stop it trembling.

Ketil cocked his eye at him.

'Have they told you I'm a monster? Don't worry, little Englishman. I don't flay men. Or hack out their lungs. Or hang them on my house-tree. Not for my own pleasure, any road. Now, whisper it in my ear.' He beckoned with a crooked, swollen finger.

Wulfgar tried to clear his throat.

'From Athelwald Seiriol, Atheling of Wessex.'

Ketil grunted and nodded at him to continue.

'We light the fires at All Hallows,' he muttered.

Ketil seemed to frown then, though with that face it was hard to be sure.

'You have been to Lincoln.'

Wulfgar nodded. How in the name of Heaven did Ketil Scar know that?

'This message was also for him?'

'For Jarl Toli, you mean, my Lord?'

'*Já. Silkiskegg.*' He spat into the straw. 'Toli the child. Why did he get the message first?'

'He – I – when we came to Leicester before, your brother had just died. We didn't want to intrude . . .'

Ketil was silent.

'Was this message for me, or my brother?'

'For –' he swallowed, and lied '– for both of you.'

'I was expecting it,' Ketil said. 'My brother hid nothing from me.' He growled, deep in his throat. 'Go back to your master. Tell him, I hear what he says. I am honoured. But Leicester does not dance when he pipes.' He jerked his head at the guards. 'When I have need of your hungry little Atheling, I will send him a message of my own.' He gave Wulfgar a long, level look. 'I understand your visit to *Silkiskegg* now. But I am still puzzled. What do men of Mercia have to do with Eirik of Bardney?'

Wulfgar thought, Queen of Heaven, how does he know that? He knows so much more about us than I'd realised.

'Pottery trading,' said a voice at his back.

CHAPTER THIRTY-TWO

'*Já?*' Ketil was turning that dreadful battle-mask in Ednoth's direction. 'Go on.'

'We'd seen examples of the stuff they're making in Stamford.' Ednoth's face was bright and open, his voice cheerful. 'We'd heard – Wulfgar and I – that Eirik had an interest. We wanted to offer him a deal. We were told we could corner the market south of Watling Street.'

Ketil was already nodding.

Wulfgar was bowled over. Where had all this come from?

'Who told you this?'

'Heremod Straddler,' Ednoth went on, 'who else? For a share of any profit, of course. But he says the future is in dealing with the Danish states, not fighting them – you, I mean, my Lord.' He smiled, self-deprecating. 'Of course, you know all this much better than I do. We didn't think you'd be interested in a little venture like ours, but we'd be more than happy to have you on board. In fact, we'd be honoured.'

Ketil scowled.

'But why deal with Eirik?'

'His was the name we were given, but we haven't committed ourselves to anyone yet.' Ednoth was wide-eyed, frank, utterly plausible.

Ketil was definitely frowning this time. 'But Eirik looks to Toli *Silkiskegg*. And he's too far north. Why should you go to him if you want to deal with Stamford?' He looked from Ednoth to Wulfgar and back again.

To Wulfgar's amazement, Ednoth took this, too, in his stride.

'Ermin Street, of course, my Lord. We thought that the man who controls the great south road would be the right person to talk to.'

'You thought wrong.' Ketil swung round and summoned one of his men. 'Wine. Stools.' He turned back to them. 'You want the man who holds Watling Street. Me. And, in any case, little *Silkiskegg* does not hold Ermin Street, no matter what he might claim. We need to talk about this.' Ketil waved a hand towards the group of women. 'Serve us. Is that you hiding there, Bolladottir? Bring us some wine.'

'An honour, *herra*.' If Gunnvor was being sarcastic there was no sign in her reverent face or her deep curtsey.

While she was doing the rounds with the great horn, Ketil looked back at them.

'So, is this a deal? I get you all the pottery you want to sell south, and you give me a share? How much were you giving Eirik?'

Wulfgar blinked. Again, he wasn't given a chance to reply.

'Forgive me, my Lord, but we need to know whether the goods you can provide are fine enough for us.' Ednoth's expression said, *I'm being perfectly reasonable.* 'We're thinking of supplying the Lord and Lady of Mercia, you know. Possibly even the West Saxon court. We can't accept anything but the best. Eirik's pottery samples were superb. Wonderful yellow glazes.'

Wulfgar felt panic rise in his throat. You might have the old dog-wolf safely trapped but you still don't goad him with a stick.

But Ketil stretched his face into a smile. It was a terrible sight.

'Not a problem. You've seen what Gunnvor Bolladottir uses at the Wave-Serpent? What Heremod has here?'

Wulfgar nodded, trying not to wince.

'Good enough for you? We can get you yellow if you want yellow, or green, or red. Cooking pots, lamps, tableware, storage jars. Tell my men how much you need. We can arrange packing, transport.' He was in his element.

And so, it seemed, was Ednoth.

Ronan caught Wulfgar's eye and winked at him.

Wulfgar turned his head away and closed his eyes. He didn't want to be there, didn't want to think about how Ronan had bullied him. How the priest had flirted with the fires of damnation, just to ingratiate himself with Leicester's terrifying Jarl.

'Come along and sit down.' Ronan reached out a hand from the other side of the fire, gesturing at a stool. 'Well done, subdeacon. You and the boy are learning fast, aren't you?'

Wulfgar went over to Ronan and stood in front of him, spoiling for a fight. 'What sort of a priest do you call yourself?'

Father Ronan's face went still. 'Not the kind you're used to, I'm guessing. I'm sorry, Wuffa. It was a dirty trick.'

Wulfgar just listened, his face tight, incapable of speech.

Father Ronan rubbed his beard. 'But I had my reasons. I don't think you realised the danger you were in just now, you and the lad. How could I have known you were planning to sacrifice the Bishop's ring?'

'Your reasons?'

Father Ronan shook his head. 'I wouldn't break the seal of the confessional lightly, lad. But we needed to keep Ketil at bay, just long enough for his temper to cool.' He sighed. 'I'm sorry.'

As Wulfgar ruminated on the priest's words, he found the first blaze of his anger subsiding. Buying time for me, he thought. It's only what I hoped I was doing myself, for the Lady. He nodded slowly.

'You mean, he would really have hanged us? If we hadn't found the right things to say?'

'Oh, yes,' Father Ronan said. 'Hanging would have been the least of it.' He reached up and ruffled Wulfgar's hair. 'Tell you what, lad, if we can lay our hands on a harp, I'll teach you that song about the raven and St Oswald. That'll brisk you up.'

The trestle tables were being laid with enormous platters of food. Gunnvor was still holding the great horn, now empty, on her knee, as she sat with the others on the stools around the hearth. Red hair and gold and silver jewellery glinted in the firelight as one of Ketil's hangers-on came forward to squat down on his haunches between Gunnvor and Wulfgar.

'All right, Cat's-Eyes?' he said to Gunnvor. He turned to Wulfgar. 'All right, Englishman?'

Wulfgar nodded. The man looked hauntingly familiar. Where, he wondered, had he seen that combination of glittering bullion and fox-coloured hair before?

'Yes, thank you,' Gunnvor said, without turning her head. She was still listening to Ketil and Ednoth's cheerful haggling.

'Where's my drink, Cat's-Eyes?'

'Get it yourself, Ormsson,' she retorted. 'I'm busy.'

And Wulfgar trapped the elusive memory. The sun slanting though into Father Ronan's little Margaret-kirk in Leicester, and Orm Ormsson glittering like motes of dust in a ray of light. And then that watershed of a conversation in the yard at the Wave-Serpent. How could he conceivably have forgotten? But so much had happened to him, in the interim.

Orm Ormsson sighed and shook his head.

'Word is you're going soft, Cat's-Eyes.'

This did get her attention. She didn't say anything, but she shifted round on her stool and gave him a long stare. He balanced himself by holding on to the edge of her stool with one hand and toyed with the trinkets at his neck with the other, looking up at her from under his long lashes.

Father Ronan was talking to another of Ketil's men now, still apparently on his quest for a harp, and Wulfgar had nothing to do but drink and listen.

Orm shook his head sadly.

'First you turn down the chance to fund my eastern trip. Where's the fun in that? Then I hear you're buying more land – that's an Englishman's game, Cat's-Eyes. A fool's game. You want to stick to portable goods. Keep to what you know.' He jingled his pendants at her.

'I'm not short of silver, Ormsson. Unlike you, I have the taste not to wear it all at the same time.'

'And now you're jaunting around with these English. Pets of yours, are they? Someone told me you'd bought them, but I said you had a better eye for a bargain.'

His tone was taunting.

Wulfgar, wincing, didn't know where to look.

'Pets?' she said. 'You could say that, Ormsson.' She looked over his head and straight into Wulfgar's eyes. 'But I prefer to think of them as my friends.'

She held Wulfgar's astonished gaze for a moment, and he tried to find something to say.

But by the time he had gathered his wits and opened his mouth, her attention was already turned elsewhere: she had shifted back to watch Ednoth and Ketil again, over the far side of the fire. He looked at her back-lit profile. *My friends*, she had said. Gunnvor Bolladottir, I am proud to be called your friend, he thought. But was it even possible for a man and a woman to be friends? What's more, she's one of the lost, he thought. A heathen. One of the damned.

And you, Wulfgar of Winchester?

Where had that voice come from? He swung round on his stool.

Are you so cocksure of your own salvation?

Clear as a bell in his ear. But there was no one there. He shivered, suddenly and violently. Nobody else seemed to have noticed anything.

Orm tossed his russet hair back and rolled his eyes.

'As I said, Cat's-Eyes. Soft.' The firelight caught the gold and silver at his throat, a dozen or more filigreed and chased and embossed and chip-carved ornaments hanging against his breast-bone, jingling gently against tiny hammers and spears. Most of his hoard looked like English work, or Irish, and Wulfgar wondered bitterly how many of those trinkets had been gouged from reliquaries and book-bindings.

Then his face froze. What was that?

He blinked and looked again.

There must be hundreds of such things. A little slip of silver wire, looped round and twisted back on itself, to make a ring.

Hundreds, thousands, of such things, yes. But Wulfgar would have laid his hands on the Holy Cross itself and sworn that he knew that particular one.

He had dangled it in front of Electus's fascinated little hands just – he counted – four days ago, outside Leoba's hut at Hanworth. He only had to close his eyes to see her unlooping that strand of blue wool from around her neck and pressing the ring into his hand. He squinted. Three twists, yes, and a protruding end of wire, and surely that was a snag of wool caught on the end?

He had never thought to check whether the ring on its loop of yarn was still around Leoba's neck, before they had done what little they could to bury her.

He was very cold of a sudden, despite his proximity to the fire.

And here was Ronan, holding a harp aloft.

'Success! Make room, boys. Time for the glee of St Oswald and the Raven!'

I've got to know, Wulfgar thought. But how?

'It's not exactly my Uhtsang,' Ronan said, 'but it'll give us a tune.'

Wulfgar leaned in close to Orm.

'Didn't you say something about looking for St Oswald, back in Leicester?' he breathed in the other man's ear. 'Any luck?'

Orm shifted almost imperceptibly towards him.

'What's your interest, Englishman?'

Under the cover of Ronan tuning the harp and uttering loud complaints about the quality of its strings, Wulfgar breathed, 'I speak for the Lady of Mercia. We can pay . . . almost anything . . . for the right bones.'

A sideways flicker of the amber eyes.

'Count a long hundred, then come outside.'

Wulfgar clasped his cold hands between his knees, forcing himself to hold them loosely, to keep his shoulders slack, his breathing even. He had no idea what he was going to do. He wasn't even sure if Orm Ormsson had really left the hall, or whether he was being watched from behind a pillar.

He didn't dare say a word to Gunnvor.

Ednoth was still engrossed with Ketil.

'Straw for packing?' he heard Ednoth ask, and 'Moss is best,' Ketil replied. It was an elaborate game that the boy was playing. Wulfgar wondered what Ketil would say when he learned that Ednoth had no intention of following through with this deal.

He counted his heartbeats.

'Where are you going, Wuffa?' Ronan bellowed. 'I've just got this wretched lump of bog-oak tuned!'

'Skitter-house,' he said.

'Men use the stable,' said Heremod, 'ladies the byre.'

Traitor. Turncoat. Wulfgar squeezed his way through the crowd.

The courtyard was dark now, and quiet. The mounds of provisions had been packed into Ketil's carts, and the cobbles stood bare under the moon. There was no sign of Orm Ormsson. Wulfgar took another few steps and the hall door swung to behind him, cutting off the cheerful roar within.

'Where's your money, Englishman?'

He had heard nothing, but Orm was at his back, breath warm in Wulfgar's ear, his sweet musky odour mingling with the smells of the stable. Wulfgar tried to turn and found himself seized by the left elbow, a cold blade at the right side of his throat.

'Don't move,' the voice said behind him. 'Where's your money?'

'I haven't any.'

The blade pressed closer.

'Don't lie.'

'I'm not.' He almost shook his head, stopped just in time. Cutting your own throat, how foolish would that look? 'Search me, if you like. But I've nothing on me. You'll need me alive if you want money for the relics.'

A quick, intimate hand, groping and patting his armpits, waist, groin. A sigh, and the knife was taken away.

'How unfortunate.' Orm moved round to stand in front of him. 'It was worth a try, though.'

'Indeed. Now, St Oswald.'

'The stable.'

Orm led the way sure-footed in the dark and Wulfgar stumbled after him. A heap of straw, a pile of bags, the smell of malted grain, the rustling and squeaking of rats, a pale rectangle of moonlight in the doorway.

'Here.' A bulky leather bag in Orm's hands. He stepped into the moonlight. 'Look.'

Wulfgar knelt and opened the neck of the bag. Long bones, small bones, ribs, those strange winged elements of the pelvis, footbones like dice . . . everything seemed to be there. His fingers danced along a femur: he knew that strange, polished sheen. He bent his head.

'My Lord. My King. Pray for us.'

Orm was restless in the doorway, his knife still drawn. He held his hand flat, palm down, balancing the point on the back of his hand, catching it by the hilt when it toppled and fell, over and over.

'So?'

'Yes. The real thing.' Wulfgar stood up. You unspeakable murdering filth, he thought. 'How much?'

'How much will you pay?'

'I'll have to take them to Gloucester to be verified,' Wulfgar said, thinking on his feet. 'You'd better come, too, and you can agree a price with the Lady, and the Bishop.'

'Oh, no. No, no, no, *no*. Why should I sell them to the first bidder?' Wulfgar could hear the smile in Orm's sing-song voice. 'Now I know you want them, I might try Winchester next. Canterbury. York. Chester-le-Street.'

Wulfgar breathed deep, keeping his anger at bay, though he could feel the hot blood mounting into his face. 'That's your privilege, Ormsson. Tell me one thing, though.'

'What's that, Englishman?'

'Where did you get that silver ring you're wearing on your neck?'

'Ring?'

And Wulfgar leapt. He had drawn his belt-knife while he had been kneeling over the bag of relics, and now he stabbed wildly where Orm had been, but the other man had twisted and jumped, so like a fox, and was somewhere to one side, fending Wulfgar's knife off with his forearm and stabbing in his turn.

'Ednoth!' Wulfgar found he was shouting. 'Ronan! To me! To me!' He hurled himself sideways like a battering ram and knocked Orm off his feet, but fell himself as he did so and sprawled awkwardly on his side, with Orm's legs trapped beneath him, kicking and flailing. And then Orm was up, kneeing him in the belly and winding him, knocking the knife from his hand. He heard shouts, footsteps on the cobbles, and then Orm's knife came down.

CHAPTER THIRTY-THREE

'Wuffa? Wuffa! Open your eyes! Is he dead?'

He knew that voice. Ednoth.

He opened his eyes obediently.

'No. I'm all right.'

Wulfgar put his hand to the back of his head. He had whacked it hard when he fell, but it was an earthen floor, thick with straw and muck. No lasting harm done.

'Don't sit up! That knife—'

Knife? He squinted down at his chest. Why wasn't he dead? Orm's knife appeared to be embedded in his heart. He shifted his shoulder-blades, breathed deeply. Pain, but not the sort you would expect. *Was* he dead? He reached out and tried the handle of the knife, but the angle was awkward.

'Pull it out.'

'You need to be careful, lad.' Deeper. Father Ronan's voice. 'Pull it out, do more harm than good. It must be stuck in a rib. Stay where you are for the moment.'

'No,' he said. Why couldn't he explain? His head swam.

'Oh my dear God.' Ronan was bending over him. 'Sweet Lord and Saviour. St Oswald, Luck of the English, pray for us. If you survive, Wuffa, they'll be calling *you* Luck of the English.'

'What *happened?*' Ednoth sounded peevish.

There were more footsteps, more voices.

'The knife's not in me,' Wulfgar said. 'Pull it out.'

Ronan knelt at his side, and palpated his chest. 'Ah.' He gave a tug. 'What have you got under there? Ring-mail?'

'St John. And St Oswald.'

'What?'

'Who were you *fighting?*' Ednoth sounded on the verge of tears.

'Give me a hand up.' Wulfgar brushed the straw and dung from his tunic and leggings. When he was steady on his feet, he said, 'It was Orm Ormsson. He killed the little girl. And Leoba.'

'What?' Ednoth and Ronan in unison.

'He had her ring, that's how I guessed. And he had the relics. Where is he?'

'*Ormsson?* Damn.' Father Ronan gusted a sigh. 'I never thought of that.'

'Where is he?'

'Leading the hunt for your attacker, or so he told us.' Father Ronan shook his head. 'We came running in here, to find you on the floor and Ormsson scrambling onto his horse, or someone's horse, shouting that he was after the man who'd killed you.'

'He's gone,' Ednoth said. 'God damn his filthy soul. He's out through the gates and a mile away by now.'

Gunnvor stood in the doorway, silvered by the faint moonlight.

'I'll find him,' she said. Her tone sent a shiver down Wulfgar's backbone.

Father Ronan pushed at the stiff wool of Wulfgar's tunic.

'Nasty rip you've got there. But you're right. There's no blood.' He pulled out the bag that held the gospel book, and that tiny toe-bone that Wulfgar had found abandoned with Leoba's pannier. The little volume's already-battered binding was now further defaced by a long score that had ripped across the leather and dislodged a silver boss.

'And that's what turned Ormsson's blade.' He opened the book. 'How long have you been carrying this? St John, beloved disciple—'

'Pray for us,' Wulfgar joined in. He took the little book and the bag gently from Father Ronan's hand and pressed them to his lips.

'What's this?' Ednoth stood by the stable door, holding a bag. 'It's – is this what I think it is?'

'He left the relics.' Wulfgar felt a great fountain of joy burst through him. Only his exhaustion stopped him from leaping to his feet and squealing like a child. 'He left the saint.'

CHAPTER THIRTY-FOUR

He had confessed his sins, all the way back up the road in Lincoln, and Father Ronan had absolved him. But as Wulfgar rode down to Gloucester shortly before noon on Tuesday, the little imps of pride were at it again. *Tell us,* they murmured, *how are you going to do this?*

Will you seek a private audience with the Bishop, tell him the whole story, keep him in suspense until the last minute, then produce the relics at the very end, to be embraced and wept over?

Why not go straight to the Lady, say nothing, throw yourself at her feet and hold up the bag of bones? Think of her face when she opens it!

Or ride through the streets of Gloucester, shouting, 'A miracle! A miracle', get the crowd following you, all the way back out to Kingsholm, go to the Lord's bedside – 'I bring all the medicine the Lord of the Mercians needs.'

Wulfgar sighed. They were all attractive prospects, but the last, he thought, was the most appealing.

He was riding alone but for the swaddled and, mercifully,

sleeping baby in his pannier. He had insisted on keeping the child with him: it went a tiny way towards assuaging the guilt and pain he felt over the deaths of Thorvald, and Leoba, and the baby's older sister.

Ednoth, to Wulfgar's astonishment, had said he was going to stay on in Ketil's train for a little. Wulfgar had blinked, his hand frozen on his horse's girth.

'But there'll be a big ceremony when we get to Gloucester, celebrations, everyone will want to hear what happened. You'll be the centre of attention. Surely you'd like—'

Ednoth had shaken his head.

'I'll come on behind you, in a day or so,' he'd said. 'Less, even. You need to hurry, I know that. But there are a few things I have to sort out here first.'

A sickening, leaden dread had seized Wulfgar's guts.

'You – you're not doing what Heremod did, are you? Swearing allegiance to Ketil?' It was too appalling to contemplate.

Ednoth had laughed, and, then, at the look on Wulfgar's face, he had stopped laughing and seized him by the elbows.

'Wuffa, look at me!' His brown eyes had been round and serious. 'Never, never, never. After what the Lady did about our land? What I'm staying for –' he had looked at his feet then and Wulfgar had seen a red flush creep up the lad's neck '– well, it's my secret. But there's no shame in it, and it won't be a secret for long, not if all goes well. All right? Trust me? And I won't be long behind you. The party will probably still be going on.' He had smiled, his cheeks still flushed. 'On your horse!' He had clapped Wulfgar on the shoulder and gone back into the hall.

Wulfgar had frowned, still unable to make anything of Ednoth's words. What could there possibly be, to keep him the wrong side of Watling Street? A girl? His mind had darted to Gunnvor in a jealous flash but his more rational side knew he could dismiss that idea without further thought. No love lost between those two.

And what right would he have had to feel jealous, anyway? He would never see Gunnvor again.

She hadn't even said goodbye. The last he had seen of her was in Heremod's stable, just before the confused crowd had come pushing in, demanding to know what all the shouting was about.

But, he'd thought, she still owns me. Legally I'm her slave, and the five øre she paid Eirik the Spider is the least of what I owe her. He'd shaken his head. There would be a hefty bill coming in one of these days.

And he would be proud to pay it.

Now here he was, a world away from her, riding down to the silvery branching Severn, looking at Gloucester spread before him. Hardly a city at all, yet, for all the Lord and Lady's lofty talk of a new capital for Mercia to replace the lost citadels of Tamworth and Repton – just the patched-up ruins of the Roman walls, and market gardens, and churches. The ancient stone minster of St Peter was furthest away, to its right the tall timber church of St Mary Lode, and closest to him the bright white plastered tower of the Lord and Lady's new church, as yet unhallowed and unnamed, all standing proud of the low, thatched roofs of the huts and farm buildings.

Much closer to him, outside the walls, he could see the splendid carved and gilded shingles of the roof of the royal palace. Kingsholm, his destination.

What difference would the relics of St Oswald make to the future of Gloucester, and Mercia?

He smoothed an anxious hand over his shaggy hair, still feeling for the absent comfort of his tonsure. His clothes were creased and grimy, with a long, three-cornered tear in the breast of his tunic, and despite his best efforts he was blood-stained still. He was bone-weary, having ridden the long miles from Wappenbury hard, with many silent apologies to his borrowed horse – something else for which he would have to repay Gunnvor. But he couldn't repress his sense of bubbling triumph, here, so close to the end of his journey, the saint riding pillion with him.

Since saying goodbye to his friends at Wappenbury he had kept the parcel of St Oswald's bones tucked inside his tunic in a sling, close against the skin of his chest. A dull ache in his neck and right shoulder paid testimony to his faithfulness. Ten days ago the saint had been little more than a misty presence to him, a name in an old song. Now he was his bosom friend. And his protector. They had not been waylaid over the last three days, not by Orm Ormsson, nor by Garmund, nor by Eirik the Spider, though all three had been haunting his dreams.

But, for all his elation and relief, Wulfgar's heart still had room to entertain a tiny, worm-like niggle of unease. Word on the road had been that the Lord of the Mercians was barely clinging on to life, and that he had been brought by barge downriver here to Gloucester, to die.

The same informant had told Wulfgar that the Atheling had gone back into Wessex, down to the nuns' minster of Wimborne in Dorset, to pay his respects at his father's grave. What that might signify, Wulfgar didn't know, but he had been glad to hear it. It would be easier to tell the Lady about her cousin's machinations if he wasn't around in person. And it would further defer the moment when Wulfgar would have to tell the Atheling about Toli

Silkbeard, and Hakon of Leicester being dead, and about him having given the message to Ketil Scar instead.

He rode up the broad track to Kingsholm, past the first out-buildings, under the great-timbered gate, and into the courtyard. His heart pounded, and his breath was quick and shallow. This was it, at last.

Home, and dry. Now for the hero's welcome, the tears of joy, the story-telling . . .

Where was the Lady?

Where was everybody?

The stables stood empty, doors ajar. No clang of hammer from the smithy. No children playing knucklebones in a sunny corner. A solitary cat asleep in the sun on the steps up to the hall.

'Hallo? Hallo!'

Silence.

He tugged his horse's reins, circled him to look round the whole yard.

Deserted.

And suddenly he realised what must have happened.

The Lord had died.

Surely nothing else could have emptied the palace like this. The Lord of the Mercians had lost his last and hardest fight, and even now they must be burying him in one of the city's churches. A chill hand clutched his heart. He slumped in the saddle, his eyes closed. Too late, said his heartbeat. Too late.

My Lady, he thought, I'm so very sorry.

She would be in despair. And he had failed. If he had done what the Atheling had claimed was possible, if he had brought the relics home in a week . . . Oh, Queen of Heaven forgive me. Her husband might have been saved. At the very least,

St Oswald would have been a source of extraordinary comfort and hope.

Would have been . . .

As if in sympathy, a fretful whimper came from the pannier. Oh, don't wake up, he begged the child silently. Please. Not now. Holy Mary, Mother of us all, what shall I do with this child?

'Can I help you, master?'

He turned his head. A slave-woman stood at the door of the kitchen, drying her hands on her apron.

'What's going on? Where is everybody?'

'Don't you know, master?'

He shook his head, bracing himself to have his shock and grief confirmed.

'The King of Wessex is coming into Gloucester. Bringing the relics of Holy Oswald.'

'The King – St Oswald – what? *Edward*?' Wulfgar stammered out in disbelief. The parcel of bones against his heart seemed to burn him.

'Aye. And I've got to stay here and tend the hearth-fires, curse my luck.' She looked at him strangely. 'Word came, two, three days back. It's a holiday, even for the slaves. Where've you been, master, that you don't know that?'

'Now, do you mean? He's coming *now*?'

'He's here already.' She looked up at the sun. 'Noon at the Old Minster, they said. They're meeting there and going round the bounds to the new church.' She looked at him more closely. 'Is that a baby you've got there?'

Electus chose that moment to whimper again, and then to bawl more loudly.

'Thank you,' Wulfgar said hastily. 'I – I must go after them. Important business.'

'And leave the poor little thing in that state? He sounds perished with hunger.' She walked over to him, hands twisting the fabric of her apron. 'Leave him with me, till your business is done?' She looked up at his face, something unfathomable in her eyes. 'I've lost my own. I'll feed this one for you.' She lifted Electus out of the pannier, not waiting for his answer. 'Hungry, are we? You're terribly thin, little heart. There, there.'

Wulfgar felt affronted. The child was rather cleaner than he was himself, and at least as well fed. But it seemed she was giving him no choice. He eyed her more closely. Well, she looked capable, and sober.

'My name is Wulfgar. I'm the Lady's secretary. Care for him well, and you will be rewarded.'

She gave him a long look, cradling the bundle of baby against her shoulder as she tugged at the neck of her dress.

'That would be welcome, master. Take your time. I've milk and to spare.'

'Thank you, again,' he said. And a candle owed to the Queen of Heaven.

CHAPTER THIRTY-FIVE

Now that he knew what he was looking for, he could see the shimmer of the procession in the distance, winding its way down through the city. The crowd was around the Old Minster. They were meeting now, making their joint way to the new church, whose freshly lime-washed walls glittered in the sun.

Wulfgar caught up with the tail of the procession as the vanguard paused outside the southern porch, beside a wooden dais which looked as though it had been thrown up hastily for the occasion. The Lady rode a magnificent bay mare, her brother a matching gelding. Edward was escorted by a clutch of his own hearth-retainers, armed and anonymous in blue cloaks and burnished helmets. Then followed a litter with a woman and two young children; Wulfgar recognised the woman as Edward's long-standing mistress. Could her presence possibly mean Edward had actually married her in church at last? Acknowledged his son as heir to Wessex? He was out of touch with the Winchester gossip, but even in Worcester, surely, he would have heard news of that magnitude.

They were reining in, turning to the crowd, holding up their hands.

Whispers in the crowd.

Silence.

Now? Wulfgar cleared his throat. He shook, and his heart thumped.

Too late.

'My beloved people.' The Lady's voice carried over the heads of the crowd. It was as though she spoke in Wulfgar's ear. 'My brother, the King of Wessex, has this day brought us the greatest gift.' After each phrase, she paused, allowing the crowd to seize her words, pass them back. 'He, through his wisdom and courage, has penetrated the dark heart of heathendom to free our beloved St Oswald from his captivity. And in his love for us, he has given the relics into our keeping, to enshrine in our new church.' She waved one glittering hand and in response the bell began to toll. 'Pray with us, my dear people. Pray for the health of your Lord, my husband, and pray that, under the leadership of St Oswald, Mercia, too, will be returned to health.'

How much of that carefully crafted rhetoric did she believe?

Edward was speaking now, standing in his stirrups for the extra advantage of height. 'A strong kingdom has a strong faith! St Oswald will unite us – West Saxons and Mercians, brothers under his banner – yes, and the men of Northumbria, too! We will fight the heathen in his name, and he will lead us to victory, as he did when he was still in his body – this very body here!' He threw his hand in the direction of the reliquary. 'Victorious in the days of our forefathers, we will see him victorious again!' A roaring cheer.

The Lady and her brother dismounted and climbed the steps to the dais.

Wulfgar tightened his lips. Something was trying to escape them, and he wasn't sure whether it was a sob or a most untimely laugh. Edward is choosing to leave rather a lot out of St Oswald's story, he thought.

But, to give my old schoolmate his due, he must have been paying more attention than I thought in our rhetoric classes. The crowd is loving it. They're loving everything today, even our overlord of Wessex.

Now came the procession of churchmen on foot. Wulfgar, still on the verge of hysteria, clutched the parcel of bones in their sling under his cloak as if they might be snatched from him. From his saddle he could see over the heads of the crowd to the reliquary borne aloft by four deacons, all of whom he recognised. Four Winchester men. He frowned. Surely for diplomatic reasons two of them ought to be Mercians. That spiteful, sneaking Kenelm, for example . . .

And Winchester choristers. Faces he recognised. To think he'd been praying to hear Winchester music again. What had Father Ronan said, among the ruins of Leicester Cathedral? *Be careful what you ask for . . .*

He caught glimpses of carved and gilded wood beneath a gem-encrusted pall, which dazzled with sunlight, preciousness and sanctity. Every cleric in the city, with other faces he recognised from Worcester and the surrounding minsters, must have assembled in the courtyard in front of St Peter's to escort the saint up and down and round the churches and huts and market gardens of Gloucester before coming here to the new church. The Bishop of Worcester was in the vanguard, in a cope which flashed fantastically in the sun, so stiff with gold that it would have stood up on its own. More flashes of light glanced from the processional cross onto the pink, freshly scrubbed, newly tonsured scalps of the priests and lesser clerics.

The grubby bundle he held couldn't possibly compete with all this.

But what was in there, behind the glitter?

There must be something. No one would arrange this ceremony for an empty box.

Wulfgar nodded, breathing deep and slow as realisation dawned. It had to be the bones of the nameless monk of Bardney, and the rune-carved fragments of the old wooden reliquary.

So, Garmund had got safely back to Wessex.

Wednesday, Garmund had taken the bones. Two days, maybe, hard riding on good horses from Bardney . . . Garmund had good horses.

King Edward must know they're not the real relics, Wulfgar thought savagely. Or must guess, at least. Denewulf of Winchester may look like a fussy old wether, but he's not that big a fool, not where matters of the Church are concerned.

So, Friday, he guessed, they must have received the bones in Winchester. And seen at once that they weren't the real thing. Edward wouldn't risk St Oswald's wrath falling on Winchester. So he's palming the false relics off on his sister. Trying to undermine Mercia, put something false, something rotten, at its core . . .

Wulfgar felt the hairs on the back of his neck prickle. Edward must have sent word that he was bringing the relics straight away – two, three days ago, they heard, that's what the woman at Kingsholm said. Saturday, probably. Queen of Heaven, they've been working hard. And I didn't leave Wappenbury till Sunday.

He closed his eyes.

If I'd been quicker, more decisive, I'd be up on that dais now.

With the true bones of my Lord and saint. I couldn't manage the job in a week, but I might have done it in ten days . . .

Lips stiff with righteous anger, he thought, I've got to get this over with. This is my moment. He shortened his reins and tensed his thighs, preparing to urge his horse ahead. Ride forward, throw back your cloak, bring out your bag, and proclaim the presence of the saint!

There was a sudden commotion in the crowd at the entrance to the square.

Clerics and lords and dairywomen and ploughboys all turned as one, voices stilled and necks craning. The Lord of the Mercians' litter had arrived. Wulfgar sagged again. He couldn't interrupt this, not now.

The crowd parted, falling back, some spontaneously falling to their knees. Wulfgar sneaked another glance at King Edward, curious to see what he would make of this display of devotion to his rival. But as far as he could see Edward was serene and smiling. Now everyone could see the litter-bearers advancing – a litter, Wulfgar thought miserably, that looked more like a funerary bier. The Lady walked to meet it, resting one hand lightly on the embroidered cover that covered her husband's motionless form. The Bishop gestured and the reliquary-bearers moved forward.

A strange symmetry here: the laymen bearing the body of the ailing Lord of Mercia coming to meet the clerics carrying the bones – the putative bones – of the dead King and Martyr of Northumbria. The Lady had a set expression on her face, as though she were struggling to keep her feelings hidden, no matter what might happen.

Does she know they're not real, the relics? Surely not, Wulfgar thought. She's got too much integrity to go through with this if she did.

The Lady might be determined to keep herself under control but the crowd knew no such restraint. Tears were flowing freely. In the last few days the man they had known for so long as the Old Boar, the Lord of Mercia, had vanished. In his place was this stranger, a wasted figure apparently sitting up but all too clearly propped and held by cushions. Those blue-veined hands, mottled and claw-like, flopped loosely on the cover with every step the bearers took. Had his hair always been that ash-pit grey? His eyes were closed, his head lolling to one side, a sheen of spittle in the corner of his mouth. The bearers lifted him up onto the dais.

Wulfgar glanced at Edward again. The contrast was agonising. He chewed at his lip and looked down at his hands gripping the pommel of his saddle. The knuckles stood out white.

All the bells had stopped ringing now; the word must have got back to the minster and St Mary's. The crowd was growing all the time.

Everyone watched the two biers. The bishop nodded at the choir. It must have been a prearranged signal because they at once began singing an anthem, soft and haunting. *O Oswald, builder of churches, champion of faith, a lion in battle* . . . The priests set the reliquary down on the dais. The Bishop went over to it and removed the gold-tasselled pall to reveal the casket underneath, its paint and gilding looking barely dry. He lifted the lid and took out a purple silk bag. A sigh hushed through the crowd. The thurifers stepped forward and swung billowing clouds of incense over the bones.

The Bishop moved slowly towards the bier. Even standing downwind Wulfgar could hardly hear anything, just a mumble, which could have been prayer or the Bishop having a word with the Lady. She stepped away from the litter and made her way up to the dais to join her brother. The Bishop took her place. He bent over the corpse-like figure, concealing the Lord of the Mercians entirely for a couple of minutes in a shroud of gold. The crowd was tense and silent; not even a baby cried. Finally the Bishop stepped back, still holding the silk bag. But no one looked at him: every eye was on the sick man. He lay still as he had been before, his head slumped to the side, the fragile white-clad body swamped by cushions. The silence held.

Wulfgar became aware of the shuddering of his own heart, counting out the moments as they waited. And waited. He looped his reins over his saddle-bow and, unseen beneath his cloak, folded his arms around the lumpy bundle of bones.

King Edward might think otherwise, St Oswald, he thought, but you are really here.

What was it Father Ronan said? *A bell you can ring, to get the saint's ear. And the saints plead for us to God, if they choose.*

St Oswald, St Oswald, *please*. I know I'm asking a lot, but look at what I've been going through for you. Do this for me if for no one else. Or do it for Thorvald, and Leoba, and their little girl. For Electus. For all the holy innocents of this world. I've compromised my own soul for you. Killed. Lied. Surely I deserve something in return. *Please*.

And suddenly there was a change in the air, as though the wind had shifted its quarter. The Bishop, who had been standing quietly by, hands folded and eyes downcast, snapped to attention. The crowd began to murmur, and then fell still.

The Lord of the Mercians turned his head, and lifted a hand.

Two of his attendants came forward swiftly. He was plucking feebly at the coverlet. They pulled it aside from him.

Beneath it he was fully dressed.

That pale cloth, which had looked so like a winding sheet, was only the finest of lambswool cloaks. He even had shoes on. They arranged his arms over their shoulders and gently levered him to a standing position. His sword-bearer stepped forward and deftly buckled the sparkling harness around his waist and shoulder, and then buttoned the sword and scabbard in place. The Lord raised his right hand, his left arm draped around the shoulder of a retainer, and the crowd went wild.

Now Wulfgar did look at King Edward. He was watching the scene with veiled eyes and set mouth. He looked down to his side and said something to his son. His wife bent and put her arms around the boy. Wulfgar couldn't guess at any of what they were saying, as the air was too full of shouts for the Lord and Lady of the Mercians, and the Bishop, and St Oswald.

The Lord of the Mercians turned to lift his hand to first one side of the crowd and then the other. His feet shuffled – he was utterly reliant on the men who were helping him – but there was no doubt that he was standing. He was opening and closing his mouth, too, but no one could hear what he was saying. He was surrounded by hundreds of people who'd served under him for over twenty years, people who had heard only rumours for the last weeks, people who half-believed that he was already dead, that Mercia was about to be plunged back into foreign invasion or worse: civil strife.

Now they had their Lord restored to them. No wonder their happiness verged on hysteria. The man standing next to Wulfgar had tears pouring down his bluff, red face.

But none of the shouts now was for King Edward.

The south door of the church opened, and the glittering procession moving inside.

I ought to be there, Wulfgar thought. But it's impossible. I can't get through the crowd in time. I'm filthy, unshaven – the guards here in Gloucester won't know my face.

And what will I do, anyway? Shout, *That's not St Oswald?*

I can't do that – not now.

They've had their miracle. They'd pull me from my saddle and tear me limb from limb.

So, what? Wait here? Or ride to Kingsholm, and wait there until the Lady comes home?

The crowd surged forward then, avid for a last glimpse of the saint, and Wulfgar found his horse going willy-nilly with their flow. He was less than a dozen yards from the south porch when a hand took hold of his bridle.

'Wulfgar of Winchester!'

CHAPTER THIRTY-SIX

He looked down in surprise to see a smooth, narrow face, bland light-blue eyes, straw-fair hair with a newly shaven tonsure just visible under a pristine lambswool hood.

Kenelm. The Bishop's nephew. And, like everyone else in the square, he was smiling.

Wulfgar returned his bow but found a smile harder. He was such a mixture of conflicting emotions – exhilaration, outrage, fear, exhaustion – that he couldn't speak for a moment.

Kenelm's own smile began to fade as he looked Wulfgar up and down.

'One black eye, fading. Unshaven – un*tonsured*, even. Filthy clothes. Filthier nails. And—' he fingered the hem of Wulfgar's tunic '—is that a *bloodstain*? Wulfgar, what in Heaven's name have you been doing?'

Wulfgar, still awash with new and unmanageable feelings, couldn't find an appropriate answer.

'Getting filthy, as you've so astutely observed.' He tried to soften the waspish edge to his voice. It was good to see any familiar face, even this one. 'Do you know where I could get washed? And find a bite to eat? I need to see the Lady, and I can't come before her, or your uncle, looking like this.'

Kenelm looked him up and down again.

'You're right about that.' He thought for a moment. 'I'm lodging at St Peter's,' he said. 'Come back with me? It's not far, and they –' he jerked his head '– should be in the church for a couple of hours yet. We can drink to the Lord's restored health. And you can tell me where you vanished to.' His eyes were eager. 'You wouldn't believe the rumours.'

Wulfgar nodded slowly.

Oh, I probably would, he thought. How close are they to the truth?

He dismounted and the two young men walked side by side, pushing their way through the festive crowd, Kenelm leading the way past the south side of the new church.

'Why aren't you inside?' Wulfgar asked. 'Bishop's nephew, and all.'

'Me?' Kenelm pulled a face. 'Oh, I'm not important enough, apparently. What with King Edward, and the Bishop of Winchester, and all the West Saxon hangers-on, it seems there's not enough room.' He shrugged. 'Anyway,' he said, looking sideways at Wulfgar, 'I could ask the same of you. The Lady's secretary, *and all*.'

Wulfgar slid away from that question. 'Bishop Denewulf is here, too? I didn't see him.'

'He was waiting inside the church.'

Edward's hearth-retainers had lined up their horses either side of the south door. Wulfgar eyed them without curiosity, until he found his gaze returning with a jump to one cloaked and helmeted figure.

Garmund.

He was sure of it.

And, just as the thought passed through his mind, the man-at-arms spotted him. Their eyes locked. Almost against his will, Wulfgar found himself handing his own horse's bridle to a startled Kenelm and walking towards the mounted man. The man glanced quickly at the door of the church. Still closed. He swung himself out of his saddle with a creak of leather and a whiff of sweat.

'Brother,' Wulfgar said, with more calm than he felt.

'Litter-runt. What a surprise.' Garmund's voice was low, his eyes shadowed by the helmet. The sun shone on his red lips, his white teeth, his black beard, the massive gloved hand gripping his horse's cheek-strap. 'She didn't have you killed, then.'

'She?' Gunnvor? The Lady? It took a moment for Wulfgar to understand. 'No. No, she didn't.' The Spider's wife. He felt light-headed for a moment. Garmund had no idea of how that story had ended, he realised. Indeed, how could he?

'Are you listening to me, Litter-runt?'

He blinked.

'Sorry. What did you say?'

'I said, *good*. Because it's giving me great pleasure, beating you at your own game. I can do the saint-hunting as well as you. Better, even. And telling my Lord King and his stupid bitch of a sister how badly you failed them. And now I can tell you, too. And see what happens to you, which is an unexpected pleasure.' He grinned. 'King Edward's asked for you back, to face trial in Winchester.'

'*What?*' Wulfgar felt the ground shift beneath him. 'What lies have you been peddling?'

Garmund glanced at the church door again.

'That's the beauty of it, Litter-runt. I don't have to tell them anything but the truth. What a fool you are, to come back to Gloucester.'

While Wulfgar was still groping for an answer, there was a stir in the crowd. One of the other hearth-retainers shouted a warning.

Garmund looked round, swore, and vaulted back onto his startled horse.

Wulfgar snatched his chance to turn away and vanish into the throng of people. The church door had swung open on its massive wrought-iron hinges, but it proved to be a false alarm. No one emerged.

'Who was that?' Kenelm asked, agog.

'My brother.'

'Your *brother*? I didn't know you had a brother.'

He nodded, his thoughts racing. 'Two. And a sister.' What in Heaven's name am I going to do now? he wondered. I can't go to the Lady if Edward's going to ask her to arrest me.

And, he thought, will she even want to see me? What has Garmund told her? She must be thinking of me with – well, with what? Disappointment? At the very best. He wondered what lies his half-brother had been spreading – that Wulfgar had been killed? That he had failed in his quest? Or – and his heart stopped – that he had betrayed her?

Yes. That last. That would be it.

Wulfgar the traitor.

That would be his story.

Oh, what a sorry contrast I must make to Edward, her beloved brother, and Garmund, his trusty servant, coming to her rescue like the Hand of God. She thinks she's got the relics; she thinks the story's over. She'll be ready to hand me over to Edward, without listening to a word I have to say.

He swallowed the misery and the rage he could feel ready to build in his throat.

But surely Garmund must know he and Edward have fobbed the Lady off with fakes? Oh, he thought with disgust, but that would just add to the pleasure he's patently taking in the whole sorry tale.

And – with a chill – now that Garmund knows I'm here, he'll want to find out whether I still have the real relics . . .

He'll be after me.

He turned to Kenelm, finding a smile at last from somewhere, false and strained across his face.

'Can I stay with you tonight? And maybe you could tell me what the rumour-mill has been grinding out?'

'Aren't you going to the feast at Kingsholm?'

'I'm in no mood for it. Don't let me stop you, though.' He ran through the conversation with Garmund again in his head. Something was niggling at him but he still couldn't put his finger on it.

Kenelm raised his eyebrows.

'Is there something you're not telling me?' He put his head on one side and smiled his crooked smile. 'I know we started off on the wrong foot, but I would like to be your friend, Wulfgar.'

Wulfgar, already sad and weary beyond expression, found it even harder then. I need a friend in Gloucester, he thought. But are you really someone I can trust? Slowly, he said, 'Kenelm, can I tell you a story?'

The other man's face lit up. 'Are you going to tell me where you've been?' he asked.

But the story had to wait. After Wulfgar's welcome encounter with a bucket of hot water and a linen towel, he rolled the relics in his cloak and left them with his saddle-bags while their hosts escorted them to Vespers in the ancient church of St Peter's. Aching and distracted, Wulfgar found it hard to stay awake.

There was a beautiful cycle of wall-paintings on the opposite wall, and his eyes kept drifting back to three images in particular: Christ entrusting St Peter with the keys of Heaven and Hell; St Peter's denial of his Lord, his stricken face turned away from the curious maidservant, and the cock crowing; and, finally, the story only found in St John's gospel, of Christ telling St Peter, 'Feed my sheep'.

St Peter had been a coward, and a liar, and he had abandoned his Lord and friend in His hour of greatest need. And yet, somehow, he had been forgiven. Wulfgar's hand groped for the little gospel-book in its bag around his neck.

After Vespers, they were invited to share the canons' meal in the refectory. While Kenelm joined in with the gossip along the table as vigorously as any of them, Wulfgar drifted in and out on a tide of weariness, overhearing snatches of conversation as he cradled his horn beaker of damson beer.

'I heard he had been earmarked for Pershore . . .'

'You wouldn't believe the amount of honey the estate has to pay . . .'

'Well, he claims she's his wife . . .'

'No, no, he's gone to Evesham . . .'

Trying to show willing, he asked, 'Who's earmarked for Evesham?'

A dozen faces gaped at him. Eventually Kenelm said, 'Edwin. The Lord's old secretary. The man whose job you've got.'

A young priest snorted.

'The man whose job we all wanted.'

Wulfgar hoped the firelight hid his blushes.

'Yes, I remember . . .'

They all stood for the closing grace.

Finally they had a quiet moment. Wulfgar and Kenelm huddled by the banked hearth in the hall while their hosts snored around them. Wulfgar opened his bundle, spread the dry, brittle contents out before Kenelm's disbelieving eyes. He told him the bare bones of the story. He watched disbelief slowly change into wonder and acceptance. He saw Kenelm's hands tremble as they touched the relics, and Wulfgar knew he had found somebody who, for all his shortcomings, felt the power of the saint as forcefully as he did himself.

'But – the miracle . . . the Lord was healed . . .' Kenelm's voice died away.

'St Oswald was there, remember,' Wulfgar said. 'Just not in the reliquary, where everyone thought he was. If there were a miracle, he was responsible.'

Kenelm nodded.

'But why did my uncle choose you to go, and this boy – this Ednoth . . . ? ' Kenelm's voice tailed away, but Wulfgar saw his lips tighten.

'He must have thought we'd do the job—' Wulfgar saw something flicker in Kenelm's eyes. 'Oh, when he could have asked you, you mean?' He sighed. 'I was on hand, that's all.'

Kenelm glanced sideways at Wulfgar and seemed on the brink of speech, but he closed his mouth again and turned his gaze back to the mound of glowing charcoal.

'What is it?'

Kenelm smiled, but it didn't reach his eyes.

'It's – Wulfgar – I'm sorry I kicked you at Vespers, the other evening.'

'What? Oh, at Worcester, you mean?' It seemed a lifetime ago. 'It was on purpose, then?'

'I'd just come from a meeting with my uncle—'

Wulfgar held out his hand. 'Thank you. Now, forget about it. We all do childish things sometimes.'

Kenelm's fair skin flushed as he took the proffered hand. 'Childish – yes, I suppose I deserve that.' He squinted at Wulfgar. 'You – you seem different, somehow.'

'Grubbier?' Wulfgar, gritty-eyed, stifled a yawn.

'No, it's changed you, what you've done. Look at what you've achieved!' Kenelm gestured at the little pile of bones, heaped on the sacking.

Wulfgar nodded, a thrill going through him at the other man's words. This is what I had been hoping for . . . I may never get any public recognition, but at least Kenelm knows.

'It wasn't just me. I couldn't have managed without Ednoth, although he could be really annoying. Too young to know any better. And Ronan – Father Ronan – I wish you could meet him. He doesn't look like a priest at all, big and burly, with a pied beard like a badger's pelt and no tonsure, but I've never met faith like his . . .'

'Who did you say his bishop was?'

'I didn't.' Wulfgar frowned for a moment. 'I've no idea, now you mention it.'

'And you never thought to ask?'

Wulfgar shrugged. 'Other things seemed more important.'

Kenelm raised his eyebrows but said no more on the subject.

'And your brother? That big horseman? Will he be at Kingsholm?'

'Half-brother.' Wulfgar nodded, feeling the familiar shiver in the small of his back. 'And he'll be after me, now he knows I'm here in Gloucester and I can prove the relics they've brought are fakes. He'll want to make sure I'm kept quiet.' He hugged himself. 'And he'll probably guess I've got the true bones. He'll want them back. What do I do now?'

Kenelm looked anxious. 'I believe your story, Wulfgar, but I don't think I can help you. I wasn't there. You need Ednoth, or that priest of yours. Without them, it's your unlikely story against the King's very plausible one.'

'No.' Wulfgar knew he looked grim. 'It's more than that. It's St Oswald, against a pack of lies.'

CHAPTER THIRTY-SEVEN

'We must go to the Bishop. Now.' Wulfgar stood up. 'If you can believe me, then maybe your uncle will.'

'Now? It's not even dawn yet. Wouldn't we be better getting some sleep?' But Kenelm's yawn was unconvincing.

'Now.' Wulfgar was already reaching for his cloak. 'We owe it to the saint. But I'll go on my own if I have to.' He ached in every bone. He made for the door as Kenelm got awkwardly to his feet and followed him slowly.

The street was cold, the sky above clear, but the stars were paling and a greying in the east showed where the night was coming to its close. The first cocks were crowing.

'I just want all this to be over.' He felt as though his soul were floating somewhere above his body, a body that was slow-moving and clumsy. He tripped over a pile of kindling that had been stacked just inside the gate and only Kenelm's quick snatch at his arm saved him from going headlong.

'You do look tired. Would you like me to carry the relics for a bit? It would be an honour . . .'

Wulfgar pulled away, out of reach, as though Kenelm had threatened violence.

'No! They're not heavy, just awkward—' He stopped and looked at the other man's face. 'Sorry.' Trust had to start somewhere: why not here? He unfastened the pin at his throat and shrugged his cloak back over one shoulder. 'Here.' He pressed his lips to the improvised sling and held it out to Kenelm. 'That goes over your head, and your arm through – that's it.'

The two clerics moved quietly through the sleeping town, Kenelm's face shining, his arms hugging his body, his steps careful. After the great events of yesterday, the festivities had lasted late into the night and there would be more than one aching head in Gloucester that morning. From behind a set of shuttered windows the sound of a baby crying reminded Wulfgar of little Electus, whose very existence had slipped his mind for the last few hours. How could he have forgotten about his own godson? Another reason to hurry to Kingsholm. That woman – was she honest? Was she kind? She had looked it, but how could one be sure?

They were at the city gates now. The guard stirred at the sight of them and unlatched the little wicket gate to let them out. So, we don't look like trouble, Wulfgar thought. I don't look like a killer, or a thief, or a wanted man.

They walked through the dewy fields, the hedgerows alive with birdsong and the fluttering of wings. Despite the dawn chorus, Wulfgar could hear his heart thudding in his breast.

'The Bishop will be at Matins,' Kenelm said. 'We can wait for him outside the chapel door.'

The palace courtyard was barely recognisable from the previous day, when it had stood so empty. Despite the early hour, it was buzzing with horses and rumpled soldiers, yawning women carrying jugs of beer, scrambling dog-boys and turnspits.

The two clerics were admitted through the main gate without question, and nodded towards the chapel.

'Come for the service of Thanksgiving, have ye?' The guard was bright-eyed for all the early hour. 'Best shift yourselves. They've been singing their "*Te Deums*" since first cockcrow.'

They were at the chapel's very threshold when Wulfgar stopped. A shift of the pattern, and suddenly the meaning he had been seeking was clear to him.

'He didn't know.'

'What?'

'They don't know.'

Kenelm stared at him.

'Garmund, and King Edward. And Bishop Denewulf,' Wulfgar explained, to himself as much as to Kenelm. 'They don't know that the relics they've brought are false. If they knew—' He stopped and shivered.

Kenelm stared at him.

'If they knew what?'

'Garmund would have grabbed me yesterday, if he thought for a moment the real relics were still out there. They think they've brought the true relics to Gloucester.' He put his hands to his eyes. Which was riskier? To connive in their unwitting fraud? Or to unmask the King of Wessex and the Bishop of Winchester as gullible fools? He groaned. He was right, he had to be. Garmund would never have exuded that well-fed, smug air if he had had a clue that Wulfgar had outwitted him.

'Master!' Suddenly a slave-woman was at his elbow. 'Such a lovely baby, bless him. Suckling like a lamb! Shall I keep him by me today as well?'

He blinked at her, his thoughts miles away. 'Baby?'

'Aye, master, you left him with me yesterday.'

'Oh, that was you, was it?' Both Kenelm and the woman were staring at him now. 'Yes, please do. Thank you. Bless you.'

'Baby?' Kenelm asked tentatively.

'Did I not say? My godson.' He moved his fingers to his temples. They hurt. Why, in the name of Heaven, if King Edward thought he had the true relics, would he give them away?

The sun was lifting clear of the horizon, flooding the courtyard with light. The white-plastered boards of the chapel were suddenly dazzling. A door opened up like a dark hole in front of him.

'Wulfgar!' a voice said.

And another voice shouted over the first one, 'Arrest that man!'

He was face to face with Edward, King of Wessex.

Cold blue eyes, narrow and intent; a thin, bony nose; an abrupt and haughty gesture of the head – Wulfgar remembered how Edward had always reminded him of a bantam cockerel. He also remembered why the Litter-runt jibe always stung so much: Edward had never been any taller than Wulfgar was himself.

'Arrest him!' came the shout again, from somewhere in the courtyard. He turned to see whose the accusing voice was, but the sun was right in his eyes.

'Take him in charge,' the King said.

The whole royal party was in the courtyard of a sudden, with both the bishops, and a bevy of attendants. How had so many people packed into that tiny chapel? Wulfgar felt his elbows seized. No, not the whole party.

Miracle or no miracle, there was no sign of Athelred, Lord of the Mercians.

His Lady was in front of him now. He had imagined this reunion so many times, but he had never couched it in these terms: her mouth a set line, her brows narrowed, cheeks pale, sea-grey eyes remote and cold.

'We will go to the hall,' she said. 'Bring him to us when we command.'

'My Lady—' But she had turned on her heel and was walking away in a sweep of white and silver.

'Don't look so worried, Litter-runt.' Garmund was leering at him at him, and Wulfgar realised whose voice it had been, shouting for his arrest. 'They won't hang you, worse luck, not for this. It'll be exile. You can scuttle back the far side of Watling Street where you have so many new friends.'

'What did you tell them?' Wulfgar's voice was no more than a rasp.

'What?'

He tried to clear the frog from his throat.

'About what happened at Bardney? What do they think happened, Garmund? The bishops, and King Edward. And – and the Lady? What did you tell them?'

Garmund grinned again and tapped his index finger against his nose.

'Me to know and you to find out, Litter-runt. And you will. Find out, I mean.' He looked past Wulfgar to the guards at his elbows. 'Tie his hands.'

Wulfgar closed his eyes.

'Garmund, is that really necessary?'

'It might be a long wait, Litter-runt. They'll be preparing your trial. We don't want you overpowering your guards and escaping, do we?' The men standing round found this much funnier than Wulfgar did. Sycophants, he thought. But that means they think Garmund is someone worth flattering. He must be doing very well under Edward.

But the summons came before the rope.

CHAPTER THIRTY-EIGHT

Wulfgar had been cherishing the faintest of hopes that the meeting might be no more than an informal debriefing with the Lady. That hope died as he was jostled into the hall.

This had all the trappings of a formal trial.

The Lady sat in the place of honour in the middle of the high table, under the embroidered red cloth. King Edward was placed on her left. The Bishops of Worcester and Winchester, still vested for Mass, flanked them. A small wooden casket decorated with silver-gilt plaques stood on the table before them. The Kingsholm steward, tall and grey-haired, holding his staff of office, was there at one end of the dais. Clerics and hearth-retainers and the Lady's women were lining the walls, but Wulfgar was only mistily aware of their presence.

The four pairs of eyes at the high table watched his approach.

Wulfgar looked at each face in turn as the guards propelled him up the length of the hall, past the cold, scoured hearth-place. The Lady had no expression at all. Edward's thin face looked, if anything, amused. Denewulf, Bishop of Winchester, looked like an old sheep, but Wulfgar hadn't served in his cathedral for more than fifteen years without learning that a lot went on behind that bland, bell-wether façade. And Werferth of Worcester? A thunderstorm, ready to break.

A small rush mat stood below the dais, in front of the Lady's chair. He was frog-marched to it, and the guards took a step back and to the side. He felt very small.

The doors opened again, and he heard the sound of many feet pounding on the boards. Half-turning, he saw Garmund marching towards him at the head of a dozen or so men. Was it the same troop he had with him at Offchurch, and at Bardney? Wulfgar didn't recognise any of their faces, but then, why would he?

'Answer when you are spoken to!'

Wulfgar nearly jumped out of his skin. It was King Edward who had shouted, in that booming voice that belied the King's slight build.

More gently, the Lady said, 'Wulfgar of Winchester?'

He tried to speak, nodded instead.

She raised a hand. 'Proclaim the charges,' she said.

Somewhere behind him, the familiar voice of the steward said, 'Wulfgar of Winchester, you are charged with the following crimes against the King of Wessex, against the Lord and Lady of the Mercians, and against your Saviour in Heaven. Firstly, that you did hinder Garmund, servant of King Edward, in carrying out his duties, and precipitate an attack on him and his men. Secondly, that you yourself were responsible, directly or indirectly, for the deaths of three of those same men. Thirdly, that you did, in flagrant contradiction of your clear orders, procure for yourself the sacred relics of the Most Holy Oswald and then sell them to the aforesaid Garmund for thirty pounds of silver coin, which you kept as private profit.'

The Bishop of Winchester stirred in his seat.

'*Nefas est sacras reliquias vendere,*' he intoned. 'It is absolutely forbidden to sell sacred relics.'

Or to buy them, for that matter, my Lord Bishop, Wulfgar thought. But I don't see Garmund standing on this mat.

The Lady held up a hand again, in mild reproof.

'All in good time, my Lord of Winchester.' She looked at Wulfgar again. 'You have heard the charges. This casket contains a holy relic, a bone of St Oswald, whom you have also wronged. Do you lay your hand upon it and swear to tell the truth, the whole truth, and nothing but the truth, knowing you invite damnation if you lie?'

But it doesn't, he thought in a blur. Contain a relic, I mean. It can't. Not of St Oswald. It must be a bone from the monk of Bardney. Dizzy, he found himself stepping forward, resting his hand on the casket, swearing a meaningless oath. No, not meaningless, he realised. Invalid, perhaps, but heartfelt for all that. If he swore by St Oswald, and meant it, then surely the oath had meaning. And who knew but that brother of Bardney was one of God's many, many nameless saints, whose holiness was only known in Heaven? Better to assume virtue, he thought, sanctity, authenticity. He bowed his head.

The Lady spoke again. 'How do you plead?'

Wulfgar lifted his eyes to hers. The hall was silent. He searched her face for some sign that she knew the truth, but she was pale, her lips set, apparently implacable. Surely, he thought, his Lady could do better than this. What were her instincts telling her? He took a deep breath.

'Not guilty, my Lady. Not guilty to any charge.'

She was the first to look down.

The buzz of chatter in the hall died away as the steward called, 'Garmund, also of Winchester, called Polecat. You are summoned to bear witness. Please take the oath.'

And suddenly Garmund was standing there, not next to him but an ostentatious ten feet to his right, as though any closer contact would contaminate.

'My Lord and King, my Lady, my Lord Bishops.' He bowed and stepped forward to lay his hand upon the shiny box. 'I do so swear.'

'The full oath, please.'

He swore again. Did his voice waver? Was there a hint of anxiety in his eyes? None that Wulfgar could detect.

Certainly, when he began his story, his voice was clear and confident.

'I first travelled to Bardney, with great hardship, in the dead of winter, on my Lord King's errand, arriving there on the Feast of the Holy Innocents. There I spoke with the wife of the Dane who holds Bardney. She is an Englishwoman and a Christian. She was overjoyed by our coming, and she gave us leave to return and search for the relics of the Most Holy Oswald.' He bowed again. 'It had long been in my Lord's mind that the relics would be a fitting gift to the Lord and Lady of Mercia, on the completion of their new church.'

The Lady was smiling, Wulfgar saw to his horror – smiling at her brother and holding out her hand for him to take.

Garmund paused, waiting for them to finish their tender fraternal moment.

'When the earth softened, after Easter, I returned as planned. I was warmly received by the Lady of Bardney. She fed me and my men, and bade us rest, but in my eagerness to find the resting-place of the saint I asked her to take me out in the churchyard, with a lantern, as by then darkness had fallen.'

Wulfgar wondered whether this farrago of truth and lies had been composed by Garmund himself. He always had had the knack of sounding plausible when up in front of authority.

'To our horror,' Garmund went on, 'we found Wulfgar and his band of desperate hired ruffians digging illicitly in the churchyard. I challenged him, and he set his men on me and the Lady of Bardney. I shouted to summon my own men and there was a battle. Before making good his escape, Wulfgar had killed three men of Wessex and one of the Bardney servants.' He paused again. Muted but disbelieving uproar in the hall.

'Did you pursue them?' the Lady said, leaning forward.

Was this whole story new to her, Wulfgar wondered, or had she heard the outline, but not the details?

Garmund shook his head in sorrow. Wulfgar could see he was enjoying himself hugely.

'We were outnumbered, and afraid. We had our injured to tend to. And we did not realise until daybreak that he had made off with the relics.'

'And then?'

'They sent us a messenger at dawn. In return for the silver that we were bringing for the Lady of Bardney – and I must stress that this silver was a gift, and a token of our respect and thanks for her hospitality, and in no way a payment for the relics – Wulfgar and his gang would sell us the bones of the Most Holy Oswald.' Garmund raised his eyes to the roof-tree and looked suitably outraged. 'What can I say? We were shocked and saddened by the sacrilege. But the Lady of Bardney said, and I could only agree, that we should see the money as a ransom, and its payment as a pious act. We duly exchanged the money for the priceless bones, and I returned to my Lord, King Edward, who was then in Oxford, arriving there last Friday. Overjoyed by the news, full of love for his sister, he commanded us to travel to Gloucester at once.' He turned then to look at Wulfgar. 'I never thought you would have the nerve to show your miserable face in Gloucester again, let alone at the sacred ceremony for receiving the relics.' Garmund shook his head sadly. 'Oh, Wulfgar, my brother, what would our father, God rest his soul, have said?'

'Have you quite finished?' There was an impatient edge to the Lady's voice that gave Wulfgar just a flutter of hope.

Garmund turned back to her and bowed once more.

'Only this, gracious Lady of Mercia, that the hardships, deaths and injuries we underwent were incurred in your service, and we would gladly have undergone twice what we did to give you joy.'

Wulfgar could feel his heart pounding and the blood burning in his face. His hands were shaking. It was rage, but he knew it would be read as guilt. He tried to smother his emotions but he could feel them like charcoal, smouldering at his core.

I've killed one man, he thought, and I tried to kill another, but I didn't hate either of them as much as I hate Garmund and Edward right now. Queen of Heaven, he prayed, forgive me my anger. Help justice to be done.

The Lady's teeth were worrying at her lower lip.

'And when Wulfgar sold the relics to you, did he know that my brother the King planned them as a gift to me, that the relics would be coming to Gloucester anyway?' She glanced at Wulfgar then, scanning his face, looking puzzled rather than angry.

Garmund shook his head.

'Oh no, my Lady. In fact, from what he said I am quite sure that Wulfgar wanted the bones to go to Winchester.'

Wulfgar opened his mouth in furious indignation but the steward quelled him with a look.

The Lady winced. 'And who can swear to the truth of your story?' she asked.

Garmund gestured behind him to his troop. 'Twelve witnesses.'

'That's more than the law requires,' Edward said, 'for any crime.'

'But none of them is a Mercian.'

No, my Lady, Wulfgar thought, that won't hold water, you're grasping at straws there.

'All men of sworn standing in Wessex, my Lady,' Garmund said. 'My Lord King himself can vouch for them.'

The Lady looked at her brother.

Edward nodded.

One by one, Garmund's oath-swearers came forward and rested their right hands on the reliquary. With every name, every repetition of 'I do solemnly swear, as I hope for salvation . . .', Wulfgar could feel his chances dwindle. It'll be exile, he thought. And confiscation. He thought about the box he had entrusted to Worcester's sacristan before setting out with Ednoth, so full of hope. His books – would she really take those from him? And the silver brooch her father had given him?

He closed his eyes. If she didn't trust him any longer, then he didn't care where he went, or what he did.

He was still Gunnvor's thrall, he remembered. And if his property were confiscated by the court he would have nothing left to repay her with. He could hear her voice now: *I'll keep you to sit at my feet and teach me English love-songs of a winter evening.*

396

Singing with Gunnvor, and serving at Father Ronan's altar in his little Margaret-kirk. It wasn't the future he had planned, but he could imagine worse.

'Wulfgar!' The Lady sounded really angry this time.

He blinked.

'I'm sorry, my Lady.'

'Have you an answer to these charges?'

CHAPTER THIRTY-NINE

'My Lady, my Lord King, my Lord Bishops.' Wulfgar took a deep breath and bowed. He wasn't going to let Garmund outdo him in courtesy, and it gave him a moment to collect his thoughts. There was still that hot fire of dark red anger in his belly, but he noticed that his hands had stopped shaking. 'I have good news for my brother and his men.' A rustle of interest in the crowd behind him. 'They have committed perjury – a grave enough sin – but they have not imperilled their immortal souls.'

'What?' The Lady sat up.

'And for the same reason, my oath is void.'

'Explain yourself.' Her voice was terse but her face told another story.

'That box does not contain a bone of St Oswald.'

'Nonsense! What are you talking about?' This from Denewulf of Winchester, watery blue eyes narrowed in annoyance. 'I chose it from the relics and placed it there myself for the Kingsholm chapel.'

Wulfgar turned to his former superior and bowed, hand on heart.

'With all love, my Lord, you have made a mistake. The bones that Garmund took from Bardney, that were placed in the church yesterday, are not those of St Oswald.' His eyes met those of the Bishop of Winchester and held them. He said softly, 'They are the remains of a brother of Bardney who died no more than thirty winters ago.'

'What did you say?' It was the King, this time.

Wulfgar repeated his last sentence, word for word, in a steady, carrying voice.

Uproar followed from the hall behind. Bishop Denewulf was leaning forward, wagging a finger, trying to make himself heard above the commotion. King Edward had masked his mouth with his hand, his narrowed eyes flickering back and forth between Wulfgar and Garmund.

And now the Lady was on her feet, holding her hands up, quietening the hall by sheer effort of will. She turned to her steward, attentive at the side of the dais.

'Clear the hall. We will hear this case *in camera*.'

He came forward, thumping his iron-tipped staff.

'Everybody out! Witnesses for the prosecution, you are reminded not to leave the palace courtyard. We may need to call on you again.'

Garmund turned to leave, but the steward called him back with a summary command. Wulfgar used the hiatus to recruit his thoughts into some sort of order. He had the Lady's attention now. But he had to regain her faith.

She raised her eyebrows at last.

'We are listening.'

He nodded.

'Yes, my Lady.' Think. *Think*, he told himself. Choose every word with care. 'Garmund's story does have some truth in it,' he said slowly. 'He was already in negotiation with Bardney on King Edward's behalf, unknown to us. He rode there with those men whose oaths you have taken, and their arrival coincided with mine. He did indeed negotiate to purchase the relics from the Lady of Bardney – and I stress the word *purchase*. But who was the true guardian of St Oswald? Not she, my Lady. She didn't even know the saint was there, and she was no daughter of the Church. The true guardian was Thorvald, reeve of Bardney, grandson of the last sacristan of the shrine. He chose the Bishop of Worcester as the best person to receive the relics, and it was Thorvald, God rest his soul, who guided me to the saint's haven.'

'God rest his soul?' Bishop Werferth's voice was sharp.

'Thorvald was slain, my Lords, my Lady, by one of Garmund's men.' Wulfgar closed his eyes briefly. 'In turn, I killed that man, in an unsuccessful attempt to save Thorvald's life, and I have confessed that killing and been absolved.'

The Lady looked at her brother. 'Killing the reeve was not in Garmund's tale.'

Edward shrugged. 'It's hardly germane.'

'By your leave?' Wulfgar asked.

She nodded.

'The saint had been hidden thirty years ago in what was at that time a new grave. In the dark we could not distinguish St Oswald's bones from those of the Bardney brother who had been buried there. We took them all. Garmund's men attacked us without warning as we were escaping Bardney. We got away from them and sorted out the bones, but we were captured. Two of our party escaped with the true relics, and we fobbed Garmund off with the other bones.'

A screech of protesting wood sounded as Edward pushed his chair back.

'Rubbish. A mish-mash of lies. Bishop Denewulf has verified the bones.' He turned on the Bishop of Winchester. 'You swore they were the real thing.'

Bishop Denewulf nodded. 'And the old reliquary, my Lord King. Don't forget that.' He smiled. 'That's proof.'

Wulfgar shook his head. 'No, my Lords. I'm very sorry. Those pieces of wood belong with the saint's true relics, not with the bones Garmund brought you.'

The Bishop of Worcester steepled his fingers, tapping tip against tip, his good eye squinting balefully at Wulfgar. 'Then,' he asked, 'where are these true relics?'

'Yes,' the Lady said slowly, 'where are they?'

Garmund couldn't contain himself. 'My Lords! My Lady! You heard my men's oaths? You've seen the relics! How can you doubt me?'

Wulfgar's hand had gone to his breast in a familiar gesture, but he remembered even as he did so that the relics were no longer there.

He had entrusted them to Kenelm.

Kenelm.

Where was Kenelm?

He was by my side, Wulfgar thought wildly, when I was arrested. He said he wanted to be my friend. But he kicked me at Vespers, he remembered. His heart seemed to stop. Had Kenelm betrayed him, too?

'Where are the true relics?' the Lady repeated.

'We should send to St Oswald's Church,' the Bishop of Worcester said. 'Bring the reliquary here.' He snapped his fingers for the steward. 'That may establish part of the truth.'

'Wulfgar?' the Lady said. 'To whom did you give the bones?'

'Kenelm has them,' he said in a very small voice.

Bishop Werferth turned from his muttered conversation with the steward.

'My sister's son?'

Wulfgar nodded. 'He was with me when I was arrested. We were bringing the relics to you, my Lord.'

'This is farcical.' King Edward was really angry now. 'Who is this Kenelm? Wulfgar has no witnesses. My man has twelve attested oath-swearers and the Bishop of Winchester himself to vouch for the worth of my gift.' He was rattling his fingers on the table; and Wulfgar thought, he always did hate looking a fool, even more than most of us.

'You'd better be telling the truth, Wulfgar,' Bishop Werferth said, 'or you'll pay for dragging my family's name into this unspeakable mess.' The steward was summoned forward again by a wave of the Bishop's bony, ring-laden hand and ordered to send men out to look for Kenelm.

'Now what?' Edward said. He stood up and began pacing up and down behind the high table, and Wulfgar was suddenly, forcibly, reminded of the Atheling. The cousins might look so different but there was something akin in them that transcended the physical: that restless appetite for action, that need to control, which Wulfgar found so alien. The King turned suddenly to lash out at the flinching Denewulf of Winchester. 'You said you had no doubts! You were full of praise for Garmund! Now what, Bishop? Still no doubts?'

The Lady, ignoring his outburst, said, 'Now we wait.' She looked down at her folded hands, then, unfolding them to grip the edge of the table under its white linen, she said, 'Edward, as a matter of interest, why were you going to donate the relics to Gloucester?' Her voice was calm, almost casual, but Wulfgar observed the slight hunching of her shoulders. He also registered the tense of her question. Not *why did you* . . . but *why were you going to* . . . He felt a sudden rush of hope.

She was still speaking: 'Why not keep them for Winchester? For the cathedral? Or your own new church? The great saint of the English!' She half-turned in her seat to look up at him. 'Why do you care for me so much, all of a sudden?'

'Oh, for God's sake, Fleda!' Irritation riddled the King's voice. 'Don't pretend to be so naïve. If I'm to rule Mercia as well as Wessex, I need the Mercians to love me.'

'Rule? Mercia?'

Her brother didn't seem to notice the shock in her voice.

'Of course rule Mercia. It's been such a messy, *de facto* arrangement for the last twenty years or so. Typical of Father. It's time to sort it out, now that the Old Boar's on his death-bed. When he dies I'll take over *de jure* as well.'

'He may not die. We had a miracle yesterday, if you remember' The chill in her voice now made Wulfgar think of the three-year winter that would herald the Last Judgment.

Edward made an impatient gesture. 'He's an old man. One way or another, he'll never be well again.'

'So Mercia will be taken over?' she said slowly.

Edward nodded.

'It's only common sense. We'll absorb Mercia into Wessex. As Kent has been. Sussex. And then I'll be able to take an army against the Danes in East Anglia . . .' He smiled and pulled out his chair to sit down next to her again. 'All the English peoples will be united in the end, Fleda. Under one king. One law. Mine.' He was still smiling. 'You're in safe hands.'

'And you think the Mercians will just . . . roll over for you?'

'They love you,' he said, taking her hand. 'They've done what you've told them for nearly twenty years.'

'Not me, Edward. My husband. And he's the grandson of Mercian kings.' She pulled away.

A slave brought in wine for the high table and, under cover of the ceremony on the dais, Garmund sidled close enough to hiss to Wulfgar, 'Is it true, Litter-runt, what you said about the relics? The bones I brought are the wrong ones?' His eyes flickered to King Edward.

'Of course it's true. I don't lie on oath, unlike some people.'

Garmund's eyes contracted and darkened.

'If it's true, I'm going to kill you.'

Wulfgar found he was rolling his own eyes to Heaven.

'I've heard that before.' Astounded and delighted, he realised that Garmund's words didn't frighten him. He smiled at his half-brother. 'You should be thanking me, for not mentioning Offchurch.'

Garmund had clenched his fist before remembering where he was, and in whose presence. Lowering his hand again, he said, 'You little – I *will* kill you.'

'On Edward's say-so, was it, the Offchurch raid? A foretaste of his policy towards Mercia? Does the Lady know?' Wulfgar broke off at the sound of a knock at the great doors, turning on his heel in sudden, wild hope.

The reliquary had arrived from St Oswald's church.

But there was still no sign of Kenelm.

CHAPTER FORTY

St Oswald's reliquary had been smuggled up to Kingsholm disguised in a bundle of sacking and hidden in a rush basket. The whole ungainly parcel was placed on the table by the indignant sacristan of the new church. Werferth of Worcester quelled his brother prelate with one ferocious look.

'Give me the keys, and then you may withdraw,' he said to the sacristan, who had been hovering like a broody hen.

Outraged, the man opened his mouth, but one more glare from his Bishop had him backing out, bowing all the way to the doors.

'Have you looked inside before, godfather?' the Lady asked.

He shook his head without looking at her, intent on removing a second wooden box of new, golden oak, much smaller but still large enough to need both hands. He turned the second key. The slight click sounded loud in the silent hall.

As Bishop Werferth raised the lid of the inner box, he gave a bark of laughter. Wulfgar saw Denewulf of Winchester flinch.

Bishop Werferth reached in with both hands and lifted out the skull.

'Come up here, boy.'

Wulfgar looked at the Lady. She nodded, and he made his way up onto the dais. What a difference it made to his morale, looking down at Garmund.

Quiet, conversational, the Bishop said, '"The Death of St Oswald", Wulfgar, how does it go?'

Wulfgar gaped.

'Sing? Now?'

The Bishop nodded.

'Just the account of the martyrdom, please.'

Wulfgar, baffled, groped after his singing voice but that seemed to have betrayed him too. It came out as a stammering croak.

'*Merciless Mercians   martyred the king,*
Hacked off his head   and his noble hands,
Set them on high   as a horrible sign . . .'

His voice sounded very small in that great, echoing space.

Thankfully, the Bishop cut him off with an abrupt gesture.

'So they do teach the classics at Winchester? I did wonder. Bishop Denewulf doesn't appear to know the story.' He turned to his colleague. 'Thirty years a bishop and you can't do better than this? You ignorant fool.'

Denewulf held up his hands, shying away from Edward rather than his fellow-prelate.

'I knew full well there shouldn't be a skull among the Bardney relics! The other bones – the fragments of the coffin – I never said *all* the bones were those of the saint!'

'The fragments of the coffin. Yes.' Werferth's voice had

changed, softened, gentler than Wulfgar had ever heard him. 'These I do remember . . .' He closed his eye. 'The last time I ever went to Bardney, only a few years before the Danes –' he crossed himself '– I had just been ordained priest, and I went as a pilgrim to give thanks to St Oswald. The good brothers made me so welcome. This man –' he rested a hand on the smooth brow of the skull '– this very man must have been among them.' He shivered suddenly and groped at the table for support. Wulfgar peered into the Bishop's time-ravaged face, trying to make out the lineaments of a fit and vigorous man of thirty, full of pride in his new ordination. 'The brothers opened the reliquary for me, and inside was an ancient wooden box.' The Bishop put his other hand to his own forehead. 'Our Lord and His Blessed Mother on the lid. Prayers incised around the rim in runes. Angels. And this is it. Wulfgar, my stool.' He sank onto it. 'Hand me one of those pieces.'

Wulfgar crossed himself, and lifted out an intricately carved piece of wood, the length of his foot and the width of his hand, damp, rotten and crumbling.

The Bishop pressed it to his lips.

'Forgive an old man,' he said under his breath.

There was a sudden crash as Edward banged his fist on the table, rocking it on its trestles. Wulfgar leapt to save the skull from falling off the edge.

'But this proves *nothing*!' the King shouted. 'Wulfgar duped Garmund with false bones. So? He was always a slick little sycophant. Garmund was a fool to trust him, I'll grant you that. Let's have a judgement here.'

From the floor, Garmund called, 'My Lord! If I may venture to speak?' His tone was humble and ingratiating. 'I admit it, I was a fool to trust Wulfgar, you're right, my Lord. But he is my own brother, and a man of the Church. I never thought he would lie about these sacred matters.'

A shiver of disgust went through Wulfgar as he gently laid the skull back with the other bones. Slick little sycophant, was he? The King of Wessex could look to his own follower for the truth of that statement. He had a sudden onrush of memory: rough bark against his back, Garmund roping his arms, and Edward taunting him that they were going to re-enact the martyrdom of St Edmund . . . And the Lady – ah, but she was only Fleda then – rushing in from nowhere, plaits flying, bashing the big boys about the heads with her embroidery frame . . . How could she possibly think he would ever betray her?

But she was nodding now, her face pinched thin and pale with sorrow.

'Wulfgar, you have no proof. I accept that these bones cannot be the bones of St Oswald. But that only makes matters worse. Garmund would never have believed these to be the real bones if you hadn't put them together with the true fragments of wooden reliquary and sold the whole package to him. Your brother trusted you, just as I did.' Her voice wobbled. 'Implicitly. To find the saint. And there is no saint.'

'But, my Lady—' It was hopeless, though. She had turned away. He didn't understand how she could credit any of Garmund's lies.

'Never mind the saint, where's the silver?' Edward leaned across, moving into the gap the Lady had left. 'Thirty pounds of silver. My silver. Where have you hidden it?'

'Thief!' Garmund shouted from the floor.

Bishop Denewulf shook his fleecy white head.

'Wulfgar, I never knew you properly, did I? Your uncle's heart will be broken.' He pursed his lips, heavy pink jowls quivering. 'Where did we go wrong?'

'We should wait for my nephew,' the Bishop of Worcester said.

Wulfgar turned to this unlikely saviour with his heart racing, but, 'No,' the Lady was already saying. 'It is time for judgment. Prisoner, please return to the floor of the hall.' She looked at him. Her eyes were winter-grey again. 'Will you get down? Or do I have to ask the guards to help you?'

Numb and exhausted, he shook his head, and climbed back down to the floor and his place on the square of rush matting.

'Wulfgar of Winchester,' the Lady said, 'you have not been able to produce a single oath-swearer. Garmund has twelve. I have no choice but to find you guilty on the following charges. You have yourself confessed to killing one of Garmund's men, and I find you guilty of manslaughter.'

'Murder!' Garmund shouted. 'My man was stabbed in the back, in the dark! He had no chance.'

'Silence!' The thunder in the Lady's voice was eerily reminiscent of her husband in his prime. 'We will establish the status of the dead man and you will pay the appropriate fine to King Edward and to the man's family. Next, that you stole and sold holy relics, in defiance of canon law. This is a Church matter, and I will ask the Bishops to come up with a suitable penance. I hope it will be a heavy one.'

She swallowed and glanced down at her hands, folded in front of her, white even against the white linen.

'Then we come to the matter of deceiving Garmund with the false relics. A very rare crime, and not one which is mentioned in the dooms of Mercia. However, it appears to come under market law.' She cleared her throat. 'It seems to me to be comparable with a moneyer who mints false coin, and for that crime the penalty is to have the offending hand struck off at the wrist-joint and nailed above the mint.' She blinked furiously. 'The right hand.'

'Where shall we nail Wulfgar's hand?' Edward was tight-lipped and bright-eyed.

'I – I don't know yet. Finally –' she paused for a moment '– finally, you disobeyed your orders. You are my man, oath-sworn by head and hand. The Bishop of Worcester and I told you to find the relics and come back to us here in Gloucester. Instead, failing to find the relics, you stole those bones –' she gestured at the piled skeleton in front of her '– you sold them under false pretences, and then you came to Gloucester and told us this web of lies. For the crime of oath-breaking, the only penalty the law allows me to impose is confiscation and exile. If you are ever seen within the borders of Mercia again, your life is forfeit without further trial.'

'And Wessex,' Edward said, cracking his knuckles. 'And Wessex. What can I say, Fleda? I was going to ask you to give him back to me for judgment, but I couldn't have done better myself.'

Wulfgar's ears were ringing. He shook his head to clear them. Hard to breathe. No, there was no fault in her judgment, or her knowledge of the law. Only, he thought bitterly, in her haste, and her ignorance of the hearts of men. He clasped his hands together, the fingers of his left hand stroking his right. Warm. Pulse in the wrist. Calloused fingertips. Stubborn ink-stains which even now left their grey ghosts.

His pen-hand, he thought.

His harp-string hand.

He pressed it against his breast.

'Do you have anything to say?' She sounded wooden.

He couldn't meet her gaze. Lips cold and numb, staring at her chin and veiled throat, he stammered, 'My Lady, if all this were true, if I had thirty pounds of stolen silver hidden somewhere, why in the world would I ever have come back to Gloucester?'

Her eyes were wet.

'Only you know the answer to that.' Her lips tightened. 'Open the doors. We need to make the judgment public.'

Wulfgar heard steps retreating away over the resounding floorboards, noted the change in the light as the doors far behind him opened, letting daylight into the gloom of the hall. He heard voices from outside, raised in argument. His shoulders tensed. Would they cut off his hand at once? In the courtyard? Using a kitchen knife? A butcher's axe? Summary justice was the custom, after all. Done, and seen to be done.

CHAPTER FORTY-ONE

'My Lady.' The respectful voice came from somewhere over Wulfgar's left shoulder.

'Is this important?' The King sounded impatient.

The Lady held up a hand.

'Wait, Edward.' She nodded. 'Continue.'

It was the steward who had spoken.

'My Lady, there are some men outside who claim to carry news with a bearing on the case.' He cleared his throat, diffident. 'I know you have already given your judgment, my Lady, but one of them is the deacon, Kenelm.' He bowed in the direction of Bishop Werferth. 'The Bishop's nephew, whom I was commanded to find.' He bowed again to the Lady. 'And one of them is your cousin, the Atheling of Wessex.'

Wulfgar tightened his grip, hand clutching cold hand till they blotched a numb white and red.

Don't open the door to hope, he told himself. Judgment has been passed. Nothing can change that.

'Too late.' Edward thumped a fist on the table, satisfaction in his voice. 'As your man says, judgment has been given.'

The Lady had gone even paler.

'In an ordinary case, yes,' said Bishop Werferth, leaning forward, 'it would be too late. But, Fleda, this is not an ordinary case. The saint himself is on trial here.'

Denewulf of Winchester nodded. He opened his mouth as though to speak but glanced at Edward, swallowed, and reconsidered.

And now Edward is going to sulk, thought Wulfgar.

Sure enough, the King was pushing himself back in his chair and folding his splendidly embroidered arms across his chest.

'Go on, then,' he said. 'Bring them in if you must. I can't imagine anything they say will make a difference.'

The Lady nodded.

'Let them in.'

Wulfgar concentrated on his stance. Feet evenly planted on the mat. Deep slow breathing. His hands were still clinging to each other: he managed to unclench them to hang at his sides. Head up. Eyes open. He stared unseeing at the high table. He was determined not to turn round. The back of his neck prickled.

'Seiriol!' The Lady sprang to her feet, her face alive with sudden delight.

The three men seated at the table had all gone very still.

Wulfgar heard the light, confident step coming up the length of the hall. It stopped at his side. A hand rested on his shoulder.

'My Lord . . . King. My Lady. Bishops.' But the greeting was only courtesy. He had nothing to say to them, not just then. 'Wuffa? You seem to have got yourself into a little difficulty.'

Wulfgar found he couldn't turn to look at the Atheling. Staring ahead, he muttered, 'My Lord.'

'I found some friends of yours down in the town. They told me they have something for you.' The hand squeezed his shoulder and let go.

'Why are you interrupting the court?' Edward's voice was harsh with barely suppressed rage. 'Sentence has been passed on the traitor.'

And the Atheling actually laughed.

'Oh, Eddi. This is Wulfgar we're talking about. Traitor, indeed.'

'He's one and you're another.' Edward shoved his chair back. 'You're trying to undermine Fleda, now, aren't you? You and your damned meddling – get out of here, do you hear?' His voice rose as he unleashed his anger. 'Get out!'

The Atheling shook his head.

'You're not in charge here, Eddi. We're not in Winchester now.' He turned to Fleda. 'What do you say, cousin?'

The Lady was still standing, her cheeks pink but her voice dignified and steady.

'Seiriol, it would give me great pleasure if you would join us.' She indicated a place beside the Bishop of Worcester. 'Steward, a chair. You are a neutral voice in this case, cousin: your opinion would be highly valued.'

'Neutral!'

The Atheling vaulted up onto the dais.

'King for half a year, Eddi, and you still can't control your temper?' He waved at the steward. 'Never mind a chair. Let my witnesses in.'

Wulfgar's heart fluttered as wildly as a bird caged in the fowler's hands, for all his slow, careful breathing. He turned his palms outwards. *Mother of God, Queen of Heaven, ask your Son to have mercy on me, a sinner . . .*

More footsteps. Several pairs of feet. Not just Kenelm, then.

He heard the Lady's voice, asking a question.

And then a voice he'd never really thought to hear again: 'Father Ronan, priest of the kirk of St Margaret, in Leicester.'

He turned, mouth gaping.

'Ronan!'

The steward thumped the ferrule of his staff on the floorboards. 'Will the prisoner be silent?'

And next to Father Ronan, Ednoth. And next to Ednoth, Kenelm, holding out to him a bulky and familiar parcel. He reached for it, hands shaking.

The next minutes passed in a blur. He was only vaguely aware of the formalities of the court: of Father Ronan and then Ednoth being sworn in and asked to summarise their adventures; of Kenelm taking his oath that this was indeed the bundle with which Wulfgar had entrusted him.

'Wulfgar of Winchester.' The Lady's voice brought him back to his senses. There was a softness in it now, but it didn't move him as it would have once. He would have taken her word against Edward and Garmund and all the world beside, but she hadn't trusted him. 'Would you please open that bag?'

He didn't think to climb up to the dais. He knelt on his rush mat and carefully unfolded out the sack-cloth before taking the bones out of the pile and arranging them in some kind of meaningful pattern.

Clavicles and scapulae.

The long line of strange, three-flanged vertebrae.

The smooth sickle-curves of the ribs.

Angel-wing pelvic bones.

The long scaffolding of femur and tibia.

Foot-bones like something children might use in a game, like cherry-stones for counting: *Merchant, Ploughman, Shipman, Bowman* . . . How did it go on? *Rich man, Poor man, Beggar-man, Thief* . . .

Soldier, Scholar, King, Saint . . .

Fragments of a man who had blazed so brightly for a few years and then been treated so cruelly. Wulfgar weighed a weightless rib in his hands, thought about it flexing and relaxing in life and breath and prayer and song, forming part of the cage of that mighty heart.

A heap of brittle kindling.

No, Wulfgar. He raised his head, listening. *I am more than that. I am here. I am with you now.*

He was barely aware of the other hands reaching out for the bones, lifting them, stroking them. Only when the bony blue-veined hands of the Bishop of Worcester reached to wrap them again in their sacking did he come blinking back to himself. He offered the rib to the Bishop, and noticed that the old man, kneeling at Wulfgar's side, had tears streaming down his face. Both the good eye and the empty socket were weeping.

The Lady was offering him her hand. He looked at it for a long moment before taking it in his. Her skin was clammy.

'I should never have doubted you,' she said. After a long heartbeat, she took a deep breath and looked around her. 'However, if we accept Wulfgar's story, and the corroboration of his oath-swearers, then we have to decide what to do with the false witness borne by Garmund Polecat.'

They all looked around the hall.

Garmund had taken advantage of the diversion caused by the relics' arrival. He was nowhere to be seen.

King Edward, still up on the dais, said stiffly, 'I can deal with my own, thank you, sister. Garmund is my faithful man.'

'And I wish you joy of him,' she said, smiling.

'We need someone to care for the saint,' Bishop Werferth said. 'Transfer him to the reliquary and get him back to the church, discreetly. Find a suitable box for the carved wood. Arrange proper burial for my old friend here.' He rested a hand again on the skull, stroking a gentle thumb over the bony forehead, marking a cross. 'Wulfgar—'

Wulfgar opened his mouth to lay claim to the honour the Bishop was offering him, but as he did so his eye fell on Kenelm, hanging back, his face set with misery. 'My Lord,' He was pleased to find his voice was firm. 'May I suggest your nephew Kenelm is ideally qualified?'

The Bishop frowned for a moment, then he nodded. 'Yes,' he said. 'Yes, you may.'

Kenelm flushed and beamed.

Edward had been watching their every move, lips compressed, eyes wary.

'And what will you tell the good people of Gloucester?' he asked. 'You'll look as big a fool as I will if you confess that that show yesterday was a case of mistaken identity.'

'Edward.' The Lady went over to her furious brother. 'We all saw the miracle yesterday. And –' she drew a deep breath '– when your message came, that my dear brother was on his way here bringing me this most marvellous gift, it was amongst the happiest days of my life.' She put one hand to his face and turned it so that he couldn't help looking into her eyes. 'That gift was in good faith, and I honour you for it. And so do the people of Mercia.'

Bishop Werferth coughed.

'Edward, it may be the destiny of Wessex and Mercia to be joined one day. Look at our own family, and how many marriages have been made across the border. But Mercia will not be *absorbed* into Wessex, any more than I was absorbed into my husband when I married him.' She released him then. 'And, speaking of my husband, I must go to him.' Her tone had grown weary.

'And we will be going back to Oxford,' Edward said. He still wasn't looking happy, but the pinched fury was relaxing out of his features.

The Lady turned to her cousin.

'Seiriol, would you escort me to my husband's bedside? You will be delighted to see how much better he is. His speech was less slurred this morning than it was last night, even.'

While she was speaking, Wulfgar watched the Atheling's face. Was there the briefest flicker of anger? Frustration? Disappointment? He couldn't be sure. The Atheling took her hand and bowed over it.

'I'm sure I will. One moment, then I'm all yours.' Letting go, he turned to Wulfgar, who held himself straight and still. Here came the interrogation he had been dreading.

'Well done, Wuffa.'

'Thank you, my Lord.'

The Atheling dropped his voice to a murmur, their faces close together.

'And, tell me, did you speak to my friends?'

Wulfgar swallowed.

'I carried your message to Toli Hrafnsson, my Lord.'

'But you were too late, then, for Hakon?'

Wulfgar nodded. So, he knew about the death of Hakon Toad.

'What about his brother?' the Atheling asked.

He wondered what to say.

'My Lord . . .' Only the truth would do. 'I wasn't sure what to do, my Lord, but it seemed Ketil Scar would welcome the message, and so I passed it to him. He seemed to be expecting it.' Wulfgar watched the Atheling's face warily.

At last, he smiled. 'And?'

He cast his mind back. It felt an eternity ago. 'Toli said, "If you hear nothing from me, then, yes, let it be All Hallows".' Wulfgar glanced up. The Atheling was still smiling. He took a deep breath, 'But, Ketil, my Lord – he said, "When I need him, I will send for him". Meaning you.'

The Atheling's eyes narrowed for a moment, then he looked at Wulfgar and smiled. 'You're a true servant, Wuffa. And a true friend. If they don't appreciate you here—' he glanced briefly at the Lady, still hanging on her brother's arm '—you can always come to me. Wherever I am. Remember that. You have done a great kindness to me and my friends.'

The Atheling's friends. Toli Silkbeard Hrafnsson. Ketil Scar Grimsson. Not just names now. Wulfgar thought of touchy, swaggering, lecherous Toli, of massive, irascible Ketil, and the louring ghost of Hakon Toad. *We light the fire at All Hallows . . .* He still didn't know what it meant.

He bowed. 'Yes, my Lord.'

The Atheling nodded. Softer than ever, he said, 'And if I ask you to help me another time?' He held up a hand. 'We'll talk about it later. But remember, Edward is only King of a very small part of these islands.'

'Yes, my Lord.'

And it's true, Wulfgar thought. To think I once believed Winchester was the whole world.

'Thank you. Later.' That warm clasp on his shoulder again.

'Thank *you*, my Lord.'

The Atheling saved my hand, Wulfgar thought. My life, really. And he had made King Edward look petty. Wulfgar half-smiled at the memory of the King's expression. He would be in the Atheling's debt for that these many years. But he still didn't trust him. Wulfgar watched the Lady and her cousin walk arm in arm down the hall and out of the great doors, her smiling face turned up to his like a flower to the sun. The familiar sight made him uneasy for some reason.

Edward, at his shoulder, said, 'You were only doing your duty, I suppose.'

Wulfgar jumped, and bowed.

'As was Garmund, my Lord King.'

Edward's face tightened.

'Why do they all love you so much? Fleda? Seiriol? My father? He always thought your shit smelt of roses.' He raised a clenched right fist, and then lowered it slowly. 'No, don't bother answering. I don't really care.' He walked away.

Wulfgar had no answer for him, anyway.

CHAPTER FORTY-TWO

'Holy Blood, they've all taken themselves off at last!'

'Ronan, I can't believe you're here.'

Father Ronan smiled. 'Faith, I like to think I'm not easily cowed, but put me in a room – even a muckle great room like this – with the Lady of Mercia, the King of Wessex, two bishops and a prince of the blood, all staring daggers at me, and I find I'm quaking in my shoes.' He shook his head, still smiling. 'What, Wuffa, did you think I could come so far with you, and not see St Oswald put to bed?'

Ednoth clapped Wulfgar's shoulder, and then gave him a clumsy hug.

'What on earth's been going on?' he asked, letting go.

Wulfgar looked at him, and then at Kenelm. 'I don't know where to start. Where did you get to?'

Kenelm had flushed an unbecoming shade of puce. 'I'm so sorry, Wulfgar. I panicked. When they were shouting for your arrest, I mean.' He swallowed. 'I ran away.'

'Don't be too hard on yourself, boy,' Ronan said. 'The saint took a hand. You ran slap into us.'

Kenelm nodded. 'Just outside the city gate. I recognised Ednoth, of course, from the court,' he went on. 'And I guessed who Father Ronan was, from the way you'd described him.'

Ronan raised an eyebrow. 'Oh, aye? What have you been telling him, Wuffa?'

Ronan here, Wulfgar thought, in Gloucester. It seemed miraculous. Was it conceivable that Gunnvor was here, too?

Ednoth was grinning more broadly than ever. 'Oh, it took a little doing, but we got the story out of him,' – he prodded Kenelm's arm – 'and convinced him to take us here. And then the guards weren't going to let us in. And then the Atheling rode up to the gates, and he recognised me!' His face was radiant. 'And, of course, the guards had to do what *he* told them.'

'We should go back into Gloucester,' Ronan said, his eyes twinkling. 'I hear there are some fine ale-houses.'

'They speak well of the beer at the Lammastide,' Kenelm said. 'The canons, I mean, at St Peter's.' He looked from face to face. 'I'll show you the way – if you want me to come?' He bit his lip.

'Come with us if you like,' Ednoth said, 'but I think we'll go to the Holly-Tree.'

Wulfgar shrugged. Any ale-house, and any company, would be welcome just then. Suddenly remembering a duty he had wholly forgotten, he said, 'I should just check on Electus.'

He found the wet-nurse in a sunny corner of the courtyard. She had put her broom down and was suckling the baby, seated on an upturned half-barrel, leaning back with the sun on her face and her eyes closed. He stopped a few feet away, feeling shy, and reluctant to disturb such obvious contentment.

'Call it a miracle, master.' Another young woman had paused at his elbow, yoked buckets of milk swinging. 'She lost her little one only last week. It never thrived.' She shook her head. 'Now someone's brought her this brave boy.' Her eyes brimmed with easy tears.

Wulfgar nodded. When he found his voice he said, 'Tell her I'll be back later. I'll provide for his care.' That poor woman had lost her own baby, and now she could feed Leoba's. Who was he to question the ways of Heaven?

Preoccupied, he followed the others back along the well-trodden path to the gates of Gloucester. Like everywhere else in the city, the Holly-Tree was teeming with holiday custom. They found a long bench outside and a bowl of the house cider.

'Absent friends,' Ronan said, and they all lifted their cups. The priest caught Wulfgar's eye, and they both smiled.

A heartbeat later, Wulfgar's smile froze as he stared at the earthenware cup in his hand. Smart, wheel-thrown, skilfully spattered with yellow glaze. He looked up from it to encounter Ednoth's eyes.

'Oh, the cups?' Ednoth's offhand air didn't fool Wulfgar for a moment. The boy was insufferably pleased with himself. 'Ketil's going to be very happy with the deal we've already made this morning, with the ale-wife here,' Ednoth went on. 'And I've taken several more orders. I just hope he can keep up supplies. I still need to sort myself out a trader's licence, but that shouldn't be a problem. I suspect the Lord and Lady will think they owe me a favour.'

Wulfgar shook his head, smiling through his disbelief. 'So, this is why you wanted to linger with Ketil? Pottery trading? But you were so scornful!'

Ednoth brushed his doubts aside with an airy gesture. 'Oh, I didn't know what I was talking about.' His eyes lit up. 'Wuffa, this is just the start! Gunnvor's introduced me to some lads from an island somewhere away east. Gotland, Father Ronan? Would that be right? Anyway, they're looking for backers for an eastern venture. Beyond Miklagard, they said. Serkland! *Saracens!*'

'And are you going to invest?' Wulfgar asked.

'Might do.' Ednoth was pink with elation. 'I might even go along. Maybe not this trip, but there will be others. And it'll make a change from sheep-farming. There's a great big world out there, Wuffa! Let's drink to it.'

'What a shame,' Ronan said over Wulfgar's shoulder. 'The lad seems quite deranged.' He lifted a hand to draw the attention of the pot-boy.

'Ronan, Gunnvor hasn't come south with you, has she?' It was a forlorn hope, and Wulfgar wasn't surprised to see the priest shaking his head.

'No.' He cocked his head. 'And I can't tell from the look on your face whether you're glad or sorry.'

'Where is that pot-boy?' Ednoth got to his feet. 'No, you stay where you are, Father Ronan. I'll look for him.'

'I'll come with you,' Kenelm said.

Ronan shuffled along the bench and gripped Wulfgar's knee.

'How are you doing, lad?' His eyes were dark and intent.

Wulfgar smiled but he couldn't put his heart in it this time.

'Still brooding on the man you killed?'

Wulfgar nodded.

'That, and other things.' Leoba. Thorvald. Their little girl. Some things would be etched on his heart for ever.

'We're all bearing that burden with you, you know,' Ronan said. 'Even Gunnvor, though you might not think it.'

'That's different. She – she—' Wulfgar fell silent. He wasn't sure what he wanted to say. He shied away from thinking just how ruthless, how efficient, Gunnvor had proved in that nightmarish fight on the Bardney causeway.

'She'd done it before?'

He didn't want to hear that, although he suspected it might be true. Eventually, he said. 'She isn't in holy orders.'

Ronan snorted.

'Hardly! And there's nowt in her commandments or her upbringing to tell her not to kill.' He paused for a moment, eyes opaque. 'I've killed men myself before now, you know, Wuffa. It was only by chance – and ill-chance at that – I didn't at Bardney.'

'Have you killed anyone since you became a priest?'

Ronan was quiet for a long time, contemplating his empty cup. Then he said, 'No, as it happens I haven't, not since I was ordained. But, lad, my path to the priesthood was a long and winding one. It was what my father wanted for me; it was why he freed me and had me taught my letters. But I fled it, over land and sea. I went as far away as I knew how.' He shook his head. 'Dublin was the least of it. I did a lot of bad things, Wuffa. I was full on forty when my vocation cornered me at last.' Then, his voice brisker, he said, 'That man you stabbed – he would certainly have killed you, you know, as well as Thorvald.'

Wulfgar nodded.

They shared the silence.

Ednoth was making his way back to them.

'What does a man have to do to get a drink around here? I've never seen an ale-house so packed.' He squeezed himself in on the end of the bench. 'The pot-boy says he'll get round to us when he can.'

'Where's Kenelm got to?'

Ednoth shrugged.

'Need-house?'

'Be kind to him, Wuffa,' Ronan said. 'He let you down very badly, and he knows it. It can't be easy, being the Bishop's nephew. Especially not that Bishop.'

Wulfgar let the priest's words sink in. He nodded, thoughtful.

'The Bishop!' Ednoth said. 'He says I've got to walk through Gloucester in a white shirt, barefoot and carrying a candle, and then he'll let me go to Mass again. It hardly seems worth it.' He grinned, ignoring Wulfgar's frown. 'Do you want to hear a riddle?'

'Not really.'

Ronan put his hands over his ears.

'Of course you do,' Ednoth said, undaunted. 'It's a new one. I am the hard thing that hangs by a man's thigh. I lift my head in search of a hole – what am I?'

Wulfgar and Ronan groaned in unison.

'A key, of course,' Wulfgar said.

'Oh, before I forget!' Ronan said. He leaned over to one side and rummaged in the big bag he'd brought with him. 'Gunnvor gave me this for you. She said you must have left it behind, that last time you were in the Wave-Serpent.'

He handed a small linen-swathed parcel to Wulfgar, who turned it over, curious. He looked up at the priest.

'Do you know what it is?' Wulfgar asked.

Ronan shrugged.

He unfolded a small bag of unbleached linen to find it contained something flat, no larger than his hand. Bewildered, he untied the strings to take out a rectangular metal object.

He stared at it.

The others were both looking at him. He was about to say, 'This isn't mine. I've never seen it before, and I certainly didn't drop it in the Wave-Serpent', when the memory flooded back.

Squatting a few feet from Thorvald's cooling body in the darkness after moonset, ferreting through mud and damp sacking for those precious bones, his fingers coming across the embossed metal plaque. He had only ever explored it by touch. Now, closing his eyes and running the ball of his thumb over the bumpy surface, there came a stomach-churning jolt of recognition.

This plaque had been among the bones when Gunnvor had gone off to sort them. That morning seemed half a dream, now. *A wren singing, and Gunnvor singing, and the sun coming up . . .*

She had found it.

Taken it.

Stolen it, in fact.

He thought of everything they had gone through together since she had asked him to sing 'The Death of St Oswald'. And all the time she had been hiding this little treasure from him. It was his old refrain: treachery everywhere.

But now she had returned it. It was tantamount to confessing the sin, he thought, and he forgave her from the bottom of his soul.

He tilted the plaque the better to catch the light.

Ronan inhaled sharply.

Chased and embossed silver gilt, the gold worn in places and the silver tarnished, but still a beautiful thing. A tall, graceful figure of a man with a large, heavy-beaked bird on his shoulder and a tree growing behind him, the whole scene framed by a rounded arch. Panels around the edge showed more birds and beasts caught up in a tangle of richly fruiting vine.

Ronan and Ednoth were both craning over his shoulder to see.

Ednoth looked at Wulfgar.

'Did you find that in the grave?'

Wulfgar nodded, speechless.

'They don't make them like that nowadays,' Father Ronan commented.

'What is it?' Ednoth asked.

Wulfgar turned it over, finding his voice at last.

'A plaque from a book cover,' he said, looking at the rivet holes. 'Or perhaps from the lid of a box to keep a book in.'

'A little box,' Ronan agreed. 'A single gospel.'

'Would that be St John, then, with his eagle?' Ednoth asked.

Ronan frowned.

'Let me have a look.'

Fighting his reluctance to part with it, Wulfgar handed the plaque to the priest.

'Faith, no, that's not St John, not with a sword,' Ronan said.

'And wearing tunic and leggings?' Wulfgar said.

They were both shaking their heads.

Ednoth looked from one to the other.

'Who is it, then?'

'St Oswald, of course,' Wulfgar said happily, taking it back. He looked at it hard. The man's face had been chased into the metal with light, sketchy lines. A frank, open face, with neat moustache and beard. Wulfgar tilted the metal and let the light flicker across its patterned surface. Was that a faint smile on the lips?

My Lord, he thought, it's good to see your face at last.

'I suppose I ought to give it to the Bishop. It might make up for giving away his ring.'

Ronan raised his eyebrows.

'What your dear Bishop doesn't know won't hurt him. And Cat's-Eyes seemed very sure that it was yours.'

Wulfgar looked at him, wondering how much he knew or guessed.

'She said you can thank her when you're next in Leicester. When you're settling your account.'

The pot-boy had arrived at last with a fresh bowl of cider, burnt apples bobbing. Wulfgar pulled out the little bag he kept around his neck and tucked away the image of St Oswald next to his gospel-book. They were very much of a size, and he wondered if maybe once, long ago, they had belonged together.

'Father Ronan, do you have Uhtsang in that bag?'

The priest nodded.

'Why?'

'Because we're not leaving this bench until I've learned that song about St Oswald and his raven.'

Author's Note

The Bone Thief is set soon after the death of Alfred the Great of Wessex. In Alfred's lifetime, the ancient English kingdoms had collapsed under the weight of Viking attack. Alfred had held on to Wessex, but the eastern half of Mercia had been lost to the warlords of the Danish Great Army. Western Mercia had been saved with West Saxon help but at a great price – the loss of its independence as a kingdom. When the story opens, the new king of Wessex, Edward, is planning an aggressive programme of conquest that not only involves defeating the Danes but also assimilating Mercia. Athelfled (Fleda), Lady of the Mercians, has to resist him on her own, as her husband is incapacitated with illness. One possible solution presents itself: heavenly protection and earthly inspiration in the form of the bones of St Oswald, the mighty king and powerful saint who had died nearly two-and-a-half centuries earlier.

All this is historical enough. Two manuscripts of the *Anglo-Saxon Chronicle* refer briefly to St Oswald's bones coming from

Bardney, in modern Lincolnshire, to Gloucester, in Mercia. They give no detail, and while the D manuscript has it happen in AD 906, the C manuscript files it under 909. Tantalising glimpses like this, riddled with contradiction and possibility, are the raw stuff of Anglo-Saxon history. There is no hint in any source – historical or archaeological – of *how* St Oswald's bones survived the fall of the monastery at Bardney to the Danes, to reappear over a generation later. Wulfgar and his companions are almost entirely fictional and, given the contradiction in the *Chronicle's* own dates, I have taken the liberty of bringing the rescue of the relics back a few years, to the immediate aftermath of Alfred's death.

It is hard now even for many devout Catholic Christians to understand the fervour with which saints' relics were venerated in the Middle Ages. Fragments of saints' bones, their clothing and possessions, objects which had come into contact with the relics, were believed to be imbued with extraordinary power. In a profoundly hierarchical age, God the Father and Christ could seem remote figures. Christ's mother, the Blessed Virgin Mary, was a more approachable figure, however, and the saints, especially the local ones, could feel like personal friends and patrons. Wulfgar, my fictional hero, feels a profound connection with St Oswald.

Wulfgar may be imaginary, but his dilemmas about his future are very real. Priestly celibacy was not the norm at this period, and even many senior clerics had wives and families. There were very few centres of learning left after the Viking depredations. The Anglo-Saxon clergy of 900 bore considerable resemblance to the 'hunting parsons' satirised by Anthony Trollope in the 1860s, their way of life differing very little from that of the landed gentry and aristocrats whose kin they were. Anyone whose faith was centred on ideals of scholarship and service would find this a challenging environment.

Athelfled, Lady of the Mercians, is very much a historical character, however. First with her husband, and later alone, she ruled Mercia. The *Anglo-Saxon Chronicle* tells us that she won battles and built fortresses. She and her husband founded St Oswald's Church in Gloucester, and the ruins of her church are still visible, although the relics have been lost once more. Nonetheless, we do not know when she was born, or how old she was when she married, or whether she led her army into battle in person. Any attempt to flesh out her historical bones moves instantly into the realms of the imagination, but we do know that Mercia stands out among the Anglo-Saxon kingdoms for the number of strong women in its history.

Other elements of my story are matters of historical interpretation. What were relations like, between Mercia and Wessex, once Mercia had been demoted to a lordship rather than a kingdom, particularly after the men who had brokered that deal – Alfred the Great of Wessex and Athelred, Lord of the Mercians – were out of the picture? Many historians see the siblings Athelfled of Mercia and Edward of Wessex as happy partners, united against the Danish threat. But I find it hard to believe that all Mercians readily acquiesced in their subordination, especially as, on several occasions in the later tenth and eleventh centuries, the prospect of Mercian independence was to raise its head again.

In some ways, I have exaggerated existing contrasts for the sake of the story. In Wessex and English Mercia social values are based on family, land, Christianity and tradition. Across the border, in Danish England, loyalties are fluid, a person's background is less important than his or her actions, wealth is based on portable bullion, religion is polytheistic and personal rather than institutional. Englishmen and Danes both value silver, but the English want it stamped with the king's head, whereas a Dane will accept it in any form – Arabic coin, broken jewellery, ingots – then get out his little scales and weigh it.

This is the world of Gunnvor Bolladottir. Most armies attract camp followers and the Danish Great Army was no exception. By the 880s there are references to its soldiers needing to defend their 'women and children'. Were these women Scandinavian, or local? What can life have been like for those children? We have no answers, but the depiction of Bolli, Gunnvor's father – coming from Hordaland in Norway in the 860s, making his fortune, his daughter growing up as part of the tough raggle-taggle gang of children trailing in the army's wake, and then inheriting his ill-gotten hoards of treasure – is at least a plausible speculation.

As is, I hope, is the rest of the story.

GLOSSARY

Abecedarium – a written alphabet, from the letters A-B-C-D

After-gangers – from Old Norse *aptrgangr* (after-goer), a malevolent walking corpse

Army-law – the East Midlands (Eastern Mercia) fell to part of the Viking Great Army, which further subdivided to govern the Five Boroughs (Leicester, Lincoln, Derby, Nottingham and Stamford). We have very little idea of how this worked in practice, but the Scandinavian homelands had complex legal systems, and armies need discipline. I have combined these to come up with the idea that Toli and his father Hrafn governed Lincoln by what we might call 'martial law', a comparatively arbitrary form of justice

Atheling – the title *Atheling* comes from the word *athel* (noble) and literally means 'of a noble family'. It was applied to all the men of a royal house who were eligible through birth and character for the throne, and is often translated by modern historians as 'throne-worthy'. The Anglo-Saxon monarchy was, in a limited sense, elective – the eldest son of the reigning king had no more automatic right to the throne than any other atheling

Bone-garth – graveyard

Byre – cattle shed

Catafalque – a raised bier

Chape – a metal fitting decorating and strengthening the tip of a scabbard. Chapes, like other Anglo-Saxon sword-fittings, could be very elaborate and made of bronze or silver

Clarnet – a (modern) Mercian dialect word meaning 'idiot'

Coldharbour – Coldharbour is a place-name often associated with Roman roads. It used to be thought that it represented a Roman ruin in which Anglo-Saxon travellers would shelter. This idea has been comprehensively debunked (until fairly recently almost all English main roads had their origins in Roman roads, so that's where the settlements were, and the name is only attested in early modern times) but it's much too good a word to relinquish

Dais – a low raised platform

Dalmatic – a wide, long-sleeved tunic worn by deacons as part of their official vestments

Eke-name – an extra name, recognising a personal quality, which might or might not be flattering. The Anglo-Saxon and Norse were very fond of these. The Modern English 'a nick-name' is a corruption of 'an eke-name'

Ergasteri – a Greek word, meaning workshop

Ettling – Northern dialect word meaning 'intending'

Forbye – Northern dialect word, meaning 'besides'

Frankish – French, only France hasn't quite been invented yet

Gildsmen – gilds were formal social groups of people with something in common, formed for mutual advantage. Members took an oath of loyalty to each other, feasted together regularly, funded gild-members' funerals and prayed and paid for Masses for the souls of deceased brethren

Gospel book – a manuscript containing one or more of the Four Gospels – St Mark, St Matthew, St Luke, St John – of the Christian New Testament. They are the main account of the life and deeds of Christ

Grikkland – the Old Norse (and indeed modern Icelandic) name for Greece. Here referring to the whole Greek-speaking eastern Roman empire, not just the modern Greek nation state

Herra – Lord, just like Modern German *Herr*

House-carls – a Norse term for household troops in their lord's personal service, often used as a bodyguard

Jarl – an Old Norse word essentially meaning 'top aristocrat'. It becomes the Modern English 'Earl'

Kist – chest, a Norse word still used in Northern England

Laiking – Northern dialect word, meaning 'playing' (compare Modern Swedish *lekpark*, playground)

Lectionary – a book containing the readings from the Bible needed by the priest for each day of the year

Matins – the first of the seven hours (church services) of the day, at cockcrow

Midden – where domestic rubbish was dumped; a compost heap, in effect

Miklagard – the Old Norse name for Constantinople (Istanbul) – literally 'Big City'

Muniments – documents indicating ownership of land or other assets. In the tenth century, in the absence of bank vaults or domestic safes, many people would lodge their muniments at a church for safe-keeping

Necessarium/Need-house/Skitter-house – Latin/Old English/Old Norse for the loo

Numinous – possessing *numen*, a spiritual guiding power residing in a particular person, place or object

Oblates – a child on whose behalf binding religious vows have been taken, who grows up in a clerical or monastic institution. It was common practice in early medieval Western Europe to dedicate a child to the Church at a very young age – at or even before birth in some cases – but seven was the normal age to leave the birth-family and enter the religious house

Precentor – in charge of the cathedral music

Prestr – Old Norse, priest

Quires – the folded sheets of vellum (calfskin) from which a manuscript is made

Ragr, nithing – these are both Old Norse insults which call a man's heterosexuality into question

Reeve/Port-reeve – a reeve was an administrative official. Calling Thorvald the 'Reeve of Bardney' may be anachronistic as it isn't until the eleventh century that we can see clearly that reeves are what we might now call an agent or a factor, managing the estate in the landowner's absence. But someone must have done the job, and reeve is the best word for it. The port-reeve whom we meet in Lincoln is the Jarl's agent in charge of overseeing the market

Reliquaries – the elaborate and valuable boxes which contained the bones and/or other relics of a saint

Sacristan – the church official responsible for guarding its treasures, such as the sacred vessels, the candlesticks, books and vestments

Serkland – the Old Norse name for the Abbasid caliphate, the Islamic empire whose capital was Baghdad

Shire-court – shire-courts were held twice a year, presided over by the lay and clerical authorities and dealing with the most important legal cases. It may be a little anachronistic to refer to a Mercian shire-court in 900. Wessex was divided into shires at this point, but Mercia had to wait until later in the tenth century for the modern shires (Worcestershire, Herefordshire, etc) to be imposed. However, there must have been an institution along these lines

Southron – a Northern form of 'Southerner'

Thanes – most famous nowadays from Shakespeare's *Macbeth*; they were (to generalise wildly) wealthy men, but not normally top aristocrats, who owed military service to the king. There were ranks within the thanely class; Wulfgar's father was a king's thane, which was the top rank. If anyone killed a thane, he paid to pay a manprice (*wergild*) of 1200 shillings

Thorndyke – thorn-hedge

Thralls – from the Old Norse word for slaves. It gives us Modern English *enthrall*

Thurifers – men or boys carrying thuribles, i.e. incense-burners, from Latin *thus*, incense

Tonsure – a circular shaven patch on the crown of a man's head, indicating that he is ordained

Trash (in its original meaning!) – dead twigs, dry leaves, too small to be useful even for kindling

Trumpery – valueless

Tunicle – a wide, long-sleeved tunic worn by subdeacons, but not quite as elaborate or wide-sleeved as the deacon's dalmatic

Utlendingar – Old Norse, outlanders, i.e. foreigners

Vespers – the late afternoon or evening hour (church service), held at dusk

Wadmal – from Old Norse *vathmal*, a densely woven, warm, hardwearing woollen cloth

Wave-Serpent – Old Norse poetry is full of *kennings*, poetic phrases which describe one thing in terms of another. *Wave-serpent* could be one of these and refer to a dragon-prowed Norse ship – maybe the one Gunnvor's father sailed from Hordaland to England in?

Wergild – literally 'man-money'. Everyone in Anglo-Saxon England had a wergild, which was the compensation a killer had to pay to the family. The amount varied according to social status, gender and ethnicity. It was an attempt to limit the damage that could be caused by a violent feud

Wether – a castrated ram

A note on currency:

In 900, the English unit of currency is the silver penny. Twelve of these make a shilling (but there is no shilling coin), and 240 pennies weigh a pound. Paying two shillings as a toll thus involves counting out twenty-four silver pennies – a very considerable sum. Scandinavians did not mint their own coins yet at home, but when they settled in England they began to imitate the coinage of the English kings. The Norse word *øre* comes originally from Latin *aureus* (gold coin). An *øre* was very approximately an ounce of silver, or about one-and-a-half English pennies. In Ireland a slave-girl was valued at three ounces of silver.